His Heart

Copyright

Opening Quote

I love to watch you. You're like candy to my eyes. Like a movie that you've seen, but gotta watch just one more time. But that smile you're wearing. It's a beautiful disguise. It's just something you put on to hide the emptiness inside. And you seem so lonely. But you don't have to anymore. If you're a heart without a home. Rebel without a cause. If you feel as though you're always stranded on the shore. Like a thief in the night, let me steal your heart away. Baby if a reason's what you're looking for, I'll be yours.

Heart Without A Home by Nick Carter

Chapter One

✖ Dani ✖

A smooth timbered voice cuts through the serenity I had been enjoying. The beautiful sunset. The colors streaking across the sky. Pinks. Purples. Yellows. Oranges. Reds. All working together to form this almost sexy painting across the sky. I've already taken several photographs of it. It's really not often a sunset like this happens. At least not as brilliant as the one in front of me.

I sigh as I look towards the boat shed. My mouth falls open at the sight. There are several men standing around a tall, well-dressed man with a black mask covering his head. Everyone is looking around nervously. I'm confused by what I'm seeing, but some sixth sense tells me I should duck down.

"Maybe we shouldn't do this here. This isn't exactly the most remote place on the beach."

My heart nearly stops beating when I recognize the person speaking. "Sheriff Bauers?" I whisper the words to myself as I sink further into the brush I am in, becoming far more confused about what's happening.

My heartbeat quickens the more I realize the level of danger around me. I'm so incredibly close to them that I'm more thankful for the tall brush than I have ever been for anything in my entire life. I silently look around for an escape route. I don't know what's going on, but I don't want to be caught up in it.

"Just couldn't leave well enough alone, could you? It would've been in your best interest to accept our offer. Any of them," a deep voice says. He's tall and also well dressed. He's wearing black slacks and a white shirt. His tie is undone. I bite my lip and try to make myself as small as possible. His dark features are just as intimidating as his voice.

"I think the Sheriff is right. We should get out of sight. Anyone could see us out here," another deep male voice says. I squint. He's in a police uniform, but I can't see his face. His blond hair catches the sunset and looks like it's shining.

"If I wanted your opinion, Deputy Modelo, I would pay you for it. I pay you for your cover and your discretion. Don't make me regret it," the older man I've decided must be the leader of whatever is happening says. He's broody. Dressed in all black. I can't make out the color of his eyes, but they look cold. Calculating. Dark.

I swallow hard. The voice… I recognize it, but… I squint again and shake my head. No. That's not possible. I haven't seen him in many, many years. I was so young then. Barely considered a young girl. Hardly more than a toddler. I was just learning my ABC's.

"Look, you don't need to do this. I -" the man in the black mask begins.

"Shut up," a man I recognize as Deputy Sheriff Draple says. He hits the man in the head with his gun. The man crumples to his knees. I cover my mouth to choke back my screams.

"It's much, much too late for that, Mr. Rudd," the bossman says. I furrow my eyebrows. Rudd. Rudd. I know that name. Why do I know that name?

"Let's get this over with. No time to dawdle. I have a hot, young blonde waiting on my desk at the office for me," Sheriff Bauers says with a smirk.

I start slithering away as quietly as I can, praying that no one sees me or hears me. I know danger when I see it. This is it.

5

Tears have started to pour from my eyes because I know what I'm witnessing. I can't call anyone because the entire Cedar Key police force is here. A man is about to die right in front of me, and there's nothing I can do.

As soon as I hit the end of the brush and the parking lot, I stay crouched, wondering how I'm going to get to my car without being seen. There's nowhere to hide.

"I have to do something," I whisper. I have to. I can't just let a man die right in front of me. I can't. I take a deep breath to steady my breathing. I have to help. I can't just stand here and do nothing.

My camera. My fingers grasp my camera. The police here may be corrupt, but maybe I can take pictures and get them to higher people. The FBI? A different department? I don't know. All I know is I have to help whoever this guy is. I have to do something.

I crawl back to the brush I had been crouched in and lie prone on the ground. I take out my camera as I breathe deeply and as quietly as possible. I may not be able to stop it, but at least I can get evidence of what's happening.

I start snapping pictures of everyone on the beach. The Sheriff. The Deputies. The other people. I stay hidden and force myself to be calm while I think. One of the guys pulls the hood off the man. I quickly take photographs.

"Holy shit. Carter Rudd?" I whisper as my throat goes completely dry. Carter Rudd. He's one of the most powerful land developers in the country. Maybe even the world. What could they possibly want with him?

"Alright, Mr. Rudd. Let's get this over with," the boss says. I zero in on his face. His salt and pepper hair. His facial hair. Everything about him is neat and trimmed. Proper. He doesn't even have a wrinkle out of place. Just like…

I shake my head. No. I can't think of him. I won't. I have to focus on what's happening in front of me. I have to do what I can.

"Wait!" Carter holds his hands up defensively in front of him. "I'll let you keep the land. I'll scrap the entire plan!" Carter slowly rises to his feet. "We can work something out."

"That offer has long passed," the other guy that I've decided works directly for the boss says.

6

"You know where our hideout is. We can't very well keep it with a mall built over us. How are we supposed to do our business privately? And that bullshit offer to waive the rent you'd charge us to let us stay? Come on, Mr. Rudd." The boss shakes his head.

I sniffle. I can't get over his voice. It's so familiar... so terrifyingly familiar. So cool. Calm. Like nothing can touch him or affect him. It's cold. Dangerous. Unfeeling. Just like *his*. Just like the man who killed my mother in cold blood and left me. *He* felt nothing.

The Sheriff snickers as he draws his weapon. "Time's up, Mr. Rudd."

I pick up a semi-large rock and throw it as far as I can away from me. It hits the ground and clangs off something metal, making a loud noise. I stay hidden and try not to make a sound. I hold my breath just in case they can hear me breathing.

"What the fuck was that?" Deputy Sheriff Draple asks as he spins around.

Everyone looks around. I pray once more that they don't see me. I don't know what to do now. I can't keep making distractions. I can't take all five of them myself. The tears pouring from my eyes come harder. I do all I can to hide my sobs.

"Check it out." the boss gestures to the Deputy Sheriff and the Deputy. They both nod, weapons drawn, as they start towards the direction the noise came from. As soon as they get through the brush, they'll see me immediately. I have to get out of here somehow.

"We have to get this over with. If they find witnesses, we'll deal with it."

"Agreed, Sheriff," the boss says. The Sheriff shoots Carter in cold blood as I keep snapping pictures. I put a hand over my mouth to muffle the scream as Carter falls into a bloody heap on the ground.

I tremble and bite my lip to stop the scream and the sobs that threaten to escape. I glance towards the two cops searching for where the noise came from. I have some time.

Pictures.

I have to get them.

I have to.

With shaky hands, I snap pictures of Carter Rudd's body, the Sheriff, and the two other guys as they pour gasoline on him. The leader lights a match and drops it onto the body. It erupts into flames. I snap picture after picture until I know my time is up. I have to move. They're so close now.

The Deputy and Deputy Sheriff come through the brush several yards away from me. It takes them only seconds to see me and my camera. My heart pounds in my ears.

"What the fuck?" the Deputy Sheriff nearly yells.

"Get her!" Deputy Modelo screams.

I scream as I run, staying as low as I can to the ground. Bullets are flying. Everyone is yelling. Pure chaos has been unleashed as everyone starts chasing me.

I try to stay as low as I can to the ground, but the bullets are ricocheting off the pavement. I cover my ears as I sprint.

I reach my car and dive into it. I throw my keys into the ignition as I sob. I don't even have my door closed as I peel out of the parking lot. Bullets shatter my back window and ding off the siding of my car, but I don't stop.

I can't.

I don't dare look into my rearview mirror as I speed through the small town. I keep my eyes forward as I hit Florida State Road 24 and fly across the Gulf of Mexico towards the mainland, leaving Cedar Key behind me forever.

✗✗✗

(Six Months Later)

It's been six months since I fled Cedar Key.

Six months since my entire life turned upside down.

When I left, I drove straight into Gainesville, Florida. I went to a friend's house and made a copy of the pictures. Then I turned everything I had into the police. I left immediately afterwards.

The Cedar Key cops disappeared. So did the other two people. The Gainesville Lieutenant I gave everything to had kept in touch. They had identified everyone in the photographs. He thanked me for getting such clear pictures.

Of course that didn't help me at all. I know they're looking for me. I saw everything. There's no possible way they aren't looking for me.

And that's why I'm here in Chicago. I ditched my other vehicle. I had a friend get me a new one under her name. She even leased me a condo.

I don't have a choice. I can't be too careful. I'm terrified to use my real name in any situation, so I've come up with an alias. A pseudo. Lilly Alexander. To the world, that's now my name. As far as anyone knows, the old me disappeared and hasn't been heard from for months.

They don't know that I'm still here. Just… no longer a photographer. Everything I used to love is everything I stay far away from. I can't risk anyone knowing who I really am.

I breathe in the evening air as I sit on the beach of Lake Michigan.

It's become my favorite place in the city. It's also not nearly as quiet as Cedar Key. It's far busier. I've come to love that. I've come to feel safe with the hustle and bustle around me. Even at night. It's easy to get lost in a sea of people; in skyscrapers that tower over the sky; cars driving along every road.

I stand and walk the short distance to my condo. I love that the condo is close to the lake. I love how secure it is.

A few minutes later, I'm getting ready for bed and feel the tears sting my eyes. They've become such a normal routine for me that I don't even bother wiping them away.

Instead, I lay down in bed and pull my covers up to my chin as I bury my face in my pillow. The tears fall freely as I mourn the death of my former self. No more Dani Jade. As far as the world is concerned, Dani Jade is dead.

I lose track of the hours as they pass by. Eventually, as is my usual routine, I fall into a restless sleep.

XXX

My eyes fly open in the dark. I fight to breathe. I'm soaked to the bone. Freezing cold. Is it from being held down in the water? I feel all around me but don't feel water. Did I get out?

A scream fills the cool night air. I shiver uncontrollably. I feel around me again. My hands sink in something. Is it water? Is it mud? Am I in the Gulf?

It's warm, but the air is frosty. I can feel a breeze. It hits me in the face and makes me choke. The coughing hurts my already burning lungs.

I cover my ears as the screams and cries get louder. I try to move from wherever I am, but I can't. My body feels so heavy. Like I'm paralyzed. Maybe it's mud. Maybe it's quicksand. It's sucking me in. I can't get out. I fight, but I feel like I'm just getting sucked down more. It has to be quicksand. Why am I in quicksand?

Maybe it's mud. The mud in the gulf. I shake my head to try and clear it. It doesn't work. The screams. They're getting louder.

Where are they? Why can't I see them? My eyes dart around in the darkness. I know they're here. I can feel them. Smell them.

No… I sniff the air. No… I smell him. My father. I smell his signature cigar and whiskey scent. It's all over. It's surrounding me. Just like it did that night. The night he screamed he was going to kill my mother.

I shake my head. Why? What did she do?

Suddenly, my surroundings start coming into view. I'm not in water. I'm not being held down in the mud. I'm not paralyzed.

The screams and cries I hear are coming from my own mouth. I take several calming breaths, but it doesn't last.

Abruptly, I hear a loud bang!

I scream at the noise and leap out of my bed.

My bedroom door flies open. A flash of light skims across my bedroom and over my head. I duck down lower.

I cower next to my bed covering my ears and folding myself into myself, trying to make myself as small as possible.

It's no use.

The light hits me again.

They found me.

Chapter Two

⚔ Nick ⚔

"So? You intending on answering my question? Or is the plan to make me drag it out of you?" One of my brothers, Ryan Crane, is walking alongside me.

I can't help but laugh as I step off the elevator and walk through the hall to my condo. "Don't you have a gorgeous young wife to harass or something?"

"She's busy helping out Breetana. Something about a surprise for Chase. She's taken over the entire house and kicked me out."

I laugh again and shake my head. "Dude. I didn't even have to be there. I know damn well she kicked you out because in true Ryan Crane fashion, you tried to take over her decorations. You know how she is."

Ryan married the love of his life, Arianna, about two years ago. I never thought I'd see the day he settled down, but fuck if it didn't suit the guy. The two have a baby boy who is just over one year old. They couldn't possibly be more sickeningly in love if they tried.

"Come on! What's it like being on Taylor's team? Do you like it? I know you loved being a cop, and I know you missed it. Even if the shit you did in patrol pissed you off. This is far more suited to you."

I look at Ryan and sigh. Just after Ryan took down Arianna's mafia father as well as another small-time mafia boss, Arianna had decided she hated Manhattan, where we lived. I couldn't blame her. Her father was all kinds of fucked up. He had arranged for her to be married off to the son of the Ambrosio mafia. When she turned eighteen, he tried to force the marriage that very night.

Despite her age, Ryan is twenty years older than her, Arianna and Ryan were already secretly together. As soon as she turned eighteen, she fled her father's house. She and Ryan were married within a couple of weeks.

That didn't stop her father, though. By the end of the summer, Arianna had survived several kidnapping attempts, being shot at, and an attempt on her life by her best friend, all while being pregnant. Ryan and his crew had obliterated her father, the other mafia boss, and the son that Arianna had been promised to and bullied by.

Her so-called best friend, Renza, disappeared. Despite all of our attempts at locating her, she's completely vanished. While we're still looking for her, we have no clues to where she could be.

After all of that, no one could blame the girl for wanting to start over somewhere else.

Truthfully, we all really liked the idea of leaving. Manhattan didn't really hold the same allure as it had. Our family had grown over the years. We felt far too spread out. We all talked about it and decided on Chicago. It was the best decision we'd ever made.

"Yes. I missed it. I don't miss New York. I don't miss the NYPD. I don't miss the mundane calls and dealing with the same fucked up people. But I do miss the work. I miss the investigation. Solving problems. Fixing shit."

Ryan claps me on the back as he chuckles. "I knew it. I knew you'd be a good fit. Taylor needed another good guy to round out his team. Chicago's organized crime world is getting a little too big for him. He's been needing me a lot more. You know how much he hates that."

"You were right. I love working for his taskforce. This is exactly what I've always wanted to do. I feel like I am actually accomplishing something, you know? Still don't know how either of you pulled it off, though."

I've been out of the business of being a cop for eleven years. Not to say I still didn't train. I was Jason Crane's, my other brother's, Head of Security. I never looked back. Him and Ryan had become my best friends, the family I never had, after I had been adopted into their family when I was only a kid.

I grew up with them. I went on the same missions they did for our father before Ryan took over. I was just as much a part of the family mafia as I am part of the family. After our father was nearly killed, Jason and I got scared enough to follow our own dreams. While neither of us would ever leave Ryan to run the mafia himself, we both chose different paths. Me with the NYPD. Jason with his own company.

After a few years, though, I decided I needed more. I wasn't sure I wanted to go back into the mafia, but I also wasn't really sure I'd ever truly left. I still ran missions with Ryan if he needed me to. Even after becoming Jason's Head of Security, I trained all the time with Ryan's guards.

But there had always been something missing. I loved what I did with Crane Enterprises. I just missed being out there solving crimes. Helping people.

It was actually the situation with Ryan and Arianna that made me realize it. Being taken under Taylor's wing and helping him research and figure shit out was like a fucking drug I didn't realize I was addicted to until it was too late.

So, I applied to Chicago PD. I got hired. I went through the academy. I graduated at the top of my class. When I got out, I went straight to Taylor's team. I didn't go through any of the on the job field training. I still don't know how or why.

But I'm not complaining. Being a street cop is a bitch. So much fucking politics. Procedures made up by people who don't know what they're talking about. We follow those procedures and end up wrapped up in red tape; thrown under the bus to the media vultures for not following procedures. Problem is we do. But if the public doesn't like the procedure, then procedures are changed to please the world only to have the entire thing start all over again. We're the most hated profession in the world. Probably even more than lawyers.

At least on Taylor's team, I don't have to worry about having to tase someone who's holding a gun on me because me pulling out my gun to defend myself could be viewed as excessive force. I don't like the idea that punching someone in the face and breaking their nose because they were trying to get my gun can get me in trouble for being too violent.

"Suffice to say that you're where you belong. The department agrees."

"Yeah. I am where I belong. I don't think I would've come back if it meant not going directly to the taskforce."

"Lucky you have family in high places."

We both laugh as I reach my door. "It's midnight. You staying here?"

"Fuck no. As soon as Arianna texts, I'm out. I miss her."

"You've been away for what? An hour?"

"An hour too long."

"You guys are disgusting." I grin at him as I unlock my door.

He chuckles. "Asshole."

Just as my door is swinging open, Ryan and I hear a blood-curdling scream. We both jump. My hand automatically goes to my gun. "The hell?"

The screams continue. We both realize that it's coming from the apartment across the hall from me. Ryan and I both look at each other and take out our guns.

"Lucky you just got done serving a warrant," he says as he looks at the gun I'd just taken out of the holster on my hip.

"Wouldn't matter. I'm always armed. Just like you."

"I taught you well, little brother."

He's cocky as fuck, but the man doesn't lie. I wouldn't be where I am without him and Jason and the Crane family. He nods to the door. I take out my flashlight and hold it with my gun as he kicks open the door. I go in first, sweeping the room with my gun and flashlight. Ryan follows. The screams get louder as we near the bedroom.

We finish clearing the room before we get to the bedroom. I was taught many things, but one thing I was taught well was to always clear the room fully. If we rush to the danger, we risk being ambushed by unknown threats. I don't like the unknown. I do whatever I can to eliminate it as quickly as possible.

The screams stop. We start hearing sobs and gulping breaths. Ryan looks at me. I nod. He kicks open the door I assume leads to the bedroom.

14

I'm right. I move, sweeping my light and gun across the room. Ryan follows closely behind. We work quickly to clear the bedroom.

As soon as we burst through the bedroom door, I saw the girl. The scared girl who is sitting on the floor next to her bed crying and gasping for breath. She's trying to fold herself into herself. I know she's trying to make herself disappear.

"Clear." Ryan comes out of the bathroom as I finish the closet.

"Check the balcony," I command. I haven't gotten there yet.

Ryan moves quickly. I make my way to the girl. She's covering her ears as she begins screaming again, like she's trying to drown herself out. Tears are streaming down her face. She's sobbing so hard that she's choking as she screams.

I put my hand gently on her arm and unintentionally send her into an intense battle of fight or flight.

"No! No! No! No!" she screams. She throws her body into the most chaotic flails I've ever seen as she hits, claws, and kicks at me.

"Holy shit! What the fuck happened to you?" I grab her wrists and haul her against my chest, pinning her arms to her side.

"Get away! Get off me!" She's shrieking at the top of her lungs. I know without a doubt we're going to have company soon. Every neighbor on this floor has to hear her.

"It's okay! I'm not going to hurt you! I'm a cop. Okay? I'm a -" Before I can finish my sentence, a hard knee connects directly to my balls. I let her go as I sink to my knees. "Fuck!"

She kicks me in the stomach, then knees me in the face. I fall backwards onto my back, inventing new curse words as I cup my dick in my hands. The kick to my stomach and knee to my mouth hurt like a motherfucker, but it's nothing compared to the kick to my manhood.

I groan and roll to my side completely focused on breathing through the pain of my balls being relocated to the back of my head. I don't even notice her screams anymore or the fact that she's fighting Ryan and has gotten away again.

"Stop it! Stop! Stop fighting!" Ryan demands.

I distantly hear a door slam and more screaming, but I don't give one single fuck. For all I care, she can fucking choke on her cries. "Fucking hell. Jesus fucking hell."

"Get off me! No! Get off!" Her screams are suddenly muffled. I hear someone being slammed into something.

"Fuck! Would you calm the fuck down? We aren't here to fucking hurt you!"

I take a deep breath and roll back onto my back, daring to open only one eye.

Ryan has managed to get her onto the floor and straddle her, keeping her still with his weight. Stuffed in her mouth is a pair of panties.

Ryan meets my eyes and glares. "She fucking bit me. Do you know what Arianna is going to say?"

"She kicked me in the damn balls! You'll live. I'm not making it until tomorrow."

At that moment, her bedroom flies open. Ryan and I both look up as my boss, Lieutenant Taylor Reddick, busts through the door, gun pointed directly at mine and Ryan's heads. "What in the ever living hell is going on here?"

"What are you doing here?" I ask through my damn near sobs as tears roll freely from my eyes.

"I don't give a shit if you're my brother or not. I'm your superior officer. I asked you a fucking question," Taylor growls.

"Calm it, Reddick," Ryan growls. "We heard her screaming and busted in. She fought like fuck. That's all we know."

Taylor lowers his weapon and holsters it. He looks at me whimpering like a baby and holding my now completely numb cock. "What happened to you?"

"She fought. Kicked me as hard as she could in the fucking balls. Relocated them fairly nicely."

Her screams have subsided, but she's still sobbing. Taylor kneels down in front of her and takes the panties out of her mouth. He holds them up to Ryan. "Panties. Are you out of your fucking mind?"

"She bit me. She was screaming. I had to calm her down and get her to stop somehow."

"You guys busted through her door. What do you expect? Get off her." Taylor glares. Ryan slowly gets off her. She doesn't move.

I bite my lip and force myself to at least get to my knees. "She was screaming. We busted in because we thought she was being murdered and needed help."

Taylor holds out a hand to the girl as he stands. "My name is Taylor Reddick. I'm here to help you, okay?"

The girl stays unmoving on the floor. "Are... you a cop... too?" I can hear the fear resonating in her voice at the idea we're cops. I hate that she fears us. We're the good guys. What could've possibly happened to her to make her think we aren't?

"I'm a Lieutenant with Chicago PD. I promise you that I'm here to help, honey." Taylor has always had a way with women. Tonight is no different. The girl takes his hand. He helps her up, walking with her to her bed. She sits down. He kneels once again in front of her, taking her hands in his. "Let's start with your name, huh?"

"D-Dani J-Jade. No! Wait! No! That's not my name..." She starts sobbing again and shaking her head. "Lilly! Lilly Alexander! Lilly -"

Taylor hugs her. "Shh... Hey. It's okay, Dani. Nothing is going to happen to you. You're safe, okay?"

"I didn't mean to say Dani. I didn't mean to say that. I didn't mean to say my name. Please don't let them find me."

"Find you? Who?" I ask. She cries harder. Taylor and Ryan both glare at me. I look at them confused. "What?"

"Quit talking. Let him work his magic," Ryan says.

"Shh… No one is going to hurt you. Not on our watch," Taylor says into her ear.

It takes her several minutes to calm down. Taylor pulls away slightly and Dani meets my eyes. She stares at me for a long moment before taking a deep breath. "I'm sorry I hurt you." She nearly whispers the words.

Taylor slowly stands and lets go of her. He steps a few steps away. I'm just about to respond when I hear more chaos in her apartment. Taylor and Ryan look at each other and quickly move out of the room as something shatters. Dani screams again and launches herself at me. I catch her and hold her tightly, somehow keeping from tumbling with her to the floor.

"It's okay, Dani. I got you. I won't hurt you."

"Don't let go. Please, don't let them find me!"

"I won't, Dani. I won't let you go. You're safe with me." I hug her as tightly as I can as her nails dig into my back. She's shaking, and all I can wonder once more is what the hell could have possibly happened to her.

"We gotta go. Now," Ryan says as he comes in.

"What?" I meet Ryan's eyes and see a familiar spark.

I'm already moving, pulling Dani with me and ignoring the sharp pain between my legs where my balls used to be. Ryan is protective as fuck. When he senses danger, none of us question him. We act. If he says we have to go, then we believe him.

Taylor comes in and moves around Ryan. "Dani, do you have a bag? We need to get you some essentials to take with you."

I don't know what they saw, but I see the fear all over Dani's beautiful face. I don't like it.

Dani shakily steps out of my arms and walks to the closet. She takes out three bags of different sizes. "I'm... ready." She looks at the ground. Taylor and Ryan don't hesitate to grab a bag. Dani slings the last one over her shoulder. I sigh as I walk towards her, grabbing the bag from her shoulder. "I hope I can trust you guys. Because if you're leading me into a trap, I'll go out in a blaze of glory and take all you fuckers with me."

Taylor and Ryan burst out laughing. I grin like a moron. She's feisty.

We follow Ryan out of her condo. Both Taylor and Ryan have their guns out, as do I. As soon as we reach the parking garage, we jump into Ryan's SUV. Taylor follows in his truck. I still don't know what the hell is going on, but I trust my family.

Dani is sitting behind me staring stoically ahead into the night as Ryan speeds through the streets of Chicago. It's obvious the decision to trust Taylor didn't come easy to her. She struggled giving him her hand, then freaked out after telling him her name.

I'm pretty sure Ryan and I are still up in the air with her, but I also know she's running from something. Someone. No one has three packed bags ready to go on a moment's notice. No one is that willing to leave with complete strangers.

No. Dani Jade is definitely on the run. Her decision to trust us has something to do with her belief that, although we may be dangerous, we aren't as dangerous as those that are after her.

I don't know what's going on with her. But I intend to find out.

Chapter Three

⚔ Dani ⚔

Looking around the room of the crazy large mansion I'm sitting in is like looking through a shiny glass window into a life I've only ever dreamed of. The couch is made of the softest material I've ever felt. The house is warm and inviting. I've never felt so comfortable. I never want to leave. Which is truly an odd feeling for me. I've never wanted to stay in one place for long.

My eyes fall on a large photograph that covers most of the wall behind me. My mouth falls open in shock. "Oh my God... That's..."

"Cedar Key. By Dani Jade." One of the men who burst into my apartment sits next to me. I'm not sure who he is, but despite pinning me to the ground and stuffing my panties in my mouth, he's turned out to be very kind. Intimidating. But kind. "She's my wife's favorite artist. We have seven of her pieces. One is in our bedroom. Five are in her piano room. But this one? This one is her favorite." He gestures to the painting.

I blush. "Why? What is it about this particular piece?" It's the only piece I sold after I left Cedar Key. I had to make sure I had enough money. My agent mentioned this piece sold for over a million dollars. Considering

I took it the day I witnessed Carter Rudd being killed... I can't understand why it sold for so much. To me, the beauty of that day is forever tarnished.

He smiles. Despite my feelings on it, I'm genuinely curious. This piece of work is nowhere near my best. At least in my opinion.

The guy looks up as one of the other guys sits down. It's the guy I kicked. Lieutenant Reddick follows, also sitting. Everyone looks comfortable around each other. Like family. A dynamic I never really knew but have always longed for.

I look away from everyone. My eyes fall on an exotically beautiful, petite woman as she walks into the room carrying a steaming mug and a bag of ice.

She hands me the mug. "I thought you might like some hot chocolate. It's made with real milk and real chocolate."

"There really is no other way," the guy I kicked says.

I raise an eyebrow. "Water and powder. There's another way."

The guy next to me scoffs. "Like hell. Packaged hot chocolate doesn't belong in this house. That shit isn't real."

Everyone laughs, and I can't help but chuckle as I take a sip. I close my eyes and sigh. It's the perfect temperature. It's creamy and smooth and rich. Everything hot chocolate is in my fantasies but never lives up to in real life.

"Okay, I'm sold. This stuff is amazing."

"It's what makes me happy when I'm feeling anxious." The woman turns and hands the guy I kicked the bag of ice.

He immediately puts it on his manhood and whimpers, completely unashamed. "Thanks, Arianna. I needed this."

"Arianna? That's such a pretty name." I take another sip.

Arianna's smile lights up the entire room as she gestures to the guy next to me to move over. He does as she says. I can't help but look at her in amusement. The guy is big. Tall. Intimidating as hell, even though he has shown kindness. She's half his size. Warm. Kind. Such a stark contrast. Yet he just did what she wanted with no argument.

"Ryan will tell you he runs things around here. But it's really his wife," Lieutenant Reddick says.

"Wife?" I look at Arianna. She grins as Ryan puts his arm around her and pulls her to his side. She melts into him. "You're his wife?"

"Yep! I'm lucky he chose me."

20

He kisses her on the side of the head. I've always wished for a sweet love like that. It's kind of hard, though, when I've never been in one place long enough to have any kind of a relationship.

"I'm the lucky one." He kisses her again. I smile into my hot chocolate.

"To answer your question about that photograph. I love the color contrast." Arianna tilts her head. "The sunset is so vivid against the simple image of the boathouse. It's so bright and full of life. It brings an otherwise boring boathouse to brilliant existence. There's nothing about that shot that I hate." I blush as Arianna reaches over and pats my leg. "You're incredibly talented."

My eyes widen. Oh no. No. No. No. This can't be happening. It's bad enough I messed up and told them my name. It's even worse that they put two and two together and know who I really am. I have to leave.

I set down my hot chocolate and quickly stand. "I have to go. I'm sorry. Thank you for helping me."

Lieutenant Reddick quickly stands and catches me, gripping my arm, as I start running to the door. "Hey, hang on. Dani, stop."

I don't bother to fight. I'm too weak and tired. "I need to leave, Lieutenant. I'm sorry. Me being here puts you all at risk. I trust you saw something that spooked you enough to make me leave my condo. And it's because of that trust in you and whatever you saw that I need to go."

"Please just come sit down. Let's talk about it. You can trust me. Us. I promise. I know you've been through some shit, but we can help."

I shake my head. "No one can help me." I break free of his grip and take out my phone. I order a Lyft, then grab my bags. I can feel everyone watching me as I leave.

A few minutes later, my Lyft arrives. The driver gets out to help me with my bags.

"Well, well, well..." I look up and realize two things all too late. The first is that the man standing in front of me was identified by my contact at Gainesville PD as Max King. A member of the Krins Mafia. He's the one who was nicely dressed with the loose tie. "Fancy meeting you here, little girl."

The second is that the vehicle in front of me is not the vehicle I ordered. I swallow hard. "No..."

"Oh, yes." He gives me a sickeningly dark grin that sends chills to every part of my body. I start to back towards the still open gate of the house as Max stalks towards me, pulling out a gun. "You're a hard one to track down, Ms. Jade. Gave me a run for my money for sure. I thought I had you tonight. I showed up to your condo, but there were a bunch of neighbors around. I was in your house. So fucking close. And then your boy toy had to ruin it. Stole you from under my fingertips."

"No... He's... He's not..." My breath catches as Max gets closer. I try to gauge how close I am to the house. What are the chances I can make it? I nearly choke on my tears when I realize I'm too far away.

"Get in the car, Ms. Jade. I don't want to make a scene."

I put my hand up to my mouth and shake my head. Max lunges for me, catching me by the arm. I try to shove him away. I scream as loudly as I can and swing with my free arm while I shove with my other, connecting with Max's eye. "Fuck! Bitch!" His grip tightens on me as I try to wrench away.

"Let me go! Help! Help!" I fight him off as best I can, but his hand is digging into my arm. His gun is jammed into my side. "Help!"

He's dragging me to his car as I fight and try to get away. "Stop! Stop it, or I'll fucking shoot you!" he yells. I scream at the top of my lungs, begging for anyone to hear me. Pleading for anyone in the house to come rescue me from my epic stupidity.

"Let her go!" The guy I kicked appears like some avenging angel. He has a gun pointed directly at Max's head. I've never been so happy to see anyone in my life.

"Ah, yes. The boyfriend. Drop your weapon or your little toy gets a bullet in her side."

He smirks. "Yeah, that's not happening. Let her go, and I just might think about sparing your life."

Max turns slightly, showing his gun jammed in my ribcage, as he starts to back up. His other arm snakes around my neck. He pulls me hard against his chest. I meet the guy's piercing dark eyes. He doesn't flinch, looking directly at Max.

"Drop your gun, or I choke the life out of her while you watch." Max's grip around my neck tightens.

I sputter as he begins slowly crushing his arm into my windpipe. "Please..." I'm scared. I'm weakening with every breath he keeps from me.

I can feel my heart slowing as it pounds in my ears. "No..." I won't die like this. I won't. I reach up and try to claw at his arm to loosen his grip. He only tightens it more.

"See, I have all the advantage. Your girl, here, is my way out. You can't get to me without shooting her. You're all alone out here."

Through darkening vision, I watch as the guy's smirk turns dangerous. "You think I'm all alone out here?"

I hear two clicks near my head and Max's arm immediately slackens. He doesn't let me go, but at least I can breathe.

"Let. Her. Go," Lieutenant Reddick rumbles.

"Right. Fucking. Now," the other man who got me out of my condo growls.

Max slowly does as he's told. I sink to the ground in a heap. I hear someone get slammed against the car behind me, but I don't dare look.

A pair of strong arms come around me and pull me against a rock solid, warm body. All of the adrenaline I had moments earlier to fight and stay alive completely slips away. I start sobbing.

"I got you. It's okay. You're safe."

"I haven't felt safe in six months." I sob into his chest.

He holds me closer. "You are now. You are with me."

"Taylor," the guy I'm assuming is the leader of whatever this is says. "Take Dani's stuff inside. Get her set up in a guest bedroom. Nick, it looks like she feels comfortable and safe with you. Get her inside. I don't know if there's any other threats."

"Nick?" I ask quietly through the sobs.

"Yeah. That's me. Sorry we haven't been properly introduced." Nick stands and pulls me up with him. He keeps his arm around my waist.

"What do you need from me, Ry?" I look up at the new voice. He hadn't been here before. I press myself closer to Nick.

"It's okay," Nick says. "That's Luke. He's here to help."

"I'm sorry I ran. Please just take me inside. At least I felt safe there."

"You *are* safe there, Dani. No one in my family would ever let any harm come to you."

I cling to him as I walk, still shaky from the adrenaline dump I just went through. I trip over my own feet, but Nick catches me and swings me effortlessly into his arms.

"Oh! Really, you don't need to carry me."

"I don't need to, but I'm going to."

He carries me into the house as I wrap my arms around his shoulders. I hate that I enjoy the feeling of being in his arms. I hate that I love how he smells so fresh. I hate that I love every perfect ridge of his arms, and his chest against me. I hate that I love his beautiful eyes and his sexy, short, dark hair. I hate that I think he's sexy. I hate that I find him attractive in the slightest.

More than anything? I hate that I feel like I can actually trust him. I haven't truly trusted anyone except my contact in Gainesville and the friend who helped me get a car and condo here in Chicago. I haven't talked to anyone. I've kept my head down and lived completely off my savings, which I took in cold cash.

"Which room?" Nick asks.

"Arianna said upstairs. Second room on the left. She wants Ryan close in case you need help for any reason," Taylor, the Lieutenant says.

Nick nods and carries me up the stairs. He walks into a room and kicks the door shut behind him. He doesn't put me down until he reaches the bed.

I sit on the edge of the bed and look around. "This room is beautiful."

"Arianna has good taste." Nick puts his hands in his pockets and looks down at me. "I'll take the room next door to you. Arianna and Ryan are at the end of the hall." He gives me a small smile. I give him one back and look down at my hands. "If you need anything, just let one of us know." He turns with a nod and leaves the room.

I'm instantly on edge being alone. "No. I can do this. I'm strong. I've never needed anyone. I can be alone in a room in a stupidly big house." I take a deep breath and dig through one of my suitcases for something to sleep in. After I'm cleaned up and changed, I climb into the softest bed with the softest sheets and softest blanket I've ever felt. "Jesus. This is so fucking incredible." I sink into the bed and sigh in contentment as I close my eyes.

Despite the comfort, though, sleep doesn't come easy. Every bump in the night makes me jump. Every noise. Every squeak.

The shadows that play across the floor seem to get closer to me. Like they're reaching for me. Threatening to drag me to the underworld.

I try to close my eyes, but all I can see is Max's hand around my throat. His arm squeezing the life from me.

By the time the sky starts to lighten, I'm shaking in fear. I hate that I'm afraid. I worked so hard being able to protect myself and take care of myself. I don't like feeling scared and helpless.

Finally, I can't take any more. I jump out of the bed and hurry to the door. The house is quiet and dark. My heart is racing a million times faster than it should be. I feel like I'm being chased. I feel like Max is going to grab me.

Nick said he'd be in the room next to me. He gestured towards the room that would be to my right near the stairs. Maybe I can sleep on the floor. Or a chair. Anywhere near him. He makes me feel safe, even though hours ago I was terrified of him. I decided I could trust him pretty quickly. I know now that he isn't after me; that he wants me to be safe.

To help.

I quietly open the door and see him lying in bed. Taking a steadying breath, I enter the room, silently closing the door behind me. It's fairly dark, but I can make out a sitting chair in the room near the bed, so I make my way to it and curl up in it.

It's not the most comfortable place in the world, but at least I'm not alone. At least Nick is near in case something happens.

After a few moments, I hear Nick stirring. My eyes fly to him.

"Dani? What are you doing?" he asks raspily.

"I... I'm so sorry. I couldn't sleep. I couldn't stop thinking about everything. I just... didn't want to be alone." I bite my lip as the tears sting my eyes. His voice is husky with sleep. I'm silently praying to any God that's listening that he won't make me leave.

"Well, come here. I won't have you sleeping in a fucking chair."

I let out a relieved breath that he's letting me stay. "It's okay. I'm okay."

"Dani. Get your ass over here. I'm not telling you again."

My body obeys on its own at his dominant tone. Before I understand what happened, I'm lying in the bed with Nick's arms around me. My back is to him, but his fresh, earthy cologne envelopes me just as tightly as his warm embrace. I'm instantly calm and relaxed.

When I close my eyes, I don't see any shadows. I don't see Max. Wrapped up in Nick's strong arms, I fall into the first peaceful sleep I've had since I left Cedar Key in my rearview mirror.

Chapter Four

⚔ Nick ⚔

I don't know what time it is when I wake up, but there are two intoxicating scents that are battling for my attention. I'm struggling to decide which one to give into.

The woman wrapped in my arms smells like toffee and caramel. My face is buried in her beautiful hair. Her soft body against mine wreaks havoc on my libido. All I can think about is how every single one of her curves fit every part of my body like it was made for me.

She shifts slightly, her sexy ass wiggling against my cock. It has to be an accident. I try to stay still. But she keeps pushing against me and moving against my dick. Either she's having a really good dream, or she's trying to kill me.

I groan and give in to her. I move my hand up her stomach to her tits as I kiss the back of her shoulder. They fit perfectly in my hand. I've never been with a woman who fits me so perfectly. Not even the one I damn near married.

She sighs in pleasure with the sexiest whimper I've ever heard and pushes into me harder. I run my hand down to her hips as she starts grinding into me. I let her as I kiss along her neck.

"Mmm... Something smells really good." She tilts her head to give me more access.

It's those words that bring me back to reality. That and my stomach growling. My mouth starts watering, but I don't know if it's because of her or because of whatever delectable dish Ryan is cooking for Sunday brunch.

"That would be Ryan. He cooks brunch and dinner for the whole family every Sunday. We spend the entire day together."

"The whole family?" She pushes herself into me a little more.

I chuckle. "Yes. The whole family." I grind into her, giving her a little of what she wants. She sexily whimpers again. "You like that?"

She nods and melts into me. "I'm not opposed to a quick fuck. I've had a few one-night stands in my life."

I nearly choke. "Fuck, Dani. So have I, but I highly doubt this would stop with one night." Even with those words, I still push against her and let her grind into me, making my cock rock hard.

"Maybe I'm okay with that, too."

I laugh and kiss the back of her head. "I wish we had more time, but Ryan hates when we're late."

I reluctantly pull away from her. I've had my fair share of women over the years, but I'm the kind of man who wines and dines before I fuck anyone. Call me old-fashioned, but I think dinner and drink is the least I can do before I'm pounding a woman's pussy.

However, I've never had an immediate reaction to anyone either. Not any of my exes. No one. There hasn't been anyone like her. Even though she did kick my ass last night, I still have this intense attraction to her that I can't explain.

Dani gets up and tosses a smirk over her shoulder. "It's nice to know your dick still works."

My mouth falls open as she looks me up and down. She laughs. I hold a pillow over my head. "Go get dressed. If I look at you anymore dressed like that I won't be responsible for my actions."

She laughs again. I feel her get up. "Should I just go downstairs?"

"Not dressed like that." I toss the pillow aside and stand up, walking to the bathroom in my room. I don't dare look back at her. "I can see right through that sheer fabric you're wearing. It's forcing me to become possessive as fuck." When my ridiculously hard cock is safely hidden in the bathroom, I pop my head from around the corner. "I've never

28

immediately felt like this about anyone. I don't know what it is about you. But no one gets to look at you wearing that but me."

She bites her lip and pushes her hair behind her ear, trying to hide her shy smile. I groan and close the bathroom door.

✗✗✗

A little while later, I stride into the dining room. My eyes fall onto Dani, who has taken up residence in a corner watching everyone. She's wearing short shorts and a bright pink tank top. She looks completely out of her element and slightly terrified. I can't help the grin that slides onto my face as I walk to her. She gives me a barely there smile as soon as she sees me and looks up at me through her eyelashes.

"Thank you for changing. I'm not willing to share you with anyone," I damn near growl. She tries to stop the laugh, but it bubbles out. I push her hair behind her ear and lean down to kiss her forehead. "What's wrong?"

She sighs and shrugs as she looks down. "I've spent the last six months in hiding. I've been so careful about telling anyone my real name. I don't trust anyone. I never have." She looks up at me. "Ever." She takes a deep breath. "Yet here I am with a bunch of complete strangers. I blurted out my real name to Taylor. I haven't done that in so long. But I've never felt safer. And then there's you, and all of these strange feelings I've never had for anyone. I don't know how to explain them. I don't understand any of this."

I gently pull her close and hug her. "I understand how scary this is, Dani. I was in the same place as you awhile ago. I came from nothing. I had no family. But these guys?" I turn and gesture to everyone talking and laughing in the room. "They became my family. They're protective as fuck. Loyal as hell. There isn't a single person in this room who would think of betraying you. They'd all do anything for you."

"That's insane. They don't even know me."

I shrug. "Doesn't matter. You obviously need help. Help and protection. That's what we do."

"So, what are you guys? A security firm or something?"

I hesitate and decide she doesn't need to know right now. Not until I have all of the information I need about her. Like just what in the hell she's running from, and who that guy was that tried to kidnap her.

"We're just a family who would do anything for those we love and care about, Dani. We protect those who need help. We fight and do whatever is necessary when that person is one of us." She watches me for a moment. I know she knows I'm not being completely open with her, but she lets it go. I look up at Ryan as he and Arianna enter the room. They both are carrying food. Dani groans. I smile down at her. "He's an incredible cook."

"It smells so good."

"Nick, there's more stuff on the counter," Ryan says. "You and Dani grab it. Jas, grab the tea Arianna has in the fridge."

We all do as we're told and are soon settled at the huge dining room table enjoying the food spread out in front of us.

"Nick, maybe it would be nice if you introduced Dani to everyone," Arianna says.

I smile at her, silently thanking her for giving me an opportunity to do just that. "Of course. Starting at Ryan's right. That's Ethan Crane. Next to him is Jenny. She's Ethan's wife. Those are mine, Ryan's, and Jason's parents. They adopted me when I was a kid."

"And we've never looked back. He completed our family, and we love him very much," my mom says.

I smile and feel my cheeks slightly redden. "I love you too, mom. Uh... anyway. Next to her is Eve Shaw. She's Chase's and Taylor's mom."

"Taylor has a brother? Is he a cop, too?" Dani asks.

"No, no. One cop is enough," Eve teases. Dani laughs.

I smile at the sweet sound coming out of her beautiful mouth. "Taylor and Chase grew up together. It's kind of complicated. They aren't really brothers by blood, but they are as close as real ones would be. Eve adopted Taylor when he was in his teens."

Dani smiles softly. "Sometimes adopted brothers are far closer. Brothers of the heart is often a much stronger bond."

"Couldn't agree more." Ryan looks at me. I look at Ryan and Jason. We all share a smile. I point next to the guy sitting next to Dani.

"That's Chase. He's CEO of Shaw Incorporated. Next to him is his wife, Breetana."

"I'm never going to remember everyone," Dani says.

"It definitely takes awhile," Breetana says with a soft smile.

I look down at Dani. "That's Shane. He's Luke's step-dad. You met Luke last night. And next to him is Luke's mom, Sonya. The two of them just got married last month."

"Aww..." She smiles with the sexiest look of concentration on her face that I've ever seen.

I smile at Dani. I give her credit. She's really trying to remember everyone. "Let's see. You met Luke. He's Arianna's brother. You met Taylor. Next to Taylor is his wife, Nicole. And then next to Luke is Jason. He's mine and Ryan's brother. And this is Jessa. She's Jason's wife. I love all my sisters, but she's my favorite."

I kiss her on top of the head. She chuckles. "That's because without you, Ryan, and Jason, I wouldn't be here today."

Breetana smiles brightly. "We'd be jealous, but none of us can argue their bond."

"They're almost as close as me and Arianna," Taylor says, winking at Arianna.

"I thought Luke was Arianna's brother." Dani looks confused.

"I am," Luke says. "But those two have one hell of a strong bond. We have one, too, but not anywhere close to them."

"So, you all aren't actually related? You're just really close and are like a family? Or... did I... miss something?"

"Well, Jason and I are brothers. Ethan and Jenny are our parents. Nick was adopted, so not blood, but still related," Ryan starts.

"And Luke and I share a father who is no longer with us," Arianna says.

Dani's beautiful blue eyes widen. "Oh! I'm so sorry. I -"

"Don't, honey. It's not what you think. He was a true piece of shit. No one here misses him." I lay my hand on Dani's thigh and give it a light squeeze. She shivers under my touch. I fucking love that I have that effect on her. "Eve is Chase's mom, and Sonya is Luke's mom."

"And then me and Nikki are sisters," Breetana says.

I smile again. "Lastly, the three kids in the playpen over there. The taller one is Tait. He's Taylor and Nikki's son. The one looking at you is the flirt. That's Christopher. He takes after his dad, Ryan, in the ladies'

31

man department. Thank God he takes after Arianna when it comes to looks."

Everyone laughs. Ryan shakes his head as he chuckles. "Asshole."

I smile. "And then the shy one in the corner is Jackson. He's Jason's and Jessa's son."

Dani practically glows. "They're all adorable."

Ryan smiles. "Now that we've totally overwhelmed the poor girl, we should get down to business."

Jason nods. "Agreed. What the fuck happened last night?"

Dani bites her lip and looks down at her lap. She subtly leans into me. I put an arm around her, sensing she needs comfort.

"Dani? Would you like me to start with what I know, and you can fill in the blanks for us?" Ryan asks. She nods and sniffles, wiping away a tear. "Okay. Everyone. This is Dani Jade. She's a photographer. The same one whose work hangs all over this house. Last night, after Nick was through serving a warrant with Taylor, I met him at his condo. I intended on a couple drinks while Arianna and the girls..." Ryan looks at his wife. She almost imperceptibly shakes her head. "While they were working on a project. We were just heading inside when we heard screaming. We busted into Dani's apartment. We found her on the floor."

"I... had a nightmare. It felt real," Dani says quietly.

"She fought us. Someone called the police," Ryan continues.

"I heard Nick's address and took the call," Taylor fills in.

Ryan nods. "After we got her to calm down, Taylor and I heard some noises in the common area. We saw someone snooping around."

"We thought he was a nosy neighbor, but when he saw us, he took off," Taylor says.

"We knew something had scared you, Dani. We didn't know what, but that's why we decided you needed to leave."

"We both felt danger."

"After we got you back here, we weren't sure why you decided to run until I found out who the guy who almost kidnapped you was." Ryan's eyes flick to me. I don't know who he was, but I'm happy I'm about to find out.

"We totally understood why you were scared and didn't want to trust us," Taylor finishes.

Luke clears his throat and looks at Dani. "Max King of the Krins Mafia. A small time little group out of Northern Florida."

Dani sucks in a breath. I hug her tighter.

Taylor nods. "Your turn, Dani. What happened to make you a target of a mafia?"

It takes her a few minutes attempting to compose herself before she stands up. I look up at her. "Dani?" I ask.

She holds her head high, though she sniffles. "I witnessed them murder Carter Rudd."

Chase coughs. "Carter Rudd? I hold his investment accounts. They still think he's just missing."

Dani hugs herself as she turns white. I stand and put my arms around her. She burrows into me. "I watched them burn his body. I have pictures."

"You took pictures?" Jason's voice is slightly higher as his eyes shoot to her.

She nods. "They saw me. Cedar Key police were involved. I have pictures of them all." She pulls away from me and starts heading for the stairs. "I'll get them." She stumbles and sways.

Knowing what's about to happen, I quickly move to catch her. She goes limp in my arms. I lift her and head for the stairs. "She passed out."

"Do you need any help?" Arianna asks quietly.

I shake my head. "Not right now. Thanks." I look at Ryan. Reading the war going on in my eyes, he nods. There's not a chance in hell she's going to be able to talk to anyone about this right now. Her fear is still too intense.

I take Dani up to my room and lay her down, crawling in bed next to her. I'd attempt to wake her up, but I know she didn't sleep more than a couple of hours. She crawled into bed with me just as the sun was starting to rise. It was still dark. That mixed with her fear, and it's no wonder she's out.

I wrap her tightly in my arms. I don't know why I feel like I do, but I already hate that she was alone all these months fighting the fear of being found by them.

No.

No fucking way that's ever happening again. Maybe I'm fucking crazy, but there's something about this girl. Something that both appeals to me and makes me want to keep her safely tucked in my arms forever.

XXX

"For once I just wish this family could live a normal life. Run our companies and barbecue every week. Ski every winter. Boat in the summer."

"I know, mom," I say quietly.

Mom is laying in my bed on the other side of Dani. She's running a cold washcloth over her forehead and face while I hold her close to me. She's been sleeping for a while now. I don't want to wake her up, but it needs to be done.

I've learned a few lessons over the years about women from Jessa. First, no matter how tough they think they are, they all have their weaknesses. Second, if they pass out scared, they'll wake up scared. Third, the best way to handle a woman is to let her tell you what she needs. And last. Listen to her. If she can't tell you what she needs, watch her. Watch her body language. It will say everything.

"I never wanted this for any of you. I love Ethan with everything I am, but one of the best days of my life was when he handed everything to Ryan, and Ryan turned this entire mafia legal. I thought that meant no more fighting other gangs and mafias."

"And now it seems Ryan always has a battle going on somewhere."

"His sense of protection is so strikingly strong. He's always hated when innocent people get hurt."

"We all do, mom. Jason. Me. It's why I became a cop. It's why Jason got out. He hated that he could kill so easily if it meant protecting someone else."

"I know, honey. He could never let it go, though. It ate him up inside. He's not like you and Ryan. He's always been able to make the kill if he needed to, but he can't compartmentalize like you two can." She sighs as she looks down at Dani and pauses for a long moment. "She's really beautiful. Isn't she?"

I smile. Her color is starting to come back. Her beautiful, long dark hair is spread like a halo over the pillow. I know she'll be waking up soon. "She's the most beautiful woman I've ever seen." I realize my mistake far too late. My mother is like a fucking bloodhound when love and romance are involved.

"I haven't heard you say that since Penelope."

I wince. "I don't want to talk about Penelope, mom. She took everything from me. I should've seen it."

I glare daggers at the wall behind her as Dani begins to stir. I force my gaze to soften as her beautiful golden eyes flutter open. My heart feels like it grows wings. I smile and run my thumb over her bottom lip.

"Who... is Penelope?" she whispers.

I chuckle as her eyes darken in something that looks a little like jealousy. "A woman I thought I loved, but found out way too late that all she wanted from me was my money."

"When they first met, we all thought she was a very sweet girl. She'd been through a lot. She made my boy happy at first. That's all a mother can ask for. But she hurt Nick, and I'll never forgive her for what she did. We did replace the money she took from his trust fund, but I know that didn't matter to him. It was what she did. Even still. She did show him that he deserves everything good in life despite what he came from, and she did teach him how to love."

"No. You and dad did. You taught me how to love. Jessa and Jason. Ryan and Arianna. Penelope taught me to watch my back with who I trust, and who I let in. Penelope is the reason I haven't let a woman in for so many years." I know my voice is laced with venom. The same venom that always finds its way in when I talk about my ex. Dani sighs and starts to sit up, but I pull her into me. I bury my face in her hair and take a deep breath. "I'm being selfish right now. I know you need me, but right now I need to calm down. I don't know why, but you do that for me."

"I... Me? I do?" she asks shyly. I nod into her neck and lightly kiss it. I feel her shiver against me. I smile.

"How do you feel? Better?" mom asks Dani.

"I'm not really even sure what happened."

"You passed out," I tease with a smile against her neck.

She swats at me. "I know that."

God. Something about this girl. Something about having her in my arms. Something about her attitude, her fight, her spunk. She's exactly the opposite of Penelope. She's nothing like what I thought I was attracted to.

I've always gone for gorgeous model-type girls. Dani is dark. She's mysterious. She's interesting. She's intoxicating. I already can't seem to be able to get enough of her. I want her around. She's layered. I just want to peel away all of those layers, and learn everything I can about her.

Dani has sexy as hell curves. She's nowhere near model-thin. I love that I can grab her hips. I love that she has an ass. I love that she's strong and independent. That she fights instead of giving up or running away.

I love so many things about her. I'm quickly starting to realize that all of it scares the hell out of me.

I fell pretty hard and fast for Penelope, and she messed me up far more than I let anyone see. Except my family. They know everything and got me through some difficult times that I would've let destroy me if it weren't for them. I leaned on Ryan and Jason a lot more than I probably should've, but I've always been grateful that they were always there for me.

Still. Opening up to people after Penelope hadn't been easy. I never wanted to.

Not until Dani.

"I think it was all of the people," Dani says softly. "The family atmosphere. I've never had that. It was like everyone at that table was throwing these vibes at me that said I'm safe. That no one is going to let anything happen to me. And the other part of me just couldn't believe it. It just scared me. I've been alone so long that the idea I could have that... It just seemed so foreign."

"Oh. Sweetheart, everyone deserves that," my mom says. "Everyone deserves a family who loves them and cares for them and protects them. I can see how strong you are. How fiercely independent you are. But even the most fiercely independent people need help sometimes."

I smile. "You remind me a lot of Ryan. He thinks he can do everything on his own. He's gotten better about it, but he realized a lesson that I think you need to as well."

She smiles a little sadly as I look down at her. "And what's that?"

"That sometimes the family around you is perfectly capable of helping out," mom says softly.

"You just have to let them. You don't need to fight every battle alone."

She nibbles her lip. "But I've never had that. My dad killed my mom when I was a kid. I saw the whole thing. He ran. Abandoned me. I was only four. The… real… reason I passed out…" She takes a deep breath. "It was because I thought of Krins' voice. And how it's so, so similar to my dad's. My heart started racing. I got so scared." She sniffles. "After it happened, I went to foster homes. I've never really felt anything but having to take care of myself. Fight my own battles."

Mom runs her fingers through Dani's hair. "Things are different now, sweetheart. At least they can be. If you want them to be. Maybe you and Nick should talk for a little while. After, if you would like, Ryan and Nick can take you aside somewhere. You can discuss the pictures you took and everything else. I think you need to be eased into the rest of the family dynamic. So, we'll start with dinner." Mom squeezes Dani's arm as she gets out of my bed. She turns back and smiles as she closes the door behind her.

Dani looks at me, a little wild-eyed. "She's the mother I always wanted."

I laugh. "She's pushy. She'll push her way into your life until you have no choice but to let her in. It's best not to fight it. If you do, she becomes relentless."

"I like her."

"Don't tell her that. She'll gloat for days." I smile as Dani laughs and slowly sits up. I keep my hand on her stomach. "Feel okay?"

"I think so. I know she said to talk for a bit, but I think I'd like to just get the rest of this over with. Show the pictures to your brother. Maybe then I can try and relax the rest of the day."

"Does that mean no more running away? You're going to trust us to help you?"

She turns and looks over her shoulder at me. I'm still laying down, my hand under my head propping me up. I let my hand drop to her thigh and let my thumb draw small circles.

Her eyes darken a little, and she smiles softly. "I really like you. I've never really had a boyfriend. I dated a guy for a little while. The sex wasn't at all what I thought it would be. He was kind of a jerk. I left for a shoot in Australia for Time Magazine and never looked back. Never cared for sex or dating since, even though I've been with a couple of people just for a quick fix. I've been able to make myself just as happy as they all did."

I swallow hard at her honesty; her admission. "It can be pretty great with the right person."

She blushes. I can hear my own voice has gone down an octave as I look up at her. I hate admitting it to myself because I've been pretty happy on my own, but I want her. I want her for more than just a hook-up. I can actually see myself starting a relationship with her. Ever since Penelope walked out on me, I've never wanted a relationship.

I give her leg a squeeze and shake my head slightly. They say relationships that start under intense situations are doomed to fail. I really should stay as far away from her as possible.

Before I even have time to react, Dani is shoving me on my back and straddling me. Her lips crash to mine.

I suck in a breath. "Oh, fuck." My hands gravitate straight to her ass. I let her grind herself against me as I kiss her.

"What is it about you that makes me feel so safe? Like not only do I belong somewhere, but that I actually want to belong?"

I get harder and harder underneath her the longer she stays pressed against me. "I don't know, Dani. All I know is you have already managed to get under my skin. I've never felt like I needed to claim anyone or make them mine. But you? I don't want to let you go."

She smiles. Her fingers draw small circles over my abs as she sits up, her pussy staying firmly pressed against me, making me want to bust out of my jeans. Mine run up and down the smooth skin of her arm. We're quiet for a while until Dani looks up at me. I meet her eyes. Damn, I love her eyes.

"Maybe I don't want you to let me go," she says softly.

I smile as she leans and kisses me. "Then, maybe I won't."

I grip her hips and turn onto my side, flipping her with me. I wrap my arms around her, my hand coming to rest on her perfect ass. I kiss her again and again until I decide that breathing without her isn't possible.

Time slips away.

I forget about all else except making her forget about everything but me.

Chapter Five

⚔ Dani ⚔

I open my eyes to two of the most beautiful and piercing green eyes I've ever seen. I smile shyly and feel the blush creep to my cheeks as I hide my face in Nick's chest when I think of kissing him the way I had and grinding against him like a crazy, horny person.

I feel my cheeks grow redder. "I'm not entirely certain why I can't control myself around you. I'm usually very in control."

"Maybe because I'm so charming and handsome and disarming." He tangles his fingers in my hair and tugs on it until I'm looking at him. He leans in and kisses me long and demandingly.

I've never been one to let someone else have control. With Nick, though, letting him control me, take all of me, is all I want. I press myself closer to him and run my fingers through his hair. I don't understand what he does to me. I don't understand any of the way I feel or my reaction to him. It's so unlike me, but it feels so right.

His large hand finds my tits like they had this morning. He teases my nipple as his kiss turns hotter. I feel like I'm on fire. I can't get close enough. I whimper and moan. I lightly run my nails down his back as he kisses his way to my neck.

He bites, sucks, and licks it. "How do we go from you relocating my balls, to you running away and damn near getting killed, to me wanting you so fucking bad? All I want to do is claim you as mine, Dani."

"I don't know. I don't understand anything about what's happening. I can't stop touching you. I want you." My voice comes out in barely more than a breathy whisper as he kisses his way down my collarbone and back up to my neck while he tugs and flicks my nipples. "I just want to be yours." He slides his hand down my side to my ass and spanks me. Hard. "Oh, fuck!" Heat pools between my thighs and both of my hands find themselves buried in his short hair.

Oh God, why did that feel so good? He just spanked me, and I want him to do it again? He starts trailing kisses down my chest.

At that moment, a hard, loud knock sounds on the door. I jump.

"Fuck," he whispers the words to me and holds me still as I whimper. He turns his head to the door. "What?"

"We need to sit down with Dani before dinner. Gives us a couple hours. I don't want to overwhelm her like this morning." I have already come to know Ryan's deep, rich voice. I can hear the power in his tone. I have to wonder if everyone in this family is dominating and possessive like he is. I can already tell the one next to me is.

"Give us a little while."

"No. Make it quick," he growls. I feel my entire body turn red with embarrassment as my eyes widen. "We have shit to do. I don't care how long you keep her in that bed tonight, but this gets taken care of first."

"Fuck you," Nick growls back. "Give me thirty minutes."

"You two aren't downstairs in thirty minutes, I'm dragging you down there no matter what position you're in." I can't help but laugh at the humor in Ryan's voice. "I mean it!" His voice drifts off down the hall.

Nick groans. "I completely understand if you want to stop after that. I love my family, but they are truly assholes sometimes."

"Even the girls?"

"Fuck yes. All of them. They have to be in order to end up with the men they did."

I laugh again and arch into him. "I don't want to stop."

He gives me a cocky grin as he squeezes my tits. He continues kissing down my chest until his mouth falls to one of my nipples. He sucks hard.

40

I moan and arch into him again as he rubs the other. He pinches the nipple and rolls it between his fingers. He tugs it while he nips the other one and pulls it between his teeth as he rolls his tongue over it. So much pleasure shoots through me. More than I've ever felt.

I gasp, whimper, and moan as I tug his hair. "I want you."

He smiles against my tits as he kisses his way across my chest to the other one. His large hand splays across the one his mouth just left. Just as he starts flicking and twisting it, his mouth crashes down on my other nipple. He lightly bites it. I buck into him.

"You have me."

I shake my head trying to make myself say words I never thought I'd say to anyone. Let alone after a day. "I meant I want you. To be with you. To be yours. Just yours. Is that crazy?"

He grins and wraps his fingers in my hair. He shifts and crushes me to his mouth once more. "Completely. But there's no fucking way I'll let you be anyone else's."

"Why do I feel like this?" I tilt my neck to the side when he starts kissing it again. "Why do I trust you and want you like this?"

"I'd love to explain it to you, but I can't, my girl. I can't explain something I myself don't understand. All I know is that this feels right."

I've always been one to trust my instincts, and he's right. This does feel right. I don't understand why I feel the way I do.

I shiver as his hand trails down my side again to my thighs. He leaves a trail of goosebumps when he moves it back up, this time on my inner thigh. I gasp and moan when he cups my pussy over my panties. I don't know when my clothes disappeared, but I'm okay with it.

I've never thrown myself at anyone like I am, but I can't help. The instant attraction is scary as hell, but I want him.

I just want to be his. It's like some weird hand of fate or something is pushing me directly to him. I arch into him as he kisses me again and again. Deeper and deeper. I grip his hair and scratch my nails across his back. He grips my panties and tugs. It hits my clit.

I scream. "Nick!" My orgasm hits before I have a chance to stop it. My stomach tightens. My thighs tremble. I arch into him as I throw my head back. I dig my nails in his arm as he nips my neck.

"Holy shit, baby. Little pent up?"

41

I can feel his smile against my neck as my pussy clenches and pulses. I weakly slap his chest as I grip his arm and close my eyes. He chuckles as he kisses my neck. He rights my panties as I come down, moaning.

"That's never happened before…" I pant and blush releasing my grip on his arm.

He smiles and leans down, kissing me deeply again. "It'll be happening a lot more. Get dressed. We need to get down there before Ry drags us out naked."

I raise an eyebrow. "We aren't naked."

He winks as he gets up. "We will be if we don't get up."

Every fiber of my being hums at the threat. Instead of making him follow through with it, though, I gain control of myself and get up to get dressed. I watch him shyly.

I really don't understand why I feel like I can trust this family. I know nothing about them. But I feel safe. I feel safe with the family, and with Nick.

✕✕✕

Nick pulls me next to him as we sit down on a couch in yet another room in the endless rooms this house possesses.

"Wow." I look around a little nervously as Ryan sits on another couch next to us and another guy takes a seat across from us. I sink into Nick's side.

Ryan smiles. "This is one of Arianna's favorite rooms. She decorated it herself."

"I love how it opens right outside onto the patio," I comment.

"It always gets a nice breeze from the lake," Nick says.

I nod softly. "Her taste is exquisite."

Ryan smiles, and his cheeks flush just a little. Ryan's kryptonite is his wife. I can't help how comforted I am by that; how comforted I was when I first saw them together. To me, that shows he's loving and caring despite how crazy intimidating he is.

"She's incredible," Ryan says.

I smile and look at the other person in the room. "And you're... um... Ryan and Nick's brother. Was it... Chase?"

He smiles. "Close. Jason. But they call me Jas sometimes. Sounds like Chase." He has the same ruthless and intimidating look that Ryan does. They both are dark. They exude power and control. Even though Jason's eyes are blue and Ryan's are brown, they're both dark and deep.

"I see the resemblance," I say with a soft smile.

"Dani, you said you witnessed the murder of Carter Rudd. Are you absolutely positive that's who you saw?" Jason asks.

I nod emphatically as Nick hands Ryan the manila envelope that holds all of the photos I took of the murder. "Everything she took is in there. She has some clear as day pictures. I was looking through them while she was getting dressed."

Ryan and Jason look through the photos. I tuck my feet underneath me. Nick holds me tighter. I still don't understand why I feel so deeply that I can trust him. All of them.

Ryan sighs. "It's all pretty damn clear what happened here."

Jason nods as they both look at me. "Thanks for picking the condo across from my brother's, and for screaming like you did the other night. You walking into this family just saved my life."

Nick and I look at each other confused before looking back at them. Nick raises an eyebrow. "What the fuck are you talking about?"

"Well, while the two of you were napping, Taylor called me," Ryan starts.

"He said that he just got a slam dunk case put on his desk by his Captain," Jason says looking directly at Nick.

I watch as the realization of whatever is happening sinks into him. "Son of a bitch."

The three of them share a look. It's evident to me immediately that they are incredibly close. They share a bond that must be so tight that they know what each other is thinking.

I clear my throat. "Um... Care to clue me in?"

Ryan looks at me. "I went upstairs to get you both and figure it out. Obviously, you were busy."

I furrow my brows in even more confusion. "Figure what out?"

Jason takes a deep breath. "Dani... um... I'm Carter Rudd's biggest rival. A few years ago, there was a project in Cedar Key that he wanted. I

43

got the bid. I just hired Jessa, and her work was completely outstanding. She did phenomenal work, and the company asked for us to do a second project."

"The project was in a swampy area. Jason flew down and took a look and they decided it could be done, but they had to move over, and it would be half into the next lot," Nick continues.

Jason nods. "The company bought the lot over, and development and construction started. Jessa started working on the project design, but we found ourselves in a tough..." Jason looks at Nick. Nick shakes his head. "Situation. Personally. I also had a site manager who called me saying he had been threatened. That if we didn't stop construction, people were going to get hurt. We continued, despite everything going on here. One day, I get a call that everything we had done had been burned to the ground. The company that hired me backed out. They wanted a new location. Everyone had gotten spooked."

"I found out it was a small-time mafia called the Krins Mafia. We were planning to take them down, but things got very intense here. Family comes first," Ryan says. Nick stiffens. I grow more confused.

Jason shrugs. "So, we dropped it. We let it go. Haven't heard from them since."

"Until today," Nick finishes.

"Today?" My eyes dart around the room. I tense. I truly expect a fight.

Nick runs his hand up and down my arm. "Hey. Relax. I didn't mean here. I meant the information Taylor got."

I take a deep breath and close my eyes for a moment. Ryan reaches over and squeezes my leg. I open my eyes and exhale. "You're safe, Dani. I promise." I nod and lean my head on Nick's shoulder. My heart tells me he's not lying, so I force myself to relax. Ryan lets go. "He's making it look like Jason is the one who committed the murder."

My eyes fly to Ryan. "What? But that's insane! How is that even possible?"

"Shh... There has to be more to this," Nick says against my ear.

"Oh, there is." I whip around as Taylor walks in the room. He plops on the couch near Ryan and puts his head in his hands.

"What? What happened?" Ryan asks. I can feel the sudden edge he exudes.

44

Taylor groans and leans back on the couch. "I need hard evidence, because my Captain just issued an arrest warrant for Jason. He said he'll give me an hour to convince him otherwise. I told him I wanted to investigate it. Something didn't feel right. He's never questioned my instincts before. He's pushing hard for this. It's completely out of my hands."

"Fuck," Jason whispers.

My eyes widen. "He's been paid off." I say it quietly. I don't think anyone can hear me, but I know. I've seen it. It's just like Cedar Key. Only a larger scale.

"There's no doubt, Dani. He's absolutely being paid off," Ryan confirms.

I look up at him. "I feel like this is my fault. If I had stayed instead of ran... faced them..."

"You'd be dead, too." Taylor's intense look makes his words ring true.

"This isn't your fault." Nick hugs me.

I suddenly perk up. "Wait! I gave everything to a police officer in Gainesville before I left. I've been in contact with him." I quickly pull out my phone looking for his contact information. I hand it to Taylor. Taylor takes my phone and looks at the information I pulled up. "Maybe he could help."

"Dani, uh..." Taylor gives me my phone back. "Lieutenant Campbell was killed at a barbecue with his family yesterday. It's been all over the news. National headlines. He was a decorated officer. They think he was killed in retaliation for someone he put away a few years ago. A leader of a profound gang in Gainesville who escaped prison. There's a massive manhunt for the leader. Every department in the U.S. got alerted. Especially us because the leader has ties here."

I completely deflate and nearly cry. Nick kisses the top of my head. I can feel his body humming with anger. "Well, I think we have a pretty fucking good idea who killed him. I don't think it was this gang leader."

"Don't dismiss him so easily. He could be involved. What about those?" Ryan nods to my photos. "They give a pretty fucking clear picture of who did what."

Taylor looks through the pictures and nods as he stands. "Dani, is there anything else you remember about this? Anything the photos didn't catch?"

I hesitate and look up at Nick. He smiles softly, giving me all the courage I need. "I… don't want to sound crazy… but… his voice. Krins' voice. It…" I take a deep breath. "His mannerisms. The way he stood. Like… like nothing could touch him. Slightly leaning to his left."

Ryan nods. "Okay. Good. Why do you feel like all of that is significant?"

"Because it's just like my dad," I blurt out. The entire room is silent as they watch me. "My dad was… stabbed in the right leg. I remember it, even though I was really young. It scared me. He came home and bandaged himself up in my bedroom because my mom was screaming at him. He locked the door. She was banging on it." I look down as Nick hugs me close. "He walked with a little bit of a limp after, and he leaned to his left when it hurt. To… take the pain off it."

"What was it about his voice?" Ryan asks.

I look up at him. "You don't think that's crazy?"

"No. I don't. I think everything helps. And if you feel like it's significant, I want to know."

I nod and take another deep breath, relaxing slightly. "His voice. The accent. It's hard to explain… My father. He's Italian and Irish. His accent is very distinct. Hard to explain, but unusual. I've never heard it on anyone else all my whole life."

Taylor looks at Nick as he nods. "It's a lot. Thank you, Dani." He gives me a soft smile before looking back at Nick. "Crane. With me. Ryan, keep Jason here. Jason, call Jess, and get her over here. I won't be able to stop him if he raids your house or office. But he doesn't have a warrant for here."

Jason raises an eyebrow. "What if he gets one? Everyone knows we're brothers. We're two of the most powerful people in the world."

"If we call, go to Chase's and bring guards." Nick lets me go and stands.

I follow, grabbing his arm. I hate the idea of being here without him. "Wait! Nick…" He must see my panic because he turns to me and kisses me in front of everyone. When he releases me, I can see in his eyes everything I need to know.

"This is my family, Dani. No one is going to let anything happen to you. Just trust them. Trust Ryan. If he says move, do it. Don't hesitate. He'll protect you. We all will." He kisses me again, then follows Taylor out of the room.

I force myself to calm down before I turn and walk outside to the patio. I've never allowed myself to trust anyone before. The only person I've ever trusted is myself. But I'm not stupid. I know I need help this time. This is too big for me. I can't keep running. I have to face it. For Lieutenant Campbell. For myself.

It feels foreign to me to trust people I don't know, but I know I don't have a choice. Everything in me tells me I can trust Nick. And if he trusts everyone else, I feel like I can, too.

I shiver despite the warm and humid air. This is going to get bad. I feel it with every fiber of my being.

I just hope I survive it to tell the tale one day.

Chapter Six

⚔ Nick ⚔

Taylor and I are sitting in Captain Wolf's office waiting as he looks over the photos Dani took of Carter Rudd's murder.

After a few minutes, Taylor clears his throat. "As you can see, Captain Wolfe, Jason Crane had nothing to do with the murder."

"It's peculiar how you, Lieutenant, just happened to come across this evidence. How?" Captain Wolfe asks.

Taylor raises an eyebrow. "Sir, with all due respect, you've never questioned me before."

"Lieutenant, with all due respect, I've never needed to." He looks through a couple more photos. I glance at Taylor as Captain Wolfe puts the stack of photos down. "You say you have an eyewitness? Someone who saw everything?"

I nod. "Yes, sir."

"The same person who took these photos?"

I nod again. "Yes, sir."

"It's also ironic to me, Detective Crane, that these photos taken by your girlfriend, who's a professional photographer and very famous, suddenly surface on the very day your brother gets in trouble." The Captain glares at me.

I look at Taylor. Taylor meets my eyes, the same cold look in mine reflected in his. We now know without a doubt Captain Wolfe has been bribed.

No one but Taylor knows anything about Dani. Everyone knows who I am, but no one knows I'm involved in any way with Dani. We never mentioned her.

"I can't say with certainty that these photos weren't created and edited to look like this gang you speak of killed Mr. Rudd," Captain Wolfe continues. "You have nothing but the girlfriend of one of the members of that family saying it happened. I don't care how powerful Jason Crane or his family is or how in with them you are, Lieutenant. I'm sending teams to his house, his parent's house, and his brother's house."

I watch him pull a stack of papers together. There are six sheets. My heart sinks as I stand. "You're ignoring evidence. Take the photos to the forensics team. I'm sure they'll tell you they're legit." I turn to leave the office, not waiting for dismissal. Taylor follows close behind. As soon as we leave the office, I'm on my phone.

"How'd it go?" Ryan asks when he answers.

"He has six warrants. He's going to hit me, Jason, Taylor, you, Chase, and mom and dad at the same time. He only said he's hitting Jason's, our parents, and you," I respond.

"So, he's fucking dirty. I'll take care of it," Ryan says.

"Make sure Dani has everything. No trace of her. She has a flash drive with more copies of the photos."

"I'll take care of her, Nick. Don't worry."

I hang up and jump in Taylor's truck.

Taylor starts it and immediately pulls out. "He's fucking crazy."

"Unbelievably."

"I'll drop you at your condo. Be there when they show up. Let them search."

"You still have Dani's key?"

"Yeah. Why?"

"Because when they leave, I want to grab more of Dani's stuff to take to her. She has enough stuff for maybe a week."

Taylor hands me the key. "When you go to her, make sure you aren't tailed."

"You think I don't know that?"

"I know you know that. I also know you're pissed the fuck off, and that impairs judgment. Stay vigilant."

He's absolutely right. I force myself to breathe as he pulls up to my condo. "If anything happens to her, I swear..."

"I know."

"It's fucked up how quickly this happened. I won't say I'm in love with her, but I'd do anything for her. So fucking fast."

"You don't need to tell me. Nicole and I fell fast and hard, remember? We knew within a week of meeting each other that we belonged together."

I smile. Everyone in my family fell in love quickly. It's like we kept everyone at a distance, but as soon as our perfect woman entered our lives, we knew. We knew she was the one we wanted, and nothing else mattered.

With the exception of Ryan. Ryan had known Arianna for a couple of years before he realized he had any feelings for her. But as soon as it dawned on him, he waited for her. There was no one else he wanted. Damn good thing because she's perfect for him.

I sigh. "I'll head to the penthouse as soon as they're done."

"Ryan will have guards on them. They'll be safe."

"I don't question that. What I do question is Dani. I don't know if she'll run again."

"Trust Ryan. He won't let her this time."

I nod. If there's one thing about my brother that is a constant, it's how protective he is. If he says he'll keep her safe, he will. Hopefully Dani lets him.

I let myself into the penthouse much later than I wanted to that night. I took a very roundabout way to get here to make sure I wasn't followed.

Before I even have the door closed, Dani is launching herself in my arms and wrapping her legs around my waist. I catch her and bury my face in her hair. I kiss her neck. "Can you greet me like this when I come home all the time?" She nods and sniffles. It's then that I feel her tears on my neck.

"She was having a hard time. Things got really intense, and she was afraid you weren't going to make it here." Jessa rubs Dani's back as I hug her tighter.

"Hey. Why would you think I wouldn't make it here?" I say the words softly in her ear. She shrugs.

"Why don't you guys come sit down?" Jason is in the kitchen taking out food from a bag. "I ordered dinner. It's not Ryan's cooking, but it doesn't suck."

I attempt to let Dani down, but she clings to me instead. "Baby, what the hell happened?" She tightens her grip. I look at Jessa.

Jessa smiles softly. "Trust me when I say that she needs this. She needs you right now."

I nod and carry Dani to the couch. Jason carries the food in. I look up at the massive TV screen. Batman. Of course Batman. Jason's favorite movie. Dani straddles me and keeps her face hidden in my shoulder.

I look at Jason as he sits. "They searched our houses. They threatened to take Ryan in for hiding me."

I roll my eyes and chuckle. "I'm sure that went over real well."

"He threatened them with a team of lawyers. Who all showed up nearly at the same time as if on cue. They ripped the Captain apart. Dani held up well until they arrested Taylor."

Dani gasps out a sob. Jessa looks at me sadly. "She thought you were next."

"We tried to explain that Ryan would never allow either of you to be arrested, but by that point, I think she'd had enough," Jason continues.

"Christ. I'd had enough. We both spent an hour bawling like psychos on the floor." Jessa shakes her head.

I kiss Dani below her ear. "Dani, Ryan's lawyers got Taylor out before Cap even had a chance to drag him in. Captain Wolfe was arrested by our taskforce ten minutes ago. Taylor slapped the cuffs on himself. They found evidence he'd been taking bribes."

Jason chuckles. "Well, they didn't exactly *find* it. More like Robby-the-fucking-computer-genius dug it up and dropped it in their lap."

I smile. "He found shit he'd been doing for years. Cases he'd been assigning himself. Tampering and hiding evidence. Cases involving gangs and other mafias our team never saw. He was so deeply involved in organized crime that he probably could've been a mafia boss himself. He was being paid off by several different crime groups for years."

"I was just so scared they had gotten to you," she whispers.

I run my hands up and down her back. "I'm okay. I promise. They didn't threaten me. I even had time to grab some more of your things so you have more clothing."

"Then, why are we still here if everything is okay?" Dani asks.

"Because Ryan hasn't said it's safe to go home yet," Jessa explains.

Dani pushes herself up so she's looking directly at me. "Who are you guys? Really? You're more than just a family. There's guards everywhere around Ryan's house, and now here. He's obviously the leader of whatever this is."

I hesitate and clear my throat. "Why don't we eat first?"

"No. Now. I'm tired of feeling like something is being hidden from me."

"Baby, we're not -"

"Yes! You are hiding something! I know something else is going on here. I'm not an idiot! I put my trust in you and your family. The least you can do is be honest with me!" She's very obviously trying not to cry.

I look at her, proud as hell and a little turned on that she just stood up to me. Jason and Jessa are concentrating on their food, completely avoiding looking at us.

"Okay. I'll tell you. But while we're eating." I guide her off me, and we dish up. When she's settled, I take a couple bites as I try to decide what to say.

"You basically claimed me, Nick," Dani says quietly. "And I let you. I've never let anyone do that. Especially so quickly. That means I'm a part of this... this... whatever this is. I've never allowed anyone -"

"It's the mafia, Dani. We're a mafia family." I don't make eye contact with her. No one does. The silence in the room is deafening. Without saying a word, Dani puts her food on the table and stands up. We all watch her walk silently to one of the bedrooms.

Jason looks at me. "You know you need to go after her."

I shake my head. "I'd prefer to live." I take another bite of my food and nearly throw up. My stomach feels like it's turning inside out. "Fuck." I glare at the plate and put it on the table next to Dani's as I stand up. "If I'm not back in five minutes, run. She probably killed me."

Jason chuckles. "I don't think she'll kill you."

Jessa smiles. "And it will definitely take more than five minutes." She shrugs. "Fifteen, and I'll call backup for you."

I glare at both of them as I walk to the bedroom. She's not in the first one. I sigh as I close the door. I take a deep breath before I slowly open the other one.

Dani is sitting in the swinging chair of the master bedroom looking out the floor to ceiling window at the city. It was put in not long ago for the kids. For some reason, it lulls them if they're here and fussy.

"Dani, I'm sorry," I start.

"Why wouldn't you tell me that? Don't you think that's incredibly important information? Considering what I'm dealing with?"

"If I told you, would you have run?" She stays quiet as she folds her arms over her chest. I slowly walk across the room and kneel in front of her, taking her hands in mine. She yanks them free. I let my hands drop to my lap. "Baby -"

"Dani." The words are like a sucker punch to my chest. I don't want to lose her so soon. Definitely not like this.

I swallow and nod. "Dani. I didn't tell you because I didn't want to scare you. Knowing you were dealing with the mafia, then telling you that we are the mafia seemed like it would cause you to run. But we aren't like your typical mafia."

She scoffs. "Yeah. Right. Everything is legal." She glares at me.

I glare right back. "It is. We aren't involved in illegal shit. Drugs, weapons, whatever the fuck else. We aren't your typical mafia. Yes, we have a hierarchy. Yes, we have wars with other mafias and gangs, but we don't go around killing innocent people."

"All mafias are the same. All they care about is power, control, and money."

My eyes darken. I have to fight back the anger as I stand and walk to the window.

Away from her.

After taking a few deep breaths and reigning in my anger, I turn away from the city and towards her once more.

I lean against the window, not daring to get closer. "I'll deal with a lot, Dani. I know you've been through some bullshit. You can be pissed off and angry with me all you want. But I won't let you talk bad about my family. If you don't want to let me explain, fine. Leave. Deal with the Krins Mafia on your own. You seemed to be doing just fine without me."

We stare each other down. Finally, she breaks the stare and stands up, walking to the opposite side of the room.

She turns back and glares at me again. "If you expect me to trust you then you have to be honest with me. It's hard for me to trust. Everyone I've ever trusted has either betrayed me or been taken away. I won't go through that again. I will not tolerate secrets. Your family seems very close. So close that you seem to be able to communicate with looks. I won't be kept out of it. If you want me in your life, no secrets. Because I *have* done just fine on my own. I don't need anyone." I watch her deflate as she sits on the bed. "But I *want you*. I want this." She sweeps her arm across the room. "I *want* a family. I want to feel like no matter what, I have protection. I want to know I can count on them just like they can on me."

She looks down at the ground. I make my way across the room to her. It's like some magnetic force is pulling me to her. I wouldn't be able to fight it even if I wanted to.

I once again kneel in front of her and gently take her hands in mine again. I breathe an inward sigh of relief when she doesn't pull away.

Her eyes shine with unshed tears. "It's all I've ever wanted."

I reach up and tuck her hair behind her ear, cupping her cheek. She leans into my touch and closes her eyes. "That's what this is really about? You don't want to be left out of what's happening. You want to know what you're getting into. You feel like you've been accepted into the family. It both scares the hell out of you and gives you that sense of family that you've always wanted."

She nods. I stand, pulling her up with me. I lie down in the bed, pulling her on top of me. I wrap her in my arms and kiss her hair. "Then, let's talk about it. You want information. I'll give it to you." I pause a moment as she nods. "This mafia wasn't always legit. Our dad had a ridiculous amount of illegal shit going on. Money laundering. Drugs. He was part of the weapons trade. He owned Manhattan and New York. He had factions in L.A., Chicago, Dallas. He was in Florida. Las Vegas. He was considered extremely powerful. He had a lot of people in his pocket. Lawyers. Cops. Fuck. Even the DA. No one dared mess with Ethan Crane or his family."

She shifts on top of me, curling herself even further into my arms.

"Just like any other mafia, dad was training his sons to take over. The problem was that the older we got, the less we wanted it. Jason especially. He's never been good about killing someone and forgetting about it. Ryan had been wavering and that caused him to waver more. I just ran from it and became a cop."

"Wait... Killing someone?" She stiffens and looks at me.

"Bad guys. People trying to impede on Crane territory. Other gangs. Mafias. Those that threatened us. We never touched innocent people. That's one thing that's always set us apart from all other mafias."

She relaxes again and rests her head on my chest.

"Ryan was going to school for culinary arts when dad was shot during a war against another mafia. We were all in school when it happened. Ryan always knew he'd be taking over, but after dad was shot, he was forced into it sooner than he thought it would happen. He had always hated the illegality of everything that our father had been doing. Jason and I wanted out after it happened. We helped Ryan become legit. After that, Ryan did all he could to keep us out of it. We only became involved if we absolutely needed to be. Only if it involved family, and we had no choice."

Dani smiles softly as she gets up. She stands and removes her jeans, shirt and bra. My cock gets so hard it actually hurts. My eyes go directly to her tits. She keeps her panties on and neatly folds her clothes.

She glances over her shoulder at me. "Tell me the rest."

My eyes roam her body. "Honey, talking is the last thing I'm thinking about right now."

She smiles and raises an eyebrow when she catches me adjusting myself. "Maybe you should get more comfortable."

I laugh. "I can think of a lot of ways to get more comfortable."

She smiles as she walks back to the bed. She doesn't bother with a shirt. I damn near whimper as I watch her.

I get up and strip to my boxer briefs as she crawls under the covers. I crawl under with her and wait for her to settle in my arms. Why it feels like the most natural fucking thing in the world is beyond me.

She nuzzles my chest as she wraps her arms around me. "Tell me." Her tits press against my chest. While I would rather them be in my mouth, I know she needs to hear everything.

"He got Jason and I to help him out while he finished business school. Jason helped a lot with that. Within a couple of years, we'd turned the entire operation legit. Now, all Ryan cares about is helping people. He's protective as fuck about his family, but also innocent people. He's helped clean up cities. Crime rates have dropped because of him. Granted, it's not always legal how he does it, but he has contacts all over. Police. FBI. ATF. CIA. Even Interpol." I look down at her.

She looks up at me and kisses me. "So, he's sort of like a secret superhero?"

"We actually call him Batman. Rich and powerful businessman by day. Loyal and fierce protector by night. He hates the nickname, but it's part of the reason Batman is Jason's favorite movie. And superhero."

She laughs into my neck as she kisses it. "Promise me he's not dangerous."

"I promise he's not dangerous to you. He'll protect you with his life. We all will. But anyone who comes after you? He's the most dangerous man in the world."

"You all barely know me. How are you just so accepting of me?"

"It's how we are, Dani. I've never felt so strongly for anyone. That's not me. There's something about you that makes me turn into this possessive asshole. I don't want anyone else touching you. I want you to be mine. And with this family, as soon as one of us falls for someone, that's it. They're part of us. And we protect our own." She looks up at me again. I realize what I just admitted. "I -"

Her lips meet mine hungrily. I grab her ass as I slip my tongue in her mouth. She moans. I kiss her deeper. I crave her. I need her. I feel like I'm starving without her.

For several hours, Dani and I touch each other and make out like high school kids. What starts as hot and heavy turns to sweet and loving before it goes right back to scorching. When we start panting, we slow down. The touches become sensual, but only succeed in turning us on even more. We start grabbing for each other.

For each squeeze of her tits I give her, she gives me a squeeze of my dick. For every light rub of her nipple, I get a soft thumb rubbing my tip. For every pinch and tug, she returns the favor.

I follow her lead on what she's ready for, even though I want all of her. When she can't take anymore of the hot and heavy makeout session, she looks up at me shyly as she reaches into my boxer briefs and grabs my cock.

I moan and squeeze her ass as my heart skips a beat. "Fuck…"

She looks up at me through her lashes as she licks her lower lip. She starts stroking from my balls all the way up to my tip. Slowly at first, but when she starts rotating her wrist as she strokes, it becomes faster.

I let my fingers play with the waistband of her panties before trailing them down. I lightly rub her from her clit to her pussy. She lets her head fall back as she continues her strokes. I lean down and start kissing along her throat as I slide her panties aside.

I give her nothing but one finger lightly rubbing her clit. When I start feeling her shiver and tremble and grip my dick harder as she strokes, I slide one finger slowly and deeply inside her wet pussy with a low groan.

She moans as she arches into me. "Yes…"

I can feel how close she is by the way she clenches and tightens around my finger. I match my thrusts with her strokes. Fast and deep. When her trembling becomes uncontrollable and I'm close to coming, I start crooking my finger inside her pussy as I thrust. Her hand starts to shake as my dick starts to throb.

I kiss up to her ear and whisper, "Come for me."

"Oh, Nick!" She tightens and clenches around my finger. I bury it as deep as I can go inside her. She comes hard for me, arching, moaning and jerking her hips with every spasm.

"Fuck… Dani…" I moan against her neck as I come just as hard as she had. She continues to stroke me through it, soaking her hand and my dick in my come. I can feel it getting everywhere, but I don't care.

I start thrusting slowly again, not nearly done with her. She continues slowly stroking, making a mess but obviously just as much not done with me.

After numerous coming sessions, and when neither of us can keep our eyes open any longer, we drag ourselves from the bed to clean up. When we finish, we fall back into bed and quickly into an exhausted sleep just as the sun is peeking over the horizon. Dani is wrapped tightly in my arms right where she belongs.

Chapter Seven

✗ Robby ✗

There's nothing like sitting in my own place doing what I want. No one looking over my shoulder. No one telling me what to do. I love that I can live my own life without having to answer to anyone.

It's not that I don't like people. I just don't trust them. I trust very few people. The rest of them I'm sure have some kind of bizarre scheme up their sleeve.

Like some weird scheme to try and kill my sister. Well, at least the woman I consider my sister. The only person who has ever really been there for me over the years.

Arianna and I have been friends since middle school. Unfortunately for both of us, Renza, my ex, was also part of our group. They had basically grown up together and were already as close as sisters by the time I entered the picture.

The three of us immediately hit it off, though. I liked Arianna right away, but I fell hard for Renza. At least at first. We were together all through middle school and high school. But I had started struggling with my sexuality.

Renza also started changing. Becoming distant. Experiencing bizarre and uncharacteristic behavior. Jealousy towards Arianna. Outright accusations that I was fucking Arianna on the side.

The thought was nauseating. She's like my fucking little sister. Fucking her would be no different than fucking a family member to me. I love her, but that's disgusting. Renza and I started growing apart. Which was fine with me, because the older I got, the more I knew she wasn't my type. I like guys. She didn't have the right parts.

The jealousy turned to outright viciousness. Such viciousness that even though I wanted to break up with her, I was talked into staying so I could keep an eye on her. But then it turned into a violence I never thought I'd see from her. She set Ryan and Arianna's house ablaze knowing Arianna freezes up completely around fire. Arianna was pregnant at the time. Other people were in the house. Everyone got out, but Renza nearly killed them all. She fled. We still haven't found her.

I sigh and open my laptop. The sun is just peeking over the horizon, but I have a shit load of work to do. Something doesn't sit right with me with this Krins Mafia we're dealing with. As far as I can tell, and my research has never been wrong, they have four members. One of them unfortunately met his maker a couple days ago when I put a gun in his mouth.

It just doesn't make sense. They're small, yet they paid off an entire police force in Cedar Key? Granted, there were only three cops on the force, but it still doesn't make sense. They're small. They don't bring a lot of money in. Yet, the accounts of the three cops in Cedar Key were padded quite nicely. The Captain here in Chicago was receiving very high weekly payments.

Between everyone, that's far more money going out of the pockets of the Krins Mafia than they're even close to bringing in.

I don't like it. I growl low in my throat and reach for the energy drink next to me. I never used to drink this shit. But I've been staying awake far fucking longer lately the more obsessed I get with this case. Sometimes, I don't even remember to eat. If it wasn't for Luke and Arianna, I probably wouldn't.

I smile at the thought of Luke. He's an amazing man. I never really thought it was okay to be gay. Even though I've known for a while that I am, I'd seen the way some people in school were treated when it came out that they were.

It was never really about if I could handle the bullying or not. I'm a big guy. I'm muscular. I'm over six feet. People didn't mess with me in school. I had an attitude that matched my looks. People usually stayed away from me. I liked it like that. But it also hurt to see what others went through. I didn't want to be one of them.

Eventually, dating Renza was just my cover. Part of my image. One of the things that kept my dirty little secret from being blasted all over the school. And that's just what it was to me. A dirty little secret. I accepted who I was, but I also thought being gay was wrong. That something was fucked up with me.

And it was that secret that allowed me to be close enough to her to discover her sick plans. At least some of them. It allowed me to investigate my suspicions and watch her. Because for all she knew, I was just a love-sick fool following her around like a lost puppy. Too in love to see what she was really doing.

I turn back to my screen and focus. There are more important things going on right now than a trip down memory lane. But, as luck would have it, just as I'm getting into my groove, a very loud knock sounds on the door.

"For fuck's sake," I growl. I hate being interrupted when I know I'm onto something.

I get up and storm across the room to my door. I throw it open only to see Luke on the other side. The object of every fucking fantasy I think I've ever had. He gives me a cocky grin. I definitely feel like I should be concentrating, but turning him away isn't an option. I want him near me all the time.

I lick my lips and back up to let him in. Of everyone in this mafia, Luke and I have become closest. To everyone else, we're just friends. But behind closed doors? Luke is my dream. He's everything I've ever wanted, but never knew I needed.

It was after Arianna and Ryan's wedding that I realized I want that. I want the type of love they share. And the only way I'd ever get that was if I allowed myself to be who I really am and explored it.

Luke was the one who helped me do that. I was instantly attracted to him, but stayed far away. Until he approached me anyway. All it took was a subtle touch of his hand to mine; his thigh against mine when we sat next to each other. I knew he was feeling me out.

Our first kiss was late at night after everyone was asleep. We were off the coast of Greece. Nothing around us but open water and the stars. I was laying on a pool chair enjoying the serenity when he came out and sat next to me. We talked for a while. Then his lips were on mine, and everything was right.

We snuck around everyone, not wanting to ruin any plans. My job was to keep an eye on Renza. I couldn't do that if it was known that we were together.

I'm also a little fearful of coming out. Luke is the love of my life, and I'm not ashamed of it. I'm scared, though, that the family I've been accepted into won't be so accepting of me if they know who I truly am.

It's a selfish reason. Part of me even knows I'm being stupid. The idea of coming out, especially after this long, and admitting to people that Luke and I have been together for over a year and hiding it, sends me into an instant panic attack. And I don't even have panic attacks.

I close the door behind him and watch him sit on the barstool next to where I was. It's not unusual. It's just having him that close fucks with me. It's not my fault I want him all the damn time.

Luke smiles. "So, where are we at? What did you find out?"

"Uh... Well, I know something is really fucked up. This doesn't make sense, babe." I pull up everything I found out and show it to him. "It has to be a front. Look at the money going out compared to in. It's a substantial difference."

His leg touches mine as he leans over to look. I discreetly suck in a breath and force myself to breathe normally, even though heat has spread throughout my entire body, and all of my blood has rushed directly to my cock. I have to focus on what's in front of me. Luke on his knees between my legs needs to wait.

I can't help but smile, though. Of all the people in the world, Luke is the only one who has ever given me those mythical butterflies.

He looks at the screen confused. "No way anyone can survive like this. Let alone a mafia. That's not possible. Where the fuck did you find this?"

I look at him, half in astonishment and half in pure lust. "You're joking." I grab my energy drink. He laughs and drops his hand to my upper thigh. I nearly drop my can. "Holy shit," I whisper and force myself to look at him as he squeezes my thigh.

This happens every single time he touches me. My reaction to him is instantaneous and always strong. He's incredibly close to my balls. I can think of nothing now but him. With his other hand, he grabs my can and sets it back down on the counter.

"You're seriously too fucking good for that shit. You drinking those things to keep your ass awake ends right fucking now."

I can't keep my eyes off his lips, but I feel his eyes burning into mine. I swallow and lick my lips as he inches closer. His hand has ridden up my thigh so high that the back of it is touching my erection.

"Jesus... Christ."

My throat has gone completely dry. I feel like I've lost all control of everything. I can't move. I can't breathe. My body has become numb. All I can feel is his hand on me. All I can think about is his lips on mine. Every time. It's like this every damn time. His lips are so close to mine. His cologne overpowers all of my senses.

"I think you need a break," Luke says huskily against my lips. He gives me a half smirk.

"I... really... need... fuck it."

Whatever sane thought was left in my head has been violently consumed with my desire to have his lips on mine. I move in the last fraction of an inch and crush my lips into his. My arms wrap around his broad shoulders. My body melts into his. God he always feels so good. So fucking good.

"Mmm... fuck I've missed you." He stands up and pulls me with him. He's got maybe an inch on me in height, but it feels like he engulfs me in his arms as he pulls me close.

His lips meet mine in a fevered kiss as he backs me up against a wall. My back meets it with force, but all I care about is him.

His hips grind into mine. I can feel how hard he is for me. He's always hard for me. He strains against his jeans just as much as I am.

I can feel we both need the friction, so I move my hips against his with just as much force as he gives me. My hands fist into the back of his shirt right at his waistline.

"Me too. Shit, me too."

Luke grabs my ass as his tongue meets mine. It becomes a war of domination that I lose as soon as Luke's hand finds my zipper. He tugs it down with a bit of aggression as he pins me against the wall. He shoves his hand into my pants and grabs my cock over my boxer briefs. I moan, and my eyes roll back into my head.

"Fuck. I'm yours. Fucking yours." I have yet to understand why it's like the first time with him whenever we are together. But I don't care. His hand squeezing and rubbing my length and balls is the only thing my mind can wrap itself around.

"I know, baby. Fuck, I love hearing you say it."

He pulls me away from the wall while keeping one hand in my pants as he plays with me and massages my cock. His lips never leave mine. His tongue dips in and out of my mouth as he backs me down the hallway to my private sitting room. The sitting room I've never allowed anyone in but Arianna, Ryan, and him.

He backs down a couple steps, then guides me down them. As soon as he gets to the couch, he sits. I immediately miss his lips on mine. Still not taking his large fucking hand off my cock, he brings his other hand around and rips my button off my jeans. I barely hear it ping across the floor as he yanks my jeans down. He briefly removes his hand from my cock as he shoves my boxers down. I spring free.

He looks up at me and grins as he licks his lips. "I still can't believe how fucking big you are."

I look down at him with an arrogant smirk. I know I'm a good size. Thick. Long. The kind of dick fantasized about. But his opinion is all that matters.

I run my fingers through his short brown hair and tug. "Just suck it. You're killing me." I moan as he laughs and takes me in both his hands as he strokes. "Fuck yes." One of his hands drops to my balls. He rolls them around in his hand as he tugs and jerks on my cock. He keeps his eyes on me as I close mine and throw my head back in pleasure. "Aww... Goddamn." My hips move in time with his pace. Just when I think I'm going to have to shove myself into his mouth, he finally takes me. "God, yes."

His tongue swirls around my tip. His teeth scrape along my shaft. He takes me deep and ever so gently bites my tip as he continues his assault on my balls.

He strokes my shaft and sucks on my tip. So many sensations are hitting me at once that as soon as I feel that all too familiar jolt shoot down my spine, my cock immediately follows.

"Shit." I try to pull out of his mouth, but he doesn't let me. My stomach tightens as my dick thickens. "Fuck. Luke, I'm gonna come." I try pulling out again.

"Mmm…" He keeps me in his mouth and looks up at me, a devilish glint in his eye.

I can't hold back. I nearly collapse as I release. I shoot hot liquid into the back of his throat, and let out an animal cry as he sucks me dry and swallows every fucking drop I give him.

When I'm done, my pants around my ankles, I drop to my knees in front of him, gasping for breath. I love the way he makes me feel. I love how I'm exhausted afterwards.

He runs his fingers through my hair and over my shoulders before he grabs my chin and forces me to look up at him. He kisses me, long and slow, making me taste myself on his tongue. He brings both hands to my cheeks and runs them to the back of my head, deepening the kiss.

When he pulls back, he smiles. "How was that for you?"

"Best fucking blowjob I've ever had." I can't help but smile back.

"Really? Considering how many I've given you, that's a fucking compliment." Luke drops his hands to his own jeans.

I follow every move he makes with my eyes. He flicks his button open and holds himself down as he unzips them. He lifts his hips and slides his jeans and boxer briefs down. My eyes go wide as he pops out for me. His beautiful dick always astounds me.

I find myself licking my lips and swallowing. I still can't believe how right it feels being with him. Perfect even.

He smiles at me. "You planning on staring at it all day?"

I look up at him and clear my throat as he rests his arms on the back of the couch, waiting for me to make my move. I don't hesitate. I take him in my hands. He throbs as I start stroking him.

It's his turn to moan. The sound tells me all I need about how I'm pleasing him. I keep steadily rubbing him. I reach down and start playing with his balls, tugging lightly as I stroke him.

I slowly and eagerly take him in my mouth. His familiar taste on my tongue as I start sucking on his tip makes me harden again. I reach down and start squeezing my dick to relieve the pressure as I take him further and further to his own release.

He leans back and lets his head drop to the back of the couch. He gently thrusts into my mouth, quickening his pace to match mine. I stroke him more firmly as I suck harder on his tip.

"That's it. Just like that, baby."

I smile at his deep voice saying the word 'baby.' The way it rolls so naturally off his lips. His whispered words of encouragement make me start scraping my teeth lightly up the sensitive vein running along his length. His moans, and soft sounds show me he's enjoying it. I fucking love that he does it.

His hands bunch into my hair. He pushes my head down so I take him further into my mouth. He guides my head up and back down, setting a pace he needs. I smile and let him take control as he fucks my mouth. I keep pace with my strokes as I suck him off.

"Fuck, I'm gonna come... I'm gonna come." He yanks me back like he always does, but I love how he tastes. I take him back in my mouth and suck him until he comes for me. I keep sucking until he stops pulsing and spilling himself into my mouth as I swallow all he gives me.

It's his turn to catch his breath. I grin, kiss his tip, and stand, pulling my jeans and underwear up. I sit next to him as he pulls his up, too. He stands and pulls me up with him.

"What are you doing?"

"It's seven in the fucking morning. You had to be up all night considering how many cans of energy drinks there are sitting on that counter." He lays down on his side on the couch and pulls me down with him with my back to him. He kisses me on the back of the neck and pulls me closer to him. "So now we rest."

"Why the hell do I feel so safe? Like this is the most natural thing in the world? Fuck. Like I've just been waiting for you? Even after all this time, I still don't get it."

His chuckle comes from deep within, and his chest vibrates against my back. "Because you are, and you love that feeling."

I have never in my life snuggled into fucking anyone, but I do it with him. I love the feel of him against me; his arms around me. I love the feel of his warm breath against my neck.

Being with him is everything I've ever wanted but never dared to let myself even think was possible.

This.

Him.

I've finally found what I've been looking for. In his arms I found my safety. The one thing I never felt I truly grasped.

With him, I found my home.

Chapter Eight

⚔ Dani ⚔

"We'll head over. I just need to get Dani up."

I force my eyes open and blink against the sun. Nick is sitting on the edge of the bed with his phone to his ear.

He's really a beautiful man. The muscles in his back are just as well-defined as the rest of him. I could stare at him all day and never get tired of the view.

"I know, Ry. We'll be there. It was a long fucking night after a really long fucking day."

I smile and blush as I giggle. Nick looks over his shoulder and grins as I hide my face.

It was a long night. A long night of us not being able to get our fill of each other. A long night of us not being able to keep our hands to ourselves. He drove me crazy all night long. The thought of the heavy makeout session makes me want him all over again, the touching… I bite my lip as I smile. The orgasms.

"We'll be there." He hangs up the phone and quickly throws the covers off me before I have a chance to react. I squeal and laugh as he covers my naked body with his.

"Too bad you're wearing jeans," I say shyly through lowered lashes.

"No. Good fucking thing I'm wearing jeans. Or I'd be fucking you right now, and we need to get up. Ryan has news, so it's back to reality, baby."

I pout. Nick laughs and kisses me. His tongue slides into my mouth and dances with mine. After a few moments, he reluctantly pulls back.

I look up at him. "Do we really have to go?"

"I'm sorry, Dani. I know after yesterday you probably want to forget everything that happened, but that's not the way we work."

I sigh. "No, it's okay. I understand. I can't just keep running from this."

A flash of pride crosses over his face as he kisses me once more. "Your strength is something incredibly sexy, honey."

I smile and blush. "Most people find me intimidating. I've always just taken what I wanted and done what I felt was right. Stood up for myself on my own two feet. Most people run from that."

"Most people aren't me." He kisses me again as he runs his hand lightly down my rib cage to my thigh. I arch into him when he grips it.

My fingertips trail up his muscular back as I smile softly. "What are you doing? I thought we had to leave?"

"We do. But…" he grips my hip and pulls me up into him. "Some things are more important." He slaps my ass.

I jerk into him with a gasp as my fingernails dig into his shoulders. "Oh… fuck…"

He leans down and kisses my neck. I moan in response. His hand wanders back up to my tits. He fondles both of them in turn. He pinches each hardened crest. I whimper when he starts kissing down my body. He stops to lavish my incredibly sensitive peaks before continuing his tantalizing trail of kisses down to my pussy.

"Mmm…," he hums as he licks my clit. My eyes roll back in my head, and I tangle my fingers in his hair, tugging him closer. He sucks. Hard.

"Yes…" I tug his hair and arch into his mouth, begging for more. For all he'll give me.

He thrusts two fingers slowly inside of me and crooks them against my G-spot, making me scream in pleasure. Almost immediately, I start trembling. My pussy tightens and clamps around his fingers as he thrusts.

He licks and sucks from my clit to my pussy. He replaces his fingers with his tongue, sending me into pleasure Heaven. I grind against his tongue as I writhe and moan. He hums low again, sending delicious vibrations through my pussy.

My entire body seems to sing for him. Like he's the choir director and knows exactly what to do to make me hit all the notes I need to. Waves upon waves of pure ecstasy wash over me until I rise to my peak.

"Come for me," he demands as he growls possessively and dominantly.

I barely hear his whispered command over the pounding of my heart in my ears. "Nick!" I tremble and arch into him as I come. My body jerks with every spasm. My pussy pulses around his tongue and clenches hard around him.

I grip anything I can to keep myself from flying off the edge of the world. His hair. His shoulder. The bedsheets. My entire body vibrates and shakes.

After several moments of panting and aftershock after aftershock, I look down at Nick as I start to come down.

He kisses my pussy and looks up at me. "Sexiest thing I've ever seen. You coming like that for me." He kisses my pussy again and slowly gets up with a wink. "I hate to ruin it, but you need to get dressed. As much as I want to stay in bed all day, we really need to go."

I groan as I roll out of the bed and walk to my suitcase for clothing. After taking a shower, my pussy still humming, and getting dressed, I find Nick in the living room with Jason. Jessa is tending to her son, Jackson. He's cooing at her. I smile. He's really a gorgeous child.

"Wow. His eyes. They're so blue," I say, shocked I haven't really noticed.

"His eyes are really vivid. We've always said we could see his soul in them," Jason says pridefully.

"We joke about how our eyes intensified and formed his." Jessa smiles.

I smile as Jason stands and starts gathering their overnight bags. I start to head to the bedroom. "Oh. I'm sorry. Let me go grab my stuff."

"Don't worry about it. We're staying here, baby."

I look at Nick in confusion. "I thought you said we were leaving."

He stands and smiles as he helps Jason grab the rest of their bags. "We are, but we're coming back here. The penthouse is our safe house. It's well guarded. High security. No one is getting here without clearance, an ID badge, and a handprint."

"A... handprint?" I tilt my head.

Nick smiles. "Yes. This building is one of the safest buildings in the city."

Jessa laughs. "It's one of the safest buildings in the world."

Jason winks. "Nick designed it himself."

I look at Nick and smile at the smile that fills his entire beautiful face. "You designed this? I thought you were a cop."

"I am." He gives me a crooked smile. "Before, though, I worked security. I know the ins and outs of safety. Family is top priority. Their safety is everything. So, all of the security in everyone's houses and office buildings is designed by me. State of the art everything. I don't trust a security company to do it. I don't miss anything."

We all start leaving the penthouse and gathering in the elevator as Jason smiles. "He really doesn't miss anything."

"With good fucking reason," Nick says.

I watch him. "That sounds like a story."

Jason chuckles. "Several years ago, someone broke into Ryan's house. He supposedly had the top rated security system. State of the art."

Nick rolls his eyes. "My ass."

I chuckle. "So, what happened?"

Nick shakes his head. "Fucker got right through security. Didn't get far. One of Ryan's guys got to him before he got to Ryan."

"Thank God," Jason says. "But Nick calls up the security company, makes their designers come out, shows them all of the weaknesses and flaws in their system, and then designs his own. It's fucking Fort Knox."

"I didn't start my own company or anything," Nick explains. "I pulled together the best of everything and used them all."

Jessa shakes her head. "You should've started your own company. You'd be a billionaire."

We all laugh as the elevator doors open into the garage. Nick tugs her hair. "I already am. Investments are wonderful when your parents give you a giant trust fund. Anyway. If I had started my own company, I wouldn't be doing what I love." Jason and Nick throw everything in the SUV we drove here in yesterday, then Nick takes my hand. He looks at Jason. "You heading to Ryan's?"

"Everyone will be there. Ryan said this was huge and needs to be addressed immediately."

"Wonder what the fuck Robby found out."

"Something big enough for Ry to want all of us there." Jason gets in his SUV.

Nick leads me to his truck. Before I get in, he presses me against the side of it and kisses me hard. His hands grab both of my breasts. I whimper. He slides his hands over my body and grabs my ass. I moan and grip his shirt in my fists as I close my eyes. He squeezes it, making me gasp. Much too soon, he pulls back and grins.

"Holy hell." I smooth my clothes back down and get in the truck. Nick leans in and kisses me again before closing the door.

Moments later, he climbs in the driver's side. We head out. As soon as we get out of the parking garage, he takes my hand in his.

"I feel like you know everything about me, and I know so little about you."

He chuckles. "You know more about me than most women ever have." He says the words quietly as he stops at a light. He looks at me and smiles.

I sigh and squeeze his hand before looking out the window at the Chicago traffic. Making sense of my feelings over the past couple of days has been difficult to say the least. But I did it. "Can I be honest?"

He starts driving again as the light turns green. "I wouldn't want it any other way."

I turn to look at him, shifting my body slightly and taking his hand in both of mine. He glances at me and squeezes my hand in encouragement. "Nick, I don't fully understand why, but I really like you. I've never felt so strongly for anyone. Certainly not so quickly. I told you last night that I've always been on my own. I've always taken care of myself. But it's so different with you."

"Honey, you said all of this last night."

"No. I said I wanted to be a part of all of this. The whole family. I said I've always wanted this. But that's not all. I want you."

"Dani, I know. You did a pretty good job of explaining yourself last night. Over and over again." He grins and winks at me. I blush at the memory.

I shake my head. "Please be serious."

He sees the determination written all over my face. "Okay. I'm sorry, baby."

"I mean, yes, I want the family. I want everything. I've never felt so safe. Ever. But you. Nick, I've never felt this way before about anyone. I know it's only been a couple days. It's so fast -"

"Dani. Honey." He brings both of my hands to his lips. "You don't need to explain yourself. I understand. I feel the same way. And I know you think it's odd, but in this family? It's really not. Jason and Jessa? It took them a while to admit their feelings for each other, but after she started working for him, they were inseparable. Jason put himself on all her projects just to spend time with her. Chase and Breetana were the same way. Taylor and Nikki? They fell for each other the very day they met. Ryan and Arianna are the only couple in the family who didn't fall for each other quickly. Though, I'm not totally sure they didn't, despite their age. Everyone in my family falls fast and hard. Even our parents."

I let out a nervous and relieved breath. "I'm falling in love with you," I whisper. I thought I'd feel lighter after the words left my lips, but I don't. Nick doesn't say anything. I didn't know that I needed him to say something, anything, back just as much as I needed to say the words.

Nick turns into Ryan's driveway. "When we get in there, it's going to be chaotic."

Nick is still holding my hand as he parks his truck. I bite my lip. I didn't realize how disappointed I would be. I guess I didn't expect him to say he was falling in love with me, too, but I did expect some type of acknowledgement.

"Okay."

"If you get nervous, just tell me. I'll do whatever you need me to for comfort."

I shrug as he lets go of my hand. Without saying a word I open the door and start climbing out. I wipe away a tear and sniffle as I jump down and close the door.

Jessa and Jason, who arrived just before us, walk hand in hand into Ryan's house. I glare at their backs. I don't really know why. They didn't do anything. I'm the idiot who confessed my feelings and got rejected.

I start walking towards the house, trying to check my feelings. Suddenly, Nick pulls me back to his truck. He pushes my back against the door and holds me in place with his body as he takes my face in his hands, forcing me to look at him.

I glare. "What do you think you're doing?"

"Are you going to let me talk?" I cross my arms over my chest but say nothing. "If you'd waited a second before you jumped out, you would've heard me say I'm falling in love with you, too." My breath comes out in a whoosh. I nearly collapse against him. His arms wrap around me, and he pulls me close. "I'm honored that I get to be the guy who finally stole your heart."

"Does that mean you're giving me yours?" I ask into his chest.

"Promise not to break it?"

"As long as you promise me the same thing."

He pushes me back enough so that he can kiss me. "I promise."

I smile as my heart takes flight. "Me too."

He smiles as he kisses me again. When he pulls away, he takes my hand and leads me inside. Ryan and all of his brothers as well as a ton of other people are in the living room.

Ryan looks up at us as we walk into the room. None of the girls are here.

I look up at Nick. "I thought he said the whole family?"

"The girls are by the pool. You can head out there if you want."

"This concerns me. Shouldn't I stay?"

"Your call."

I lower my voice, even though no one else would be able to hear me over the voices of everyone else in the room. There's so many people I've never met. "Will Ryan mind?"

"No, baby. That's not how we work. Everyone is respected here. Male or female." He leads me to the only spot open to sit. It's on the couch next to Ryan.

Ryan looks at someone in one of the oversized chairs. "Get up. You know better. Be respectful."

The guy starts to get up but Nick sits next to Ryan and pulls me into his lap. I love being like this. "Don't worry about it. Sit. We're fine." I settle between Nick's legs as the guy sits back down.

Ryan nods. "Now that everyone's here, let me tell you why. First of all, this is Dani. Dani, this is some of my team."

"Your mafia?"

Ryan's eyes flick to Nick's, then back to mine. "Yes. My mafia." Ryan points to a young looking guy sitting next to Luke. "That's Robby. Robby is a computer genius. He can hack. He can build a computer from scratch. He can recreate shit you think you lost forever. He's part of my mafia, but more importantly, he's family. Arianna is like his little sister. Until he joined me, she was all he had. That makes him more important than just a hacker who's on my team."

Robby smiles at me as Luke runs his hand down his back. Robby blushes and looks down at his laptop. He clears his throat as he rests his leg against Luke's. I grin like a fool. I love love.

"So basically, I discovered some odd shit. First of all, the money going into the Krins Mafia is far less than what's going out. We have cops being paid off in huge sums. A mafia can't survive like this. It isn't possible."

Luke puts his arm on the back of the couch and Robby leans back into it. Neither of them struck me as gay, but they make the cutest couple. Robby sits closer to Luke.

"What about the Captain?" Nick asks.

"He was getting the biggest payments of all," Robby confirms.

Nick kisses my shoulder and tightens his grip around me.

Luke looks at Ryan. "There's no doubt that it's a front."

Ryan nods. "Are you tracking the money?"

Robby nods. "Trying. I just started, but it's already more fucking complicated than anything I've ever come across."

Luke hugs Robby to his side. "You got this."

Ryan smiles. "You're the best hacker I know. You got this."

Robby beams. I snuggle into Nick. Finding out there's something more going on, possibly something bigger than I originally thought is a distant memory. Watching Robby and Luke makes me thankful. Thankful that I finally found what I've been searching for my whole life.

Family and love.

Chapter Nine

⚔ Nick ⚔

(Two Weeks Later)

"Stop! Stop. Dani, you have to get this right," I say.

"I'm exhausted. I need a water break." Dani stalks off, mumbling under her breath. "Asshole."

"I heard that!" I sigh and rub my forehead.

She says nothing as she falls in the grass with her water bottle. I growl under my breath as I take a long drink of my own and give her a couple of minutes to cool down.

It's been a couple of weeks since we found out we're up against a bigger mafia than we thought originally. Robby had been working hard to find them, but all he's found are smaller factions, all a front for the bigger mafia. Whoever these fuckers are know how to stay hidden very well.

We'd pooled all of our resources together. Everyone on my team with the department has been pulled to investigate this, but we're coming up empty.

What's most bothersome to me, though, is that we can't even find the smaller mafia who had come after Dani. After we took out Max King, we expected we'd find the others fairly easily.

Man, how fucking wrong we were. They're all so deeply hidden that even Ryan is on edge. Ryan is never on edge. And if he is, he never shows it.

I put my water down and look at Dani. She already has defensive moves. She's taken several classes designed to protect herself. But she wanted to learn how to fight. I'd been training with her for over a week.

"Alright. Breaks over. Get up."

She glares at me and doesn't move. "I asked you to train me. I didn't ask for that to be all we do day in and day out. I'm tired, and all I want is to go be a girl and take a bubble bath. And cuddle with my boyfriend."

I sigh again. "Dani. Adam Krins isn't going to allow you to be a girl if he comes after you. And he will. You asked me to train you. You asked me to make sure you could hold your own in a fight if it comes to that. Now, get up."

She glares at me even harder as she slams her water bottle on the ground and stands up. Her glare doesn't lessen as she reaches me.

Good.

Being pissed off is a good way to get her to fight and keep training.

"You need to learn how to block his attack and use it to your advantage. Quit holding back, or you're going to get hurt. Now, do what I trained you to do the way I trained you to do it because I'm not fucking around with you this time."

"I'd rather we be fucking around," she mumbles.

I hold back the grin. I would rather be fucking around, too, but her safety is more important. She has to learn to protect herself.

I don't really blame her for not wanting to be outside. It's hot. The humidity in Chicago is a bitch today. I take my shirt off and get into my stance. Dani's eyes roam up and down my body, and she licks her lips.

I groan and take her face in my hands. I lean in and kiss her. My tongue trails over her bottom lip before delving into her mouth. She slips her arms around me and presses closer, letting her tongue tangle with mine. I love the way she tastes.

I nip her bottom lip as I pull away. She whimpers as I gently push her back. She looks up at me with hunger in her eyes as she bites her lower lip. My eyes take on a mind of their own and wander over her body.

"You're so beautiful, Dani."

"You could take advantage of that, you know."

I smile and tug her ponytail. "You need to focus. Adam Krins isn't going to take it easy on you, baby. That means I can't. Now, let's go. Stance up." She growls and glares. "Remember. I'm not fucking around this time. I'm coming at you with everything I have. Do what I taught you because if you don't, you're going to get hurt."

She rolls her eyes. "Fine. Whatever."

Her attitude is sexy as hell. I shake my head as I get into my own stance. Giving her little time to prepare, I step forward and make my move, throwing a right cross at her.

She blocks it perfectly. I throw a left. She blocks. I advance on her throwing punch after punch. She expertly blocks, but misses every opening I give her to attack me.

"Watch for your openings, Dani."

She narrows her eyes as I continue my assault. Watching my every move, she throws a kick at my ribs. I block her.

She immediately throws one at my other side. I block her again, She stumbles but quickly recovers and throws a punch. It connects with my shoulder.

Her eyes widen in fear. "Sorry!"

"Don't. I can handle it." I don't let up on her. I throw a spinning kick and connect with the side of her upper leg.

"Ah!" she screams and falls backwards, trying to catch herself with her hands.

My mind screams at me. I try to catch her because I know what's about to happen. "Don't! Just fall!" Her hand connects with the ground. She screams again. She curls up onto her side and cradles her hand as she starts crying. "Fuck!"

I drop to her side and gently take her wrist in my hand. I touch the side of it and wince as she screams. She hits me with fury with her other hand. I swallow the gasp of surprise and force myself to take the blow.

"I fucking told you I'm tired!"

"Baby, I'm sorry. I was just trying to prepare you. Make sure you're ready for anything thrown at you." I keep my voice steady and calm even though I'm pissed at myself for not listening to her and her needs.

I pull her close. We're both sweaty and sticky, but I don't care. She's sobbing. I can't stand to see my girl cry.

"You shouldn't have made me continue."

"I know, baby. I'm sorry." I hug her closer and kiss her neck. The salt from her sweat hits my tongue. After a few moments, the sobs wracking her body start to subside.

"Part of the issue is that you're fighting your boyfriend, and you don't want to hurt him. You're holding back."

I look up at Ryan. I knew he'd been watching. He'd been watching all week. I didn't expect him to come over here. He hadn't said anything at all until today.

"Do you honestly think I don't know that?" I snap at him. I don't mean to, but I'm also pissed that he picked now to spew his Ryan Crane advice. It's not the time.

"Dani, get up. You need to fight someone you aren't attached to."

"Ryan, fuck off. She's fucking injured," I growl.

He kneels down across from me. Her back is to him. "Let me see your hand."

I glare at him. He's my brother, but damn if the possessive motherfucker in me doesn't rear his head. "Ryan. Walk away. Let it go."

Ryan stares me down as he waits for Dani to turn to him. She gives him her hand, and, under my icy stare, he cautiously examines her hand. She hisses and bites her lip.

A few moments later, he lets go and looks her in her eyes. "You need to fight someone you aren't afraid to hurt. I can go get one of my guards, or you can fight me. It's your choice."

I glare far more viciously. "Are you fucking kidding me? She's done. She's not fighting anymore."

Ryan doesn't acknowledge me. Instead he focuses on her. My blood reaches a boiling point I'm pretty sure could melt the fucking sun.

Dani sniffles. "I can't. I'm hurt, Ryan. My wrist is broken."

Ryan shakes his head. "It's not broken. It's sprained. Probably jammed. Not broken. Do you think Mr. Krins is going to give you a free pass because you fell and hurt your wrist?"

I know he has a point, but I'm just as fucking protective as he is. "Ryan. Back... the fuck... off." I stand slowly, and he glances up at me before looking back at Dani. My fists clench at my side.

"Dani. Trust me." He holds out his hand. To my complete astonishment, Dani takes it. He pulls her to her feet as he stands. She brushes herself off, then takes her stance. Ryan peels his shirt off.

I grab his arm, a little fearful. "Ry." I know what Ryan's capable of. He's the one who trained me.

He gives me an encouraging smile. "Trust me," he says. I back up as Ryan readies himself. No matter what, I do trust him. He looks at Dani. "You give me all you got. Understand?"

She nods. "Yes."

"I mean it. Don't hold back. Don't worry about hurting me. I can handle it."

"I understand."

Ryan throws a punch that Dani quickly blocks. He throws another. Dani blocks again. Ryan shakes his head. "Stop. Stop. When you block, you need to throw me off. Simply blocking gets you nowhere. Block. Push my arm back with your forearm. Got me?"

"I got you."

Ryan throws a punch again. Dani blocks and pushes his arm off. He throws another. She does the same thing.

"Harder!" Ryan commands. Very quickly, their movements are nothing but a blur of motion. "Watch for your opening! You've missed it six times."

He's right. He's given her several, and she hasn't taken one. "Come on, baby," I rumble quietly. I see her getting frustrated.

So does Ryan.

Ryan takes an opening and grabs her arm. He spins her against his chest, one arm tightly holding her around the waist, the other across her neck. "Never let yourself get frustrated. You get tired, you fucking push through it. Frustration leads to weakness. Leaves your opponent an opening. If I were Krins, you'd be dead."

He lets her go, but gives her no time to recover. I see she's tired, but I force myself to let Ryan take her through this. She needs someone who won't go easy on her. That's definitely him.

Dani shifts into a fucking determined warrior and starts fighting Ryan with everything she is.

She kicks, punches, shoves.

"Use everything you have to your advantage!" Ryan commands. "You're a lot smaller than me."

Dani takes his hint and drops to the ground, swiping at his feet. Ryan stumbles, but doesn't fall. Like lightning, Dani is on her feet. She kicks Ryan in the leg and shoves him.

He falls. "Fuck!" Ryan grabs his side.

Dani covers her mouth as she drops to her knees at his side. I know what's coming, but I stay quiet. It's a lesson she needs to learn. "Are you okay? Shit, I'm so sorry!"

Ryan grabs her around her waist and flips her over him and onto her back on the ground. He straddles her and pins her with his body. "Never let your guard down."

Dani struggles against Ryan, but he doesn't let her up. "Ugh! Asshole!"

"Good. Get mad. Then take fucking control. Get me off you."

Dani fights, then figures it out. She turns to her side, throwing Ryan off her. She straddles him, her forearm to his neck. Ryan grabs her waist and flips her over his head. She hits the ground hard. "Ow! Fuck!" Fighting through the pain, she jumps to her feet.

Ryan follows. "Watch for your fucking opening. Take me down and run. You need to learn that you don't need to kill me to win. Give yourself an opening to get out. Now, again. The right way this time."

Ryan throws a punch. Dani blocks and throws him off. He kicks. She grabs his leg. She pushes him back and turns to run, but he recovers and grabs her around the waist.

She drops her body and twists, elbowing him in the ribs. His grip loosens. She twists to the other side, elbowing him again in the ribs. He lets go.

She spins on him and drops her body. She swipes his legs out from underneath him. She jumps up and pushes him, sending him hard to the ground. She runs straight to me. I wrap her in my arms.

Ryan gets up. He brushes his jeans off as he walks towards us. "Let's go inside and get some ice for your wrist. Your punches got weaker as we went on. It's not because you were tired. I'll have Doctor Chantau look at it. I know it's not broken, but I want to put your mind and Nick's at ease. Tomorrow morning, we continue. You and me whether your wrist is wrapped up or not."

She nods. "Okay."

I kiss her on the head, then let her go. She picks up her water bottle and heads for the house. Ryan and I follow.

"I'm sorry, Ry. I know you'd never hurt her or any of us. I'm sorry I got so protective. I don't know what the fuck that was about."

He pats me on the back. "Love. That's what it was about."

I smile. Love. Never thought I'd fall in love again. Truth is, I never was. Whatever the hell I felt before isn't close to this.

Dani is everything I've ever wanted in a woman. A partner. She's strong. She's beautiful. She's compassionate. Caring. She's even become pretty fucking protective of me and this family over the past two weeks. She fits in with the girls. Fuck. She fits in with all of us. Everyone loves her.

Most of all, she fits with me. When she's not in my arms, I miss her. When she is in my arms, I never want to let her go.

Love.

It doesn't seem like a striking enough word. It doesn't seem strong enough. But I can't deny how I feel about her. I don't know when it happened, but I've fallen for her. I've fallen so far, so deep that I'll never be able to come back from it.

I don't even want to.

Chapter Ten

✕ Robby ✕

(One Week Later)

"I don't want to waste time chasing ghosts. Do you really think this is the best option?" Ryan asks.

I scrub my hands over my face to hide my frustration. I'd just come to Ryan's office to lay out my plan, but the more I think about it, the more I hate it.

"We're out of options. We need to go through each of these smaller guys to get to the big one. I've traced them as far as I can go with the information I have. I need more to go on." I close my laptop and look at him. "I like it just as little as you do, but we don't have a choice."

Ryan's gaze is intense. It always has been. Even when he doesn't intend it to be. It's the reason so many people are automatically intimidated by him. Even his office is intimidating.

Ryan sighs and leans back in his chair. "I'll send guys out to the two you found. We'll get you your information." I give him a weak as hell smile as I stand up. "Robby, hold up."

I sigh as I force myself to look at him. I know what's coming. I'm not in the fucking mood. "What?" I keep my attitude in check. Barely. I love my brother, but he's perceptive as fuck, and I often hate him for it.

Ryan watches me for a moment. I want to look away, but I refuse. "What's going on with you lately?"

"Nothing." I shrug.

Ryan narrows his eyes as he stands. "I can tell something's going on. We all can. Arianna's worried. And you know that makes me worry because her instincts are usually right on."

I bite my lip as he moves to the front of his desk. He leans on it and crosses his arms over his chest. "Really. It's nothing."

He watches me again. I very nearly give in. I can't, though. Not yet. "Okay. Just know that whenever you're ready, you have family now. We're all here for you. It's not just you against the fucking world anymore."

I nod and nearly flee from the office as tears sting my eyes. What the fuck is wrong with me? I never cry. Not even when I found out the truth about Renza. I didn't shed a single solitary fucking tear.

Ducking through the house to avoid everyone, I make a beeline for my place. My sanctuary. My little slice of solitude.

It's above an extremely large garage. I love it. I love having my own place to run to when I can't face the outside world.

I nearly sprint up the stairs. I slam the door behind me and start pacing. "Why can't I just tell them? It's not like I'm ashamed."

I'm not at all ashamed of being gay. Now that I've finally allowed myself to admit it, there's no going back for me. Luke is incredible. I've never been happier.

I know what the problem is. There's several. And I'm too chicken shit to deal with any of them. I'm too scared to tell anyone who I really am.

Especially Arianna. She's the most accepting person I've ever met, but I don't know if she could ever accept me after she finds out the truth.

Because the truth is, I've been lying to her for years. I've been lying to everyone. All because I thought something was wrong with me for wanting to be with a guy. So, I forced all of that to the back of my heart and locked it away. I liked Renza. I thought I fell for her, but during this time that I've been with Luke, I realized that couldn't be farther from the truth.

I never felt butterflies. I never felt like I couldn't live without her. Her kiss didn't send electricity through my entire soul. Her touch never set me on fire.

Now, here I am. I have all of that with Luke, and I'm hiding him away like I'm ashamed to be seen with him. But I'm not. I hate not being around him. Not touching him. I hate not kissing him. I'm totally disgusted with myself because I'm too afraid to share our relationship with everyone. Even the small affections in front of people, like leaning into him, scares me. But I do it. Sort of to test people.

I'm terrified. Terrified they won't accept me. That I'll lose everyone. "Fuck it." I grab a bottle of beer, but just as I'm about to take a long drink, someone knocks on my door. I growl and glare at the door. "No one's here. Go the fuck away."

I turn and walk towards my private sitting room, not giving a shit who's at the door. I need to think. I need to be away from everyone and think.

I plop down on the couch and take the long drink from the bottle that I desperately need. I'm so tired of hiding, but I don't know how to come out. I don't know how to tell any of them the truth.

My ears suddenly perk up as I hear footsteps coming down my hall towards me. I reach for my gun and point it at the entrance.

I watch as a tall man with a solid as fuck body leans against the frame. He folds his arms over his chest and levels me with a glare as soon as he sees the bottle in my hand, and the gun pointed at his head.

"Forget you gave me a key?" His voice is hard as I shrug. I know he's pissed off at me. I can feel it in his steely glare that's piercing through me. I put the gun on the table and take another drink. I lean back against the couch. "I thought we talked about this."

I chuckle and down the rest of the bottle. We had talked about it. I don't really drink. But sometimes I get pissed off enough that I do. It's there that the problem is. I usually drink until I pass out. "There hasn't really been a lot of talking between us lately."

Luke crosses the room and sits on the coffee table in front of me. He takes the bottle from my hand and sets it down on the floor. "Then, talk to me. Because binge drinking and passing out after isn't going to get you anywhere."

He rests his elbows on his knees and leans forward. The edge in his voice has all but disappeared. Replacing it is nothing but concern and love.

I say nothing because I don't know what to say. Instead, the tears I fought back all day break like a dam.

"Jesus. Babe, what's wrong?" Instead of mocking me in my moment of weakness, Luke sits next to me and pulls me into his arms. The sweet action forces more tears. I cling to him like he's my anchor. He lets me cry. "Shh... Whatever it is, it's okay. I promise."

He kisses my head and runs his fingers through my hair. He rubs the back of my neck and caresses my arms and back.

After what seems like hours, I finally look up at him. His shirt is soaked.

"I don't know what came over me." I grumble the words and wipe vigorously at my eyes. Showing weakness and vulnerability is not my thing. I've always been the tough guy.

Luke grabs my hands away from my face and kisses me. He holds my hands in his lap with one hand and pulls my head closer to him with the other. His tongue flicks against my lips. I open for him, greedily accepting his tongue into my mouth.

I groan as soon as his tongue finds mine. He lets go of my hands and pushes me back onto the couch. I pull him down on top of me. My hands roam all over him. They grab his ass, his arms, his back.

Our kiss is heated. His delectable weight on top of me makes me harder than I've ever been in my life.

Luke moves his hard cock against me as he starts kissing my neck. I want all of him. I want to feel him against me. All of him. Every. Fucking. Inch.

"I thought you were going to make me talk," I gasp out as he nips my neck.

"Later. I know what you need right now." He grinds harder into me. He always knows what I need.

His glorious dick against mine almost makes me come in my pants. His teeth graze against my neck and my fingers grip his hair. It's short, but there's enough of it for me to tug. I fucking love tugging his hair. He reaches between us and grabs my cock.

"Oh. Fuck."

He rubs it and squeezes it until I feel like I'm going to explode. Finally, his fingers find the button on my jeans. He tugs the button open and unzips my jeans. He pulls my cock out, and then does the same thing to himself. He lets them touch each other. I throw my head back.

"Goddamn, you feel good." He leans down to kiss me.

His tongue finds mine again and again. The pressure building in me from our dicks rubbing against each other is more than I can take. I need to stick it somewhere because I'm about to come undone.

I wrap my legs around his waist and lock him against me as I thrust myself against him. "Luke. Holy shit. I need..."

He pushes against me harder and lets me rub my cock against his. He pushes himself up and straddles me as he grabs both our lengths in his hand. He keeps himself against me and starts stroking us at the same time. I watch him.

His masterful strokes bring me closer and closer to the edge until I'm begging for release. "Please. Fuck. Please."

"Come for me… You know how much I love watching you explode." His intense, heated stare meets mine. The kind that makes me shiver in so much pleasure that all I can think of is him.

My cock throbs in his hand, but it's the feel of his throbbing against me that sets me off. My load spills into his hand and mingles with his deliciousness as he falls on top of me, gasping for breath.

Neither of us speak for several minutes as we're tangled in each other's arms. We hold each other tightly as we catch our breath.

"You always know what I need."

"I may have needed that myself." He kisses my neck as he pushes himself up again. He holds out his hand, the one not covered in our come, for mine.

I look up at him quizzically but take it. He pulls me up and leads me out of my sitting room. Neither of us bother packing ourselves away.

He stops in my laundry room and starts stripping. I raise an eyebrow. "Do you have a thing for fucking in laundry rooms now?"

He laughs as he throws all his clothes in the washer. He pulls me against him and kisses me as he pulls off my shirt. "We made a mess of ourselves. We need to clean up. Then you're going to talk to me. No later. No tomorrow. You're going to tell me what the hell is going on behind those sexy brown eyes of yours." He tosses my shirt in the washer and lets his eyes roam all over me. "God, you're gorgeous."

I blush and shake my head as I take all of him in. Every part of him is sculpted and hard. Every ridge and line looks like it's painted. I grin as I strip the rest of my clothing and toss them in the washer with his. He pours in some soap and leans over to start the washer giving me a perfect view of his muscular ass.

"It's like you're a fucking painting. Every part of you is perfect." I grin as I watch him.

He smiles and takes my hand. He leads me to the shower in my master suite and turns the water on.

With more care and love than I've ever been shown by anyone other than him, Luke slowly cleans me up. I look down as he runs the washcloth gently over me. He takes my cock in his mouth. I lean against the wall. I look down at him and watch him work me. He brings me to my climax once more.

He stands after he finishes cleaning me off and kisses me. It's soft. Not as commanding and heated as it usually is. He pours everything he feels, everything he is into that kiss. I smile against his lips as his arms wrap around me.

"I have a surprise for you," he says huskily.

"What?"

"You'll see." He turns the water off, and we step out to dry off. "Don't bother getting dressed." He takes my hand after we wrap a towel around our waists and leads me to the kitchen. Set up on the table in the living room is a romantic display.

I raise an eyebrow. "Candles and flowers?"

"Not just any flower. The Bird of Paradise." He smiles down at me.

I shake my head in awe. "How do you do it? I mean, I know what the flower is. Bird of Paradise is my favorite because it's so unique. I love the colors. Blue, orange, red, green." I shake my head as I get slightly emotional. "How are you this badass mafia man one second, then this incredible sweet man with me? How do you remember everything I've ever told you about my likes and dislikes?"

He kisses me gently. "Robby. You're my boyfriend. Mine. All mine. Obviously, I'm going to remember everything you've said to me. I love you. I want you to be happy. Make you feel special. Because you fucking are."

He guides me to the couch and sits me down. I smile up at him as he walks to the kitchen. I lean forward and run my finger along the soft petals of the flowers before lighting the candles. Luke comes back with a bottle of chilled Chateau Julien French Kiss and two wine glasses. He sets them down as I sniff the air.

"Raiding Ryan's kitchen again?" I tease.

He laughs as he heads back to the kitchen. He takes something out of the oven. "Fuck right. Ain't no way I can make Thyme Chicken with all these roasted vegetables and mushroom sauce." He starts plating everything and brings it to the couch. "I can plate it and make it look pretty romantic, though." He walks to my TV and puts a DVD in. Then he comes back and sits next to me.

I smile as the movie starts. "Damn. What's the occasion? You're pulling out all the stops today. My favorite food. My favorite movie. My favorite flower. Favorite wine. Favorite man."

"It's been stressful. With all of the information you've had thrown at you that you've had to sift through. I know how many all-nighters you've pulled. I know how tired you are. I thought you needed a break."

I nod as I focus on my food. I eat quietly a moment before looking over at him. "You know how much I love you, don't you?"

He smiles and reaches over to run his thumb over my lower lip. He catches my chin in his hand and kisses me softly. Lovingly. "I know."

I smile a little sadly. He doesn't deserve all the sneaking around. He deserves so much more than me. I look back at my plate. "So…, what did you tell Ryan when you asked for this dish?"

"Uh… I said that I knew you'd been working hard. I thought maybe I could bring over a good dinner instead of getting takeout."

I watch as he goes back to his plate. We both eat in silence. The sneaking around has been hard for both of us, but I think it's taken an even bigger toll on him than on me. He does it because of his love for me, and his desire to make sure I'm able to take everything at my pace.

But I can't do this to him anymore. I have to figure out a way to be honest about us with everyone. Luke deserves it. So do I.

After we've cleaned up, we settle into the couch. I cuddle into his arms as we watch the rest of the movie. The Departed. Something about two cops on the opposite side of the law trying to figure each other out while they infiltrate the mafia. I can't get enough of it.

Luke leans down and kisses me deeply. I smile. This is all encompassing love. The kind of love I've wished for my whole life, though, I'm only twenty-one. I know when he kisses me this way that Luke Massena is really and truly all mine.

Chapter Eleven

✗ Luke ✗

I didn't think for a second that I had a chance in hell of finding the love of my life. Truth is, I've spent most of my life throwing myself into work just to forget about the fact that I'd be alone forever.

I knew I liked guys a long time ago. When most of my friends started talking about how hot a chick was, I simply didn't see it. Didn't feel it. I never felt an attraction to a woman. I thought something was wrong with me.

My first real attraction was to a guy who was supposed to be my best friend. I never told him. I did tell my mother, though. Mostly because I was honestly afraid that I was defective. That something in me was messed up.

Leave it to my mom to give me confidence in who I am. To own it. And that's just what I did. I never flaunted it. Most people have no idea that I'm gay. When I worked for the NYPD, none of my partners knew. Working for the ATF? Same thing. None of my partners knew. My boss did, though. Shane and I had always been close. He was my mentor and became the father I never had.

I'm not ashamed. I just don't think it's necessary for people not close to me to know. I'd had plenty of hook-ups over the years. I never lacked companionship. I never lacked sex if that's what I needed. I'm comfortable with my life the way it is. I'm comfortable in my own skin.

I didn't expect Robby. As soon as I met him, I liked him. We became friends quickly. We hung out. I knew pretty fast that he was the one. But he was with Renza at the time. Though, after watching him, I realized he wasn't in love with her at all.

I saw the way he looked at me. It didn't slip by me that when I stood a little too close, he didn't pull away. I noticed how he shyly stood close to me. Or how he leaned against me before pulling away like it was an accident.

It didn't take long for me to take the leap and kiss him. Everything after that has been fucking magical. All the fucking around without a single person knowing. It was exhilarating.

When we first moved here to Chicago, I knew that his private sitting room was off limits to everyone except Arianna and Ryan. It was his place to unwind. He invited *me* to it right away, though. Like it was the most natural thing in the world. I felt honored.

I felt even more honored when our first time together took place in that room. His special place sharing such a special moment.

I wasn't always this happy. Comfortable. Understanding of who I am. But never this happy. For once in my life, all the shit I went through in life doesn't matter anymore. It's like it all led to him.

I look down at Robby and smile softly as I watch him sleep. I thought being an NYPD officer was the highlight of my life. But I witnessed some really fucked up corruption that went all the way up my chain of command. It seemed like everyone was on the take in the department. And those that weren't were totally oblivious.

There were six officers, including a couple higher up, that were stealing drugs from the evidence room. On record, they were destroying it. But in reality, they were selling. I didn't want anything to do with it, even though I had been approached about joining. I was trusted. They knew I wanted to take care of my mother. And let's face it. A cop doesn't make much.

I never totally understood how it happened, but I was approached by the ATF after attempting to report the incident. Apparently, they knew what was happening. My so-called partners tried to pin everything on me after I confronted them. The ATF hired me. I thought that was the greatest thing that ever happened to me. They allowed the official reprimand, but buried all of my files with the department.

After that, every single person involved was taken down by my team. It wasn't drugs. It was weapons too. The DEA handed the case to the ATF voluntarily because they didn't want to fuck around with the weapons shit they found themselves in. Shane and I became very close. I had a nice career going with them.

Until last year when I quit and joined the Crane Mafia. I'd never really felt like anything I had done in either the NYPD or the ATF really mattered, even though the career I had going was an incredible one. It wasn't until I really became involved in this family that I really felt like I belonged somewhere.

But it wasn't until Robby that I truly realized that the greatest achievement of my life was falling in love. Real love. The kind of love that people don't dare to dream of because it's too perfect.

Robby stirs in my arms. I look down at him. His head is resting on my chest. His silky brown hair is falling just a little over his eyes. I brush it away.

"I need a haircut."

I chuckle as he snuggles closer to me. He's so content and peaceful in my arms. I love the effect I have on him.

"I can cut it for you."

He looks up at me and smiles. "Luke Massena. Badass. Second in command to the most powerful mafia boss in the world. Hot as hell. Gay. Cuts hair." He smiles wider. I laugh. "Can you be any more perfect? Because I'm trying to find a flaw, and I can't."

I smile and turn over to my side. I cup his chin in my hand. "I have many flaws. One of which is how perceptive I am. Gets me in trouble sometimes."

I lean in to kiss him. It's time to get him to open up. No matter how pissed off it gets him. I pull back and pull him close.

I know exactly what's on his mind, but I can't help him if he doesn't talk to me. Lucky for both of us, I know how.

"Do you have any food in this place?" I ask, already knowing the answer.

"Uh... Not really. Arianna likes when I eat with them. Says she knows I'm eating well then."

I really don't blame her. Everyone knows Robby drinks a lot of energy drinks and sometimes binge drinks. He eats very little. How he still has a body like he does is beyond me.

I kiss him again. Tenderly. "Give me an hour. Meet me on the roof."

"An hour for what?"

"Robby." I kiss him, then stand up. "Just trust me. Do as you're told." I head to his laundry room and quickly get dressed. I have big plans for him. I sense he needs something like this. More than just the dinner and movie we had last night. "One hour, Robby!"

I yell the words back to his bedroom as I head for the door. "Got it!"

I grin as I close the door behind me. I quickly walk across the property to Ryan and Arianna's house. I slip through the back door to the kitchen and smile. As I knew he would be, Ryan is cooking.

"Any chance of you whipping me up something for a picnic for two?" I lean against the kitchen counter as Ryan turns to me with a spoon.

"Taste. And then we'll talk."

I take the spoon and taste the sauce. "Needs... something."

Ryan tastes it and winces. "You're right." He throws oregano in it and stirs it before making me taste it again.

"Much better."

He nods and turns it to simmer before turning back to me. Whatever the red sauce is will be simmering all day long on a low heat. It's how Ryan works. "Now, tell me about you and Robby."

I smile and damn near laugh. "You don't miss a fucking thing, do you?"

"Not typically. I've seen the way you two look at each other. I've seen the touches. And it's been over a damn year."

"He hasn't come out yet, though."

Ryan shrugs. "Technically, neither have you. Doesn't mean your family doesn't know."

I put my head in my hands and groan. "This is killing him. I can tell."

"Did you come here for food or advice?"

I look up at him. "Maybe both."

He smiles as he gathers some stuff out of the fridge and gets to work. "You've said you're comfortable with yourself. The choices you've made. Who you are. Yet, you're keeping a huge part of yourself hidden from those who love you. It's going to be hard to help Robby become comfortable in this new life if you're hiding, too. This is killing you just as much as him. We all know anyway. All of us. We've all seen the both of you."

I can only nod. He's right. I never really cared what people thought about me, but I've kept part of myself hidden for years, only opening up to a few people. I know all of them know about me. I've always been able to tell. There's never been a reason for me to tell anyone anything because they all know.

I finally have the family I've always wanted. The opportunity to protect my family as I've always wanted. How can I say I'm comfortable with who I am if I can't admit to my family who I am and confirm what everyone already knows?

"Okay. Point taken."

"I think you need to have a serious discussion with Robby about what's holding him back from telling us all that he's in a relationship with you. And while you're at it, maybe you need to figure out what's holding you back, as well."

"I know what's holding me back."

"So do I."

"It's because I feel like everyone already knows about me. Why reiterate?"

Ryan chuckles and shakes his head. "It's not easy being a gay man in a role of near absolute power like you have. But it also isn't fair to yourself to feel the need to hide it." He finishes the picnic meal and turns, searching through cabinets for something. His words are like a kick to my balls, but he's right. I never really thought of it like that.

Arianna comes into the kitchen and kisses me on the cheek before turning to Ryan. "Hey, handsome. What are you looking for?"

"Didn't we have a picnic basket?" he asks. Arianna slides in front of him and kneels in front of a cupboard. She pulls out a basket.

I grin as she hands it to Ryan. "Took her a second to find it. You would've been looking all day."

Ryan leans down to kiss Arianna. "Thanks, baby."

"You're welcome." She grabs his ass and a bottle for Christopher on her way out.

He growls. "If Luke wasn't here, you'd be on the counter." Arianna laughs as she blows a kiss over her shoulder at him. Ryan shakes his head. "She's going to be my undoing."

"Oh, I don't doubt that." I check my watch. "Fuck, I'm gonna be late." I grab the basket Ryan just finished packing and hug him.

He hugs me back. "What the hell is this for?"

"Giving me a clearer head. Thank you for everything." I pull back and head for the door.

"You're welcome."

I nearly run back to Robby's, my plan at getting him to open up unfolding in front of my eyes. I head up to the roof and find Robby laying on his back with his arms folded under his head.

He glances at me. "Took you long enough."

I chuckle and sit next to him. He sighs and turns to his side, laying his head on my lap. I run my fingers through his hair. "Ryan made some pretty badass steak sandwiches for us. There's fruit in there. Cheese and crackers. A couple sodas."

"You really like taking care of people, don't you?"

"It's my job to take care of people. That's not what it is with you, though. With you, it's different. I care about you. A lot. I love you. You know that."

"I've never snuggled into anyone like I do with you. I've always been the one taking care of everyone."

"I know. But you don't have to do that anymore. Not with me. It never has been that with me. I get to be the one to take care of you now."

Robby puts his arm around my waist and kisses my leg. The gesture is so sweet that I shiver. Not that he hasn't ever done it before, but this feels a little different. I can tell Robby feels vulnerable.

I caress his cheek. "Don't get too comfortable. You need to eat. There's plenty of time for cuddling after."

He grumbles but sits up and does as I say. I hand him a sandwich and soda. We eat in silence for a little while as I wait him out. After a few minutes, he finally talks. "I don't know how to tell anyone that I've been lying about who I am. Arianna will never forgive me."

Aww, yes. There it is. The fear that people will reject him for being who he is.

"When I first realized I liked guys, I thought something was wrong with me. I had a crush on my best friend. I thought something was wrong with the wiring in my fucking head. I trusted one person enough to talk about it. That was my mom. She helped me realize that nothing is wrong with me. Eventually, I grew to be confident in myself. In who I am. I didn't have an issue picking anyone up. But I still haven't fully come out. I feel like people probably know, but I've never confirmed it or denied it." I look at him. He's listening to me intently. I reach over and brush his unruly hair out of his eyes.

He smiles softly. "You still haven't come out to anyone in the family."

I sigh and drop my hand as I take a long drink of the soda. "No. I haven't. It's not that I'm ashamed to or anything. I'm not afraid if I will or won't be accepted. Like I said, I'm pretty sure they all know. It's why I've never felt the need to tell them. Why reiterate? Truth is, I didn't realize until today that I do have some fears. I'm afraid I won't be respected in my position. I'm second in command to the largest mafia boss in the world. That comes with a lot of responsibility, and an immense amount of respect."

"And you're afraid that if people know, they'll look at you as weak."

I smile at him and lay back on the roof, putting my arm out for him. He lays next to me on his side, putting one arm around my waist and one leg over mine. I absently rub his arm as I hold him.

"Yeah. I always kind of thought that it wasn't anyone's business what I do in my bedroom. Truth is, it isn't. But that doesn't mean that I should be hiding who I am from my family. It's not fair to me. It's not fair to them. My mom knows. Shane knows. Other than that? You. And I struggle with that. I struggle with hiding myself from my family."

I choose to leave out the conversation with Ryan. While it might be easier on Robby to know that everyone already knows, I don't want him to feel like he shouldn't tell them on his own.

Robby is quiet for a while as he ponders. Knowing him well enough to know he needs to organize his thoughts, I continue holding him and stay silent.

"I'm just afraid that they aren't going to accept me. I feel like Arianna will be pissed that I didn't tell her sooner; that I was with Renza so long using her for cover. I've been lying practically our entire friendship."

I can't help but smile. "I'll be honest, babe. I really don't think you have anything to worry about. First of all, you know Arianna better than that."

"I guess I'm not worried about her not accepting me. Not really. I'm more worried about her being pissed that I kept this from her."

"You really only just accepted it yourself. You've only been with me for a little over a year now, and I've been the only one. How can you feel like you've been lying to her when you only just admitted all of this to yourself?" I turn over to my side, facing him. I drop my hand to his hip and force him closer to me so he's flush against my body. "I have an idea. It might make things a little easier for you. I know it definitely will for me."

He looks at me a moment as he settles back into my arms, using my arm for a pillow. "What's your idea?"

"What if we talked to the whole family together? As a couple? We'd have each other to lean on for support. And in the end, our family is all that matters. Us. We're all that matters."

He buries his head in my chest. I hug him tightly. "Do you really think they'll be accepting?"

I kiss his head and smile into his hair. "I do. They haven't given me a single reason to think otherwise."

"Then why haven't you done it yet? Is it really just because you think they already know about you?"

I'm quiet for a few moments because I really only have one answer. "Because it didn't matter to me until right now. I've never been in love with anyone before. But I am. With you. And I want to shout it from the fucking rooftop."

He looks up at me, an adorable look of both shock and awe spreading across his handsome face. The same look he gets every single time I tell him I'm in love with him. He knows it. He's heard it. But he can't quite believe it.

I grin and lean in to kiss him. He willingly opens his mouth for me. I dive in with my tongue to meet his. Kissing him sends crazy sensations everywhere throughout my body. I've never kissed anyone and felt like this with anyone but him. The excitement. The instantaneous want and need. The love.

I put everything I feel into the kiss as I push him onto his back and crawl on top of him. I hold his hands above his head and press my hips into his so he can feel everything he does to me.

When I'm forced to come up for air, Robby's brown eyes become impossibly darker. He pushes himself into me as he bites his lip. His hard cock against mine sends sensations through me that only he's ever managed to make me feel.

I lean down to kiss him again and again. Our arms and legs tangle around each others until I don't know where I end and he begins.

He's everything I've ever wanted. I can't believe I've found what I've been searching for my entire life. I've always wanted true love. A man who could make me feel like I'm everything to him. Someone who I could treat like royalty, and who would do the same for me.

"I'm so in love with you, Luke," he whispers.

I smile and pull him up with me as I get up. I lead him down to his bedroom and make love to my man over and over again.

Chapter Twelve

☒ Nick ☒

I light the last candle on the folding table I brought down to the fire pit. I check to make sure the trays of food are still steaming hot, then stand back to observe my work, mentally checking off everything on the list in my head.

Pristine, dark purple table cloth. Check. Tulips. Purple and white. Check. Silver stemmed long candles. Check.

I check my watch. Almost time.

All of Dani's favorite foods. Check. Alpha Omega Chardonnay. Check. Silverware.

I look around and check the tray. "Fuck. Remember silverware," I say, making myself a mental note.

I take a last look around before nodding and turning back towards Ryan's house. I saunter through the sliding glass doors off the pool and take a deep breath heading directly to the kitchen. I grab all the utensils I need and put them in my pocket, then turn for the living room before running into Arianna. She falls on her ass before I can catch her and glares up at me.

My eyes widen. "Shit. I'm sorry. You're just… so fucking tiny." I give her a teasing smile as I help her up.

"I'd be angry, but I can't be." She pouts and looks over her shoulder.

I raise an eyebrow. "Are you… hiding?"

"Yes. And in a hurry." She tries to get by me.

I block her path and fold my arms over my chest. "Explain."

She sighs. "Ryan and Luke are dealing with an issue in London. So…, I've been trying to stay out of their way. But Chris is being really, really fussy. I have tricks. A lot of them. None of them are working. I think he wants Ryan, but he's on a call right now."

I narrow my eyes. "Okay…"

"So…" She bites her lip and looks down in shame. "I may or may not have pawned Chris off on Jason. And… he… may or may not have a meeting in the city that he needs to get to."

I chuckle. "How important is the meeting?"

"It sounds a little important, but it's not like the company will close down important."

"Air? Where the hell are you? I'm going to be late!" Jason yells from somewhere in the house.

"I'm a terrible person." She wipes her eyes. "But he's driving me crazy!"

I almost laugh, but decide teasing is far more important. Good thing she has more than one brother to help her out in times like this. "Sounds to me like we got ourselves in a little bit of a pickle."

She turns up her nose. "I don't like pickles. Ryan makes me drink pickle juice for cramps after I workout or during my period. Pickles are for demons."

"They do your body good." I quickly grab her around the waist and spin her so her back is to me.

She squeals. "What are you doing! Let go!" Her eyes widen in both shock and horror as my grip tightens.

"Jas! I got her! Hallway near the living room!" I call out.

"Fuck! Nickolas, I hate you! I wouldn't have let him be late!" Arianna squeaks.

Jason comes around the corner carrying Chris. "I'm already going to be late, Air! I'm going to have to fly to the meeting. Literally. In my chopper. Fly. Or I'm not going to make it."

"You have two hours. Give me one more. Please!" Arianna pleads as I hold her against me and Christopher starts fussing again.

"Two hours in Chicago traffic to get downtown, Arianna. I'm going to be late." He kisses Christopher on the head and hands him to Arianna as I let her go. Jason kisses her cheek and hurries from the house.

She nuzzles him and hugs him close. "I love you, little man. But I'm exhausted. Between you and this constant need to wake up at three in the morning..." She sniffles again.

"He's still waking up at three in the morning?"

"It's like clockwork. It's like he senses Ryan getting up to get his workout in. I'm so tired, Nick. And stressed out. I try to be quiet and strong for Ryan, but right now I don't feel much like a Mafia Queen. Or Princess. Or royalty at all." She plops on the floor against the wall with Christopher in her arms. He fusses and whines.

I kneel next to her and hold out my hands. "Give him here."

She shakes her. "Dani is finishing getting ready. She'll be down for your date in a minute."

I take on the dominant tone I rarely use. "Arianna." Her eyes snap to mine. "Give me Chris. Go upstairs. Take a nap. Do it now."

Her eyes widen slightly as she gives me Christopher. I stand with him in one arm and help her up with the other hand. "O-okay." She takes a last look at me as I hold her gaze. She scurries up the stairs.

I smile and shake my head as I check my watch again. I look up the stairs. I'm really cutting it close, but I need to take care of my family. I head for Ryan's office and hear the raised voices before I even open it.

"I don't care!" Ryan yells. Christopher starts crying instead of fussing. "I said I wanted it done today! That means today! Not tomorrow. Not next week. Today!"

I raise an eyebrow as I push the door open. Luke glances at me and tries to wave me away, but I shake my head and walk in anyway. Ryan hangs up and collapses in the chair behind his desk. He looks about as tired as Arianna. Christopher cries harder.

Luke winces as he stands. "I tried to warn you. It's your head." He gives me a sympathetic look as he makes a quick exit.

"You have your orders, Massena! Fuck it up, and I might drown you," Ryan growls.

"I got it, Ryan. I'll take care of it." Luke closes the door, shooting me a last look full of empathy.

I sit on the chair across from him as he rubs his temples. I bounce Christopher on my knee. "You're in rare form today. What the fuck happened in London?"

"It started with a car crash. It turned into a war with a small Irish mob. Not mafia. These fuckers can't be classified as mafia. They're fucking crazy. Terrorizing half the damn city. They should have been dealt with long ago, but the small crew I have in London are dragging their feet. They don't think that these guys are worth the time. Typically, they wouldn't be." He sits up and puts his elbows on his desk as he looks at me. "But they blew up the vehicle of the family they got into an accident with." He looks at Christopher.

I nod. "I see."

"Nearly killed a three-year-old and his mother." Ryan looks back up at me. His eyes are on fire, but I can see the exhaustion. Christopher reaches for him, whimpering.

I stand and hand him his son. "Here's what's going to happen. You're going to put this aside. Let Luke deal with it. That's what you pay him for. You're going to go spend time with your son. Come down a little bit. When you put him down for his nap, you're going to take one yourself and spend some quality time with your wife. Because she needs a fucking break. She's as tired as you are. She just played hide and seek with Jason and made him late for a meeting because she needed to be able to take a little time out."

Ryan shakes his head as he snuggles Christopher into his chest. "What? She would never do that." Christopher calms immediately.

"She would if she was stressed the fuck out. Now go."

He narrows his eyes. "Since when does my little brother give me orders?"

"You take care of this family. I take care of you. Always have. That's not changing. Now fucking go. Spend quality time with your wife and son. You need it."

He chuckles and shakes his head. "Okay."

I follow him out of his office and meet Dani at the bottom of the stairs as Ryan starts walking up them. I hold out a hand for her and guide her down the last three steps drinking her in. She smiles up at me shyly as my eyes roam unabashedly all over her.

Her long, beautiful brunette hair falls freely down her back except for the sides, which is braided and somehow tied back like a crown. Her light gray sundress ties around the back of her neck. It hugs all of her curves in just the right places and grazes halfway between her knees and thighs.

I kiss her hand and look deep into her eyes. "You look beautiful, baby."

Her eyes brighten. "Thank you." She reaches up and straightens my collar. I'm wearing jeans and a dress shirt without a tie. The top three buttons of my shirt are unbuttoned, and my black suit jacket is open. "You look pretty incredible yourself."

"Compared to you? Not even in the same atmosphere." I take a tie out of my pocket and smile when her eyes go wide.

"What… are you doing?"

I laugh. "I said I have a surprise for you." I gently turn her around and tie the tie over her eyes. "So trust me."

"I do," she says breathily when I run my fingers softly down her arms.

"I'm never going to get tired of your reaction to me," I whisper against her neck before I kiss it.

"I hope you never do." She smiles as she slides her hand down my arm into mine. I squeeze it tightly and lead her outside.

When we get to the fire pit, I stop and stand behind her. I drop my hands to her hips and pull her back to me. "I know you've been wanting to just be a girl, and I'm sorry it's been so intense with the training. I know the bubble baths and pampering I do get to do help, but they aren't what you've been wanting. So…" I reach up and untie the tie. I put it back in my pocket as she takes in the scene.

The candles have melted just enough to look ruggedly romantic. There's the gentlest of breezes coming off the lake that makes her dress billow around her legs. She shakes her head and sniffles as she dabs the corner of her eye.

"It's so beautiful, Nick. So, so beautiful."

I gently nudge her to the chair. When she sits, I push her closer to the table until she's the perfect distance to be comfortable. "You ain't seen nothing yet."

I smile as I lift the lid from the food tray, pleased that everything is still hot. I take out a plate with a metal lid and put it in front of her. I grab mine and set out the silverware. I grab the wine chilling and pop the cork. I fill both of our glasses before putting it back.

"You're pulling out all the stops, Mr. Crane." She smiles up at me.

"Only for you, Ms. Jade." I lift the lids off the plates with dramatic flourish, presenting to her loin of lamb with wilted spinach and rosemary potatoes and carrots. I bow teasingly as she laughs.

"It looks so good."

I take my place across from her and start eating as she closes her eyes and moans. "Good?"

"So good. God. I'd marry you just for your cooking." Her eyes widen as I smile. "I didn't mean... I mean... I..."

"It's okay," I chuckle. "Really. It's okay." I smile as she does and watch her as she enjoys the meal. "Is that something you think about? Marriage? Kids? All of that?"

She smiles softly as she looks up at me. "I've always kind of wanted to settle down. Somewhere in the back of mind. But I never really found a place I liked enough. And certainly never anyone I wanted to be with. The older I've gotten, I just don't really want kids anymore. I'm happy being the favorite aunt."

I reach over and tuck a strand of hair behind her ear. "I was never sure if I wanted kids or not. But seeing Jess, Arianna, and Nicole..." I shake my head and laugh. "Not a chance in hell. I like being able to give a fussing child to mommy or daddy and walk away."

She laughs as we finish the meal. I pull out cheesecake for dessert. We talk and laugh long into the evening. I fold the table down and put everything away as she lights a fire in the pit. I lay a blanket on the ground as we watch the sunset and continue our conversation. I keep her between my legs with my arms tightly wrapped around her until the sun has long set, and the fire is nothing but embers.

She shivers and cuddles into me. "Getting chilly out here."

I hug her a little tighter before releasing her long enough to take off my jacket. I put it over her shoulders as I stand. "I'll get the fire out, and we can head inside." I reach out my hands to pull her up.

She takes them and kisses my jaw when she gets to her feet. "Okay."

After I get the fire out, I take her hand and lead her inside. "So? How'd I do?"

She giggles as she leans into me. "I had a really good time. Thank you. I needed this."

I put an arm around her. "Not done yet."

She looks up at me as we walk up the stairs. "Oh? More romance?"

I smile. "Dream level." I lead her into our bedroom and close the door. "I'll be just a minute." I kiss her on the forehead as I head for the bathroom. A few minutes later, I come back out. I take off my shirt and lean against the doorframe, folding my arms over my chest. She's sitting quietly on the edge of the bed.

"Come here," I say huskily.

She smiles softly and obeys, walking to me curiously. I take her hand and lead her into the bathroom. I shut out the lights before tugging her gently so she's standing at my side.

She inhales sharply. "Nick…" She walks towards the bathtub in awe taking in the candles and purple and white tulip petals strewn throughout the bubbles in the water filling the tub. She smiles softly as she looks at me with tears filling her eyes. "Nick, it's so… beautiful. Sweet. Romantic. No one has ever done anything like this for me."

I smile into her hair as I hug her. "You said you wanted to be a girl. And I need you to know how important you are to me. I'll give you anything you want, Dani. You need this. Time to relax." I kiss her neck softly and smile teasingly. "And to be a girl."

She giggles and hugs my arms to her chest as I sway with her. I feel her take a deep breath. "Join me?"

I stiffen and clear my throat. The constant yearning I have for her stirs to life. "I don't think that's a good idea, baby. You won't get to relax much." I keep her wrapped tightly in my arms.

She turns in my arms and wraps hers around my shoulders. She stands on her tiptoes and kisses me gently. She closes her eyes and smiles.

"Please join me?" She opens her eyes and gives me the sexiest pleading look she can muster. Though, I'm positive she has no idea just how seductive it is.

I groan. "Okay." I smile against her lips and kiss her. "I'll join you."

She smiles so brightly that any darkness in my world is completely outshined by her light. My heart beats faster as she starts to undress. I close my eyes to center myself. I have no idea what the hell is wrong with me. It's not like I haven't seen her naked before. I've had my head between her thighs.

I slowly step into the bathtub after I finish undressing. Something about this time... I've never been terrified of the potential of sex. The idea of it with her, though, is both exhilarating and scary as fuck. I don't want to scare her. Or disappoint her. Or assume she's ready when she isn't. She may have been with others, but it's been awhile for her. She's admitted that.

I close my eyes to stop myself from overthinking. Everything that's happened so far between us has felt totally natural. Fast, but absolutely natural. Why the hell our first time together wouldn't is something I need to stop thinking about. It will only ruin it.

She steps into the bath and settles between my legs with a soft moan. "Perfect. The temperature is perfect." She leans against me and drops her head on my shoulder.

I wrap my arms around her. "A nice relaxing day and night. Just what you need."

"How do you always seem to know what I need?"

"I don't know that I always know. But I do try to read you. I've never really been this way with anyone else. I guess I'm just more in tune to you then I've ever been with anyone else. Except my family. Then again, I've never felt this way about anyone else either."

She nuzzles my neck. "I haven't either. I know that's been said before and is repetitive, but it's still just unbelievable to me."

I kiss the side of her head as we fall into a peaceful silence as she enjoys her bath. After she's had her fill and we get out, she leads me to bed and curls up next to me. She traces my abs and kisses along my jaw until she gets to my lips. She kisses me softly.

I've never spent hours just kissing anyone and touching them like I do with her. I've never wanted to. There are things that I do with her that make no sense to me, but I do them because I'm so in love with her. I've never cared to make anyone as happy as I do her. In such a short amount of time, she's become my entire world.

After spending time getting my fill of touching her silky soft skin, I lean in and kiss her deeply. I roll on top of her and pin her wrists above her head. She arches into me with a sexy whimper and breathy moan as she turns her head to the side giving me access to her neck. I nip the soft flesh and suck softly. I kiss it as I pull away and kiss up her jaw to her lips.

She wraps her legs around me and kisses me softly. My body hums for her. I suck her tongue lightly as I dip mine in her mouth. My hard and throbbing dick grazes her, begging me to sink my entire length into her soft, warm, wet pussy.

"Nick…" She writhes underneath me and arches, begging.

"Fuck, Dani." I nudge her entrance with a shaky breath as I look at her. She arches again, meeting my eyes. I wrap my arms around her and sink into her, though not all the way, with a low moan into her neck.

She hisses as she wraps her legs around my waist. "Oh…"

I stay still, letting her get used to my size, and relish in how tight she is. So taut. Perfect. She pants against me as she pulses around me. Her arms come around my shoulders. Her nails dig in. I hold her close to me.

I kiss her gently. "You okay?"

She nods and starts moving against me, closing her eyes and arching. "I'm okay."

Reading her, I start moving slowly, thrusting only about half way. She meets my thrusts with sweet sighs and quiet moans. She clenches around me, bringing forth a groan from deep within. Her nails scratch gently down my back to my ass. She grips it and digs her nails in.

"Holy… shit… Why the fuck do you feel so good?" I slide my hand down her side and grip her hip.

I kiss her before she has a chance to respond. I close my eyes as they roll back in my head. The pressure builds inside me as her pussy tightens and squeezes my dick with every thrust. She grips my ass harder, pulling me into her as she pants and moans.

"Nick. Oh…, fuck me! So…, so good!" She meets every one of my thrusts, but squirms and writhes as she arches. Like she can't get close enough or take me deep enough.

I growl deeply and thrust harder. Deeper. Faster. I pull her hip up to me again and slide even deeper. I nip her lip then kiss her again and again, harder and more passionately than the last. She tightens her legs around me and pulls me into her.

I know I have a big dick. Thick. I haven't given her my full length because I don't want to rip her apart. But when she pulls me into her, I can't help but sink all nine inches of my cock into her sweet heat.

"Jesus, Dani." I pause because I know she needs to get used to all of me. I'm buried balls deep now.

She moans low and gutturally. Her grip on my ass loosens as she completely submits to me. I get impossibly harder when I feel the shift. Her hands damn near flop onto the bed as her head drops back. After a couple of moments, I feel her nails trail up to my shoulders once more. I start thrusting again.

"Oh… God…" She moans as she moves with me.

I kiss her throat, giving her deep, hard thrusts. She grips my shoulders. I kiss along her neck and jaw to her lips. She greedily kisses me, but relents and submits to me once more when I demand control. I deepen the kiss, sucking lightly on her tongue.

"Tell me you're mine," I say against her lips, as I look deeply in her eyes.

They burn for me. "Yours. All yours."

I keep giving her hard, deep thrusts. "All mine."

"All yours, Nick. All yours."

I kiss her hard and long. My tongue twines with hers as I thrust faster. She gives me soft whimpers and moans of pleasure as her beautiful face flushes a gorgeous pink. Her thighs start to tremble uncontrollably as her pussy quivers and pulses.

My dick throbs and thickens. Her nails dig into my back. She scratches along my shoulder blades. I run my hand up and cup her tits. I massage and rub them, teasing her nipples. Her pussy clamps down on my dick.

I groan as she squeezes my cock tight. "Come for me, baby. Fuck. Come for me now." I thrust as deep as I can into her pussy and hold myself there as jolt after jolt of pleasure shoots down my spine.

"Nick! Yes!" She trembles as she comes. Her pussy pulses and tightens as her hips jerk against mine. "Nick!"

I nuzzle my cheek against hers and feel her tears as I come with her, spilling everything I have into her pussy. "Baby… Shh… It's okay." I kiss her cheek and lick her tears. I run my thumbs under her eyes and lean down to kiss her again and again.

"Oh… Nick…," she sniffles. "I'm sorry. I…"

I shake my head and kiss her again. "Don't. Don't apologize."

"I've never… had… anyone make love to me… before." She pants into my neck, holding me as tightly as she can against her.

"Get used to it. Because I'm never letting it happen with anyone else. You're mine." I kiss her again, pouring all of the love I have for her into it as she nods. She starts thrusting under me again, slow and sensual.

I make love to my girl all through the night until we both are too spent to move. It seems to be a trend with us. One I'm never going to tire of.

Dani falls asleep on top of me with my dick buried so deeply inside her it's like we're one person. I hold her as tightly as I can, not believing how I ended up with this perfect woman falling in my lap.

Finally, as the sun starts peeking over the horizon, I fall into the most peaceful sleep I've ever had with the only woman I've ever loved with every part of me.

I know without a doubt that I'll never love anyone else as deeply as her. She owns my whole heart and soul.

And I wouldn't want it any other way.

Chapter Thirteen

☒ Dani ☒

(One Week Later)

"Dani, stop. What are you doing?"

I wince a little at Ryan's commanding tone. I feel like I've been training for hours. I'm so tired that I'm flailing against Ryan instead of fighting.

I groan and sink against him. Somewhere during the fight, he got a hold of me, and I haven't been able to get him to release me since. "I'm tired. And hot." I know I'm whining, but I don't care.

Ryan chuckles. "Krins isn't going to give you a break because you're tired and hot."

"I know! I just feel like I've been training every day for years. I feel like I haven't seen Nick in days. I hate the penthouse. I feel isolated and alone. I hate that feeling. Which is so weird because I've been alone most of my life. I used to love it. I just want Krins to attack already!"

"I get it, honey. I do. I know you're angry. I know there's a lot of shit going through your head right now. But when I took over your training, I promised I would show you how to fight and survive. Right now, you need to channel all of your anger into kicking my ass because I am *not* letting go of you until you start using your training." His muscular forearm is around my neck. The other is tightly around my waist.

I'm not moving, and I can't help but feel defeated. "I don't know how."

"Dani, yes you do. I'm six feet five. I have over a foot on you. I tower over you. Use what you have to your advantage. Free yourself, and we'll hit the pool. Talk."

"Promise?"

"Cross my heart."

Over the past month, since I've met everyone, Ryan and I have become close. I would even go so far to say the guy has become my best friend. I feel comfortable with him. Safe.

I can talk to him and not feel like a complete idiot if I don't understand something, or if I need advice about something stupid. Like what my boyfriend likes for dinner so I can surprise him.

"Now. Take a deep breath and focus. I'm not going to go easy on you just because you're fucking tired."

I do as I'm told. I close my eyes and take a deep breath. "Okay. I'm ready."

He says nothing, but I feel him tense as his grip tightens. I become slack, letting him support my entire body weight.

I drop my body like a one hundred and fifteen pound weight, and Ryan struggles to shift enough to support my change.

I turn and elbow him in the ribs. His grip loosens. I turn and elbow him on the other side, then continuously and quickly twist my body back and forth while I'm elbowing him until he lets go.

"Ha!" I quickly make my escape and run.

"Alright! Alright! Get your suit. I'll meet you in the pool."

I grin over my shoulder but don't stop running. I run up to the guest bedroom that Nick and I left swimsuits for when we are here and quickly change.

I make my way down to the pool and dive in without thinking. I needed this. I need the cool water against my skin after such a long and grueling day of training.

When I resurface, Ryan is diving in. I watch him glide through the water with practiced grace. He resurfaces next to me with a splash that makes me squeal. He laughs, and we start splashing each other like we've entered a contest. It's a good thing both of us are already wet.

"Okay! I surrender! I give up!" I raise an imaginary white flag.

Ryan grins before splashing me once more. He dives under the water before I have a chance to retaliate and swims away.

After wiping the water out of my eyes, I swim after him. He's leaning against the edge of the pool smiling at me by the time I reach him.

I laugh. "You're such a dick."

He winks. "I know. Yet people still flock to me." He smiles. I laugh and lean against the side of the pool next to him. "So? Talk to me. You were so off your game today, I thought we jumped back in time. It was like your first day all over again."

I sigh, and the small smile that had been on my lips falls away. "It's been a month. And we have no information on the Krins mafia. We don't know where they are. We don't know anything. I'm so tired of being scared. I don't like the feeling. I worked so hard to make myself into what I am. It's just not fair. I feel like that little girl who watched her dad kill her mom all over again. I hate it."

"Dani, I can assure you that you're safe here. No matter what happens, you don't need to feel scared."

"And I don't. At least not here. I feel safe here. I feel safe when I'm with Nick. It's the going between that I have a problem with. Not just because of the drive and not being surrounded by…" I gesture to him. "Family. It's because the penthouse is so lonely. I feel isolated. Especially when Nick isn't there. And I know it's high security, but being alone just sucks."

"I only put you guys up in the penthouse because I thought you might want some privacy to get to know each other. You can't go back to your condo. Nick can't go back to his. I don't trust they aren't being watched. There isn't any reason for you not to stay here, though. The place is big enough. And even if they are watching my house, I have far more security than they could ever dream of getting through. Cops are done looking for Jason since Wolfe was arrested and fired."

I look at him with hope. "I love being around everyone."

"Then stay. I'll have some guards grab yours and Nick's stuff. If this is where you feel safe, then here is where you need to be."

"What about Nick?" I say the words quietly. I know Nick likes the penthouse. He likes being alone.

"Dani, Nick will go where you go, honey. If this is where you want to be, Nick isn't going to have a problem with that. He loves you. He wants you to be happy. And safe." Ryan puts his arm around me. "As for the loneliness and the isolation, have you talked to Nick?"

I shake my head and focus on the water. "No. Not exactly. I don't want to add to his stress."

"Well, you know you can talk to me and Arianna. You haven't said anything to us either." Ryan squeezes me a little, pulling me closer. I say nothing, instead biting my cheek. "I think I know what you need."

I look up as Arianna comes out of the house. "Bree and I are leaving now. Just wanted to let you know."

Ryan smiles as he looks up at her. "Think Dani could tag along?"

My heart leaps out of my chest at the thought of being included, but I really don't want to intrude on whatever is going on. "Oh! No, Ryan. It's okay. I don't want to impose."

Arianna shakes her head. "Don't be silly, Dani. You're not imposing. I'll go get Breetana and meet you back here."

"I'll assign extra guards," Ryan says with a smile.

"Thanks, my love." Arianna smiles and turns to leave.

I turn to Ryan. "Ryan, I really don't want to impose. I love the idea of being included, but -"

"You're my brother's girlfriend. Like it or not, that makes you a part of this family. You're not an imposition, so stop it. Go get dressed."

"Where are they going?"

"Shopping. Now hurry up. If there's one thing Arianna hates, it's being kept waiting."

I kiss him on the cheek. "Thank you."

"You're welcome." I jump out of the pool and grab a towel from the chair Ryan left it on. I quickly dry off and wrap it around myself. Ryan does the same. "I'll talk to Nick while you're gone, but I assure you he won't mind coming back here."

I smile and hug him before hurrying to change. After a few minutes, I nearly run directly into Nick as I'm running down the stairs.

"Woah. Where's the fire, baby?"

I smile as I pull him in for a kiss. His arms snake around my waist. He pulls me into his rock solid body and kisses me deeply. "I missed you."

He smiles. "I missed you, too."

"Ready to go, Dani?" Breetana asks.

Nick raises an eyebrow. "Go where?"

I smile. "Shopping."

A protective look crosses his eyes as he looks up at Ryan. Ryan smiles. "I have a detail on them. They'll be fine."

"Maybe I should go for extra protection," he says worriedly.

"Nick, we have shit to do. Ryan has ten guards on them," Taylor says.

Nick glares at Taylor as he holds me tighter, but just before he has a chance to say anything, Arianna steps in and puts her hand on his arm.

"Dani needs girl time. Believe me. You'll thank me later."

Nick sighs as he leans down to kiss me. "If you need anything, if anything happens, call."

I stand on my tiptoes to kiss him. "Promise."

He releases me with a pat on my ass. I smile as Arianna takes my hand and leads me out to the waiting black SUV. There's a matching black SUV in the front of us and another in the back. Ten guards. Just like Taylor said.

"It may look like overkill, but Ryan has his reasons," Arianna says.

"We've all learned to trust him," Breetana says quietly.

I nod. "I do. I trust him. Without question." The three of us climb into the backseat of the SUV. "I feel incredibly protected. I don't feel like it's overkill at all."

Breetana blinks, a little shocked. "Damn. You're going to fit right in."

Arianna laughs. "I liked her the second I met her."

I laugh. "Really? I ran away and nearly got kidnapped the first time you met me."

She laughs with me. "But you're independent."

"And you kicked ass," Breetana says.

Arianna smiles again. "You're perfect for Nick. He needs someone strong and independent like you."

"Don't forget badass. None of the rest of us are brave enough to fight Ryan," Breetana says with a smile.

Arianna and I both burst out laughing at Breetana's wide eyes. I grin. "I'm training. Not fighting."

"Even still. He's not easy on you. I should know since I learned all I know from him," Arianna says.

Breetana shakes her head. "He's not easy on anyone."

We chat as we're driven to downtown Chicago. Before long, we pull up in front of a boutique. I start to open the door.

Breetana stops me. "Let the guards do their jobs. As soon as they do their check and make sure everything's safe, they'll let us out."

I nod. "Oh. Okay. Sorry."

Arianna nudges me. "It takes getting used to. Believe me."

A few minutes later, Arianna's door opens. A guard I've come to know as Drake pops his head in. "Mrs. Crane. Ladies. Please just slide across. We don't want anyone getting out in traffic."

"Thank you, Drake," Arianna says.

I smile as I slide out behind Breetana. We're ushered into the boutique. I can't help but stare open-mouthed at my surroundings. "Is... someone pregnant?" I'm surrounded by baby clothing and... things.

Breetana laughs. "No. We're just shopping for the kids."

"We wanted to get out of the house for a while. So, we thought we'd spoil the kids." Arianna picks up an outfit and compares it to another.

"So..., I know Arianna and Jessa have a child. And Nicole." I look at Breetana curiously. "Do you have kids?"

Breetana shakes her head. "I went through a lot as a kid and teenager. I was molested. I was physically abused. It's questionable if I can even have kids because of the damage."

"I'm so sorry..." My eyes widen. My hands fly to my mouth. I instantly regret asking and allowing my curiosity to get the best of me.

"Don't be. It only made me stronger." She smiles. "I am who I am because of the hand I was dealt. We all are. We can either let it destroy us, or we can grow from it."

I blink back the tears stinging my eyes at being confided in on such a personal level. "That's an amazing perspective."

Through shopping at several different shops, I've realized that I'm having a lot of fun, and that Ryan was right. I needed this. I needed to get away. Clear my head. Think of nothing more than just being a girl.

Breetana holds up an adorable red hoodie. "What do you think? Tampa Bay Buccs!"

Arianna laughs. "Yes! Get Tait that. Taylor will have a tantrum!"

"Why?" I ask. "I like the Buccs."

Breetana laughs. "We live in Chicago. Taylor is a hundred percent Bears fan."

"Ick." I make a face. "They're the worst team in the NFL."

She laughs again. "That's why I'm getting him a Buccs hoodie." She hugs me. "But you and I are going to get along splendidly! Kronk for life. Don't care that he's retired. That is all."

I smile and hug her back. She beams at me as she hurries to the counter to pay. I watch her as I take a deep breath.

Arianna squeezes my arm. "All us girls are like sisters. You'll get used to it."

I smile. "I've never had sisters or any siblings at all."

"And now you have four sisters and six brothers."

My smile grows wider as we walk together towards Breetana. "And parents. Ethan and Jenny are so amazing. I can't believe how they've accepted me."

"We all have. We all see how much Nick loves you." I look towards the door at two of Ryan's guards. They're both focused on the door. I can't get over how safe I feel. How I feel like I belong. Arianna squeezes my arm again, and I look at her. "And how much you love him. You both are perfect for each other."

"I really do love him. He's amazing. Incredible. He's everything I ever dreamed of but never believed I would ever find. I was content with my life before... all of this. But now? Everything is so different. I'm so happy, but I'm afraid to be."

Breetana turns to us. "You're afraid something is going to happen?"

I nod. "So afraid."

"You wouldn't believe it, but all of us have felt the same way. We've all been where you are, Dani. Breetana and Chase just got together when everything blew up. Taylor and Nikki we're only just married. Jason and Jessa weren't technically even together until everything started with her. Me and Ryan had been together a while. Everything was great. We had plans for me to leave my dad's house and move in with him as soon as I turned eighteen. But life threw a wrench at us."

We all start heading for the door. Breetana links her arm with mine. "You just have to put your trust in this family. I promise you. Nothing is ever going to happen to you as long as you trust all of us. Ryan and his guys put safety and protection of family above everything else."

"He'll stop at absolutely nothing to make sure you're safe. Ryan's power base comes from family. We all protect each other."

"That's what makes him so powerful."

I smile and nod as we leave the store. The two guards by the door follow closely behind.

As we near the SUV, one of the guards grabs my arm. "Excuse me, miss. Ryan asked that you ride with us. He asked that we get the rest of your things from your condo."

I know the voice. I know who it is before I even turn around. It's the same voice that's haunted my nightmares for months. Modelo. Deputy Modelo. My heartbeat quickens.

"Ryan asked that we make it quick. He doesn't want you gone for long," Deputy Sheriff Draple drawls.

No... How? How could this happen? How?

My condo.

Ryan would never send me back there. He said he'd send guards. Knowing this information solidifies what I already know in my mind. The two are not guards. It really is Deputy Sheriff Draple and Deputy Modelo. I'm not imagining things.

I look around, trying to make eye contact with any guard as I'm led away from Arianna and Breetana to a third SUV. Will they know I'm gone? Is this a nightmare?

The SUV is different from the others. It doesn't match. There's no red stripe on the side. I briefly think about screaming until Deputy Sheriff Draple tightens his grip and leans into me.

"Don't scream, or I'll shoot you. And then I'll kill your two hot as fuck friends while I make your cop boyfriend and that fucking mafia boss idiot watch," he hisses in my ear.

"You obviously have no idea who exactly you're fucking with." I jerk my arm trying to free it, but he holds tighter.

I once again try to make eye contact with anyone else before I'm shoved into the other SUV. I know if they get me there, I'll be forced to fight. Judging from the gun Deputy Modelo holds against my side, I know surviving isn't likely. But fuck them all if they think I'll go down quietly.

"Watch that pretty little mouth of yours. You might end up with something stuck in it," Deputy Modelo growls.

"Anything you stick in my mouth is liable to get bitten off," I growl just as viciously.

"You're a fighter. Damn I like that," he says.

I glare. "Go fuck yourself."

"I'd rather fuck you."

"Hey! What the fuck is going on? Drake!" one of the guards yells. Thank God. Thank fucking God for Ryan's guards.

Deputy Sheriff Draple keeps his grip tight as he turns to the guards. He pulls me in front of him. Deputy Modelo puts the gun to my head. Six of Ryan's guards all have their guns pointed at Draple and Modelo.

Deputy Sheriff Draple tightens his grip. "Shoot us, you lose her."

Two of Ryan's guards are with Arianna and Breetana shoving them in the SUV. Drake glares. "You're outmanned and outgunned. Drop the gun and let her go."

"Fuck if that's happening. You all drop your guns, or she gets shot." Deputy Sheriff Draple points his own gun at my head. My eyes dart around. We're missing two guards.

At that moment, I sense them behind me before I hear their guns click.

"It would be a wise fucking idea for you to drop your guns right about now, and let the girl go," one of them growls from behind us.

"Either of you shoot us, we shoot her." Deputy Modelo pushes the muzzle of his gun harder against my temple.

"Not happening." Drake doesn't flinch. I meet his eyes, surprised to find that I'm not scared. Both of these assholes are going to regret ever meeting me. Drake nods ever so slightly. I make my move.

I shove both guns away from my head simultaneously and drop my body. Shots ring out. My ears immediately start ringing.

Deputy Sheriff Draple lets me go. I fall to the ground, kicking out both of my legs and toppling both Draple and Modelo. One of them lands on top of me, shoving my head hard into the sidewalk. I feel my head bounce off the hard pavement. The edges of my vision immediately darken.

"No..."

"Dani!" I hear someone calling my name.

I feel the weight on top of me lifted off. Seconds later, I feel like I'm flying, then like I'm sinking into the pillowy softness of a cloud as I fall onto it.

"No..." I close my eyes and let the darkness wash over me, unable to fight anymore. "Nick..." Nick's face finds its way into my mind. I reach for him. He fades away as the darkness surrounding me becomes thicker. I can't breathe. "Nick..."

I can't feel anything.

I can't see anymore.

The midnight blackness envelops me.

I close my eyes and give in.

Chapter Fourteen

⚔ Nick ⚔

"That doesn't make any sense, Dane." I watch as Taylor paces the room. He's talking to another member of our team. Dane is a Sergeant who works under Taylor on our taskforce. "What about the intel we got this morning? They were in New Mexico." Taylor pinches the bridge of his nose as he listens. "Fuck. Find them." He hangs up the phone and turns to Ryan. "Get the girls back here. Now."

My heart beat immediately quickens. "What happened?"

"Nothing good," he says.

The three of us look up as Robby walks in with his laptop. Luke follows closely behind. I watch as Robby takes a seat on the couch. Luke sits next to him, their legs touching. I can't help but smile a little. We've all known for a while they're together. Though, they've never said it.

"Sorry to interrupt, but I got a hit on some credit cards I've been tracking. Not a fucking trace of anyone until today," Robby says.

I raise an eyebrow. "Who?"

"Let me guess," Taylor begins. "Draple and Modelo." We all look at Taylor in surprise.

"How the fuck did you know that?" Luke asks him.

"I just got off the phone with Dane. We had surveillance set up at the airport, bus stations, car rental places. Everything."

"Modelo and Draple just rented a black SUV from Enterprise," Robby finishes.

"You've got to be kidding me." Ryan says as his phone suddenly rings. We all fall silent. "It's Drake." My ears perk up. It's not often Ryan gets a call from Arianna's head of security. All of us focus on Ryan as he answers the phone. "Drake. You're on speaker."

"Mr. Crane. We have a serious problem. I need you, Luke, Taylor and Nick to meet me in front of the house."

"What? Why? What happened?" I ask. I can hear the wind rushing and the whine of the engine as they speed through the streets of Chicago. I'm on my feet and crossing the room to Ryan before I have a chance to take a breath. All I can think about is Dani and my sisters.

Ryan's face drains of color. "What the fuck happened, Drake?"

"Two guys just tried to grab Dani. We detained them, but during the fight, Dani was knocked out. Doctor Chantau is meeting us at the house. We'll be there in a few minutes."

All of the air whooshes through my body. "What? How the hell could this happen?"

Ryan puts his hand on my arm and firmly shakes his head. I fix him with an icy glare. "We'll meet you in front of the house." Ryan hangs up.

I swipe my hands down my face as I turn around. "Fucking Christ. I knew I should've gone."

"You can't blame yourself. It still would've happened whether you were there or not." I look at Luke. He's standing with Robby cradled against his chest. I watch as he kisses Robby on top of the head. I follow Ryan and Taylor out of the room. We all walk to the driveway to wait. A few moments later, Luke and Robby join us.

I can't help but smile at them just as a car flies into the driveway. Despite all of this, I'm happy for them. Feeling more comfortable expressing their love in front of their family is what actually calms my heart slightly.

Doctor Chantau parks his car far out of the way of the returning guards. He jumps out, carrying his black doctor bag, and hurries to join us. "How far out are they?"

"A few minutes," I answer. "Can't be soon enough."

Ryan lays a hand on my shoulder. "Nick, you'll be going with Dani. Taylor, stay with them. Be on guard. Organize the other guards. Lock everything down. Entire property. Robby, stay with Bree and Arianna. Call Chase and Jason. Luke, with me. Questions?"

Like I'd be leaving Dani's side. No fucking way. I shake my head. "Nope. None."

"We got it," Taylor says.

The SUVs speed into the driveway and skid to a stop. Guards jump out in a flurry of motion. Arianna and Breetana both run to Ryan, but time stops moving as I watch Jake, a guard, pick my girl up in his arms.

Dani is completely limp.

Dead weight.

Blood drips from the side of her head.

"Shit..." My heart stops pumping blood to my body. I sway.

"Hey. Snap out of it. She needs you. Go," Luke commands. I hear him, but my limbs feel heavy. "Robby, get him inside with Dani."

"I got him." Robby forces me to walk, but I don't know how he manages.

My eyes are completely focused on Dani. My blood rushes to my ears as I stare at her lifeless form. I feel the tears on my cheeks, but I don't feel them fall. "Fuck. How did this happen?"

"Nick. Focus. You have to focus. She needs you," Robby says.

I try to shake myself out of my haze as we follow the guards into the house. Breetana and Arianna are both close.

"Set her down here," Doctor Chantau says. "Someone get me water and ice."

Jake lays Dani on a couch. Doctor Chantau puts something under her head. "I got the water and ice," Jake says.

I drop to my knees next to Dani and take her hand in mine. "Come on, baby. Wake up. I can't lose you. I need you, Dani."

"Look at me." Arianna kneels next to me and forces me to look at her. It takes me a second, but my blurred vision finally begins to clear. "Remember when you were bringing me from Manhattan to here? After I escaped my father?" She runs her fingers through my hair. I slowly nod my head. I can't breathe. I barely register the doctor cleaning Dani up and dealing with her wound. "What did you say to me?"

"I..." I swallow. I'm shaking. I can't think. All I can see is Dani. Her too still body in front of me.

"Her breathing is too shallow. Nick, you need to give me room to work. I'll take care of her." Doctor Chantau looks at me pleadingly.

I shake my head, gripping Dani's hand harder. "I can't leave her."

"Nick." Arianna forces my face back to her. "Look at me. You have to look at me. What did you say? What did you tell me?" Arianna's hands are on my cheeks. My mind clears just a little more. I shake my head again, trying to clear it.

"Nick, I'm going to lose her if you don't move," Doctor Chantau pleads.

"Nick. What did you tell me?" she whispers.

I look into Arianna's eyes and take a deep breath. "To trust me."

"Yes. And now it's your turn. *Trust me.*"

I nod and kiss Dani's hand as I stand. "I love you, Dani. Wherever you are, I need you. Don't leave me like this." I lean over and kiss her lips before I let her hand go and let Arianna push me away.

Doctor Chantau immediately scurries around her, and within seconds he's giving her more oxygen. I'll give him credit. He's fucking efficient.

I sit in a chair and put my head in my hands, making myself take deep breaths. "I can't lose her, Air. I can't. I won't be able to come back from it."

"You won't lose her. Doctor Chantau won't let that happen." She stands in front of me and pulls my head against her stomach. I wrap my arms around her waist, hugging her tightly.

"I'll get pulled so far into the darkness, I won't ever come back from it. Nothing will matter but revenge. Just like before. I won't survive it this time."

"None of us will let that happen. I promise."

"It was like I was devoid of emotion. Nothing mattered then. I didn't care about shit."

"You cared for your family just like you do know.

I take breath after breath. "The kills meant nothing. I was a monster then."

"Not happening this time…," Arianna whispers. "You're different now. Everything is different."

124

I cling to her like she's my lifeline. Like she's my only hope at surviving. Like she's the only thing that can keep me from crossing the line drawn between good and evil.

And she is.

I let anger consume me for a long time in my younger years. Anger and not having answers about my parents. Anger about what happened to them. Every evil doer we took down, every rival mafia… They all were a way for me to vent my anger. Take my revenge for what happened to my parents.

I can't go back to that. I barely survived it before.

XXX

Hours pass. I still haven't released Arianna.

I can't.

I tried, but I felt myself being dragged back. Back to a world I kept locked away in the deepest part of my memory. A world I never wanted to see again. A person I never want to be again. I worked so hard to change. So hard. I can't go back.

At least I've managed to get her into my lap so she's not standing anymore.

"Nick." Ryan says quietly. I look up. Ryan is standing in front of me.

Arianna runs her fingers through my hair. "He hasn't let me go. He tried a few times. He's fucking terrified."

Ryan nods. "I know, baby. I can see the war being waged."

"I don't want to become a cold-hearted killer. I can't go back to that."

"Nick. I know. I know better than anyone." He takes Arianna's hand and gently tugs her away from me.

Arianna looks at both of us before she looks up at Ryan. "Are you sure this is a good idea? I'm the only thing keeping him together."

He leans down and kisses her. I force deep breaths because I can feel myself hardening. I can feel the hatred turning me to ice.

"Go. I'll take care of him."

Arianna smiles down at me.

125

I can't breathe. I feel like my heart is being squeezed by some unseen force. I look over at Dani. She's lying peacefully on the couch under the watchful eye of Doctor Chantau.

"If she dies... If they took her from me..." My voice deepens to an octave I don't recognize. Demonic.

I feel my eyes darken as the ice in my veins turns to fire. Ryan kneels in front of me. I look directly at him. I can feel the shift. I try to fight it. I can't. I feel myself slowly turning into the young, hardened kid that followed Ryan around on missions and killed for sport.

It was never sport for him. It was for me. I was the kid who took pleasure in it. Who didn't feel a fucking thing for so many years that I honestly believed I was possessed by a demon. That I was a monster.

Except it's different now. Now, I'm a grown man. More dangerous. Capable of far more violence than I was all those years ago. Far more calculating.

Evil.

"Nick. Listen to me. I know where you're going in your head right now. I know it scares the fuck out of you. I know you're fighting it." He looks directly into my eyes. I wait for him to talk me down. To pull me back from the edge I'm about to step over. "Don't. Don't fight it. What we're dealing with is nothing like we've ever dealt with before. We're all going to have to cross the line if we expect to survive this one. I need you, Nick."

My eyes don't leave his. I see my own anger looking back at me; the demons I fight reflected in the depths of his eyes.

All at once, I realize what he's talking about. What he needs. What he's asking of me. Why he pulled Arianna, the only thing keeping me from crossing the fucking line, away from me.

I let it take over.

"To protect this family..." He points to Dani. "To protect her... I need the ruthless son of a bitch that feels nothing on a kill. I've tried to keep you out of this life. I tried to protect you from all of it. I can't anymore. What we're dealing with, it's fucking bigger than any of us thought."

I fall over the edge. Just like that, my evil side that I worked so fucking hard to eliminate takes completely over. The raw heat running through my body turns cold. I can feel that demonic fucker taking back over.

"I need my brother, Nick. I need you."

"How big?" I growl.

"Big enough that they have several small mafias as fronts. Robby thinks he found them. But he can't be sure. Every smaller mafia he finds is a little larger than the last. But the trail stops with these guys. I need intel. Surveillance. We're going to fight, Nick. The battle is going to be bloody, but we have no choice. They came after my family. They tried setting up Jason for murder. They tried killing Dani."

"They brought this fight to us."

"And we need to end it."

I look over at my girl once more. No one fucks with my family and lives to see daybreak. No one comes after my girl and expects to survive to see the sunrise.

I stand and walk over to Dani. I feel Ryan's watchful eye on me as I turn to Doctor Chantau. "Can I hold her?"

"Move her carefully and slowly."

I do as he says as I situate Dani in my lap. I cradle her tightly to my body. Doctor Chantau said she'd be okay. It's just a matter of her coming to now. He said it could take awhile. Ryan sits next to me on the couch.

"I can't believe how close I've gotten with her over this past month or whatever it's been. You're her best friend. She told me that. The brother she never had."

He puts a hand on her leg. "She's going to be okay."

"She will be. I won't. I can't come back from this this time. You're asking me to be that person I was when I was fourteen, Ryan. You know how difficult it was to change. To become who I am today."

"I wouldn't push you to cross the line if I had a choice. I don't. Everyone is going to have to. Chase, Taylor, Jason. I've kept them away from this. I can't anymore. I need my family."

I look at him. "There's only one thing that could have ever pulled me back over the edge. I never wanted to become that cold-blooded monster again."

"I know. But we're all in danger if what Robby found out is true."

"What aren't you telling me? We've taken on big mafias before."

Ryan nods and looks away. Finally, he takes a deep breath and lets it out. He doesn't look back at me. "Matthew Lucinio."

I look at him completely dumbfounded. "What about him?" My heart skips a beat.

Ryan looks back at me. "Robby just found evidence that he may still be alive. That this mafia... might be him."

I suck in a breath and hug Dani closer. "No fucking way. You watched him die. We all did. The house. We burned it to the ground."

"The house may have been burned to the ground. We may have thought we killed him. But... what... Robby found suggests that the person we killed... wasn't him."

Fuck. No way is this happening. No wonder he said we're all going to have to cross the line. If Matthew Lucinio is back from the dead, we'd better all pray that we find him before he comes for us.

I can see our future.

The battle ahead will be long.

Gruesome.

And I'm not sure we'll win the war this time.

Chapter Fifteen

☒ Dani ☒

Nick... His scent. It surrounds me. Comforts me. It envelops me. Pulls me back from the darkness that's overtaken me.

"Nick..." The words come weakly. My mouth feels like a desert. Cactuses sprout from my tongue. I try to wet it, but I can't.

"Dani?" His voice is so soft, but alarmed. I can hear it.

"Nick..." I cough and feel something tighten around me. Something comforting. Something that keeps me from falling back into the abyss I fought my way out of. Water is pressed to my lips. I greedily drink it, feeling sweet relief.

I burrow into the comfort that's grounding me. My head feels heavy. There's a stabbing pain behind my left eye that nearly blinds me.

"I got you, baby. I'm right here."

I feel myself being pulled away from the comforting tightness. His arms? "No... Please don't let me go..." I try to speak louder, but I still can hardly hear my own voice

"Examine her the best you can in the position she's in," Ryan says. Dominant. Commanding.

Safe.

"She needs to be laying down so I can do what I need to do," someone says. I don't recognize the voice.

I grip the soft fabric that's against my hand in my fist. His shirt? "Nick..."

"I'm right here, baby. I'm never fucking letting you go again."

I feel myself being shifted and then lifted in the air. I open my eyes slightly and whimper at the pain, choosing instead to close my eyes again and burrow into Nick's neck.

He walks somewhere with me before I feel myself being laid down on something. A bed?

Nick pulls away. I start to panic. My eyes fly open, but immediately close. I grip his shirt tighter. "Don't leave!"

"I'm not. Dani, I promise. I'm right here. I'm not going anywhere."

The sudden surge of panic subsides as he lays down next to me. He wraps me in his arms and pulls me close to him. "Please stay. Don't let me go."

"I promise, baby. I'm right here." He caresses my face and neck as he leaves a soft kiss on my nose. With the pad of his thumb, I feel him wipe away my tears.

"How is she?" Ryan's voice and Nick's arms and scent make me feel safe. Like everything will be okay again.

"She's going to be okay. But I need to see your eyes, sweetheart. Just for a minute."

Nick kisses me on the forehead. His lips are warm. Comforting. Safe. "Do what Doctor Chantau says, baby. You're safe now. I'm right here."

I take a deep breath as I open my eyes. The pain behind my left eye is excruciating. I whimper.

"Tell me what hurts, Dani."

I squint into the kind eyes of an older man I've never met. Nick called him a doctor and seems to trust him. I decide I can, too. "M-my left eye. More my head. Behind my eye."

"Like a headache?" Doctor Chantau asks.

"Like the worst headache known to man."

"I expected that. Fuck." The tone of Ryan's voice makes my heart beat rapidly. I can feel the fear.

"Hush, Ryan," the doctor says. I look at the doctor in amazement, fighting the pain. I've never heard anyone talk to Ryan like that. Not even his father. I smile. Nick hides his smile. Ryan chuckles. "Dani, this is going to be bright for just a second, but I have to look, okay?" Doctor Chantau takes a pen light from his pocket and gives me a kind smile. "Try to keep your eyes open."

I bite my lip and frown. He quickly flashes the light over my eyes and turns it off. My eyes snap closed immediately.

Nick pulls me close to him. He kisses my forehead again. "You're doing great, baby."

"Dani, I know this is going to be hard, but can you remember anything?" Doctor Chantau asks.

I turn on my side to Nick and burrow my head in his chest. "I remember everything." I sniffle. Nick kisses my head and hugs me tightly. I feel the bed next to me press down as someone sits. A warm hand rubs my back as Nick cradles me.

"I need to know what happened, honey. Anything you remember," Ryan says softly.

I take a deep breath and let it out slowly. "We were leaving the boutique. Arianna and Breetana were led to the middle SUV, the one we went to the boutique in. I remembered there were three SUV's when we left the house. They all looked the same. All had the same markings and detailing. The same red stripe. I counted ten guards with us. But when we left the boutique, there were four SUV's, and the last one didn't look like the others. Also, there were twelve guards."

Nick kisses me. "Good girl. So fucking observant. Detail-oriented. That helps so much, baby."

"More than you know." Ryan squeezes my back comfortingly.

I smile into Nick's chest. I've never been complimented for being who I am. Details are how I make my living. "One of the guards said that you, Ryan, wanted them to take me to my condo. But I knew you didn't want me to go there. I knew you were sending guards there and to the penthouse to get mine and Nick's belongings." I take another deep breath. "And the voices. I'll never forget the voices of Deputy Sheriff Draple or Deputy Modelo. I won't forget any of their voices or faces. I didn't see their faces right away. But I knew it was them. I knew the voices."

Nick leaves a gentle kiss on my temple as Ryan continues rubbing soft, comforting circles on my back. They give me the strength to continue.

I take another deep breath. "I tried to think of a way to get away. I tried to think it through. But they were dragging me towards the SUV. There was a gun on me. I couldn't scream." I find myself getting angrier and angrier as I tell them what happened, but the angrier I get, the more the stabbing pain hurts. "The guards saw what was happening and stopped them, but Draple and Modelo kept me near them with their guns on me. I remember Drake and I making eye contact. He nodded. I did what you trained me to do. I knocked their guns away. I dropped. I fought. But someone fell on me and knocked me into the ground. My head hit really hard. I tried to fight, but I must have passed out."

Ryan leans over and kisses the back of my neck. "I'm so fucking proud of you. I need to brief everyone. Nick, you already know everything. Stay with her."

"Please. She needs the rest, Nick," Doctor Chantau says.

I look up at Nick. I know I don't need to say anything. He knows. He doesn't break eye contact as he starts talking. "I promised Dani that this family doesn't keep secrets from each other. That she'd be as much of a part of this as she wants to be." Nick looks up at Ryan.

I hear Ryan sigh. "You're so much like Arianna. Stubborn and strong as fuck."

I smile softly as I turn and slowly get up. Nick helps me until I'm sitting with my legs dangling over the edge of the bed. I sway a little with the dizziness.

Doctor Chantau glares at both Ryan and Nick as he digs in his bag. "Ryan, go get her water."

"Yes, sir."

I gap at the doctor as Ryan obeys his orders. Unreal. A few moments later, Ryan returns with a glass of water.

The doctor hands me two pills. "This will help with your headache. When you get downstairs, you will lay down on the couch." His voice is firm. I can only nod as I take the water from Ryan. I take the pills and chase them down with a long sip of cold water.

"I'll make sure of it," Nick confirms.

"Sometimes, I question why I decided to continue to work for this family. So many gunshot wounds, pregnancies, and the innate sense you all have for being completely stubborn. It's enough to make anyone hang themselves," Doctor Chantau says.

Ryan bellows and Nick howls with laughter. Ryan pats Doctor Chantau on the back and gives him a side hug. "You're like the grandfather none of us had. Everyone loves you. The kids adore you. And you can't deny that you love all of us."

Doctor Chantau's scowl is replaced by a soft smile. "I suppose that would be accurate. Now, for once, Nickolas. Be the good one of all your brothers and do as you're told."

"Yes, sir." Nick stands and offers me a hand.

I take it and get unsteadily to my feet. Nick sweeps me into his arms. I smile and wrap my arms around his shoulders as I lay my head on his shoulder. Ryan smiles at me from over Nick's shoulder.

"Thank you for letting me be a part of everything," I say with a soft smile.

He returns the smile. "If I didn't, my girl would kick my ass. And Nick's right. We don't keep shit from family. Everyone, including all the girls, will be down there. You're a part of the family now. You should be there, too."

I smile as Nick carries me downstairs. As soon as Jason and Jessa see Nick carrying me, they stand up from the couch. Nick smiles as he sets me on my feet. He lays down on his side and waits for me to lay next to him. I settle with my back to him, and he pulls me tightly to him. Being in his arms is like Heaven. It's my safe place where nothing can ever hurt me.

"This okay with you, doc?" He smirks teasingly at the doctor.

Doctor Chantau laughs. "I'm trusting you with my patient."

"Aye Aye, Cap."

Doctor Chantau leaves the room with a smile and nod. Nick chuckles as he holds me tightly. My head rests on his bicep. I breathe in his masculine and intoxicating fresh scent.

"I called all of you here because we have a huge problem," Ryan begins.

Everyone looks to Ryan as he stands in the center of the room. The entire family is here. Arianna looks worried. Robby looks exhausted. Luke looks concerned for him.

I get a little nervous as I take in the tone in the room. I hadn't noticed until this moment, but everyone is on edge.

133

Nervous.

Ryan meets my eyes. My heartbeat quickens at the intensity he holds in his own. "I promised you I'd always be honest with you, Dani. I meant that. All of us did."

I look around the room again. Some people are watching Ryan. Others have cast their eyes to the floor. "U-um... did I do something wrong?" My words are soft, unsure.

Nick kisses the back of my head. "No, baby. He just meant that this is not going to be easy to hear. For you or any of us."

"Everyone but Dani knows who Matthew Lucinio is. Dani, a brief background for you. Matthew Lucinio was a crude mafia boss. Our families were bitter rivals for years. Especially after I took over. My father was shot in a battle with Matthew. I took over very young. I started to grow more powerful than Matthew. Bigger than him. We were rivals, but our war stopped because I became close friends with one of his sons. Alex Lucinio is just as much of my brother as anyone in this room." Ryan pauses and looks at Jason and Jessa.

Jason nods and takes a deep breath. "In college, Jessa and Alex dated. They were together the entire four years. Over that time, Matthew became completely obsessed with Jessa. He used Alex's twin brother, Josh, in a sick and twisted scheme to get her to give him an heir to the Lucinio mafia. Alex didn't want control. Josh did, but being the younger twin, Matthew didn't give a shit what Josh wanted. He barely acknowledged him as his son at all."

Jessa burrows into Jason's side. I feel Nick take a deep breath before he starts talking. "At first, Josh was coherent. He wanted to protect Jessa from his crazy father so he pretended to be Alex in order to get Jessa and Alex to break up. He thought it was the only way to protect her. It worked. They broke up. Alex was torn up about it, but he eventually decided it was for the best. His father wouldn't be obsessed with her. He thought the break up and his leaving and giving his dad what he wanted would protect Jess."

Ryan continues. "So, he took off to Italy. He took over the international part of the Lucinio Mafia to get his dad off Jessa's back, and to force him to hand over control of the US to Josh. Only, it didn't work that way. Matthew grew more obsessed. He fucked with Josh even more. Drugged him with a serum to make it easier to brainwash him. Made him believe he would never be as good as Alex at anything. Crazy shit. Josh continued to pretend he was Alex. He got word that his father was going to go after Jessa. So, after a year of Alex not being a part of her life, Josh started pretending he was Alex again to protect her. Got Jessa to believe it. Got her back."

Jessa wipes away a tear and peeks up from Jason's chest. "Almost five years after Alex left, I still didn't know he had a twin. I thought Josh was Alex. Things were actually going well until we got into a fight one night. I ran to my friend Cole. He's a cop with LAPD. I stayed with him a while. He helped me get a restraining order."

"Didn't do a fuck of good," Jason growls. "He found her. Beat the shit out of her. She spent a month in the hospital."

Ryan continues. "Alex, the real one, got word that Jessa had filed a restraining order against him. He had been in Italy for almost five years, so he didn't know what was happening. When he got back here, it made sense. So, he tried to protect Jessa without his dad or Josh knowing. He had one of his guys guarding her. But, the night Jessa was hospitalized, this guy got knocked out by Josh. Alex got there just before the cops. The cop who showed up was Cole."

"Thank God." I breathe a sigh of relief, but I can sense whatever news Ryan has is going to be bad considering they're taking time to explain all of this to me. It doesn't sound like the short version.

I feel Nick take another deep breath. "After Jess was released from the hospital, Alex paid to move her from L.A. to Manhattan. But he didn't tell her. He did it all through Cole because he knew how badly he had fucked everything up with Jessa. He just wanted her out of his dad's grasp. And, I guess, Josh's at that time, too. Matthew had really fucked Josh up. He didn't even know right from wrong anymore."

I gasp as tears well up in my eyes. "That's so sad."

Ryan smiles sadly. "It gets a lot worse. Jessa got hired by Jason to work at his firm. After a year, she'd really started to settle in. She came into her own. One day, she didn't show up to work. Josh found her. But again, she thought it was Alex. Jason and Nick went to her condo because Jess is a creature of habit. She'd never been late to work. She showed up at the same time every day. Jason had a check run on her within the first couple hours of her not being there."

Nick kisses my shoulder. "We found her restraining order against Alex. Doing a check on him, we found out he was mafia. We immediately called Ryan."

Ryan runs his hands down his face. "I knew who Jessa was. I mean more than just that she was working for Jason. I knew about their relationship. Alex asked me to help take care of her. Keep her safe. I knew everything she said happened couldn't have been Alex. It had to have been his twin. So, I called a meeting. We found out that Matthew was behind everything. He had even tried to kill Josh for failing to get Jessa back to L.A. like he had ordered. So we went after him. Came up with an attack plan. Josh shot Matthew. I watched him die with my own eyes."

"So..., Matthew is dead?" I watch Ryan share a look with Robby and Luke.

I narrow my eyes as Nick buries his head in my hair. The pills the doctor gave me are starting to clear my head and make the stabbing pain lessen. I'm able to think a little clearer, but I'm having trouble understanding why Ryan is telling me all of this.

Ryan sighs. Luke squeezes Robby's thigh. I smile. I knew something was happening between them.

"I found some information today that I need to verify, but basically it looks like the Lucinio Mafia is somehow tied to all of this." Robby says the words quietly and doesn't take his eyes off his laptop. It looks like verbalizing the words that leave his mouth are painful for him to say.

Jessa lets out a quiet sob. A few others gasp.

"You can't be serious," Jenny says, looking fearfully at her son.

"Oh, he is." Taylor lets out a breath and looks at the ceiling as Nicole molds herself to his side.

Ryan takes a deep, unsteady breath. "What I'm about to say are words that I never thought I would have to. But here we go. I know Alex and Josh aren't involved. I trust both of them with not only my life, but also the life of my family. Alex was an invaluable part of saving both Jessa and Arianna. So was Josh. If the Lucinio Mafia is involved in this, then it has to be a leak or Matthew himself. Which means he somehow survived."

"Unfortunately, that evidence Robby needs to verify is regarding Matthew," Luke says. "It's possible the person they killed that they thought was Matthew... wasn't."

"And it's going to take me a lot of time to track this down," Robby says. "It's buried deep. Someone didn't want it found. I happened on a piece of this by accident. The rest of the pieces aren't easy to find."

"Jason, Taylor, Chase, Nick, and even you, Shane," Ryan begins as he looks at them. "I've done everything in my power to keep you from having to cross lines that I do on a daily fucking basis. I've always said that I will never allow you to cross over into illegal territory. But this just became a dangerous fucking problem. He's gone after Dani. He's gone after Jason. He's gone after Taylor. He's gone after Jessa before. I know Robby hasn't verified yet, but I have a feeling. You all know I don't ignore my instincts." He closes his eyes and sits down next to Arianna. He pulls her close as he exhales and opens his eyes. He looks at everyone in the room.

Chase's eyes appear to light on fire. "There's no doubt in my mind it's Matthew. And I'll do whatever I have to do to keep my family safe."

"Hell. We all will," Shane growls.

Taylor shakes his head. "You don't even need to ask. The only one any of us worry about is Nick."

"I'll do what I need to," Nick says.

Jason looks at him. "We know. And that's the fucking problem."

I stare at everyone, slightly confused, before I turn to Nick. "What are they talking about?"

"Nothing, baby. We'll talk about it later." He gives me a soft kiss on the lips before I turn back to everyone.

All of the couples in the room are sweetly cozied up to each other as the realization of the danger we are seemingly about to face sets in. For a few moments, everyone is quiet as we all get lost in our own thoughts.

I watch as Robby leans his head against Luke's shoulder. Luke puts his arm around him. I smile. The two of them and their sweet relationship is like a beacon of light through all of the darkness.

Robby puts his hand on Luke's thigh and gives the room a soft smile as all of our eyes fall on them. Luke looks at Robby as Robby clears his throat. "It might not be the right time... but... Everyone's here. We just got some fucked up news. Maybe this will help to brighten everything a little." He takes a deep breath. Luke takes his hand. My heart nearly beats out of my chest. "Or maybe it won't."

His soft smile weakens a little as he looks down at the floor. All eyes are riveted on Robby as he takes another deep breath and stands...

Chapter Sixteen

☒ Robby ☒

I stand in the room trembling in front of the only people I've ever considered my family. They all stare at me intently as I take breath after breath.

My heartbeat quickens.

I start to sweat.

I've never had an issue being the center of attention. I've never had a problem speaking to anyone in this family, let alone all of them at once.

I look at Luke, still sitting on the couch. He smiles encouragingly, but my breath quickens anyway. I realize all at once that I can't do this by myself. I never considered myself a chicken shit, but I fit the bill right now.

"I can't. I can't fucking do this." I fight to breathe as I flee like a fucking coward from the room.

I rush down the hall to Ryan's office and close the door behind me. I can't catch my breath. I start to realize real fucking quick what Jessa goes through when she has a panic attack. My heart feels like it's going to beat so hard and fast that it will explode.

"Robby? It's me, babe. Let me in." I hadn't realized I had collapsed onto the floor with my back against the door until I feel Luke pushing on it as he talks.

I force more deep breaths as I get shakily to my feet. My cheeks feel wet. Luke slips inside the office as I walk to the couch in the room.

I collapse again as soon as I reach the soft cushions. My head falls into my hands, and my body is immediately overcome with emotions I don't even know how to deal with.

"Robby. Baby, look at me." Luke sits next to me and rubs comforting circles on my back as I try to regain my composure.

"I can't do it. I can't."

"Robby. Look at me. Come on."

My body refuses to obey. All I can do is shake my head.

Luke gets on his knees in front of me. He takes both of my hands in his and squeezes them gently as he kisses the top of my head.

"Tell me what happened. Tell me what you're thinking."

I shake my head. "They won't accept this. I know they won't."

"Why do you think that? Why do you think they won't accept this?"

I don't have an answer. I don't know why my heart is racing out of control. I don't know why I can't just do this. "I don't know."

Luke gives me a soft smile. He leans forward, and his lips brush across mine. "I know you better than that, Robby. And I think I know how to help you."

I look him in his beautiful dark eyes. Eyes I find myself lost in more times than I care to think about. "I feel like a total loser right now. A complete coward for running off. I'm so fucking scared that everyone is going to turn on me. I don't want to lose them. This family is everything to me." I squeeze his hands and bite my cheek, trying to stop myself from losing control of myself again. "I'm embarrassed."

Luke lets go of one of my hands and reaches up to my cheek. "Do you trust me?" The pad of his thumb caresses my skin as he wipes away my tears.

"You know I trust you."

"Do you love me?"

"More than anything."

139

Luke kisses me, then stands. He pulls me up with him and draws me close to his chest. He hugs me tightly. "You don't have to do this alone. I'm here. I told you that we'd do this together. I meant that, baby. You have to stop taking on the entire fucking world by yourself. You don't need to do that anymore. You have me."

I cling tightly to him, reveling in how strong he makes me feel while still making me feel safe and comforted. I can't envision my world any other way. I need him. It's more than just love for me. Luke is everything.

"I'm terrified."

"I know. I won't discount your feelings, but I know that this will work out. I know how close this family is. How much we all care for each other. Trust me." I nod into his shoulder and take a deep breath. He slowly pulls away. "If you aren't ready, we don't have to do this."

"I want to do this. I need to. I love you, Luke. I don't want to hide anymore. It's not fair to either of us."

He smiles and takes my hand tightly in his. He leads me out of the office and down the hall. "I told everyone to stay while I talked to you. They'll still be there." He stops in front of me and turns to face me. I take a deep breath. "Remember. Together. You and me." He leans down and captures my lips with his. He keeps my hand in his.

I send up a silent prayer that the kiss never stops. I step closer, my body drawn to him.

Unfortunately for me, he pulls away. He kisses my forehead and turns again, leading me back into the large room where all of our family waits. I try to let go of his hand, afraid of people seeing me holding it. He grips it tighter.

I'm both delighted and filled with fear at his show of solidarity. My entire life is about to change.

"Everyone. Robby and I have something we'd like to share. It's difficult for both of us, but we have no doubt that you'll be supportive and continue to love us the same as you do now." Luke tugs me closer to him, feeling the tension in my body. I want to bolt again, but he won't release my hand. "I think most of you, if not all of you already know. Honestly, until a little while ago, I didn't give a shit about sharing my private life with anyone." Ryan and Arianna smile at us. I feel a little fear melt away.

"About a year ago, Robby and I decided to act on some feelings we had for each other."

"I'm in love. With Luke." I blink. I hadn't meant to blurt it out like that, but fuck if I don't feel better. Getting it out there is a huge weight off my chest. Doesn't stop my heart from beating out of control, though. It's racing so fast I doubt I'll be able to ever get it to slow again.

Luke looks at me and grins. "And damn if I don't feel the same way."

He turns and leans down. He takes my face in both of his hands and kisses me. I feel it all the way in the very tips of my toenails.

My ears ring. My cock starts getting hard when his tongue slips in my mouth and tangles with mine. I force myself to pull back before I make a mess in my jeans.

I slowly come to my senses and realize that everyone is whistling, clapping, hooting, and hollering. My eyes meet Luke's.

He runs a finger across my swollen lip. "See? Everything is just fine."

I look at everyone. Not a single one of them seem upset or grossed out. They all look at us with support. Love shines from their eyes. My heart feels like it actually might burst.

I watch Arianna run towards me. She's beaming as she leaps in my arms. She wraps her legs around my waist and kisses my cheek. "I'm so happy for you!"

My heart leaps into my throat as I try to find anything insincere in her eyes, or her voice. I find none. I let out a breath I didn't know I was holding as Ryan walks up behind Arianna. "Really?" I ask.

"Of course, silly! Did you think I wouldn't be?"

"Uh... I was completely fucking terrified you would hate me. I didn't want you or anyone to look at me differently."

Ryan laughs. "Robby, please. You're family. We all love you. It doesn't matter if you're gay or bi or straight or a camel."

Arianna and I burst out laughing as I let her drop to her feet. "A camel? Couldn't think of anything better?" I ask?

Arianna shrugs. "An elephant?"

Ryan smiles. "An anteater?"

The three of us start laughing again as Luke's arm snakes around my waist. He pulls me close and kisses my cheek. "Feeling better?"

141

I lean into him. The tension and adrenaline I felt washes from my body, leaving me feeling just as exhausted as I do after a mission. "Relieved. And I just went through an adrenaline dump. So, kinda tired."

"Me, too, honestly," Luke agrees.

"Looks like some other people want to talk to you." Ryan winks as he leads Arianna away.

"It's about time you two came out. We all fucking knew." Nick looks at both of us teasingly.

"It was time. I don't know why I couldn't do it. We planned on telling the family we're seeing each other today, but with everything going on with fucking Lucinio, I was going to just say tomorrow," I say. "But I didn't want to hide anymore. Wait… you knew?"

Nick laughs. "We've known for a while."

"I'm glad you guys didn't wait any longer. We're happy for you. We have been for a long time, but we knew you needed to tell us in your own way," Taylor says.

Nicole leans into his side. "We really are happy for you. And proud."

I look around at the family gathering around us. I breathe another sigh of relief. Part of me can't believe I'd kept this a secret from them. That I let my fears gather and stand in the way of my happiness.

Luke squeezes me a little tighter. "He was pretty nervous about how everyone would react."

Jessa's eyes widen. "Oh, no, Robby. No one here would ever judge you for who you love. Ever."

My eyes fill with tears at the show of support as Jason hugs me. "We're your family, Robby. Family supports each other, loves each other, and protects each other. So, anyone who gives you any shit, send them my way." Jason smirks. We all laugh.

Ryan damn near howls. "Why? So you can send them to me?"

Jason winks. "Fuck yes. What's the point of having a mafia boss for a brother if you can't use that shit to your advantage?"

We all laugh again as Ryan shakes his head. The heavy heart I had this morning disappears completely as we all fall back into the easy family vibe that I crave. That I love so much.

"Um... I know I'm really new to all of this, but I just wanted to say congratulations. On finding love." Dani smiles up at me shyly. I grin, pulling her in for a hug. As soon as her arms wrap around my waist, the tension I felt throughout her body dissipates as she exhales into my chest. "I'm never really sure how anyone will react with me interjecting myself into family things."

Nick kisses her neck. "Dani. We talked about this. We love each other. We're together. You're a part of this family."

"Couldn't have said it better myself." I release her. Her megawatt smile could light up the room as she steps back next to Nick.

After more hugs and conversation and words of encouragement and support, everyone starts to head to their respective homes for the night. Luke stands in front of me in front of the chair I long ago collapsed in.

He holds out his hands. "Ready to head home?"

"And pass out on my bed. Today has been a long fucking day." I take his hands.

He pulls me up into his chest and kisses me. "I was thinking we'd go to mine tonight."

I grin like an idiot as his hands travel to my ass. He gives it a light squeeze. I let out an involuntary whimper and close my eyes. I lean into him. My cock immediately hardens. "Jesus."

Luke kisses my forehead, then takes my hand. I open my eyes and see the same amount of desire I feel reflected back at me.

Luke glances over his shoulder, then reaches down and grabs my cock with his free hand. I shiver and groan as he smiles devilishly.

"Fuck."

"Hard for me already, huh?" He strokes me over my jeans.

My cock twitches and strains against my zipper. He gives me another squeeze. I jump. "Shit. You're sucking my dick as soon as we walk through that door."

He licks his lips and lets go of my cock as I turn and drag him out of the house.

I feel lighter than air knowing that my family accepts me. The real me. That I don't have to fucking hide who I am in front of the people that I love.

I squeeze Luke's hand as we nearly run to his cottage on Ryan's property. I can't believe how happy I am that I don't have to hide the love of my life, my heart, from anyone anymore. That we're free to be a real couple. No more stolen kisses in the hallway or secret hook-ups.

Luke pulls me to his bedroom as soon as we arrive at his place and shoves me backwards onto the bed. He unbuttons my jeans and tugs them and my boxer briefs off me. He strips his own clothes as I pull off my shirt.

"I believe I promised you a blowjob." He looks up at me teasingly and gives my cock a long lick as he settles between my legs.

I moan as I lay back on the bed, propping myself up on my elbows so I can watch him. It's one of my all-time favorite things to do. He reaches between his own legs and gives himself a couple of tugs.

My cock is vibrating with anticipation as his tongue swirls around my tip. He continues stroking himself. My hips thrust upward, begging for his warm mouth around it.

"Fuck. Luke, come on." I thrust my hips again as he chuckles.

His tongue licks from my balls up to my tip. He sucks softly. Teasingly. I throw my head back and do all I can to get him to take me further. Instead, he pulls back and sucks on each of my balls. I moan. He teasingly sucks up my length to my tip and sucks softly again.

I'm done. I grab the back of his head and push his mouth down onto me as I fall back on the bed. My eyes roll back as he takes me as deeply as he can. I hit the back of his throat again and again.

Gripping the sheets as Luke's magical tongue brings me to my peak, my stomach tightens and my cock stiffens. I feel a jolt shoot down my spine.

"Come on, baby. Come for me." He straddles me and puts his dick against mine. He strokes them together.

I explode. Warm liquid spills from me in gushes intermingling with his as he shoots jet after jet of his come onto my stomach. He collapses next to me and pulls me against him, hugging me close.

"I feel like I belong. Here. With the family. You," I say breathlessly.

"You do belong here. With us. Me. You're fucking mine, Robby. Remember that."

I kiss his chest and hug him tighter, not giving a shit that both of our stomachs are covered in come. We can both clean up in a few minutes… after I get my fill of his arms.

"I will," I whisper.

Chapter Seventeen

⚔ Nick ⚔

(One Month Later)

"How is this possible?" I'm lying on the floor in my bedroom in Ryan's house with all of the blackout shades drawn. I've been fighting the worst fucking migraine in the history of migraines.

I never get migraines. I barely even get headaches. Breetana is the one who suffers from these bullshit monsters. Not me.

"I wish I had those answers for you, bro," Jason says.

I growl dangerously keeping my eyes closed to block out any light that may be breaking into my room. "Things can't just grow cold. There has to be a fucking trail."

"Robby said it just stops. There's nothing," Jason says.

I fight a wave of nausea as I roll very slowly from my back to my stomach. The blinding stab of pain that radiates on the left side of my head takes me by surprise. I groan.

"You take anything for that yet?" Jason asks quietly.

I drop my head into my arms and whimper. This is worse than any hangover I've ever been through. "It'll go away." I hope. I hope it'll go away and I don't die of the pain before then.

I groan again. This day can't get worse. It began with this damn headache. Dani, my angel of a girlfriend, tried to make it subside by giving me the best shower sex I've ever had to relieve the stress.

For one glorious hour, my headache didn't exist. All I could think about was how tight my girl felt around my dick. How her pussy milked everything from me when she came.

Too bad that didn't last. As soon as I got dressed, the fucker hit me full fucking force.

"I'll grab you something," Jason says.

"Forget it," I groan.

"I know you're tough, but why suffer?" Jason asks. I say nothing as I try to ignore the pain. "Fine. Fuck. Suffer."

"Let me die in peace. Can we deal with this shit tomorrow?" I whimper.

I hear my door open. "No. What the hell is wrong with you? Why are you laying on the floor?" Ryan asks.

"If you two don't leave me alone, I'm going to take the gun in my shoulder holster and shoot both of you. I'll probably die from the noise, but it'd be fucking worth it."

"He has a headache," Jason says softly.

"I surpassed headache this morning. I'm at nuclear fucking explosion. Get the fuck out of here."

All I want is to sleep this off. The floor isn't that comfortable, but the thought of crawling into bed makes every fiber of my being protest.

I'm not even sure how I made it home from the precinct. Christ. Maybe I died on the way and am paying right now for every fucking person I've killed over the years. This pain is my own personal Hell.

"You need to get over it and get your ass downstairs. We found Krins," Ryan says.

I raise my head and look at him. Waves of nausea begin in my toes and roll up my entire body. I take deep breaths to try and tamp it down as I drop my head in my hands once more. Fuck looking at him. Not puking on the floor is far more important.

146

Nothing makes sense. If it did, I sure as hell can't follow it. The pain is excruciating. This fucker is clinging to me with the sharpest fucking nails I've ever felt.

"Hang on. Jas just said they disappeared." Trying to follow what those two are talking about sends a sharp pain directly to my brain.

"They did. But they turned up," Ryan says.

My head is swimming. I feel like I'm in a pool of Jell-O. I'm trying to reach the surface, but I fucking can't. "You guys have to get out. I'm fucking dying. The sound of your voices is more than I can take."

Ryan is silent for a moment. I know he's looking at me with concern. I don't need to see him. I know my brother well. "I'll send Dani up with ice and meds."

"Just go the fuck away. I don't care what you do as long as you leave." I vaguely hear the door closing behind them as they leave the room. I pass out seconds later, unable to keep my eyes open.

In the fuzzy edges of my mind, I feel myself being picked up and laid in the bed. Something cold hits my neck. A warm body wraps around me. I feel fingers run through my hair, rubbing my head before I pass out again.

XXX

Groggily, I open my eyes, feeling like I'm coming out of a sea of spider webs. It takes me a minute to realize that the groans and whimpers I hear are coming from my own lips.

"Nick? Can you hear me?" someone asks. Doctor Chantau?

"Mmm…," I groan.

I know someone is talking, but I can't see him. Didn't I open my eyes? I try again, but my eyelids won't cooperate. It's like they're super glued to my face.

"Babe? Please come back to me."

"Dani..." I reach for her, feeling the silky strands of her hair in my fingers. I shiver as her arms encircle me.

She hugs me tightly. "Don't leave me like this. Please? I just found you. I haven't even gotten to show you how much I love you yet."

Leave her? What the fuck is that about? I'm not going anywhere. I open my mouth to speak, but my words are cut off by stabbing pain throughout my body. I grit my teeth and let out a howl that's foreign to even my own ears.

"Jesus Christ." Ryan. Why does he sound scared?

"Tell me he's going to be okay. I won't lose my fucking brother." Jason... Why is everyone thinking they're going to lose me

"None of us want to," Taylor damn near whispers.

"We fucking won't," Chase growls viciously. I've never heard Chase growl. At least not like that.

"No way we're losing him. Do whatever the hell you have to, but save him," Luke says. Save me? The fuck is this about saving me?

"I'm doing everything I can. The poison is taking over. All we can do is wait for the lab to find me the antidote." That *is* the doctor. Doctor Chantau. I try to follow.

"You have no choice here. Find the antidote. He dies, so do you," Robby threatens.

Wait. Poison? I fight through another stab of misery centered directly in my stomach. Waves of pain and nausea course through me.

No.

No fucking way I was poisoned. I've only been around my family, and my team. I trust them. No way I was poisoned.

Then it suddenly hits me as explosions of agony erupt in my head.

Zekeih.

He's been on Taylor's task force for years, but he's been acting suspicious. It threw a huge shadow of doubt about his loyalties in my mind. I had been doing a little digging on him and found some interesting things.

The problem is I can't remember what they are through the gold stars that are bursting in my head.

I try to fight the blackout I know is coming, but every fiber of my being betrays me. The pain is too much. My body can't handle the intensity.

Despite me trying to muscle my way through it on sheer will and adrenaline alone, I give in. The darkness falls on me once more. I blissfully feel nothing as it takes control.

XXX

(Four Days Later)

"Nick? Please, please come back to me. You tell me how strong I am all the time, but I'm not. I'm only strong because of you." I feel something warm and wet drop onto my cheek as Dani sniffles. She's plastered to my side like I'm her life raft and she'll drown without me. I swallow and lick my lips. My throat is so dry I feel like a sand dune lives inside it. "I love you, Nick. I love you so much. I'll die without you. Please don't leave me."

I feel another warm drop hit my neck as she buries her head in it. I cautiously lift my arm and wrap it around her as I slowly open my eyes. The room is dark, but I can just make out the soft edges of her beautiful face as I turn my head.

For the first time in what feels like years to me, my head doesn't feel heavy. My body doesn't feel weighed down. I don't feel excruciating agony with every movement. Every thought.

"Baby..." I wrap my fingers in her long hair and tug a little as she looks up at me. Her gorgeous eyes reflect the small amount of light allowed in the room. Her eyes are bloodshot and puffy.

"Nick?"

I smile as I grip the back of her head and push it towards me. A sob escapes when she buries her head in my neck. Her grip on me tightens as another sob escapes.

I kiss the top of her head. "I'm okay."

"I was so scared. So, so scared. I thought I lost you."

"You'll never lose me." I hug her as tightly as I can, I'm still feeling weak, and run my fingers through her hair as she clings to me. A light in the room is flicked on, but my main focus is my girl. I don't care about anything else but making sure she's okay. "I'm okay, baby."

"Fucking Christ. He's awake." Jason lets out a shuddering breath.

"Thank God," Luke gasps.

"Baby. Oh, sweetheart." Mom's arms wrap around me from behind. She breaks down in an uncontrollable crying fit.

"Mom, I'm okay."

149

"Doc needs to check him out, sweetheart," Dad says.

Mom shakes her head. "One more minute. Please. I almost lost my baby. One more minute." Her arms tighten around me. So do Dani's.

I smile into Dani's hair. "You guys are going to squeeze me to death."

"Don't joke about that. You almost died. Nick. We almost lost you." Dani starts hysterically crying again. "*I* almost lost you."

I pull away and tilt her chin up to look at me. "Dani, I'm here. I'm right here." I take her hand and put it against my chest so she can feel my heartbeat. Mom presses her face against my back and kisses it. With my other hand, I grab hers and press it to my chest, as well. "Mom? Feel that? It's gonna take more than a little fucking poison to take me out."

"You remember being poisoned?" Taylor asks, shocked.

Chase's eyebrows shoot up in surprise. "Who did it?"

"No. I don't remember being poisoned. I remember a migraine hitting. I remember blacking out. After that I remember going in and out of consciousness. And I remember you guys talking about me being poisoned. But I don't know when or how it happened."

"We'll find out who did this, bro. That's a fucking promise," Ryan says darkly.

Mom lets me go and pats my back as she stands. Seconds later, someone else takes her place.

"Just need to check you out, son," Doctor Chantau says. "I need a blood draw and a few other things. Have to make sure the poison is gone."

I pull back gently from Dani, but she grips my waist as I roll onto my back. "Can you do this with her where she is?" I keep an arm around her as the doctor takes my other one and puts on a tourniquet.

He smiles softly. "Shouldn't be an issue." He starts preparing his blood draw kit as Dani buries her head into my chest. Her nails dig into my side as she shivers next to me. Her hot tears against my chest break my heart.

"What the fuck happened? What do you remember?" Robby asks. I look up at Robby and sigh as the Doctor sticks a needle in my arm. I shake my head and close my eyes.

"When did the headache start?" Ryan asks.

"Dude, I don't even know how long I've been out." I open my eyes and look at him.

150

"Four days. We didn't know if you were going to wake up." Dani clings to me.

I take a deep breath. The more I'm awake, the less foggy my memory is. My mind becomes clearer. Sharper. And I become more and more angry. "I had files on my computer at work. I was investigating Zekeih." I meet Taylor's eyes as he registers what I just said.

I can see the shock as he shakes his head in bewilderment. "Why the hell would you feel the need to investigate a member of our taskforce?"

I look him square in the eye. "Because his behavior has been off, man. Ever since Captain Wolfe was arrested, he's been fucking weird. Suspicious."

Taylor rubs his hand down his face. "Fuck, I know. I fucking know. It's been going on even before then. I thought I was being crazy. Why didn't you tell me?"

"I wanted proof before I came to you with that shit. He's been on your team since you started."

Taylor nods. "I'll look at the files. Text me your password for your computer."

Chase looks at me confused. "You think he had something to do with this?" He gestures to me.

"I don't know, Chase. We had a late fucking night. I drank a lot of coffee. Taylor and I didn't leave the precinct until two in the morning. I woke up with the headache. I thought it was lack of sleep or stress. It went away when Dani I were fucking in the shower."

Dani makes a choking sound and looks up at me, wide-eyed. Her eyes are red rimmed and blood shot but dry. I grin as I squeeze her shoulder.

Ryan chuckles. "Don't be embarrassed. It's nothing any of us haven't heard before."

Dani clears her throat and lays her head back on my chest. Her nails have loosened their grip on my side. I feel her relax a little more as she chuckles. She kisses my chest. I start to sit up as soon as Doctor Chantau finishes his blood draw and exam.

"Easy now. You have a lot of shit hooked up to you," Doctor Chantau says.

It's only then that I realize there's a numbness and tingly sensation below my waist. I lift the covers slightly and growl as I realize I'm completely naked and have a tube coming out of my dick.

"Everybody out except the doctor and my girlfriend." I glare at all of them.

They all grin and get up to leave.

Chuckling.

Fuckers.

All of them.

✕✕✕

Hours later, after my entire family has made sure I'm okay, I lay in bed again. I'm tired and fucking weak. I don't like it.

Dani curls up next to me. "I was so scared, Nick."

I wrap her in my arms and kiss her. "I know, baby. But the doctor is staying here. I'm still under observation. He said the poison is gone. The antidote worked. I'm okay."

"I almost lost you. I haven't even gotten to love you nearly as much as I want to. Which is my entire life."

My heartbeat quickens at her words. I gently untangle myself from her limbs, but she holds tight to me, terrified to let me go. She hasn't been far from my side since I woke up. Hell. I doubt she's left my side for the past four fucking days.

She clings to me and looks up at me slightly terrified. "Where are you going?"

"Baby, I promise I'm not going far. You can even sit up on the edge of the bed."

She does and watches me with hawk-like eyes. I smile and open my dresser drawer. I take out a diamond ring and kneel in front of her, holding it up. My heart slams into my ribcage, but I know what I want.

Her eyes go wide. "Oh my God."

The purple colored diamond catches the low light and shines like the tiny gems in the corner of her irises.

"I love you, Dani. I know it's only been a couple months, but I love you. I can't imagine my life without you. Your love kept me going, baby.

152

Your voice. Your touch. Marry me." It's short and sweet, but I've never been a man of very many words.

She nods. "Yes… Yes… Nick… Yes!"

I grin as tears shine in her eyes. I take her hand in mine and slip the ring on her finger. I stand and pull her up with me. She gently wraps her arms around me, and my heart soars as I pull her into the bed with me.

I bought that ring a week ago now. There's no better time to give it to her than right now. She's my air. Every breath I breathe.

I wrap both of us in the comforter and pull her close to me again. "I love you, baby. I'd show you how much, but I'm still fucking weakened."

"I don't need sex. I just need you. I love you, too. More than anything."

I kiss the top of her head and hold her tightly as we both fall into an exhausted sleep.

Chapter Eighteen

⚔ Dani ⚔

(One Week Later)

Nick takes my hand as we finish breakfast. I haven't left his side this entire week. I hate the fact that he's intending on going back to work today. A stupid Saturday. I glare at my plate. He squeezes my hand and chuckles.

"I have to go back eventually, Dani."

"I know, but why not Monday?"

"Because Zekeih isn't going to be there today. Taylor and I have the ability to recreate what was destroyed."

I sigh and look down at our entwined hands. When Taylor got into Nick's computer, he found nothing. Nick's computer had been wiped. All of the files he had on Zekeih had disappeared.

"Dani, don't worry. The only people who will be there are me, Nick, and Dane. Reed and Jesse will also be there. Nick will be safe. I promise," Taylor says, trying to reassure me.

I shrug, tears stinging my eyes. "Don't make promises you can't keep."

"I'm not. We're onto Zekeih. We'll recreate the files he had. Nick will be safe. I won't let anything happen to him, Dani."

I force myself to look at him. To trust the resolve and sincerity in his eyes. "Promise me again."

Nick chuckles once more and squeezes my hand. Taylor reaches across the table, signaling me for my other one. I shakily give it to him.

He gently squeezes it in his large one, looking me directly in the eyes. "I promise. Nothing will happen to Nick. I won't let it." He rubs his thumb in small circles over the top of my hand. I give him a watery smile as I nod.

"I've got a good team." Nick puts an arm around me and hugs me.

I close my eyes and let his strength comfort me. I've had to be the strong one for him over the past week as he healed and gained his own strength back. Carrying the both of us when all I wanted to do was fall apart was one of the most difficult things I've ever done.

One I wouldn't change for anything.

Later on that evening, after everyone has left for the night, I wander around the property. I'm restless. I don't like that Nick isn't here. It's not that I don't feel safe. I do. It's that I don't feel like *he's* safe.

I trust Taylor. I trust Nick. I trust both of their abilities. The problem is, I believe we're stronger together. I've learned so much about this family since I've been with them. It's only been a couple months, but I already know that this family is far stronger when they're all one cohesive unit.

"What's got you all mopey?"

I look up at Jason as he sits in a chair next to the one I've plopped in next to the fire pit by the lake. "I don't like that Nick and Taylor aren't here."

"You don't need to worry about anything happening to you. We -"

I shake my head and lay a hand on his arm. "I'm not. I'm not worried about my safety. I'm worried about him. He's not around the family."

Jason chuckles. "Man. You're a lot different than the other girls. You're a lot like Lyric."

I look at him with a raised eyebrow. "What does that mean? Who's Lyric?"

"Nothing bad. Lyric is Josh's girlfriend. It's just you're so much more independent. Fearless even. I'm not saying the other girls aren't. I'm just saying it's different with you. All of them have asked Taylor or Nick to teach them defensive tactics. Ryan taught Arianna. Josh taught Lyric. But you're different. You've asked to learn defensive and offensive tactics. You've asked to learn how to handle weapons. All the girls have asked to be kept informed of what's going on, but you? You want to be a fucking part of it. That's why I say you're like Arianna all the time. Arianna and Lyric. They didn't have much of a choice in what Ryan and Josh taught them. They didn't complain about any of it, though, because they knew it could come in handy. The fact that you asked to be taught it all is what makes you different."

I shrug and focus on the sparkling water of the lake. Peaceful. "I've been on my own for a long time. I've never liked the idea of being weak or not being able to do anything for myself. I've also been around you guys long enough to know that we need to stick together. Taylor and Nick are alone."

Jason chuckles again as he stands. He drops a hand to my shoulder and squeezes gently. "They aren't alone. Dane is with them. Taylor called in Jesse and Reed. The five of them are like a solid, impenetrable wall. Trust me. They'll be fine."

"I hope you're right."

"I am. Ryan wants to talk to you. I'll tell him you just need some time by yourself. He's in his office when you're done. Take your time."

I smile. "Thanks, Jason. And thanks for talking to me. It helped. I feel less nervous now."

"Anytime. Just remember. We *are* stronger together. But we're only stronger together because we trust each other. Trust that both Taylor and Nick know what they're doing."

I return his smile as he turns to leave.

Looking back out over the water, a sense of peace washes over me. I love this family. I love Nick. I'm going to marry him. And no one is going to stand in my way. Not some stupid, small mafia. Not some big mafia. Not some past enemy. No. I finally found my life meaning. My family. No one is taking it from me.

I sniffle a little as my mind drifts. I can't help but wonder what my life would be like if my father hadn't killed my mother. I'd like to think I would have met Nick. Somehow. Like somehow, fate would have intervened and brought us together.

It hasn't happened in a long time, but sometimes, I can't help but fantasize about how it could've been. I loved my father. I really was the definition of Daddy's Little Girl. Four-year-old me worshiped the ground he walked on.

Four-year-old me even helped him bandage his wounds. He had many of them over the years. I don't remember all of them, but I know it was a lot. I remember his leg wound. I remember his bloody knuckles. His black eye.

I close my eyes and rub my hands up and down my arms. I remember the worry. The confusion about what happened. But what I remember most is hiding under the couch while he was screaming at my mother. I remember the blood that seeped from her head under the couch covering my hands. I remember wanting to scream but being too afraid.

I remember him running around the house looking for me. I remember fighting myself to go to him. Wondering why I was so afraid of my father. The man who sung me to sleep. The man who taught me my ABCs.

I sniffle again. There were so many things I never understood. I never understood what happened. I never understood why he did what he did. Why was mom yelling at him? I can't even remember what she was screaming at him about. I always thought that if I could, I would understand everything better.

I never understood why I never saw him again after that. Or the stupid need that I have always had to see him. The need that I've never shared with anyone because it makes me feel crazy and dumb.

The man killed my mom. In front of me. Yet, here I am pining for the love lost and wanting to see him. Wanting to ask the questions that have always burned in my heart. I think most of all I wanted to know if he ever really loved me, or if it was all an act.

"Hey, Dani." The deep voice behind me is unfamiliar, and I'm instantly on guard as I look up. The man is tall and dressed in black tactical gear. Police is printed across the front of his vest.

"You're a hell of a track. Getting to you was harder than any of my other marks."

"Who are you?" I cautiously begin to stand.

"Oh, I wouldn't do that if I were you." The man moves a little closer behind me.

I let out a small sob and tears sting my eyes when I hear the telling sound of a gun cocking. "No... Please. Who are you?"

"Name's Zekeih. And you will do everything I say. Starting with getting up right now. If you scream, I'll shoot. I have a silencer. No one will hear the shot. Now, get up."

My mind is racing with all of my options. I do as he says and get up slowly, attempting to buy myself as much time as I can.

My eyes dart around the property. Ryan has guards everywhere. Someone will see me. They have to.

Behind me, Zekeih jams the gun into my back and chuckles. "If you're looking for guards, forget it. I've been casing this place for a week. I know the guard's schedule. I know Ryan switches out patrol every six hours. I took out his patrol. All nine of them. No one will have a fucking clue they aren't here until shift change."

I sniffle as my heart stops. "Why are you doing this?"

"Money, Dani. I have a family. Wife. A kid. I can't live off the salary Chicago P.D. pays me." Something in his voice makes me think he's lying.

I have to keep him talking so I can think. He couldn't have taken out all the guards. I know Ryan. He always has back up. Extra layers. I just need to figure it out.

I only look around with my eyes and decide to play on that small quiver I heard in his voice. "That can't be everything. You're part of Taylor's taskforce. Everyone on his team is loyal to a fault."

"Not everyone, Dani. A lot of us are sick and fucking tired of your perfect boyfriend. Can't do anything wrong in the department's eyes. Or in Taylor's. He's fucked up more times than I can tell you, and Taylor still keeps him around." He's still lying. I can hear it.

Come on. Come on. Where's the other guards? Where's Ryan's back up plan?

Zekeih almost has me to the gate. I'm running out of time.

"What do I have to do with this? Why not just try and poison him again?"

"Because that's not the mission, Dani. That was a vendetta. I underestimated how good that fucking doctor is. Won't make that mistake again. He's next on my list." That quiver. I still hear it. He's still lying. "First, I need to get you to my boss. Then, I can focus on Chantau and your asshole boyfriend. No one makes a fool of me and gets away with it."

A fool of him? No... Something doesn't sound right about that. It sounds almost as wrong as his voice. Like he's trying too hard to throw me off; make me believe something that isn't true. He's nervous.

"Taylor knows about you. He knows you're dirty. Nick has evidence."

Zekeih laughs and shoves me forward. We're at the gate. There are no guards. I'm out of time. I have to do something. "Taylor doesn't know shit. He trusts me. Get fucking moving. Now."

I stomp on Zekeih's foot, praying he doesn't pull the trigger. As soon as I feel the gun drop and Zekeih groan in pain, I spin and kick him in the knee. "Get back!" I scream as I shove him.

"Fuck!" As he collapses to the ground, I grab the gun he dropped when I took out his knee. I let out a loud scream. If there really are no other guards, I pray to God someone inside the house hears me.

"Help! Help!" I start to run, but he grabs me.

"What the fuck are you trying to do?" He easily twists the gun away from me and wrenches my wrist behind my back as he quickly gets to his feet.

"Get off me!" I shriek.

I know if I run, he'll shoot me if I can't get the gun. So, I have to fight. I elbow him in the ribs. He grunts. I keep twisting my body enough to elbow him until he lets go of my arm.

"Goddammit!" He tries to hit me, but I duck and knee him in the balls. "Son of a...! You fucking bitch!" He swings. His fist connects with the side of my head.

He hits me so hard I see stars and fall to the ground. "Ow..." I shake my head, even though my vision is blurring. I see him ambling

159

towards me. I kick my leg out, connecting with bone, which one, I have no idea, but I'm not giving up.

I hear a sickening crunch as he falls backwards, screaming and holding his knee. "Shit! Shit! Oh, shit!"

"Don't move. Not a fucking inch."

I can hardly see him, but I whimper in relief. "Robby. Thank God."

Robby picks up Zekeih's gun and kneels next to me, keeping his gun and eyes trained on Zekeih's head. "You okay, Dani?"

"This is why I need to learn how to use a gun. And keep it if I have it in my hand..." I stand and brush myself off, ignoring the pain and wiping my eyes to clear the blurring.

"I think you did pretty damn well without it. You fucked him up."

I look at Zekeih holding his knee and groaning on the ground. "I don't think he tried very hard."

"I don't think he was expecting a fight. Luke and Ryan are on their way out here."

"Thanks for coming out. Zekeih said he shot all nine guards on patrol tonight."

"There's more than nine guards. He shot the ones patrolling the perimeter, but they switch every ground rotation. That's why I was out here. I was called after none of the guards showed up at the checkpoint to switch off."

"What does that mean? Ground rotation."

"We have three sets of nine guards patrolling. They walk the grounds and make one complete rotation. Then they switch. It's a seamless switch. We switch one guard at a time; the entire team after six hours. Anyone watching would be none the wiser."

"It's not going to stop with me. He's still out there. He's not going to stop," Zekeih growls through the pain as he whimpers.

I glare at Zekeih. Rage overtakes me. I leap towards him, but Robby blocks my way. "Your first mistake was coming here in the first place!" I yell. "Your second was coming after me!"

"Damn. Remind me not to fuck with you," Robby says with a proud smile. Zekeih watches me a little fearfully.

I lunge for Zekeih again. He can't do anything but open his mouth, but no sound comes out. Robby stops me once more. "And poisoning

160

Nick! You fucking asshole!" I push past Robby in a fit of anger, but a set of strong arms wraps around me from behind and hauls me tightly against a solid body.

"As much as I would enjoy watching you kick his ass, I need information, sweetheart."

I growl at Ryan as tears sting my eyes. "He poisoned Nick! He works for Krins! He came after me! He killed nine of your guards! He said he's going after Doctor Chantau. What more do you need?" I cry hot tears.

"Where Krins is? What the plan is? Thanks for taking him down, but calm down, Dani. Let me take over."

I slump against him. "I need to be taught how to use a gun. And keep it. I had his. He took it too easily from me.."

Ryan chuckles. "I'll teach you. Well, more than I've touched on." His grip loosens, and he sets me on the ground. I glare harder at Zekeih wondering if I could be quicker than Ryan and kick the asshole in the head.

"Crazy fucking bitch." He barely gets the words out. They're no more than a whisper.

I shake my head. "You're about to pay for all of your betrayal and sins. I hope when you get to Hell, Satan himself tortures you."

Zekeih coughs. "This... isn't over. Krins... he's... going for Taylor and Nick... now. Fucking doctor is next."

I don't miss the look in his eyes. It's not fear of Ryan. It's pleading. He's pleading with Ryan. I turn to Ryan, horrified and suddenly very shaky. I don't know what's going on, but all those feelings about this not being right crash into me again.

"What? He... doesn't mean... does he?"

Ryan's eyes reflect the same fear I feel as he takes out his phone. He turns to Luke. "Get guards to Doctor Chantau. Bring him here. Then, we deal with him."

He takes my hand and yanks me towards the house. I have to run to keep up with him. "Ryan?"

My heart is racing. I can't think past the fact that I know Nick is in danger. Ryan's phone is against his ear. "Taylor! Get out! Get out of the fucking precinct now!"

"Ryan! What's he going to do?"

Ryan pulls me through the door of the house. "Aria! Get in here!"

"Ryan? What's happening?" The hot tears turn to lava and seer my cheeks.

Arianna runs into the room. "What? What happened?"

"What? Taylor, I said now!" Ryan is yelling into the phone as Arianna and I watch him. I can barely breathe because I'm so scared. Ryan squeezes my hand and pulls me towards his wife. "Get her upstairs. Take Chris and lock yourselves in the bedroom. No one gets in except me. You know the code word. Go!"

Arianna tugs on my hand as she turns and runs up the stairs. "Okay," she says over her shoulder.

"Wait! What about Taylor and Nick?" I try to pull away, but tiny Arianna is a lot stronger than she looks.

"Dani, when Ryan says to do something, do it. Don't question because he knows something we don't." She pulls me into the nursery and grabs Chris. She hands him to me and grabs his blanket and a duffel bag. "Our bedroom is the safest room in the house. Ryan had it completely reinforced. No one is getting in. Let's go." She leads me to her bedroom as Chris starts crying. I rock him, trying to soothe him, but I know he's just as panicked as I am.

"Shh... it's okay, little guy."

"Ari! Are you in the bedroom?" Ryan yells up the stairs.

"Just now!" she yells back.

"Lock it down! All of it!"

Arianna does as Ryan says as soon as the door is closed. After she locks it, she runs for a remote and hits a button. Metal shades drop over the windows.

"Oh my God. What the hell is happening?" I hug a screaming Chris close to me and cry with him.

Arianna finishes her lock down, then walks back across the room to me. "Ryan had to have gotten information that scared him. Something that made him fear for our safety. But we're safe in here."

"Zekeih. He tried to kidnap me. He killed nine of Ryan's guards and found me at the fire pits. Robby helped me get away from him, but he said that Krins is going after Taylor and Nick and Doctor Chantau."

A dark look crosses Arianna's face as she gently takes Chris from my arms. I follow her to the bed and sit next to her. "If Zekeih was able to get past the guards and get to you on the property, it's possible there's more where he came from. Until Ryan gets a sweep done to make sure, we're safest here."

"What about Taylor and Nick? And the doctor?" I ask fearfully.

"Taylor won't question Ryan's orders. If Ryan says get out, he will. And they'll get the doctor."

"But Taylor. He had to have questioned it because Ryan said again to get out. Arianna, I can't handle it if something happens to Nick. I can't."

Arianna cradles Chris with one arm and hugs me with the other. "I know that this isn't much to go on, but trust me when I say that Ryan won't let anything happen. I promise, Dani."

Arianna and I stay in the room for what seems like hours. We both cuddle Chris on the bed. I wish I could be as peaceful and blissfully ignorant to all of the bad things in the world like this innocent baby is.

Unfortunately, I'm not. I've seen too many terrible things to have a prayer of being that way again. No matter how hard I try to calm myself, each second that passes makes me fear for Nick's safety.

Not being with him to help him is killing me.

Not knowing if he's okay is breaking me.

Every possible horrible scenario of what could be happening to him right now plays out ever so slowly and detailed in my mind that breathing physically hurts.

I lay in the bed and think. Anything to keep the air flowing through my body.

It's the thinking that kills me.

Chapter Nineteen

⚔ Nick ⚔

The words on my screen are actually blurring together. I've been looking at it for hours trying to recreate everything Zekeih wiped out.

"I still don't understand how in the hell he could do this," Reed says.

"Money is a huge fucking factor. Look how much he's getting paid." Jesse nods to the screen.

Reed shakes his head. "I don't care. It's all about loyalty and morals to me. Being bought off? Come on."

"Wait. Go back," Dane says. I look up at my Sergeant and stop scrolling. He glances at Taylor. Both are leaning over my shoulders. "You see that?"

"I wish I fucking hadn't. We're gonna need Robby for this shit," Taylor says.

I shake my head. "See what?"

"Scroll up a little." Taylor leans in. I scroll back slowly. "That. Look at the deposit."

I furrow my brows. "Yeah? Fifty grand every week. I already told you that."

Dane points at a withdrawal. "But not about the withdrawals to other accounts."

"I figured that was offshore accounts. I planned on having Robby track them," I say.

Dane shakes his head. "That's not an offshore account number. That's onshore."

Jesse crosses his arms over his chest. "Which means he's dividing it among other accounts."

"Or other people." Taylor glares at the screen then looks at me. "Get Robby to track all of this. Make a copy of everything we recovered."

"We keeping the department out of this one?" Reed asks, though I'm sure he already knows.

Taylor nods. "Zekeih had to have help. He's smart, but no way he knows how to wipe a computer. I don't know what the hell is going on, but the only people on this team I trust are right here. Adam and Mark?"

Dane nods. "They have excuses for a lot lately."

"Adam has been acting pretty fucking flighty," Reed agrees.

Jesse yawns. "And Mark has been zoned out."

I sigh and shake my head. "We don't know anything right now."

Taylor stands and stretches. "He's right. We need the money tracked." He leans over and then back up stretching his back. I insert a flash drive and start downloading the files.

Dane runs his fingers through his hair. "I don't want to believe it, but fuck. It makes sense."

"No one wants to believe a betrayal of this level." I watch as it starts downloading.

"Especially one that goes as deeply as I think it fucking does." Taylor paces behind me. We all fall silent as I continue downloading. Jesse yawns again.

"Why don't you guys head out? Nick and I can finish," Taylor says, reading the team.

Reed chuckles. "I won't say no to that. I miss my girl."

"Damn, I miss mine, too. She had a late night at the bakery and was looking forward to a quiet night at home," Jesse says.

"I can't say the same," Dane chuckles. He's the only one of us who hasn't been hooked by a woman. "But I was looking forward to a quiet night by myself."

165

Taylor grins as everyone else stands. "Dane, maybe you need some of my old tricks and tips. Before Nicole, I rarely ever spent a night alone."

Dane laughs. "You rarely spent a day alone. How many girls did you fuck in your office?"

Taylor grins widely. "Too many to count!"

We all share a laugh as Taylor winks. After everyone is gone, Taylor turns back to me.

I look up at him. "We're close. Ninety percent."

"Good. Keep it going." His phone rings and he takes it out of his pocket, looking at the caller ID. He narrows his eyes as he looks at me and answers it.

I raise an eyebrow. "What?"

"Hey, Ry. What's -" Taylor glances over his shoulder. I watch his entire demeanor change. He's suddenly on edge. "Nick is finishing the download. We're at ninety-five -" He looks at me, eyes panicked as he stops breathing. I swallow hard, my heart forgetting how to beat. I immediately stand and take out my gun. Taylor follows my lead. "Understood."

He hangs up and looks at my computer. "Download complete. Ryan says we need to leave."

I eject the flash drive and stick it in my jeans pocket as I lock my computer. Taylor leads me out of the squad room, both our guns are ready if any unexpected threats come at us.

"Do we need to evacuate anyone in the building?" I ask.

"Not many here, but we need to head to dispatch."

I nod, following him as his cover. We reach the dispatch room. Taylor lets us in.

We're one of the precincts that houses a dispatch unit in Chicago. It's small, but if the main center or another smaller center goes out, they can help with the call load.

Taylor opens the door. "Everyone listen up! Code one! Switch your calls to call center three immediately and move!"

Each of the seven dispatchers jump into action, not questioning Taylor. They all rush for the door in a surprisingly orderly manner.

I usher them all out. "Let's go. Quickly please."

"Out the back door. Go!" Taylor commands.

"We checking the rest of the building?"

166

"Not much more to check. Check the bathrooms. I'll check the offices."

We split up and quickly move through the rest of the building, meeting in the middle where we started. "No one."

"Me either. Let's move."

We keep our guns drawn as we make our way to the backdoor we just sent everyone out of. Very suddenly, Taylor stops and puts a closed fist up to halt me. He listens, then turns to me as he sniffs the air.

I do the same. "Gas." I mouth the words to him. He nods as he turns and moves quickly to the door. I sniff again and smell smoke. There isn't a lot of it, but it illuminates a trip wire. I grab Taylor, yank him back, and hiss in his ear. "Stop! Tripwire."

He looks down and takes a deep breath. "Shit."

"Let me take the lead," I whisper. "I've been on more missions then you, and this is starting to feel like a fucking mafia set up." I step forward as he nods. "Follow my movements. They have to be in the building. This was set up after the guys left and the evacuation or they all would've been blown up."

He nods again. The smoke is getting thicker the farther we move towards another exit. It's stinging my eyes. I fight the cough I feel and stop to rip the sleeves from my shirt. I nod to the bathroom and Taylor covers me while I wet the sleeves down.

Covering both my mouth and nose, I tie the sleeve around my face. When I'm done, I keep watch while Taylor does the same.

"It's getting hot. We need to get out right now," he whispers.

I lead him to another backdoor and growl. "Fuck. It's wired, too"

"What? What the fuck do you mean wired?"

"We go out, it blows. We need to get to the garage." I lead him through the building to the garage, stepping over another tripwire. Once again being stopped by the wiring of the door.

Taylor is starting to panic. It's getting hot and so smoky that we're both fighting to keep our eyes open. Flames are starting to lick across the walls. It's fucking dark.

"They had to have gotten out. How?" he asks.

"They probably wired the door as they left. It's getting too hot. We have no choice. We have to try the front door. The way the flames are licking across the ceiling and how hot it's getting, we're going to have a huge problem soon."

"Backdraft?"

I shake my head. "More like a flashover."

"Then we go out a window. Let's get back to the offices. No other area has windows."

I nod and quickly lead him to the squad room and offices. We're running out of oxygen and starting to see far more flames dancing across the ceiling and streaking down the walls.

As we near the squad room we both stop. It's completely engulfed.

I'm starting to feel a little helpless as I look around. The calm demeanor I felt is dissipating slowly. "What now?"

"We aren't dying in a fucking fire. Nicole would never forgive me. And Dani would resurrect me just to kill me again." Taylor looks around as I chuckle.

"Fuck, she probably would."

Both of us have tears streaming from our eyes. The smoke is stinging our eyes and burning our throat. Not coughing is completely out of the question. Both of us are going through fits of it.

Crippling fits that double us over.

"The coroner." I grab Taylor's arm and backtrack a few doors. "He has a window." One of the only offices that have one.

"Let's hope we can get there. Everything else is blocked." He's not lying. We can't get through the squadroom to get to the front door, even if we did have the time.

"We're getting out. We have to." I scan the door for wires, then feel it for heat.

Satisfied we aren't going to be burned alive or blown up if we go through it, I kick it open. Taylor and I practically fall through the door.

He slams it behind us. "Find a chair or something. Or shoot it. Fuck. I don't care. We need to bust through." Taylor breaks into a coughing fit again as he tries to grab his gun.

Knowing neither of us are lasting much longer, I aim my gun at the glass and shoot, praying it isn't bulletproof. It shatters. "Thank fucking God."

Flames immediately start licking at the door searching for the source of oxygen I just gave it, and Taylor pushes me forward to the window.

"We gotta go. Now!" Taylor yells over the roaring of the flames.

Both of us lunge for the window. We take our makeshift masks and wrap our hands so that we can shatter the glass further to get out. The flames climb the walls and billow across the ceiling as we break the glass.

I stare in horror when the door and wall erupt in flames. "It's looking for oxygen! We're about to have a backdraft!" I don't know what's worse. A flashover or backdraft. Either one will kill us violently.

"Out! Get out now! We're jumping!"

We both leap and smash through the glass. We fall to the pavement a few feet below us. We're on the first floor, so it's not a long fall, but hitting pavement is never fun.

"Stay down!" Taylor yells.

We both lay prone on the ground covering our heads. Behind us, the building rumbles. The window we just jumped out of explodes. Glass and sparks fall around us. Before I have a chance to react, Taylor is pulling me up. We run to our trucks.

I grab him as a realization suddenly hits me. "Wait! Wait! Stop. They could be wired. We need to get out of here and call Ryan."

At that moment, a black SUV skids to a stop in front of us. Taylor and I both point our guns as the window comes down.

"Get in! Hurry up!" Drake yells.

"Thank fuck."

"No shit." Taylor jumps in the front.

I dive in the back. Drake takes off as we're closing the doors. It's then I realize I'm not alone in the backseat. "Doctor Chantau? What are you doing here?"

"Good question. Drake showed up and ushered me out. He said Ryan would explain."

The rest of the ride back to the house is silent. It's not until Drake flies into the parking lot that anyone dares speak.

"Why is everyone here?" Taylor asks when he sees all the vehicles.

"Because Zekeih tried to kidnap Dani," Drake answers.

"What? Why the hell wouldn't you fucking tell me that?" I ask glaring at him as my heart reaches a new level of racing.

"I just did."

"You just... Are you kidding me? Who do you think you're talking to?" I growl the words at him, seething.

He glares right back. "Knock it off. I have my fucking orders. Ryan said no one talks to you about it but him."

"Relax, Nick. You know as well as I do there's a reason. Don't take it out on Drake. He's following orders," Taylor says.

"Fuck you both," I growl.

Drake winks and smiles. "You aren't my type."

I glare but can't help the laugh that bubbles out despite the anger simmering. As soon as the SUV stops, I jump out and run to the house. As soon as I get inside, I start yelling for my brother. "Ryan?" No answer.

I sense Taylor behind me. "Family room." We quickly head for the family room, but find no one. "Ry! Where the fuck are you?" Taylor bellows.

"Quiet! Christ!" Ryan comes around the corner with a rifle.

"What the hell is going on?" Taylor asks. His voice betrays him. I can hear all the panic I feel.

"I just cleared the house. Grounds are cleared. Nikki and everyone else are at the guard's house," Ryan explains. Taylor turns and runs for the door. I follow, but Ryan grabs my arm. "Not you."

"I need to get to Dani! Let go!"

"She's not there!"

I glare at him and wrench my arm free. "I just escaped an attempt on my life. Barely. I find out Zekeih almost got to my fiancé. And now you're telling me she's not here? Fuck! Ryan, I'm going insane!"

"You think I'm letting her out of my sight after there was just an attempt on her? On my fucking property? How long have you known me? She's with Arianna and Chris. Fucking Christ." He turns and heads for the stairs. I follow as he sprints up them. When he reaches his bedroom door, he knocks. "Ari? It's me, baby. Okeania."

"What?" I look at Ryan, confused, as the bedroom door comes flying open.

Arianna leaps in Ryan's arms and Dani appears behind her. She looks at me completely exhausted, and like she's about to cry, though it's obvious she has been. I simply hold my arms out for her. She steps into them, though I want to sweep her into them and never let her go.

I hug her tightly as quiet sobs wrack her body. "I'm okay, honey." I don't give a damn about what I went through right now, but I know she needs to hear those words.

"I was so scared. Everything happened so fast. And then Ryan locked us in here. I don't even know what happened. Or why you smell like a fire."

"What happened, Nick?" Ryan asks.

"You called. We finished the download of everything I found by the time Taylor hung up with you. We evacuated the building. After we cleared it, we were leaving. Taylor nearly hit a tripwire. They were on every door. We couldn't get out. Someone set the building on fire, but they waited until we were the only ones left in the building. They had to have been there and seen everyone else leave. We went through a window." I run my hand up and down Dani's back as the other tangles in her hair. Dani's grip tightens on me.

"See anyone?" Ryan asks.

I shake my head. "Didn't see anyone or hear anyone. We sent Dane, Jesse, and Reed home. We were a little suspicious of Adam and Mark. On the way home, though, I started thinking they were involved even more than I had been thinking before. If Zekeih is the one who tried to kidnap Dani, then whoever set that fire has to know the ins and outs of that building. They had to have been watching. They had to have seen everyone leave."

"Walk me through what happened. The tripwires."

"I thought it felt like a mafia hit as soon as we hit the first tripwire. I took the lead. All the doors were sealed. All of them. There was no way out, Ry. So, we went back to the squad room. I thought we could go through an office window. I wasn't even going to try the front door. I knew if the others were wired, no way that one wasn't, too. By the time we got there, though, the room was fully engulfed. The flames were so hot, computers were melting. Shit on the walls were melting off and dripping down. Places that didn't even have flames was experiencing the same heat. I knew we were going to have a flashover. We backtracked to the coroner's office. He has a window. Small, but big enough that we could jump through. Taylor closed the door, but it felt like we were being chased by the heat."

"Accelerant?" Ryan asks.

"Gas. Diesel to be exact. Distinct diesel smell. When Taylor closed the door, we could still hear the roaring of the flames. I shot out the window. We wrapped our hands up and started punching out the rest of it. But the flames were already licking up the fucking door. They were billowing across the ceiling. We knew we had to get out. So, we crashed through the window just as the fucking backdraft hit. Damn near didn't make it." I let out a shuddering breath as Dani whimpers.

"Anyone shoot at you when you got out?"

"No. But there wasn't much of a chance. We started running for our trucks but decided that they could be wired. Drake got there right then."

Ryan nods. "I'll brief the others. You and Taylor need time alone with your girls. Come down a little. We'll talk more in the morning."

I nod as Dani takes my hand. She leads me to our bedroom. As soon as the door is closed, she jumps on me. Her mouth is all over me. Her legs are wrapped around my waist. It takes me a second to regain control of myself and keep from mauling her.

"Baby. Dani, honey. Let me clean up."

"No." Her mouth meets mine again.

She tightens herself around me. Her tits press against me and make me groan. I walk her to the bed and let her slide down my body. As soon as her feet hit the floor, we're tearing each other's clothes off. Moments later, she's pulling me on top of her on the bed. She wraps herself around me.

I sink balls deep into her. "Oh, fuck. You're so tight. Fucking perfect."

"I need you. I was so scared, Nick. I fought. I got away. Then I found out about you. I need to feel you. I need you to convince me we're both still alive."

"Shh... baby. It's okay. I'm here. You can feel me. Everything's okay."

I start to move inside her. She closes her eyes. She moves harder and faster against me, her body begging for something more than what I'm giving her. She looks at me pleadingly as she thrusts against me frantically.

172

I smile as I grab her arms, pinning them above her head. "I know what you need."

"Please."

"Trust me. I know what you need." I feel the second she relaxes and completely gives herself to me. I kiss her and give her the hard and fast thrusts that she needs.

"Yes! Oh, God, yes!" Her usual quiet whimpers and cries are screams and moans. The harder I thrust, the tighter she feels. The faster I move, the hotter and wetter she gets. The deeper I hit, the more she bucks into me.

"Holy God. You're perfect."

The bed creaks and hits the wall with every hard thrust. My dick hits so deeply within her, I couldn't get out if I wanted to.

I feel her thighs tremble as her pussy tightens around me. Her stomach quivers. I reach down, finding her clit with my thumb. I flick it back and forth. She clenches and pulses so hard around me I can't stop myself from releasing deeply inside her. The force of the explosion takes my breath away. I almost forget what I'm doing.

Dani's scream brings me back to reality. "Nick! Please! Please!" She claws at my back and arches up into my thumb. I give her the pressure she begs for as I continue my thrusts inside her. "Ah! Yes! Yes!"

"Come, my girl. Come for me."

She clenches tighter around me, forcing my orgasm to prolong. I keep rubbing her clit and empty inside her until she finally relaxes and collapses underneath me.

I kiss her, hard, my tongue lashing hers as we stay connected in the most intimate of ways. After a few moments, I pull out of her and carry her to the bathroom.

We spend hours in the shower pleasing each other, then hours of the wildest and most passionate sex I've ever had until we fall into an exhausted sleep. I wrap her in my arms completely intending on never letting her go.

Chapter Twenty

☒ Luke ☒

I throw a handcuffed and gagged Zekeih on the ground in the interrogation room of the guard's house. It's nothing but a basement. Cement surrounds us. It's cold. Dank. I reach up and turn the light in the middle of the room on before closing the door.

There's no windows. No way out of here except that one door. And it's an entire level below the main floor in the guard's house. Above us is their gym.

I smile a little darkly as I watch him try to sit up. I casually walk to the middle of the room. I turn the single chair around and sit, resting my arms over the back as he squirms.

He glares at me before letting out a loud as fuck scream. "Help! Help!"

I can't help but laugh. "You honestly think anyone can hear you down here? Well, at least anyone who might care. Only people who might hear you are the guard's working out in the gym. And... well," I shrug. "You know they don't give a shit about you."

"When I get out of here, you're first on my list." He tries to glare, but I can see what's hiding behind the tough guy facade.

I place my hand over my heart and give him a mock shocked look. "Me? Well, fuck. I'm honored. I'm just a boy from a small town in New York. Or Texas. Or maybe it was Colorado." I smile again and shrug. "Could've been Montana."

"Fuck you."

"Hard pass." I look him up and down. "You ain't even a little bit my type."

"You're fucking dead. You don't know it yet, but you're dead."

I stick one hand in front of my face. "Don't look translucent." I extend my arm. "Don't feel tingly." I take out a lighter and run my fingertips over the flame after I light it. "Still feel." I look at him, unyielding, pausing with my fingertips just over the flame before passing them through it again. "At least a little."

He manages to sit up. "You really think you're so fucking tough, don't you?"

"Think?" I shake my head. "Thinking only gets people killed." I slowly stand and walk very casually to the far corner of the room. I smile as I open a door. Can't get out of this one, though. I take out a metal bat and look it over like it's the most interesting thing in the world to me as I watch him out of the corner of my eye. "Actions on the other hand."

He gives a dangerous growl. At least I'm sure he thinks that's what it was. "Fuck you."

I smile wider as I stalk him like prey. "I thought I already answered you on that." I stop in front of him and grip the bat. He watches me.

I grin demonically. Time for a little scare tactic.

I swing the bat hard. He flinches and jumps back curling up on the floor when it sails right by his ear.

"Shit…" He lays on his side on the floor and closes his eyes a moment before looking up at me.

I make a huge show of adjusting my grip. "I used to play baseball." I study the bat. "I had one fuck of an average. Led my high school team to State all four years." I look down at him. "Did you play any sports?"

"No," he growls as he shoots a fierce look at me. Still, I can see that fear. It's not directed towards me. There's something else happening here.

"Now, now Zekeih. No need to lie. We're friends, right?"

"No. We're not friends. No. I didn't play sports."

175

I nod and look at the bat again. I swing and connect hard with the ground near his head. "I hate when people lie. I never understood the reason."

He groans and coughs curling himself into a tighter ball as he closes his eyes. "Fuck..."

"Sorry, Zekeih. Did I scare the shit out of you?" I shake my head and look at the bat. "Thing doesn't have a grip. Must have slipped." I make another show of bettering my grip on the bat. "You see. I usually don't ever ask a question I don't know the answer to. I know you were a star track runner. Mile was your jam. I learned well. Being a cop. Working with Taylor. You remember Taylor, don't you? He's your boss, right?"

"Fuck Taylor." The fear. It's definitely there.

I raise an eyebrow. "Me? Shit. Do you think he's interested? Think I have a shot? He's fucking hot."

He shakes his head again and fights through the pain of his shattered knee. Dani did a hell of a job. I'm sure his ears are ringing, too. Metal against cement. That had to reverberate through his head. "I won't tell you... anything," he grunts.

I chuckle. "Well, that's not nice. I told you things about me." I look down at him. "Tell me, Zekeih. How's your wife and son? What is he now? Two?"

His eyes flash with both rage and fear. "Stay away from them!"

"Aww... yes.... There it is. Tough guy's kryptonite. We all have it. So, tell me what I want to know. Because if you don't, I'll make sure they have no protection from the storm coming this way. None."

He struggles to get up. "Stay the fuck away from them! Don't touch them!"

"Then let's start talking, Zekeih! Because my patience is wearing real fucking thin!"

"Just don't touch them!"

"Tell me what you want with Dani."

"I'm not telling you anything! Don't you get it?"

I swing the bat again, connecting hard with the wall he's leaning against. He jumps and jerks his knee. He tries to scream, but can't. "I'm not fucking around, Zekeih. Tell me what the fuck you want with Dani."

He looks up at me gasping. "Orders... He gave... orders. Dani... alive."

176

"Who?"

"Krins... Adam... Krins." He squeezes his eyes shut as he tries not to move.

"The money."

"Krins... For Dani... He... said... unharmed." He coughs and sobs silently. "Alive."

I kneel next to him. "We know he's not the one pulling the strings. So, who is?"

"I... I don't know..." He moans in pain. "I don't know."

I stand with a nod. I believe he doesn't know. "Tell me everything you know, Zekeih. If you do, I'll protect your family. If you don't..." I shrug as I sit in the chair. I rest my hands over the back of it again and set the bat against my leg.

He looks at me like he's trying to figure me out. Finally, he sighs. Suddenly, all of the fear I know he's feeling is all at the forefront. "Adam and Mark..." He winces and pauses. "We all were approached... by Captain Wolfe. He... threatened us. Said that this... huge drug deal that the drug task force did... we'd go down for it if we didn't help."

"Help with what?"

He winces again as he moves. "He said... there was a bounty out. Whoever brought in Dani Jade would get a handsome reward. Fuck..." He pauses again. "That... the payor wanted her. Alive. He pulled me aside after I... got into... it with Taylor. We... haven't been getting along. I felt like... he wanted me to leave the taskforce. Adam and Mark disagreed with me. But I felt it. Taylor... wasn't listening to me.... anymore. He was the golden boy. His way or the highway. Wolfe... said he was going after the Crane's. That... he was under orders to take them down."

"Why?"

He shakes his head. "He didn't say. Just that... he was under orders to destroy them. Get Dani. Destroy the Cranes."

I watch him as I think. "Whose idea was it to poison Nick?"

"Captain Wolfe. He... knew I'd do it. Because if I didn't... he'd go after my wife and kid. Nick was... on to me. All of us... He knew that if Nick figured it out... he'd be in trouble. He... was arrested before I could do it." He winces again and coughs.

"But you did it anyway, Zekeih. Why?"

"Krins. Because after Wolfe was arrested… he quickly covered our tracks. He started depositing the money in my account… I… dispersed it. Me, Adam, Mark, a weapons guy, and IT guy."

I lean back. "So, Wolfe gets arrested, and you all still went ahead with this plan. He's out of the picture. Why did Krins go directly to you? Why didn't you go to Taylor?"

"Krins… He came to me… because I have a family. He used them… against me. He still wanted the Cranes… destroyed. He still wanted Dani. He never said… why. Just that he had his orders. Like… I.. had mine."

I watch him again as I think. Running through details has always been one of my strong suits. It's one of the reasons I've been so good at every job I've ever had. My attention to detail has saved my ass and those of every team I've been a part of.

"When did all of this start?"

"Months ago. After Carter… Rudd went missing."

"Walk me through it, Zekeih. Rudd goes missing. Wolfe approaches the three of you. Threatens you all. Pulls you aside. Says what, exactly? Hey, I have a special project for you. Kill your boss, or I kill your wife?"

He lays still with his eyes closed. "Krins. He told us… about Krins. Said Krins would kill my wife and my child."

"And then after. Krins approaches you because of your wife and child. Says follow through with the plan or I kill them both."

"Yes. Fuck. Yes."

"Where's Adam and Mark?"

"Dead. Krins shot them both. They were going to Taylor. Tonight. He told me… To get here. Get Dani. I hadn't figured out the schedule completely for the guards. I told him...that. He… told… me… to just get it done." He squeezes his eyes shut. "He has my wife and son."

"And that's the motivation for you following through."

"I had to." He opens his eyes and looks at me. I can see everything he'd been trying to hide. The fear. The anger. The sadness. But the thing that actually makes me empathetic is the helplessness.

I stand slowly. He winces again, this time in fear. I leave the bat by the chair. "Why weren't you and Taylor getting along?"

He looks at me. "Because…" He sighs. "Because I wanted off the team. I didn't tell... him that. I just didn't care, and it caused fuck-ups. Taylor... approached me a lot about what was going on. I wouldn't... talk to him. I shut him out. Eventually, though, I wanted... things to go back the way they were. I hated the tension. But by then, Taylor... was fed up. I lashed out. Adam and Mark tried to get me to talk to... him. Taylor kept telling me he... was available to talk." He takes a few shallow breaths. "But the anger I felt... at myself and the whole fucking world had taken over. That's when I was... approached."

"Captain Wolfe was arrested. You took over the payment distribution and became Krins' direct contact. You've seen him. Talked to him." I watch him as he nods. "He told you to poison Nick. Stick to the plan."

"Destroy the Crane's. Bring him Dani."

I shake my head. "And he never said why. You never heard anything to give you a clue about why he wants the Cranes so bad. Why he wanted Nick dead. Or why he wants Dani."

"He… only tipped me off. To… Nick being onto us. He never told me why. Just that his… contact told him. He said nothing about Dani… Just that he wanted her back."

"Back?" I glare at him as he nods. It looks like he's starting to pass out. "Dammit." I nudge his feet. "Zekeih. Up."

His eyes snap open as I start helping him. "Ow! Fuck!" His eyes roll back in his head as I prop him more against the wall so he isn't slumped. He grits his teeth. "I don't care what… Fuck…" He hisses in pain. "You do to me… He has my family. Save... my... family." His head lulls to one side as he loses consciousness.

"Son of a bitch." I head for the door and open it just as Ryan is about to walk through.

His eyes flick to Zekeih. "What did you get from him?"

"I got a little bit, but he passed out. I'm calling Chantau."

Ryan raises an eyebrow. "You think he has more information?"

"No. I think I got what I needed. But…" I scrub my hands over my face.

"But what? Take him out. We don't need him anymore, and I'm not about to have a fucking traitor on my team."

I shake my head. "Ry, he's not really the bad guy here. Krins is using his family against him. So was Wolfe. And I know what you're going to say. That's his words. Verify it. I will. I am. But we need Chantau until then." I look back in the room. "Krins killed Adam and Mark. He said that he has his family." I look back at Ryan and reach in my back pocket. I hold up Zekeih's phone. "It's coded. I can't get in. He passed out before I could get it. I'm going to have Robby hack it, but if he's telling the truth?"

Ryan nods. "Then we need to help him. Get him the fuck out of this mess, and save his family."

"I'm getting a team together now. Get Chantau. We already know he was injured from the beating he took from Dani. I don't know what kind of damage she caused trying to get away from him."

Ryan takes out his phone with a nod. I jog up the stairs. I don't know what I'm walking into, but as I'm making my way to Robby's, I start calling in guards to go with me. Wherever it may be. I take the stairs to Robby's two at a time as I'm barking orders into my phone. I don't bother knocking as I walk in.

Robby looks up at me with furrowed eyebrows as I hang up my phone. "What happened?"

I lean down and kiss him as I hand him Zekeih's phone. "Zekeih's phone. I need it open. It's coded."

He raises an eyebrow. "That's it?" He takes the phone and hands it back to me in less than a minute.

I shake my head. "How did you do that?"

"Codes on a phone for security purposes are becoming obsolete because people like me can get around them so easily. Now…, what's going on? What did he say?"

I quickly start looking through texts. "Just a sec." I open texts to an unknown number and find what I'm looking for. I hand the phone back to Robby. "Track that number. Krins has Zekeih's family. I'm getting a team together. I need to know where they are."

Robby doesn't question me. He takes the phone and sets to work. "I can't give you a lot unless he's using the phone or it's on and has GPS. If he's as smart as he's supposed to be…" Robby laughs and turns his laptop. "I take back everything. He's stupid."

I look at the screen as Robby gets up and grabs his gear. "Is that the abandoned warehouse near the dock? The one with the missing roof and missing wall on the entire Eastern side?"

"Looks like it." He swings his duffle bag over his shoulder and grabs the laptop. "Let's go. I'll track it. If it moves, I'll know. Either he ditched it or they're there. Could be a trap."

We jog down the stairs to the garage where we meet the rest of the team. I count heads. "Good. All twenty of you are here. I don't know what we're walking into, but it's an evacuation mission. Woman and child. Teams of four. Five SUVs. Everyone behind us. Robby is tracking, so I'll lead. When we get there. I want a team of four out and surveilling. I want to know if anyone so much as breathes in that building. I want to know how many people we're dealing with. This isn't a typical mission. We need to get in there and out. Treat this like a SWAT mission. I know you've all gone out with Taylor on at least one mission. Things run differently. Fast. Questions?"

"Teams? Does it matter?" one of the guards asks.

"No. But the team in the SUV following directly behind me and Robby is the surveillance team. You'll only have a few minutes. I want to get in and out in less than ten. We're hitting. We're hitting hard. Any other questions?"

I look around as everyone shakes their heads. I nod and turn to the SUV. Robby is already in his seat. I speed towards the warehouse trusting my team to keep up. One thing I've never had to worry about is this team following orders without question. They know what they're doing, and they're damn good.

I stop a block from the warehouse and look at Robby as my surveillance team all jump out of the vehicle. They quickly grab their gear and run to the shadows where they become one with them.

"Have they moved?" I ask.

"No. Still the same place."

"We're out of sight. Where are we going, sir?" one of the guys asks over his earpiece.

"Warehouse off the dock. No roof. Whole Eastern wall is gone. It's the one that had the blowout last year," I say.

"Yes, sir. We have visual. Setting up now."

I look at my watch. "Ten minutes starts now."

181

The guard quietly clears his throat. "Looks quiet. No one in the area. No vehicles. Two guards by the door. Looks like semi-automatic weapons." He pauses. "One guard, second floor. AR strapped to his back. Third floor. Three guards. All semi-automatic. Pistols in a shoulder holster. Two people in the middle of the room." He pauses again. "Tied to the chair. No explosives that I see. I have two guards heading to the other side of the building just in case we missed something."

"Good." I look at Robby. "Ready?"

"Fuck yes."

We both get out of the SUV as the rest of my team does the same. We all quickly grab gear and run to meet the other part of our team. We duck behind a building near our target as we all finish strapping on gear.

"Surveillance," I say into the earpiece as I strap a gun on my thigh. "What do you got?"

"Entrance point on the East side of the building. No guards. They're making rounds. Walking towards the West side now. We can sneak by them and take them out and the one on the second floor at the same time. Silencers mandatory. We see two wired barrels this side of the building on the third floor. One guard near them. Total of four guards that we can see."

I nod. "Be silent. Stealthy. Let's move."

We all run towards the other side of the building taking all precaution to stay completely out of view of anyone in the building or out. We meet up with the other two members of our team. Taking one last check of our weapons, we wait for our move. When the two guards are far enough away, we make our move, staying silent and hidden as we enter the building through the blown out wall.

I make eye contact with part of the team. I point at the last half, keeping my eye on the two guards, and signal them to take the stairs. They all quietly run up the stairs staying down and hidden. The leader looks at me. I hold up three fingers and countdown. When I hold up my fist, we take our shots. All three guards on both floors fall silently to the ground.

We all run up the stairs, keeping an eye out for any surprises. Other guards, tripwires, traps. When we get near the top of the stairs leading to the third floor, I duck down. I glance quickly around the corner into the room. There are two guards near the stairs and two more in the room. One of those two is near the explosive barrels. I don't know what's in them and have no desire to find out.

I feel like there's another one somewhere, but I can't see him. I've learned very well to never ignore instinct. I poke out just enough and move the scope on my gun so that the light reflects on it just enough to gain a little attention. Hopefully, from the woman in the middle of the room and not one of the guards.

She looks at me when she catches the light movement as I turn my gun slightly back and forth. I hold up four fingers. She shakes her head slightly and blinks five times. I nod towards each of the four guards I can see. She tilts her head ever so slightly to her right. Right towards the explosives. I nod as I drop back behind the corner.

There's a wall that has a blindspot from this position, but now that I know he's there, I can act accordingly. I turn back to the rest of my team holding up five fingers. They all nod, understanding that we have a hidden man.

I turn back to the room and ready my AR-15. I hold up three fingers and again count my team down. When I make a fist, we all stay low and quickly enter the room. I take out one of the guards near me while Robby takes out the other. I point to the hidden wall. Two of my team goes for the wall while another two take out the guy near the explosives and the other guy in the room.

Robby and I move towards Zekeih's wife and scared as fuck, wide-eyed child who is just barely a toddler. I quickly remove the tape over Zekeih's wife's mouth.

"The phone!" she screams. "It's counting down!"

I look at the floor and swallow. My heart instantly kicks into high gear. "Shit… Two minutes!" I yell. Robby and I work quickly to free them, but they're both handcuffed behind their backs to the chair with some ancient cuff my key would never work on.

Robby looks at me as wild-eyed as the little boy. "What the fuck are we going to do?"

I look at Zekeih's wife. "We're going to have to lift you up and drop you to break the wood. It's going to hurt. I'm sorry."

"Just get us out of here!" she sobs.

183

I signal for my guys to come to where I am. "Lift her. Drop her. Hard. Wood has to break." I look back at her. Keep your head tucked the best you can."

She nods, and I move to the kid. He's started screaming more than he already was. Robby and I both lift the chair high and turn it. He's smaller. We can drop it to the side and have a lower risk of hitting his head. We drop it hard on the floor. The wood splinters enough for us to break it. I glance at the phone as we both hurry to get him free.

"One minute, Luke," Robby says shakily.

I nod. "As long as we're downstairs by the blown out wall so we can get out by the time the explosion happens and floors start collapsing we'll be okay. Don't panic. Just move."

I lift the screaming boy into my arms as one of my team members throws Zekeih's wife over his shoulder.

"Let's move!" Robby commands.

No one needs the command, though. We're all already running down the stairs. I'm mentally ticking down the seconds in my head as we hit the second floor landing. Less than thirty seconds. We hit the last set of stairs. My heart is racing out of control, but I force myself to breathe.

Lead.

Just lead my team out of here. Save the girl. Save the boy.

In front of me, one of my guys fall. I don't need to see the bone, to know it's protruding through his knee. I heard the snap. His scream is echoing in my head. I look up as Robby starts doubling back. I hand him the kid.

"Go! Get out of here!"

He looks at me terrified as he takes the kid and does as I say.

Runs.

Ten seconds.

Nine...

Eight...

I pick up my guy with a grunt as he howls. He throws his arm over my shoulder as he cries out in pain.

Seven...

Six...

Five...

One of my other guys throws his arm around my injured guy's waist. We both lift him and run for the relative safety of that blown out wall.

Four…

Three…

Two…

I don't need to see it. I don't need to hear it. My mind is completely tuned in to whatever fresh hell is about to go off upstairs.

One…

The rumble of the explosion reverberates through the building. The ceiling starts to crumble around us.

"Luke!" Robby screams.

I make eye contact with him and push through the last few yards to that empty space. His screams and horrified expression as he looks up is what propels me the rest of the way. Using every last ounce of momentum I have, I leap to the opening.

Chapter Twenty One

⚔ Robby ⚔

I watch in unabashed terror as the building starts crumbling around Luke. I meet his eyes screaming his name as he runs. "Luke! Fucking run!"

Just as the entrance is about to be blocked by falling debris, Luke and the guy he's carrying as well as the one helping him spears me. We topple to the ground as the building collapses on itself. We all scramble to get up, carrying our injured man with us.

We barely make it to the stable wall of the factory next to this one before the entire building crumbles in a heap of bricks, stone, and metal.

Luke collapses on the ground with our injured man. "The kid. Where's the kid?" he pants and looks up at me as I kneel on the ground next to him.

I kiss him long and hard. "He's safe. I handed him off and went back for you."

"Thank you," the injured guard says. "For not leaving me there."

"Not a fucking chance. No one gets left behind." Luke sits up and rips the sleeve from his black shirt as he looks down at the injured guard. "It's going to hurt."

"Fuck, I don't care. I can't feel it. Too much adrenaline."

Luke nods and ties it around his knee tightly. To his credit, the guard doesn't even wince. I don't think that's a good thing. We help him to his feet and make our way as quickly as we can to our SUVs. We all get in. We put our injured man in the backseat and speed away from the scene.

"Call Chantau. He should be there already for Zekeih."

"What happened?" I ask as I take out my phone.

"Long fucking story. Zekeih isn't the bad guy. We need to have a family meeting."

I shake my head as I reach over taking Luke's hand. I quickly tell Doctor Chantau what's happening. Luke squeezes my hand as he navigates traffic on the way home. His hand shakes slightly, and I know he's thinking of how close he was to the building collapsing on him.

I can't blame him. I'm thinking the same thing. I wouldn't be able to live without him. I raise his hand to my lips and kiss it softly as I tighten my grip.

I plan to show him just how thankful I am that he got out. Again and again. Just as soon as that family meeting is over.

I yawn and rub my eyes as Luke turns into the driveway. Home. I know we have a lot of work to do. I have a long night ahead of me. But I lost all the energy I had long ago. I think as soon as we got into the SUV it was like everything just whooshed out of me. I feel like my arms are Gumby. My entire body is just limp.

I squeeze Luke's hand as he parks. I haven't let go of it since he took it in his. I look over at him. "We did good."

He smiles as he nods. "Yeah. We did." He reluctantly lets go of my hand. I know him well enough to know when he needs grounding.

I waste no time taking his hand back in mine when we get out of the SUV. The shaking and trembling he works so hard to hide is evident to me. I can feel the slight twitch of his muscles. I can feel the jerk of his hand that no one can see. I know Luke has seen a lot of shit and been in a lot of fucked up situations, but I don't think he's ever been that close to death.

I soothingly run my thumb over the back of his hand as he leans against the SUV waiting for our team to get Zekeih's wife and son out. I watch as Doctor Chantau scurries out of the house and rushes to us.

"Which SUV is he in?" Chateau asks.

"This one," Luke says. I can hear the quiver in his voice as he opens the door.

Doctor Chantau looks at the guard, gently lifting Luke's makeshift bandage job to look at the wound. "I need to get him into surgery. Judging how wet that is, I'd say he's also lost a lot of blood."

Luke nods and points to two guards. "Drive him to the hospital."

They both nod at the command and jump in the SUV. Doctor Chantau jumps in the backseat.

We watch as they take off before I lead Luke to Zekeih's wife and son. They're both still restrained with the rusty and very medieval looking cuffs. One of the guards has the crying boy in his arms as we all walk into the house.

Ryan meets us halfway. He looks at Luke. "Zekeih is okay."

I can feel a little tension release as Luke nods. "Broken bones?" He's quiet. I can feel the guilt radiating off him.

Ryan shakes his head. "Surprisingly, no. Knee is a little fucked up. Dani got him in the ribs. He's bruised, but Doc wrapped him up good. Zekeih doesn't blame anyone. He just wants his family back. He's beating himself up right now. Taylor is talking to him, but he feels like shit for not going to Taylor in the first place. Said he felt like he didn't have a choice as soon as family became involved. All he could think of was them and keeping them safe."

Luke shakily squeezes my hand. "I'd be the same way."

"We all would," I say.

Ryan looks down at the woman who the guards are escorting. They stop with her and the boy at my side in front of Ryan. He raises an eyebrow. "Why the hell are they still cuffed?"

I gently turn the woman around. "We don't have keys for that. And we had to get out. Building exploded. Luke..." I look up at him before looking back at Ryan and taking a deep breath. "We almost lost a guy. He fell on the stairs. Broke his leg. Luke and one of our other guys got him out, but barely. The building was rigged to explode."

Ryan's eyes flash, but he stays quiet as he looks at the guards. "We're going to have to break them out of them. Probably cut the cuffs off."

The guard nods. "Yes, sir."

Zekeih's wife pulls away and looks up at Ryan. "Where's my husband?"

Ryan smiles softly and puts a hand on her shoulder. "Safe. Let them get you and your son out of the cuffs. My wife is making some tea. Tell me what you and your son need. I'll have it ready for you."

She sniffles as she looks down and then at her son. "He's scared. Starving. We were taken as I was feeding him. He needs clothes. He's been shivering. The shorts and t-shirt aren't conducive to this weather. He doesn't have shoes. Please. Just a blanket for him."

"I'll take care of it. Go with them. When they get you out, they'll bring you inside." He pats her shoulder. She nods and lets the guards lead her away. He looks back at us. "What happened?"

"Fuck. I don't know, Ry," Luke says as he looks at me. "Robby was tracking the phone. It hadn't moved. I sent in four guys to figure out where the guards were. We went in. We took everyone out. We went to untie them, but saw those weird fucking cuffs."

I shake my head and keep Luke's hand tight in mine. "As soon as we had the gag out of her mouth, she started screaming about the phone. We looked at the phone and saw it was counting down. We had two minutes and a few seconds to get out, but we couldn't unlock the cuffs. We walked right into a trap."

"We had to slam the chairs on the ground and break them. We got them free from the chairs and ran. We were running down the stairs when Wes fell and broke his leg. I gave the boy to Robby and told him to get out of there. I was counting down in my head. We didn't have time. Me and Henry picked Wes up and just ran. We barely got out when the explosion happened. The building just started crumbling."

Ryan hugs Luke and me both. "You got out. You got everyone out. That's all that matters. You both did a damn fine job." He squeezes us both tighter before pulling away and leading us inside.

When we get inside, Arianna flings herself at us both. "Oh God, I'm so glad you both are okay. So glad."

189

We both cling to her and each other a few moments before pulling back. I kiss her cheek. "We're okay."

"Aria, the boy could use food and clothes. So could Zekeih's wife. Both are shaken up and cold," Ryan says quietly from behind her. He kisses her neck.

Arianna smiles softly at us both. She turns to him and kisses him softly. "I'll take care of them. You deal with all of this. Something is…" She shakes her head. "Wrong."

"I know, baby." He watches as she hurries off. He looks back at us. "It was a setup from the beginning. It was expected that Zekeih would be caught."

"I know," Luke agrees. "It felt like a setup to me as soon as Zekeih said Krins has his family."

"What else did he say?" Ryan asks.

"He said that Wolfe was involved. We knew that. He said that Krins approached him after Wolfe was arrested and threatened his family. He went along with it. He didn't talk to Taylor because he felt like there was bad blood between them caused by his own issues over the past few months. I asked him why they wanted Dani. I wanted to see what he knew. All he said was that Krins wanted her back."

"Back?" I ask. "That has to mean he wants her for witnessing the murder of Carter Rudd. Right?"

Ryan shakes his head. "Maybe. When I talked to him, he said Krins wants Dani back, but he was talking about her like he's known her for her whole life. Like he lost her a long time ago."

Luke looks confused. "That doesn't make sense."

"I know." He looks towards the den at the back of the house. "He's talking to Taylor. I'm hoping Taylor can get more out of him." He looks back at me. "Take Luke somewhere. He needs you." He pats me on the back as he heads for the kitchen.

Luke pulls me down on the couch near us and wraps his arms around me. He buries his face in my neck. I hug him just as tightly as he is me. We say nothing. We don't need words. Both of us are just happy that we're alive. That he's alive.

A few minutes later, one of the guards comes in with Zekeih's wife and son. Luke and I both stand and lead them to the den where Zekeih is. I poke my head in the room when I see the door closed.

I make eye contact with Taylor. "They're here."

Taylor nods and stands. He helps Zekeih up. "Let them in."

I step back and let Zekeih's wife, who is carrying their son, in the room. Taylor steps back as Zekeih, his wife, and his son all burst into tears. She carefully hugs her bandaged husband as they all tremble.

"I'm sorry, baby," Zekeih cries into her neck. "So fucking sorry."

Taylor walks quietly to the door as they hug each other. We all step back as he closes the door and hugs us both. The three of us stand in a circle for a few moments before he pulls back and looks at us both.

"I'm really fucking glad you both are okay," he says. He looks over our heads as Ryan and Arianna walk towards us. He lets us go as Luke and I turn.

"How are they?" Arianna asks, carrying clothes and a blanket.

"Happy it's over," Taylor says.

Ryan nods to the door. "She said their son was starving and cold. I sensed they all are. She can't be very warm in that sundress she's wearing."

I reach for the door and open it. Ryan and Arianna slip quietly inside with delicious smelling soup that makes my mouth water. I close the door behind them and take a deep breath.

I look up at Luke. "I have a lot to do tonight. We should get going."

His eyes burn with the same need I feel. The need we both have to feel each other. Really feel each other. But not for pleasure. Not for the passionate desire we both have for each other; the insatiable sexual drive that stirs to life when we're near each other.

No.

This need is something far deeper. It comes from the demand to know both of us survived.

ХХХ

I lift my cup to my lips fully expecting hot, bitter liquid to hit my tongue. I growl when I'm met with air. "Damn all-nighters."

I go back to my computer screen, forcing my eyes open, as my front door opens. I glance up and smile, completely forgetting everything as Luke cockily strides through the door.

"I brought coffee and breakfast." He grins and holds up two mugs and a plain paper bag.

I eye the bag hungrily. "Tell me that's Ryan's breakfast croissants."

"With egg and bacon."

"Fuck, I want that."

Luke laughs as he comes behind me. He sets both the coffee and the bag on the counter in front of me and puts both hands on the counter on either side of me. Trapping me between his body and the counter, he leans in and kisses my neck. His solid chest against my back makes me groan as I lean into him. I feel him smile against my neck.

He drops his arms around my waist as I turn my head to meet his lips. He greedily claims my mouth. I open for him and his tongue darts into twine with mine. His hands roam from my stomach to my thighs, then up until they both are squeezing my dick.

"Oh, shit!" I thrust into his hands as he bites my lower lip and slowly pulls away. He gives me a couple rubs and squeezes before he backs off. "Oh, no you don't." I turn and capture his lips again, grabbing his hand and putting it back on my cock.

He laughs against my mouth as he pulls his lips away. He leaves his hand where I put it. I moan as I rub it against me. He smiles. "Tell me what you found, then I'll do something about that hard-on you have going on." He squeezes.

I close my eyes. "Fuck." I open my eyes and gauge how far it is from my kitchen counter to the couch. Too far. I need him now. I look back at him. Both of our eyes are on fire. "Suck me off. Then I'll tell you."

He gives me an arrogant half smile as he drops to his knees. "Only because I can feel how much you need it. After I'm done, you tell me what you found. Then, I want those hot as hell lips around my cock."

"Deal. Make it fast because I'm already close." I unbutton and unzip my jeans as I stand. He yanks them down and pushes me back so I'm sitting on the stool again. He shoves my legs apart and settles between them.

He grins up at me. I can't help but think how sexy this big, powerful man looks on his knees between my legs. "You know I don't do things like this quickly. I like taking my time with you."

"You like it quick today. Because I'm horny as fuck. I need to get off. The tension is going to kill me."

He grins. "You asked for this. Remember that."

I have no chance to respond before his mouth is on my cock. My eyes roll back in my head. "God, yes." I slide my fingers in his hair as I let my head fall back.

His tongue slides up and down my length as he grabs my balls. I look back down at his head bobbing up and down on my dick.

He lets his teeth scrape up my length before he takes all of me in his mouth. I feel myself slip down his throat until I can't go on any further. He lets me all the way out, then takes just my tip in his mouth as he sucks.

"Damn you taste good."

He takes me all the way in his mouth until I'm hitting the back of his throat again and again. I can't take any more. With a satisfied groan, I release. Luke swallows everything I give him.

"Holy shit..." I pull him to me and kiss him.

He presses me against the counter and kisses me back. I can taste myself on his tongue. He knows it. Pulling away, he smirks and winks. "Now, tell me what you found out."

I grin and pull my pants back up, zipping and buttoning myself back in. I turn back to my laptop as Luke sits down next to me. "Well, there's a lot. But it goes fucking deep." I turn my laptop towards him. We both take our sandwiches and hungrily wolf them down. "I traced all of these deposits starting with that fifty grand to Zekeih. Forty grand goes to other accounts. We have Adam and Mark from Taylor's team. And we have Cooper Killington. He's a tech expert with the department. Lastly, we have Lucius Alistair. He's a weapons and evidence keeper."

"So, we have a total of three members of an elite task force being paid off as well as two other key members of Chicago P.D."

"That's not even the tip of the iceberg. I found a lot of shit that doesn't make sense." I pause and look up at him. "This stays here. I don't know what I found."

He narrows his eyes. "What did you find?"

I shake my head and look back at my laptop. "I don't know. But…" I sigh. "Nick."

"What… about Nick…?" He looks a little fearful. I don't blame him. Everyone fears Ryan. But really, Nick is far darker than Ryan will ever be. Something even Ryan knows.

I scrub my hands down my face. "He's been looking for years for the people who killed his parents."

"Yeah?"

"I… don't know how to say this. I think I might have found something that will help him. But fuck, it makes no sense."

Luke looks at my screen a little hesitantly. He shakes his head. "What am I looking at?"

"I don't know. I have to dig deeper. But…" I shrug because I know he sees what I do.

"But… it looks like somehow Nick's parents are connected to the Lucinio's." He sits back and links his fingers behind his head. "How the fuck is this even possible?"

I shrug. "I don't know. I don't know what any of this means." I look at him. "I have to dig deeper. I don't want to give him this right now. Not when I have so much more to look into."

"You will never hear me say this again, but… we can't go to Nick or Ryan with this until you know more. Nick will destroy the universe, and Ryan will be right by his damn side when it happens."

"You think he'll destroy the universe on that?" I click to another screen and point.

"What is that? Tabloid article on Lucinio and some chick he's dating?"

"That's Nick's mom," I say quietly.

Luke nearly chokes. "That can't be fucking true." He grabs my laptop and reads the article. "How the hell would Nick not have found this? He would've been all over this."

"I almost didn't find it. It was buried. Archived fucking deep. The only reason I found it…" I turn my laptop towards me again. "…is because of this." I click into another screen and take a deep breath before turning it back. "I knew when I saw this… there had to be something. Matthew loved the tabloids when he was alive. He was fucking everywhere. So, I started digging through archives. Took me all night. But I found it."

194

He squints as I zoom in. "Shit…" He blinks a few times. "Shit…"

"Yeah." I turn my laptop back towards me as I pinch the bridge of my nose.

"So, you're telling me… not only was that article completely buried, but that Nick's mother and Matthew Lucinio were married?"

"I don't know. I don't know if they actually got married. That's just an application for a license. I don't know if it was approved. I haven't found a license. I'm not even sure how I stumbled into that." I lean back and stretch. "Did you notice how similar Jessa and Nick's mom look?"

"Yeah. It explains so fucking much, but I don't want any of that to be true."

"That's not all."

"Fuck."

"Not nearly. I tracked where the money went. I tracked where all of them are putting the money."

I pause as I try to figure out how to say the rest. Luke looks at me. Sensing what I'm about to say is difficult, Luke puts a hand on my knee. "What? What else is there?"

"Not only was I able to track where it went… I was able to track it back. I… know who made the deposit." I take a deep breath and look at the computer screen. I let it out slowly as I click a couple of times, bringing up the company the deposit originated from. I know as soon as he sees it, he'll head straight to Ryan.

"Krins. We know that."

"No… I mean who's giving Krins the money."

He looks closer. "Lucinio... Tech? How is that possible?"

I shrug. "It's what I found."

Luke runs his hand down his face and looks at me. "Do you understand what you just found?"

"Yeah. The Lucinio Mafia is the head of all of this."

He shakes his head in disbelief. "It means Matthew Lucinio is, in fact, still alive."

I look at him and sigh before looking back at my screen. "Or that Josh and Alex Lucinio are involved."

"That isn't possible. Alex is like a brother to Ryan. He's known him since Alex was a fucking kid. And him and Josh have gotten fucking close now that Josh took over Lucinio Mafia." He scrubs his hands down his face. I glance at him and click to another screen. As he looks at it, I lean back and put my hands behind my head. "No fucking way."

"That's what I found."

"That's not possible."

"It's what I found, Luke. I checked and rechecked. Then checked again. And then I checked four more times just to be sure. That's what I fucking found."

"This isn't possible. Alex and Josh would never do that." Luke stands and paces, running both hands through his hair. "We have to take this to Ryan." He grabs my laptop and heads for the door.

"Fuck." I grab the charging cord and our coffees and follow him.

"There's no fucking way this is possible." He mumbles to himself the entire time we're walking to Ryan's. When we get there, we both rush inside.

"Hey, Luke! How was breakfast?" Arianna is sitting at the kitchen counter feeding Christopher. He gurgles happily. I give her a soft smile as Luke barely acknowledges her. "What the hell is that about?"

"Nothing good. Where's Ry?"

"With Nick and Taylor in his office."

"Thanks." I lean down and kiss her cheek. I follow him. Luke doesn't bother knocking. I sigh as I close the door behind us. Everyone watches as Luke flips open my laptop. He turns it so everyone can see. I plop in a chair.

Nick raises an eyebrow. "What are we looking at?"

"Robby traced the money." Luke takes a step back.

Everyone looks eagerly at the laptop. All of their faces fall at the same time. They all get confused expressions on their faces.

Taylor shakes his head. "This isn't possible."

Luke nods. "That's what I said. But he tracked it."

"Shit." Ryan paces his office. I put my head in my hands.

Nick locks his fingers behind his head and shakes it as he looks at it. "No. No way."

Ryan points to the screen. "This isn't Alex or Josh. They wouldn't fucking do this."

"The money tracks to Alex's personal account funneled through Lucinio Tech." I look up at Ryan.

He glares at me. "Alex *wouldn't* fucking do this. There has to be a logical explanation. Find out how the money is going through his personal account."

He points to his desk chair. I sigh as I stand. Exhaustion is starting to take over. The adrenaline I had earlier from seeing my boyfriend has long worn off.

Luke notices. "Ryan, he pulled an all-nighter. Let him get some sleep. We can just call Alex." I try rubbing the grit from my eyes as I sit.

Ryan turns his glare to Luke. "No one fucking sleeps until we figure this out. I've known Alex longer than anyone in this room except Nick. He wouldn't fucking betray me."

"I agree. I don't think this is him." Nick can't take his eyes off the screen.

"So, what are you saying? You don't trust my work anymore?" I'm so tired that the idea of controlling my anger makes me angrier. I stand and shut my laptop. "Find the fucking information yourself." I head for the door.

Ryan's eyes widen in surprise. I don't care. "Robby, for fuck's sake. I didn't mean it like that."

I turn on him. "I'm fucking tired. I've been working on this since last night when you gave me the file. And that was after my boyfriend damn near got killed, who nearly died right after my brothers almost did. Which was right after Dani damn near got taken. For a second time. I haven't slept, but I know what I found. That's where the money ends."

Nick lowers his voice to try and calm everyone in the room. "Look. We know. But we also know Alex. This is a set up. He wouldn't do this. There's no way." Nick looks at me pleadingly. I close my eyes and look at the ceiling as I let out a frustrated breath.

"Let him sleep. He'll be fresher and a lot more able to help," Taylor says.

I look at Taylor. "Mark and Adam were for sure involved. Along with two more people in Chicago PD."

"Zekeih told me. But fuck. I fucking knew it. Thanks for verifying." He rubs his temples.

"Take a guest room. Give me your laptop. I'll walk them through it and meet you when I'm done. You can't think straight when you're as fucking tired as you are." Luke holds out his hand for the laptop.

I sigh and give it to him. "Fine." I glare at Ryan. "But you question my skills again, I'm out."

Ryan glares right back. "You question my authority again, you won't have to worry about walking out."

Luke holds up a hand. "Enough. Both of you fucking stop it. Tensions are high. This isn't fucking great news. None of us are happy about it. Robby, go take a nap. Now. Ryan. Calm the fuck down. You know how people are when they're as tired as he is and as stressed as we all are."

"We'll figure it out. We're family. Fighting and arguing won't get us anywhere. We need each other." Nick puts a hand on Ryan's shoulder.

"I'll show you guys what we found while he sleeps. When he wakes up, we'll go from there. He isn't going to be any help when he can't keep his eyes open." Luke gives me a sweet kiss on the lips before I walk out of the room. I head into the closest guest room and slam the door.

I know it's because I'm tired, but Ryan questioning my findings pisses me off. He's never done that before. He's always trusted me. I've never gotten so angry with him that I talked back to him like that, but fuck.

I pace, becoming more and more pissy the longer I do it. I'm tired as hell, but that argument riled me up. I don't know how long I pace the room lost in my own thoughts, but it's long enough for Luke to walk in.

He sees me pacing and sighs as he puts my laptop on the dresser in the room. He grabs my hand and pulls me to him, crushing me against his body. "Why are you not sleeping?" His deep voice rumbles in my ear.

My coiled muscles immediately relax. I put my arms around him and rest my cheek against his. "He's never questioned me. Not like that."

"Everyone is tired and stressed, Robby. Come lay down." Luke releases me and takes his shirt off as he walks to the side of the bed. He strips his jeans off as I watch. All of his rippling muscles make every part of me tingle with desire.

He looks at me and grins. I let out a groan. "You make it hard to want to sleep."

"I'll let you do whatever you want to me later. Right now, I want your clothes off, and I want you in this bed."

I strip down to my boxer briefs, following his lead, as he crawls into the bed. He lifts the covers invitingly. I crawl in next to him. He wraps me in his arms. I sigh in contentment as I lay my head on his chest.

"Ryan is upset. It looks like his fucking brother is betraying him. But we all know there's something else going on. Call it instincts."

"There's nothing else. The money stops with Alex."

"I know. We all know. When you wake up, we'll figure it out. Right now, I want you to sleep. We all need you at your best. Because if Ryan is going to have to face his brother, we need to be fucking sure that this stops with him. We need to make sure that there's no other possibility that it's anyone other than Alex."

"For the record? I don't think it's him. I just can't find anything else. I didn't have a chance to look before you grabbed my laptop and took off. I can hack into the system, but I need to sleep."

"I know you, baby. I also know if there's anything else to find, you'll do it. I trust you. So does Ryan. Now go to sleep," he commands.

Luke runs his fingers through my hair and up and down my back. He's figured out when he wants me to sleep, that's the way to lull me into a deep slumber.

I can't fight it.

Before I even know what's happening, I've crashed.

Chapter Twenty Two

⚔ Nick ⚔

"I still say we need to call Alex." I watch as Ryan paces the room. I've never seen him more pissed off than he is right now.

We all stop talking as Ryan's phone rings. He glances at it before pressing a button and rubbing his head. "Lyric? What's going on, honey?" he asks. His phone must be on speaker.

"Hey, um… Luca is… on holiday… with his girlfriend… um…" Lyric pauses. We all look at Ryan's phone. The tension we all feel is suddenly far more amplified.

"What, sweetheart? What's going on? You okay?"

"I'm.. um… really sorry for bothering you…," she whispers.

"You're not a bother to me, sweetheart. What's going on? You sound upset."

"I… um… I was wondering if… you think it would be okay if I came a little early… I know we're having a memorial thing for J-Jaxon in a few days, but…" She trails off again. I furrow my brows.

"Lyric, did something happen?" Ryan asks. He folds his arms across his chest.

We can all hear her let out a breath. "It's... just that... Josh is busy with something. I was out getting a coffee and..." She sighs. "I just got approached by this girl. She just made me super uncomfortable. She was so friendly, but there was something about her... I've seen her a couple of times. She just... I don't know what it is, but she... I'm a little freaked out. Maybe it's because I'm alone and feeling vulnerable or something, but I wondered if I could come there early?"

Ryan narrows his eyes before looking back at us. I glance at Taylor. It's pretty obvious we're all thinking the same thing. With everything going on, and then Lyric calling us out of the blue saying she's freaked out, none of us are taking chances with anything.

"Yeah. I'll send the jet down for you and a car to pick you up. You'll be here by tonight. I'll get your room made up."

"Oh! I can get a ticket. I don't want to be a burden!"

"Lyric, stop that. We talked about that. You're not a burden. Listen, honey, have you talked to Josh?"

"I talked to him yesterday morning, but he's been dealing with something in San Francisco. He's been run ragged the last few months, and I don't want to pull him away from whatever has him so busy..."

Something dark crosses over his face. I know her words just inadvertently put another nail in Alex's and Josh's coffins. "I'll send the plane, sweetheart. I'll text you when the driver is on the way to you."

"Thank you, Ryan." She breathes a sigh of relief as the two say goodbye and hang up.

"There's more to this. There has to be." Taylor watches him just as closely as I am. That call put him further on edge.

Ryan holds up a hand. "Both of you shut-up or get out of my office. I need to fucking think."

I sigh and stand, glancing at Taylor and flicking my head towards the door. He stands and follows me.

I'm about to do something I've never done, but I need to snap Ryan out of this. He's in his own head and not thinking things through logically.

"What are you thinking?" Taylor follows me out of the house.

I begin the walk across the property to Jason's and Jessa's. "I'm thinking something that's going to get my ass in trouble with Ryan, but it's our only option."

He cocks his head. "Calling Alex?"

I shake my head. "Not us."

"What the fuck does that mean?" he asks. I shoot him a wink as we hurry across the lawn. As soon as we reach Jessa's and Jason's, I make a beeline for the back door. Taylor grabs my arm. "Are you insane?"

I look at him and grin sinisterly as I shrug. "Maybe." I turn back to the house.

He follows me. "You're going to get both of us shot, you fucker."

I laugh. "He'll get over it." I walk through Jason's and Jessa's back door and immediately get Jackson thrust into my arms.

"I'm going insane. I need a break. He's sick. He's fussy. All he wants is Jason, but Jason has meetings all day that he can't miss. I have to finish this project by tomorrow. I'm freaking out, Nick!" Jessa looks up at me with tears in her eyes. I pull her close. She's shaking. I can feel her heart racing. She's on the verge of a panic attack.

"Hey. I got you. I need your help, but I'll take Jackson with me when I leave. If you needed peace and quiet, Jess, all you needed to do was ask."

She buries her face in my chest and locks her arms around my waist. Taylor, recognizing the signs of Jessa's impending panic attack, plucks Jackson from my arm so I can better deal with my sister-in-law.

I wrap Jessa in both arms and hug her. "Talk to me."

"I'm just freaking out. I have so much to do and Jackson is sick. I don't want him around Tait or Chris. But he's so fussy. I can't get anything done."

"You have me. You could've called Dani." Jessa is silent. I grin into her hair as she takes a few deep breaths. A few moments later, she's breathing normally again. I slowly release her. "I got it, Jess. Don't worry about it. I'll take him with me. Dani would love to hang out with him."

She lets out a long breath. "Thank you."

I kiss her forehead. "You're welcome. Feel better?"

"So much." She smiles. I watch her visibly relax. "What did you need help with?"

"Uh... Have you talked to Alex or Josh lately?"

"This morning I talked to Alex. Josh was dealing with a gang in San Francisco that hurt one of his property owners. Why?" Jackson starts crying from another room. Jessa sighs, turning towards the room.

"Jess. Taylor has him. Don't worry. Come sit in the kitchen with me. I really need you. This is important." I take her hand and lead her to the kitchen. She sits, concern filling her eyes. I sit next to her. I know she needs a distraction to keep the panic and stress at bay. This is as good as any distraction I can think of.

"What happened?"

"I don't want to send you into another panic attack." Part of me is questioning if this is the best thing to do, but I really do need her. "I'm sorry if I do, sweetheart. I'm here if it happens, though. Okay?"

"Nick, the anticipation. That's what makes me anxious. Just tell me. What happened? And what does it have to do with Alex and Josh?"

I sigh and look at the wall as I shake my head. "Robby found some information about money being deposited into Zekeih's account. Zekeih is -"

"On your taskforce. I know."

I smile and turn towards her. I take her hands in mine. I need it just as much as she does. "Robby tracked the money. There was money going to one of our tech guys and a weapons and evidence keeper in the department. And then there was money going to two other guys on our task force. Adam and Mark."

"Oh my God." Tears sting her eyes. She bites her lip. "How is that possible?"

"I don't know yet. But, sweetheart, that's not the worst part." She looks down at our joined hands. I squeeze them. "I need to talk to Alex or Josh. But I need you to be the one to call him. Either of them."

"Why?"

"Because Robby tracked the money to Alex's personal account. If I call him, he'll go on the defensive and get aggressive. That's just how guys are. Ryan is pissed. You know how he gets. He's trying to think, but he's in his own head and not thinking clearly."

She bites her lip as she looks back up at me. "He doesn't have anything to do with this. I know it. He wouldn't do this. Neither of them would."

"I know, Jess. But it stops with him." I hold her gaze. "I need to figure this out. He'll talk to you without being an asshole. Maybe he can give you something so I have something else to give Robby. To prove it isn't either of them."

She takes a deep breath and nods resolutely. "Okay. But I'm not going to lie to him."

"I don't expect you to."

"I'm telling him everything you just told me."

"Jessa. That's what I'm asking. I don't want you to lie to him. I want you to put your phone on speaker, and get me something. Please. Ryan is torn apart over this. I can't handle seeing him deal with it. He's a fucking mess."

She nods again. I know above all else, her love for Ryan will get her to do what I want. She takes out her phone and calls Alex, putting it on speaker like I asked.

"Hey, peanut. Miss me?" Alex asks.

Jessa smiles, but it doesn't reach her eyes. "Alex... um..." She pauses.

I can almost see Alex immediately dropping his teasing tone and becoming serious. "Jess, what happened?"

She takes a deep breath and looks at me. I give her an encouraging smile and nod towards the phone. "Remember I told you about Zekeih?"

"Yeah. Ryan told me a lot, too."

"We just found out that two more guys in the department are involved and two more people on Taylor's and Nick's taskforce. Well, verified it anyway."

"Oh, holy shit. How is that going over?"

"Not really well. I'm sure you get it." She's miserable, and I feel bad for making her do this.

"Betrayal is never an easy pill to swallow, peanut."

Jessa toys with the phone and sighs again. "They tracked the money, Alex. Robby did."

"Well, that's a good thing isn't it? Why do you sound so upset about that?"

She sniffles. "Because it isn't a good thing. They tracked it to your personal account."

There's a clatter, and a slew of curse words fly out of Alex's mouth. Most of them I've never heard before. "Are you fucking kidding me? I have nothing to do with that!"

"I know. We all know. But Robby can't trace it further. It stops with you. Ryan is really messed up."

204

"What do you mean messed up? Why the hell didn't he call me?"

Jessa looks at me completely panicking. She doesn't know how to answer. I shrug because I don't either. "He's trying... to... figure it out. I don't think he's able to make sense of it. You know how upset that makes him. If it doesn't make sense -"

"I know. I know. He overthinks it until he works himself up and snaps at everyone. Peanut, listen to me. Can you get me an account number? The account number Robby says is mine?"

"Yeah…" She looks at me with wide eyes. I pull out my phone and get into my pictures. I took a picture of the screen with the account number over Robby's shoulder before he and Ryan butted heads. I hand it to her. "Yeah. Yes." She takes my phone. "I actually have it."

"Good girl. Read it to me." She does as he says. We both hear keys being tapped on his end. "I'm going to shoot you a text with all of my account numbers, Jess. I want you to give it to Ryan. That account number isn't mine. It's not even the same routing number for my bank, but I can find out where the fuck it came from."

"Okay."

"Give me a few minutes. I'll get Lance on it. I don't even know what bank that's from."

"Wait. It says it's the US Bank of America. It looks like Robby tracked the routing number that far."

"My accounts are at Los Angeles Federal Credit Union. All of them. Business accounts and personal. Give me a few minutes, peanut. I'll figure it out and call you back."

"Okay. Thank you, Alex."

"Anytime." He hangs up.

Jessa lets out a breath. "It isn't him."

"I know. But we need to prove it, sweetheart."

Taylor turns the corner carrying Jackson and a large diaper bag. "I called Dani. She's going to meet me at Ryan's and take Jackson for the day. That gives you time to work, Jess. And Nick. It gives you time to clear Alex before Ryan talks himself into going after him."

"He won't."

"You better fucking pray he doesn't. That's a war none of us want." He turns and leaves as Jessa and I wait for Alex to call back.

Finally, after what seems like years, Jessa's phone rings. "Hey," she answers sadly.

"Hey. Sorry it took so long. I had Lance do some hacking, and I needed to touch base with Josh about this."

"It's okay."

"There was a large cash deposit made to that account today. Lance hacked into the security system and pulled footage from the deposit. I just emailed it all to Robby. Lance is good, but he's not as good as Robby at putting the whole story together."

"Who was it?"

"I don't know, peanut. I've never seen the guy. I'm hoping Robby can use his skills to figure it out. All I can tell you is he isn't in the BCA database."

"Okay. I'll talk to you later. I need to check on Ryan."

"Tell him to call me, Jessa. He's my fucking brother. He should've called me when he first found out about this."

"I know. I'll talk to him." The two say their goodbyes and hang up. I take a deep breath. Him not being in the Bureau of Criminal Apprehension's database makes things more difficult.

I immediately take Jessa in my arms. "Thank you. You're amazing. I owe you. Please don't tell Ry. Let me. Just stay away from him for right now."

"You owe me your first born."

I grin as I pull away. I give her a quick kiss on her cheek as I turn to leave. "Done!"

Her laughter follows me out of the house as I make my way back to Ryan's. She knows fuck well I don't even want kids.

When I get to Ryan's, Dani is sitting on the couch. Jackson is lying next to her asleep and holding her finger.

"That's pretty fucking adorable." I lean in to kiss her but stop when she glares.

"What did you do?" She's whispering so she doesn't wake up Jackson.

I crease my eyebrows, keeping my voice low. "What happened?"

"Ryan just yelled at me, and he's arguing with Arianna. He told Taylor to leave. I know you and Taylor were talking to him this morning. He's acting like a crazy person."

"Ryan! Knock it off! If you wake up Jackson or Chris, you're going to face my wrath. You know you won't like it!" Arianna yells.

I turn as a door slams. I head towards the commotion just as Jackson starts screaming. I turn the corner as Arianna slams her hand on the door.

Tears are streaming down her face. "Ryan Nathanial Crane! Get your ass out here, right now!"

"Hey! What the hell is going on?" I ask.

"Your brother decided to pick today of all days to turn into an asshole!" She kicks the door. "And spent the last twenty minutes yelling at me because I don't think going after Alex without all of the information is the right move!"

She goes to slam her hand against the heavy door, but Ryan pulls it open. He grabs her hand before it connects with his chest and pulls her against him, wrapping her tightly in his arms. He engulfs her.

"I'm sorry, baby." He kisses her on her head, then lifts her chin so he can kiss her lips. I nearly pass out when I see he's crying. "I'm a mess right now, Aria. I don't know what to do." He looks at her like she's the only one in the world as both Luke and Robby come up next to me. I hold up a hand as Luke starts to speak. "Tell me what to do, Ari."

"Ryan... Honey." She pushes him back into his office and closes the door. The effect she has on him has always been something else.

"He looks devastated," Luke says.

"How would you feel if it looked like your brother was trying to take you out?" I ask.

"I can't imagine it. I know there's more to this. I just can't find it," Robby says slightly defeated.

"Go to the dining room. Set up. You have an email that should help you out. I need to go help Dani calm Jackson down," I say.

Robby looks at me confused. "An... email? How? What happened when I was asleep?"

"Just go. I'll explain when I get there."

Luke leads Robby by the hand to the dining room as I head to the living room. For the first time all day, I start to think everything might be okay.

Chapter Twenty Three

⚔ Luke ⚔

I watch my boyfriend work, fascinated at how quickly he's able to find massive amounts of information with such a small tip. "You found all this shit just with the information that Alex sent?"

Robby smiles as he looks at me. He cockily smirks and leans back in his chair. "You didn't doubt me, did you?"

I grin back at his teasing tone and lean in, capturing his mouth with mine. I'll never get tired of the way his tongue always finds mine, or the way he moans into my mouth when the kiss gets heated.

"Fuck, Luke. How do you do this to me?"

"Do what?" I grin, knowing exactly what I'm doing.

Robby grabs my hand and puts it on his cock. It's hard and throbbing. I bite his lip as I pull away. I give him a couple squeezes and rubs before leaning in and kissing him again.

"Alright, you two. Break it up. We have work to do," Nick says with a chuckle he tries to hide.

I laugh quietly as I slowly pull away. Robby's eyes are glazed over. I give him a last squeeze and let him go as I turn towards the rest of the group. Robby reaches down to adjust himself, and I smirk. Jason, Chase, and Taylor all sit down around the table. Nick stays standing.

I raise an eyebrow. "Where's Ryan?"

"Not joining us right now. I'll fill him later. He took Dani out to shoot," Nick says.

"What? Why?" Robby asks.

"Because this entire situation is fucked up, Robby," Nick answers. "He needs a break. And for whatever reason, Dani knows what to do. It's like she learned Arianna's skills or some shit."

"Well, not all of them." Chase winks. We all laugh.

Nick levels a glare at Chase, but cracks a small smile before he scowls at all of us. "Enough. Robby, tell me you found something. I'm not looking forward to a war with one of our brothers."

He looks at Robby, and my boyfriend fucking smirks. I grin. Not many people would dare challenge Nick Crane with a smirk, but fuck if Robby didn't just do it. I'm proud as hell that he's finding his own way to fit in with all of us. It took him a while. Robby likes solitude.

"You don't think I'd let you down, now do you?"

Nick's expression doesn't change. Out of all of us in this room, most would think I'm the most ruthless, right behind Ryan. I'm his second in command for a reason. I follow orders. I know how to get information without letting my conscience get in the way. When it comes to protecting people and my family, I'll do what needs to be done. Anyone in this room would.

But Nick? Nick is a lot more like Ryan than anyone thinks. He might actually be even darker. Ryan has the ability to make a kill without thinking about it again. Every kill he makes is for the greater good. We all know it. It's how he gets through it. How he justifies each and every kill he needs to make.

Nick came from something far more intense than mafia life. The streets of New York chew people up and spit them out every fucking day. Not Nick. They turned Nick into this dark force of nature. Something not to be fucked with.

Most people don't know it by looking at him. They don't know where he comes from because he hides it so well. But we know. His brothers and family... We know what he's shoved down deep. We know what he's afraid to let out.

One of the things that very few people really understand about him is just how hard he fights to keep his own dark depths under control. The part of him that comes from hatred for the person who killed his parents. The problem is that none of us are going to be able to hold back anymore. We all are going to have to step over that little line into scary motherfucker territory if we're going to stand a chance against the threat looming over us.

I lean back and watch him. I can see the shift. We all can. Over the past couple of weeks, Nick has become more hardened. Way less good cop like Taylor. Like how I used to be. He isn't fooling anyone anymore. His girl is in trouble. His protective side is coming out in ways he isn't able to control anymore.

I understand it. I was there when mine and Arianna's father was after her and my mother. I was there when Renza tried to kill Arianna. I know the depths he's hitting. But I also know that if it were Robby in this position, I'd hit those depths and surpass them. All of them.

Just like Nick.

Nick meets the eyes of everyone in the room before he settles on Robby. I watch Robby shiver slightly. Hell. Even I feel a chill. The icy glare he levels at Robby's statement is colder than anything I've seen.

"Stop fucking around," Nick commands. "Tell me that money goes back to Krins so we can save Alex."

Robby glances at me before he clears his throat and leans forward. His fingers fly across the keys on his laptop. In seconds, his screen is projected onto the wall in the room. Nick shuts the lights out as Robby hits a button on a remote for the blackout shades in the room to be drawn.

"This is the account I couldn't trace further. As you can see, it has Alexander Joshua Lucinio's name all over it. His social security number, driver's license number, his picture. The deposits are all cash. Every withdrawal can be traced to each member of Taylor's team and the two other department staff members we've already identified.

"Taylor, where are we with that? What's our plan?" Nick asks.

Taylor shrugs. "Set them up. Take them out. I don't know how yet, but that's what we're going to do."

"Preferably before they fuck with my fiancé or this family anymore," Nicks growls dangerously.

Taylor shrugs. "Say the word. We'll get a team to just take them out. Solve the problem. I'm tired of playing games with these guys."

Nick shakes his head. "I'm with you, but that's not how we operate. You know better."

I shrug. "I wasn't too fond of my sister being locked down in a room in this house like a fucking princess waiting to get rescued from the big bad dragon. I definitely don't like that Zekeih was able to slip by security. That's enough reason for me."

Jason shakes his head. "It isn't for Ryan. We can raid them, torture them for information, but it helps nothing. If we go after them, Krins disappears. We need to be smarter."

Robby smiles. "Good thing I know where Krins is."

"You... what?" Nick asks.

Robby nods and clicks to another screen. "US Bank. L.A." We all look up at the screen.

"Yesterday. There's one yesterday," I say with a small smile.

"Very good." Robby grins and winks at me as he clicks to another screen. "I pulled the security footage from yesterday's deposit at US Bank in L.A. Alex emailed me security footage of the person who made the deposit into Alex's account at US Bank a couple of days ago. Same guy. Let me pull up a side-by-side... and... there. Gentlemen. Meet Adam Krins."

Taylor's eyes widen. "Holy shit."

"Well, that doesn't fucking bode well for Alex," Nick says.

I look at Nick, confused, and shake my head. "How do you figure? We know it's Krins. Robby ID'd him. Driver's license and everything. All of his information is sitting right there on the screen." I point to the screen.

Nick shakes his head. "Where's he getting the money? Think like a cop. How is he getting that much money to deposit? We already know from before that the mafia he runs doesn't take in as much as it puts out."

"He's in L.A. Alex is in L.A. Who's to say he's not supplying him the money?" Chase asks.

"Come on," I huff. "I don't know him that well, but no way he's stupid enough to set up an account up in his name and give some other fucker money to deposit into it so he can pay off cops in Chicago."

Nick shrugs. "Or he's really smart and that's exactly what he did knowing we wouldn't think he's stupid enough to do it."

I know he's playing devil's advocate, but I huff again and shake my head with a glare as I fold my arms over my chest. I can't argue the logic.

Robby quickly checks something on his screen. "Shit." He clicks through several other screens so quickly that I can't keep up. "How the fuck did I miss that?"

"What? What happened?" I ask.

He doesn't answer as he flies through screen after screen. "No fucking way."

Taylor tries to follow. "What? What do you see?"

Robby looks up at Taylor and then Nick before taking a deep breath. He clicks back to the US Bank account. We all look up at the screen.

"There was this other account on there," Robby begins. "The other deposit made was for three grand. Incredibly small amount. It was buried. Only happens every other month. I tracked that account to an offshore bank in the Cayman Islands. The account has billions of dollars, but it's under a fake name."

"Not that I'm questioning you, but how do you know it's fake?" I ask.

Robby grins at me, then clicks to another screen. "Last I checked, Mitch Buchanan is a TV lifeguard on Baywatch."

Jason's eyes widen. "Son of a bitch."

"But..." Robby clicks back to the US Bank screen. "The fake account has also made large deposits into another account." He points to the screen. "This one. And this account…" He clicks back to another account at US Bank. One that I hadn't seen before.

"Holy shit," Taylor says. "All that money to this account that Krins is getting his money from."

Nick folds his arms over his chest. "Why? Why would that fake account make deposits to this smaller account when there's already money going to this other account?"

My head is spinning, but everything is suddenly clear as day. Even I can see the random as fuck smaller deposits happening. The account number, though, is only one number off from the other account. It makes it a lot harder to see that the deposits are coming from two different places.

"It's a classic organized crime move," Taylor begins as he stands. "If there are small deposits made to several different accounts across the world, it makes them harder to trace. It makes it more difficult for us as cops to find them. We have to spend time and resources to go through each and every account these deposits are being made to. And they all trace back to a larger account." Taylor points up to the screen as Robby switches to the larger account. "Like this one. So, then we have to go through these accounts to get to an even larger account. One that will have larger deposits made. By the end, we end up going through thirty different accounts to get to the source."

"Which is usually an offshore account like this one," Robby says as he clicks to the fake account.

"And usually, we can't go further than that because these accounts become incredibly difficult to trace when they get offshore," Taylor says. "We usually end up finding a hacker, like Robby, and outsource the work to them. In the end, it could take us months, even years to do what Robby just did."

"So, this is an obvious fake account," Nick begins. "Where's the real one? The source."

Robby smiles and clicks to another screen. "There." He sits back in his chair as a collective gasp echoes throughout the room.

Chase nearly chokes. "No fucking way."

Robby crosses his arms over his chest. "Matthew Lucinio. In the fucking flesh."

Nick shakes his head. "I just can't believe it. We had suspicions. But Josh shot him. Point blank in the head. I watched him do it."

"I watched it happen, too," Jason says. "Ryan and Alex were there."

"Give me a minute." Robby's fingers fly over the keyboard as he starts searching for things beyond my comprehension.

I take out my phone. "Ryan needs to see this."

"Fuck right he does. Put him on speaker," Jason demands.

I dial Ryan and put him on speaker. I walk to the head of the table and set the phone in the middle of us.

"What?" Ryan growls into the phone. We all do nothing but look at it like he's going to crawl through the phone and punch us.

Finally, I clear my throat. "Uh... listen. Robby just found some really fucked up shit. You need to get home."

"What did he find?" Ryan asks.

"Shit about Matthew Lucinio," I answer.

"It looks like he's alive. The suspicions about it were right on. You know how obsessed he is with Jessa," Jason says cautiously.

"He's not getting anywhere near my sister. How do we know he's alive? More than just suspicions." Ryan asks.

"We don't. But Robby -" I start.

"Robby just found your proof. You need to get home, big bro. This is fucking big," Robby says with a smile.

"Fuck. We're at the range in the guards house," Ryan says. "I'm sending an escort for Bree, and Nikki. I want everyone at my house if Lucinio is on the loose. What about Alex? What did you find about him?"

"He's clean. You can thank Jessa for that. She called him, and he gave her the information Robby needed to crack the case," Nick says.

He pauses as he mulls over Nick's words. Nick smirks at the phone. I shake my head and chuckle.

Ryan sighs. "We'll talk about it later. Jas, I'm grabbing Jessa myself."

"I was just about to tell you to," Jason says.

"None of us need anything." Chase says. "Taylor and I made sure all of our rooms here are restocked of everything we used last time we were all here. Just get the girls."

"Good. Makes evacuation easier. Sit tight. I'll be home shortly," Ryan says.

"Dani with you?" Nick asks.

"Yes. Not letting her out of my sight. Robby, you got a location on Krins?" Ryan asks.

Robby nods. "I tracked him as soon as I ID'd him as the person making deposits. He's at a Hilton in Beverly Hills."

"Luke. Call Josh. Have him and Alex take out Krins. That eliminates one of our problems," Ryan commands.

I nod. "I'll take care of it."

"Take care of my wife, Ry," Jason begs, obviously on edge.

"I got her. She's fine. Dani will help her grab a few things. We'll be there soon." He hangs up.

I grab my phone to call Josh. After relaying all of the information to him, I sit next to Robby. He looks at me. I smile. "I'm fucking proud of you."

"Just doing my job."

"No. You got this thing going again. I don't know where we'd be without you. I don't know where I'd be without you."

"I'm so in love with you."

I grin like a fucking fool. I love hearing those words come from his lips. "I love you, too."

I lean forward to kiss him. He's become my entire life. If anything ever happened to him, I'd burn the entire world to the ground.

Chapter Twenty Four

☒ Dani ☒

I smile as Jackson babbles at me. Jessa laughs when he reaches out his arms and grabs my hair in his still tiny hands. He tugs himself closer to me and snuggles into my neck.

"Jackson is really particular about who he lets close to him. You're a true natural," Jessa says.

"I've never been good with kids. I have a mutual understanding with them. We stay away from each other completely."

Jessa laughs and Breetana, Nicole, and Arianna all join her. We're all sitting in the living room together talking and waiting for Lyric to arrive. I haven't met her yet, but Nick says she's family. These girls have accepted me into their sisterly dynamic like nothing, and I find myself leaping for joy inside because of it. I never knew I wanted this, but damn if I don't love every second.

I've never allowed myself to get close to anyone after my mom's murder and my dad running away. I liked my life as it was. I enjoyed the idea of being able to travel the world and not have any ties at all to anywhere. It allowed me to be able to get up and leave if I wanted to.

I had a friend or two, but no one I'm still in contact with or care to be. Even the one from Florida who helped me. When she found out why I was running, she just quit talking to me. I really didn't blame her. I really liked being a loner. I liked being able to take care of myself and not need anyone.

But that all changed the night Nick crashed through my door. The night I decided to depend on people other than myself. The night I became part of something more than me. The night I became a part of this family.

We all fall silent as our guys walk into the room. Nick walks over to me and Jessa. He gives me a soft smile, then pulls Jessa onto her feet and into his arms. Jason sits next to me.

She wraps her arms around him and smiles. "What's this for? What's going on?"

"A lot, Jessa. I just want you to know that we all love you. Okay?" He lets her go. Jason pulls her into his lap. I look up at Nick. Jackson has fallen asleep in my arms. "Go with Arianna and get the kids to bed. And then both of you come down here. We need to talk. Something big is going down."

My eyebrows shoot up, but I keep my voice low. "What's going on?"

"Not now. Do what I told you to. Please, Dani." He looks at Ryan. Ryan nods as Arianna and I stand. Nicole follows with Tait, and Ryan follows us up the stairs.

"Ryan?" Nicole asks. I can hear the fear in her voice.

"Just trust me, Nikki. Please don't ask questions." I hear Ryan loading his gun.

I look back. He snaps the slide back and lets it fall forward, making sure a live bullet is in the chamber. He keeps it at the ready. I sharply inhale. He meets my eyes and gives me a slight shake of the head. Tears sting my eyes as I turn once more and follow Arianna to the nursery.

We lay the kids down and quietly leave the nursery. Ryan allows Arianna and Nicole to get slightly ahead of him, but he holds me back. I look at him questioningly, but say nothing as I fall in step with him. We follow Arianna and Nicole down the stairs. When they are safely in the living room, Ryan pulls me around the corner.

He hands me the gun strapped to his waist. "Remember when you told me you wanted to do more to protect yourself and this family?" He locks his intense eyes on mine. I nod, tentatively taking the gun from him. "Now's your chance. I'll explain everything out there, but I need you."

I take a deep breath. "What do you need?"

"I need my brothers. I need as many of my guys as I can spare. We have a lead. I'll leave Chase with you. Lyric will be here in a little while. I'll give her a gun, but I need everyone else. I need you to protect the family. Like I said, I'll explain everything when we get out there. You'll understand the why better then."

I nod and smile shakily as he takes off his shoulder holster. He starts strapping it to me. "I don't need the why. All I need is the command. I trust you. I trust this family. If you say you need me to protect them, that's all I need. You can count on me."

Ryan gives me a half and very weak smile as he finishes strapping me into the holster. "I know I can."

He turns and heads outside. Everyone is settled and looks at me curiously. Except Nick. He holds out his arm and pulls me into his lap when I reach him. He buries his face in my hair and kisses my neck.

"I love you, baby."

I turn to him and reach up to run a hand through his perfect hair. "I love you, too."

A few minutes later, Ryan comes back with a girl who is half his size. She's petite, with dark hair and gorgeous hazel eyes. Like me, she's wearing a shoulder holster. She's hugging herself and smiling softly. She nods as Ryan whispers to her. After another few moments, Ryan leads her into the living room. She takes a seat next to Arianna.

"Who's that?" I ask Nick quietly. "Lyric?"

He nods. "Yes. You'll be able to get to know her better later."

I nod and smile over at her. She gives me a shy smile as Ryan takes his place in the center of the room.

Ryan takes a breath. "Okay, everyone. Listen up. I know it's late. I know you girls are curious about what's going on and everyone is probably wondering why Dani and Lyric are wearing guns and holsters on their shoulders. Truth is we have some fucked up shit going on."

"You aren't kidding." Luke mumbles the words as Robby cuddles into his arm. Everyone looks exhausted.

At that moment, a couple guards come in with Ethan and Jenny. They're followed closely by Shane and Sonya. Eve comes in seconds after them.

Ethan meets Ryan's eyes. "Care to tell us what's going on?"

Ryan nods, standing slightly straighter. More dominant. Commanding. "Just about to, sir. Sit."

I look at Nick. I'm not used to such formality in this family. He kisses my shoulder and gives me a comforting squeeze. "It's okay."

Everyone else finds a seat and Ryan continues. Ryan swipes a hand down his face and sighs. "There's no easy way to say this, so I'm just coming out and saying it. Matthew Lucinio isn't dead."

There's an audible gulp in the room and Jessa starts instantly crying. Jason hugs her close and Ryan rushes to her side. Through the fear I feel, my heart breaks for her. I know how serious this is, but she has to be terrified.

"H-How is that p-possible?" She buries her head in Jason's chest. One of Nick's hands gently caresses her back while Jason holds her tightly.

Ryan squeezes her leg. "Jess, I know how scared you are. Trust me. But you know me. I won't let anything happen to you. I won't let him touch you. Jason won't either. You know the lines me, Jason, and Nick have crossed to protect you. Our family is bigger. We're stronger. He's not getting anywhere near you. Dani, Lyric, and Chase are going to be armed and with you and the girls the whole time."

Jessa sobs, and I shift on Nick's lap. I plaster myself to Jessa's back and wrap her in a hard hug. "I know we don't know each other well, but I think we've become really close. I only know what people told me about what happened, but Ryan is right. The family has grown. You have all of us. No way anything bad is going to happen."

"How is this possible? Josh killed him. You saw it." Jessa looks at Ryan with wide, terrified eyes.

"Josh killed a guy who looked like Matthew," Ryan explains. "Robby found the real Matthew. He found records and transactions proving he paid this guy off. He paid for the plastic surgery and sent him in the night we raided. He figured out we were coming and took off. He's always been prepared for anything. He knew as soon as he came after you, he'd need an escape plan because I'd be going after him."

Jessa lets out a choked sob before she shoves Ryan and me away and flees the room. Jason chokes back his own sob. "I got her. I'll take care of it. Just... explain the rest to everyone." Jason gets up and follows Jessa. Ryan stands once more. Nick pulls me into him again.

"There's more?" I ask quietly.

He nods into my neck. "Yes. A lot more."

"Shit...," I whisper, instinctively knowing things are going to get even more fucked up very quickly.

Ryan pinches the bridge of his nose. "We know Lucinio is alive. We know how. We also know where."

"What?" Breetana fearfully squeaks.

"Where?" Nicole whimpers. She closes her eyes.

"Here. In Chicago," Nick says.

"What?" I look at Nick as everyone starts talking at once. The room becomes chaotic.

"This can't be happening," I say, utterly confused on all of the details, but knowing it's really bad. I can read a room. And this one is filled with terror. Lyric is bawling into Arianna, who's hugging her as tightly as humanly possible.

"I never thought I'd see the fucking day." Nick pulls me close and runs his fingers through my hair.

"Enough!" Ryan's powerful voice carries above everyone else's. "We aren't going to start freaking out. We're handling this just like we handle everything else."

"Ryan, this isn't like everything else," Arianna hisses. She tucks Lyric into Taylor and stands, pulling Ryan out of the room. Nick nudges me off his lap and then stands. He pulls me with him as he follows Arianna and Ryan into his office. "Matthew Lucinio is unhinged. He always has been. You can't go into this like you usually do! He's too evenly matched!" Arianna says, keeping her voice low, though her eyes are wide and terrified.

Nick pulls me into Ryan's office and closes the door. "She's right, Ryan. You know as well as I do that this is more fucked up than last time."

He glares at Nick. "You think I don't fucking know that? We don't have a choice. We have to act on the information we have."

My eyes widen. "What... information?"

Arianna looks at me. "He wants to go after Lucinio tomorrow night."

Nick rubs his temple. "That's why he gave you the gun. He wants you, Lyric, and Chase to stay here. He'll leave a couple guards here, but everyone else needs to go in to take out Lucinio."

Ryan sighs. "I already sent in a surveillance team."

Arianna's eyes fill with tears. "This is stupid, Ryan. It takes days to plan a mission like this!"

"I think our best option right now is to listen to Ryan. He's been doing this for a long time." I say the words quietly and look down at the floor because I don't want to upset anyone.

"And I'm sorry, baby, but we don't have days. We have to act." The powerful man in front of me is scared. I can hear the small tremor in his voice. I glance at him.

Arianna wipes her eyes. "Ryan, please. Please gather more intel. For your family. What are we going to do if something happens to you?"

"Okay. Air. Listen to me," Nick cuts in before Ryan can respond. "It's not just Ryan going in there. He'll have me, Taylor, and Jason. Luke and Robby are going, and every fucking guard we have in the area. You know me. Do you think I'll let him do something stupid?" I watch a strange shift take place as Nick focuses on Arianna. Arianna looks away. "Air. Look at me, honey. Really look at me. You know what I've gone through in my life. You know how protective I am of this family and why. Do you think I'll let Ryan go into this half fucking cocked?"

I shake my head as my mouth falls open slightly. Whatever he's talking about is something he's never told me.

Arianna shakes her head. "No. You're right. I know you wouldn't."

"Aria, please just trust I know what I'm doing," Ryan says quietly.

"I know you know what you're doing, Ryan. That isn't the point. I just don't want to lose you." The tears fall freely from her eyes.

He shakes his head as he runs his large hand over her cheek. "You won't."

"I won't let it happen. Ryan has spent years protecting all of us. Who do you think protects him?" Nick asks. Arianna smiles softly.

Ryan takes her in his arms. "Out." He growls the words to me and Nick as he buries his face in Arianna's hair.

Nick winks at me and pulls me from the room. I follow him to our room and close the door behind us. I look up at him. "Nick, I have to ask."

Nick sighs. "I know. Just get ready for bed first. It's going to be a long fucking day tomorrow."

"Okay." I do as I'm told.

After the two of us are ready, we crawl into bed. Nick pulls me close. I settle into his arms with my head on his chest.

"My parents were great. My dad treated her like a queen. I don't remember a lot about them. I was young. But I remember that. We didn't live in the best neighborhood, but my dad got a really good job. He made enough to start getting us out. I had just turned ten when we moved. Started to anyway. I was in school on moving day, but they were supposed to pick me up after. They didn't. I started walking home after I waited for them for so long. All the buses were gone. Seemed like I was alone there."

He hugs me a little tighter. I curl closer, sensing he needs me. I kiss his chest and trace the outline of his abs. "I'm listening…," I say quietly.

"I got home. No one was there. They didn't come home that night. They didn't come home until the next morning."

"That's so sad."

"I asked what happened. They told me that there had been some trouble. They had to help someone. They never elaborated."

"Oh God."

"Over the next couple of months, things seemed to be okay. We moved to a little better of a neighborhood. But my parents were rarely ever home. They were secretive. One day I woke up to yelling. Something about not having money. My parents said they were getting it. They needed more time. I snuck to the top of the stairs to listen. A tall guy shot them. I never knew who he was. I hid in the closet under a pile of clothes. They looked for me, but never found me. I didn't move for hours."

"Nick... Oh God." Tears sting my eyes as I kiss his chest.

"I was still just ten. I ended up on the streets. I toughened up fast. I found a guy who seemed a little protective of me. He taught me all he knew about survival. I saw some fucked up shit, but I wouldn't let it break me. I shoved it down. One night, a guy came up to mine and Brinson's makeshift lean-to. Stabbed Brinson. He took his radio. Stabbed him for a fucking radio. He tried to take my blanket, but it was a cold night. I was pissed he stabbed my only friend. So I stabbed him with a glass bottle."

"Nick, my God. I'm so sorry."

He runs his fingers through my hair. "Brinson died in my arms."

I feel my heart shattering for him, and a sob escapes my lips. "Nick…"

Nick tugs my hair a little as he wraps it around his fist. "After being on the streets for about two months, I stumbled into a drug deal. I backed out before anyone saw me. Or so I thought. One of the lookouts saw me and alerted someone else. Before I knew it, I was surrounded by a lot of bad guys. I figured I was going to die, but no fucking way was I going down without a fight. So, that's what I did. I fought as hard as I could for as long as I could until one of them put a gun to my head."

I shake my head. I'm sobbing silently against his chest now. "Nick, stop. I can't take any more. I'm so sad for you that it hurts to breathe."

He turns to kiss me on the forehead. "There's a happy ending, baby." He hugs me a little tighter. I'm full on sobbing. Silence be damned. Nick turns and wraps me in his arms. "The next thing I knew, shots rang out all around me. I thought that was it. I thought I was dead. I passed out from fear. When I woke up, I was in the most lavish bedroom I'd ever seen. Mom was cleaning me up. Long story short, dad saved me. They adopted me. Made me a Crane. I never really knew what had happened or what my parents had been into."

I sniffle. "I'm so sorry you went through that."

He hugs me for a while until I start to calm down. Finally, I look up at him. He meets my eyes and sweetly kisses me. "I was so grateful for what they had done for me that I would do anything for them. Dad saw that, but he also saw the anger. Viciousness. All things I needed to survive the streets of New York, even though I had only been on them for two months. Dad gave me an outlet. He treated me like his own son. That meant training like his sons. Going on missions. Everything. Jason hated it. Ryan tolerated it. Both have a very clear view of right and wrong. I didn't. I enjoyed the kills. I enjoyed the missions. I didn't have a conscience. I was too filled with anger at what happened to my parents to feel anything."

"Oh…, Nick."

His arms tighten around me. He takes a breath. "Until the day dad was shot… Ryan was almost killed that day. So was Jason. I almost lost my whole family. Ryan will tell you he was a lot further from death then he was. But he didn't see it from my end. He didn't see the bullets that were flying into the walls millimeters from his head. When it was over, Ryan took over and turned everything legit. I went into law enforcement. I realized that day that I wasn't putting my energy in the right place. I was too focused on the mission when I should've been focused on my family. I vowed never to let that happen again. Since that day, I've done everything I can to protect them."

"That's why you became Jason's head of security, then became a cop again here?"

"Yes. It's why I deal with the security systems in all of our houses. Being on Taylor's taskforce gives me the tools and resources I need to find people who try to get to you or my family. Tools and resources I didn't have otherwise. I had to rely on contacts, and I didn't like that."

"So, Ryan is the protector, but you're his protector."

"Even Batman needs help sometimes. I'm that help. I don't like going back to that place, but I'll do whatever I need to do to make sure you and this family are safe. That's my job. The job that counts anyway."

"What about your parents? You never found who killed them?" I close my eyes and focus on him. His fresh, comforting scent.

"I never stopped looking. But I've always come up empty."

I nod. Even though my mind is racing with everything he just told me, his soothing touch relaxes me. I wish I could make the pain go away. I can feel how hurt he is. How sad it makes him. I've become so connected with him that I can feel his emotions just as deeply as him. I still can't get over it, but I wouldn't change anything about our love story. Even with everything going on, our story is perfect.

Nick soothingly runs his fingers through my hair and up and down my arm. I start tracing each and every ridge of his stomach. I kiss his chest softly as I shift. I kiss each of his abs and down to the waistband of his boxer briefs. I look up at him shyly, silently asking for permission to give him any type of comfort I can. Anything to stop the ripples of pain slamming into me.

Nick smiles just as softly as I had been kissing him. One of his hands tangle in my hair. The other, he rests behind his head as he watches me. I gently and slowly tug down his boxer briefs and continue my soft kisses until I reach the prize. His thick and mouth-watering cock...

I lovingly lick his tip before taking it into my mouth and sucking delicately. I dip my tongue into the dimple just below his tip with a low moan and whimper as I close my eyes and start stroking. Firmly, but slowly. I rotate my wrist with each stroke and suck on his tip slightly harder.

His breathing quickens. I feel his stomach tighten as he gets harder for me. Picking up on his cues, I smile and take him further and further into my mouth until he's touching the back of my throat. I repeat the motion again and again as I stroke faster.

"Mmm...," I hum, sending vibrations through his dick. He jerks into me. I scrape my teeth lightly over his length as I open my eyes. He tugs on my hair and thrusts his hips to my pace. His dick gets harder and harder until I can feel it throbbing.

"Dani...," he moans as he tugs gently on my hair.

I suck harder and give him a sexy whimper before I hum again around him. He jerks harder into me before holding my head still. I continue stroking, feeling his dick get stiffer and thicken as he thrusts into my mouth. When he hits the back of my throat again, he comes hard.

Mmm..." I suck and lick all he spills for me until he stops spasming and jerking and comes down. After I lick him clean, I kiss his tip softly and nuzzle his dick before crawling up to my place at his side. I kiss him deeply, closing my eyes and melting completely into the kiss.

"I love you," he whispers when he pulls back.

I kiss his jaw with a soft smile. "I love you," I whisper back. I wrap myself around him and snuggle down. I close my eyes as he runs his fingers soothingly through my hair again.

Eventually, wrapped in the arms of the most amazing man I've ever known, I'm lulled to sleep by the sound of his peaceful and even breathing.

Chapter Twenty Five

☒ Robby ☒

I watch Ryan as I pop the last of the bagel in my mouth. The entire morning, Ryan hasn't sat down. He's been on the phone. He's talked to Taylor. He's walked around the house carrying Christopher. And I've been here at this table in the conference room in the house going through each piece of the puzzle I've managed to uncover.

Nick sits next to me. "Hey. What do you got?"

I look up at him. "A lot. I…" I look back at my laptop. "I need the family here. It involves everyone."

Nick pats my back as he looks at Ryan. "Arianna is putting Chris down for his nap with Jess and Nikki. Luke is grabbing Jason from downtown. We'll all be here soon."

"Okay."

Nick, being a Crane through and through, senses my tension. He leans forward. "What's wrong? Are you okay?"

I look at him before glancing back at Ryan. I lean back and look back at Nick. "There's no one in this family that hasn't been touched somehow by Matthew Lucinio," I say quietly. "No one."

Nick furrows his eyebrows at me in complete confusion. He leans back next to me. "I know. Our families have been bitter enemies for years. Until Ryan took over. I guess even then we were."

I shake my head. "No. I mean other than just Ethan and Ryan and Jason. You. There's so much more. Taylor. Nicole. Bree. Chase. Everyone."

"How?"

I point to the laptop. "It's all here. I just need everyone."

"Okay." Nick nods and scrubs his hand down his face. "I'll grab everyone who's here."

"Thanks." I glance back at Ryan as he collapses in a chair at the head of the table. Nick leaves the room. "You okay, Ry?"

He looks at me and takes a deep breath. "I know from what Luke told me that things I've been thinking for quite awhile are accurate. But not even he could really go as in depth as you. I wanted to sit down with you and hear it first. Before everyone else. I'm struggling with having the whole family here when I hear stuff for the first time, Robby. I don't like it."

"I know. I know, Ryan. But..." I look at my screen as Jason and Luke come into the room. I wait for them to sit before I continue. Luke takes my hand. I squeeze his. "The family needs to be here, Ryan. Luke and I discussed it. You need to have the family here when you hear this. We all do. It's for the best."

"I trust you, Robby. You know that. But I still don't like it." Ryan smiles as Arianna slides into his lap.

She runs his fingers through her hair. "Sometimes, even Batman needs help."

He laughs as he kisses her. Nick comes in holding Dani's hand. They both take their seats. Lyric sits next to Luke. I wait as everyone else strolls into the room and gets settled before I stand. I hit the button for the blackout shades and project my screen up on the wall as I wait for the shades to drop.

"To begin, I wanted to dive in a little to concerns that Ryan has had for a while." I click to my first part of this fucked up presentation.

"The cartel?" Nick asks.

"Not just any cartel. The Mexican cartel that snakes up I-35 through Minnesota to Canada. Huge drug trade. Weapons trade. Sex trade," Taylor says. "But what does this have to do with Lucinio? Isn't that why we're here?"

I look at him a little sadly because what I'm about to say is going to be like a sucker punch to everyone in this room. Maybe him a little more than everyone else, though. I walk up to the screen and pause to formulate my words. There's just no easy way.

"After the plans Lucinio had for Jessa and the Crane Mafia fell through, he went off and recalculated, I guess you could say. He licked his wounds. Tried to figure out how to grow. Josh became the leader of the Lucinio Mafia. No one knew Matthew was still alive. That he still had access to so many functions and companies run by the family. After finding and tracking everything to him through the Lucinio Tech deposits, Josh gave me access to all of the companies. And I found some fucked up things. He's been skimming off the top unnoticeably for the last several years. Not just since Josh took over."

"So, we know where he's getting the money," Ryan says.

I nod. "And I wish that were all. But it isn't." I point to the screen. "This shows deposits into his account, the fake one in the Cayman Islands, from the Mexican Cartel. I tracked which one because we all know there's a lot of them. This one has control over the I-35 trade route. If you look at the dates of those deposits, you'll see that they coincide with…" I trail off and close my eyes as I swallow. I open them and turn to Chase. "When you and Bree went to Minnesota."

"What…?" Breetana asks quietly and wide-eyed.

"I don't get it. The cartel was paying him?" Chase asks as he hugs Breetana.

I shake my head. "Not exactly. At first glance, yes. But if you dig into the transactions, you get the bigger picture. The cartel keeps meticulous records. It's how they make sure they aren't getting cheated out of a single dollar. I tracked all of this and hacked in remotely to the IP address of the computer where these deposits were made from. Thank you banking apps that have no security at all. Which is damn near all banks that are used by the cartel. Small banks. No questions. Easier to pay people off. These deposits are actually being made to him for work he's done for them. Specifically, providing security along their trade route."

"Holy… shit…" Ryan stares in disbelief.

"Not even close to being done." I take another deep breath. "These highlighted numbers are deposits made to other accounts. Three different ones." I glance at both Taylor and Chase before locking eyes with Nicole. "One of them is to your ex."

She makes a small whimper and buries her face in Taylor's neck. "Why?"

"The other deposits are to Breetana's ex. And your uncle."

"Lucinio was paying them off," Ryan growls dangerously. "Why?"

"To get to you," I answer simply.

"He didn't know them then," Taylor says.

"I know. But Ryan knew you. He was close to you. What better way to get to Ryan than through his family? He already tried with Jason through Jessa. He failed at killing Ethan. He couldn't wear Ryan down with all of the small battles, which is what all of these show." I point to the blue highlighted deposits to other accounts.

"Shit…" Ryan says. Arianna burrows into him.

I walk back to my laptop and click a few things. "This one shows the deposit to the mafia you dealt with in L.A." I click again. "This one tracks to Miami." I click again. "This one tracks to Paris. He kept paying people off to come after you. When that didn't work, he looked at other ways to destroy you. He underestimated you and just how big you are. So, he went after someone close to you." I point to Taylor. "He did his research. One thing he is *definitely not* is stupid. He knew Taylor was close to Chase. He found out about Breetana and where she came from. He paid off people to get to Nicole. He knew Breetana would go to her. He knew Chase would follow. And he knew Chase would call Taylor. He knew Taylor would realize he needs help and call Ryan."

"How do you know all of that?" Taylor asks. "How did you get all of that from accounts and deposits?"

I smile a little. "I'm glad you asked. You can thank Zekeih. The laptop he swiped from Krins on his last visit with him that he gave you was a fun time for me." I click to another screen. "And I found this."

Everyone looks up at the screen. What looks like a spiderweb of red string takes over the wall. Luke shakes his head. "What the hell is that?"

I smile down at him. "Krins has been working with Matthew for years. He has more shit on him and his dealings than you can imagine.

This, however, is everything relating to the past couple of years." I highlight certain sections. These are all the small mafia's he paid off to go after Ryan." I highlight another section. "This is all related to Taylor. As you can see, he connected everything."

"So..., everything about Minnesota... the cartel, my ex, Nicole's ex. Everything. It all tracks to him?" Breetana timidly asks.

I nod. "Yeah. And I have a whole bunch more things I could show you to prove it that I found, but there's a lot more to go through. I'm highlighting everything here, but there's so much information on all of that. It would take me days to explain it all."

Ryan shakes his head. "Just... go... Keep going."

I nod again. "Okay." I highlight another section. "This part shows his plans to take down Taylor and Nicole using a small gang in Chicago." I flip to another screen. "And these are the deposits made to that gang."

"Why would he use a small gang to go after me? He knows how easy it would be for me to take out a small gang." Ryan shakes his head as he tries to follow.

"Doesn't make sense, does it?" I put up a side by side and highlight one word on the spider web chart.

"Distraction," Nick says. "He was distracting you."

"Why?"

I shrug. "To keep you from realizing he's out there so he could grow. Keep everyone off his back. If you're busy protecting your family and being thrown into these small gangs and small mafia battles, you wouldn't hear about this other mafia that's gaining traction and numbers."

"Fuck..." Ryan buries his face in Arianna's neck.

"We all felt it," Taylor says.

"We all knew something just didn't fit," Chase says.

"It all fucking makes so much more sense now," Nick says.

"So..., if all of this was orchestrated by Lucinio..." Arianna looks up at me. "Does that m-mean my father...?"

"I hate to say it, Air, but... yeah." I click to another screen and put it up side by side with the spider web chart. "It looks like he had a hand in the Massena Mafia for years. He was allies with them. He was also allied with the Ambrosio Mafia. For years. At least according to the files that Krins had on his laptop. If you look here, though." I highlight more deposits. "These accounts are Massena's and Ambrosio's. He started to pay them off. According to what I found on Krins' computer, it was to get the two of them to team up and go after you to take over Manhattan."

"Christ," Ryan breathes.

"He had to know it would never happen." I highlight another section on the spiderweb chart. "Which makes sense when you see this."

"Another d-distraction," Lyric stutters quietly as she reads the screen.

Ryan hugs Arianna tightly when she whimpers, and buries his face in her hair murmuring something in her ear that none of us hear. Arianna cries quietly. I look around the room. Breetana and Nikki are crying with her. Jessa is close. I can see the pain she feels coming from her sisters. Lyric's lip is quivering.

I sigh. Unfortunately, I'm not finished. "And... that isn't all." I sit in my chair. I don't feel strong enough to stand during this part. "Nick. I found out that Penelope, your ex, was the daughter of a very small mafia called the Carmine Mafia. It was led by her father, Ricci Carmine."

"That wasn't Penelope's last name," Nick says, shaking his head at the screen. "It was -"

"I know. She was sent undercover. As a spy. For both her father and Matthew Lucinio." I pull up bank transactions from the Carmine Mafia. "These transactions came from the Lucinio Mafia while Matthew was leading. There's also several transactions that lead to agencies Matthew used a lot to track people and spy on them. He used this agency to spy on Penelope to make sure she was doing everything she needed to."

Ryan shakes his head. "Hang on. The Carmine Mafia. We took them out a few years after Penelope disappeared."

I nod and click to another screen. "You did. They used the money that Penelope walked with to expand and move onto your territory in Sicily."

"But Penelope wasn't there," Nick says. "I was with him on that mission."

"She was." I click to another screen. "Meet Salvadore Carmine. Also known as Penelope." I wait for the very audible gasps to pass before I continue. Nick looks at me completely horrified and Dani looks utterly confused. "Penelope had a sex change. It's part of the reason that she couldn't be found. She assumed the identity of her brother, Salvadore, who was killed in a wreck. Issue is, his body was never found."

231

"So, she could assume the role rather easily." Ethan has been quiet up until this point, but I can see he's becoming about as dangerously angry as Ryan. The resemblance between the two has always been striking. But damn. Now, there's no mistaking where Ryan gets his ruthlessness from. He's sitting on the other side of Lyric and hugs her to his side.

"Yes. And she did. She was already undercover. It was an easy switch. Keep everyone thinking she'd just disappeared, but really," I point to the screen. "I found the records and everything. Lucinio paid for it. Probably what gave him the idea to pay this guy…" I pull up another screen. "To assume his identity and pay for the plastic surgery to make it work."

Everyone is quiet as they look at the screen. I look at Luke. He's the only one who knows that the hardest part is yet to come. I don't want to be the one to share the news. Luke leans over and kisses me softly and squeezes my thigh in encouragement.

He looks up at the screen again. "There's still quite a bit more." He takes my hand.

Ryan sighs and nods as he looks at me. "Go on."

I scrub my hands down my face. "Okay." I reluctantly let go of Luke's hand and click into the part that I absolutely want no part of. At all. When I get to the newspaper clipping I want, I say nothing. But when Nick realizes what I'm showing him, I can feel all the breathable air in the room sucked out completely.

"That's…" Jenny turns and buries her face in Ethan's chest. His arm wraps around her as she sobs. My heart shatters for the family who has accepted me with no question.

Jessa turns and bursts into tears. Nick stares blankly at the screen. Dani and Lyric look confused. Ryan is vibrating with anger. Arianna is wrapped around him rocking gently back and forth. Luke is rubbing my back soothingly.

Taylor shakes his head as he hugs Nicole. "He was married to Nick's mom?" He looks at me as he quietly speaks.

I nod silently. After a few moments, I take another breath. "Nick's mother married Matthew Lucinio in Las Vegas. The marriage was annulled three weeks later." I click into another screen with shaky hands. It's a birth certificate with Matthew's name. "But… that was long enough for them to conceive a child…" I look down. "Nick." I click to another screen. "It

232

looks like she re-filed with Nick's father's name after…" I scrub my hands down my face. "After Nick's father adopted him."

I've never heard Nick cry. He's always been the one that's been the hardest. Even harder than Ryan. But the sobs that rip through him as he falls to his knees and Dani wraps around him are so painful that I can't bear it. I turn and throw myself at Luke. The tears I fought so hard to keep at bay fall freely from my eyes. Luke hugs me hard. Even Lyric is freely crying right now, and she's the only one in the room who hasn't been directly touched by this… Yet…

It takes a while for everyone in the room to calm down enough for anyone to speak. I hear people reassuring Nick. I hear sobs quieting. I clutch Luke's shirt as I tremble and peek at everyone. Ryan and Jason are sitting on the floor next to Nick. Jenny and Ethan are embracing all of them. Dani is somewhere in the inner circle burrowed into Nick. Somehow, Lyric has ended up in a Nicole and Taylor sandwich.

Chase puts a hand on my shoulder. "What else do you have?" he asks quietly.

I look up at him and wipe my eyes, clutching Luke with the other hand. "How Matthew found out about Nick. The truth behind Nick's parent's murder," I say quietly. "And…" My eyes flick over to the circle Dani and Nick are buried in. "And Dani…"

Chase nods. He walks over to Ryan and kneels next to him whispering in his ear. It takes a few minutes, but eventually, everyone is back in their chairs. Dani is sitting in Nick's lap. Everyone is sitting around Nick as he keeps his face buried in Dani's hair.

I clear my throat. "Matthew found out right away about Nick, but he refused to have a paternity test done, according to these court records. He denied all responsibility. Which was fine with Nick's mother because they were trying to get an adoption. The court granted it when Lucinio said he didn't give a shit. And, yes. That's literally in the transcripts. The judge granted the adoption."

"He should have just stayed not giving a shit," Jenny growls quietly.

"Couldn't agree more," Ryan says in a voice that takes the temperature in the room down a few degrees.

I shiver. "Uh… Adam Krins… kept immaculate records," I say a little quieter than I mean to. I take a couple of breaths as I slowly release

Luke. He stays close to me with his arm around me. "He has a journal of every hit Lucinio ordered him to do. Including…" I click to the journal page about Nick's parents. "The murder of Nick's parents." I watch as Nick looks up at the screen. He glares but says nothing.

"I will kill him," Ryan growls.

I let out a breath. I close my eyes a moment before opening them and clicking into another journal entry. "This talks about plastic surgery he underwent after the murder of Nick's parents. He talks about how Lucinio paid for it." I click back to his accounts. "It took me a really long time, but I did find this in his records. It's the transaction from Lucinio in the amount of the plastic surgery. Maybe that's where his plastic surgery obsession started."

"Krins had plastic surgery?" Taylor asks.

"It seems there's a lot of that going around," Chase quips humorously.

I rub my forehead as tears sting my eyes. Dani stands and stretches as she looks at the screen. I look at her as she puts a hand on Nick's shoulder. "Ladies and gentleman." I pull up a side by side image. "Meet Adam Krins."

Dani looks at the screen and whimpers as I get up. Nick rubs his forehead and scrubs a hand down his face. I stand behind Dani, already reading her enough to know what's about to happen. She sniffles as her grip on Nick loosens. I watch as her head falls back. Nick looks up just as her knees buckle. She falls into my arms.

"Dani?" Nick stands. I gently release Dani into his arms as he sits and rocks with her.

Her eyes flutter open and she sniffles and whimpers. "Oh God. Oh my God."

Ryan looks at me. "Who is that? Who is he? What happened?"

"Adam Krins is Joey Jaydon." I give Dani's shoulder a squeeze. "Daniella Jaydon, or Dani Jade as we know her. This is her father."

Dani cries into Nick's chest as he hugs her closer. "I didn't know!" she sobs. "I didn't know!"

"Dani," Nick whispers in her ear. "Dani, shh… It's okay."

"Please don't hate me!" She grabs his shirt in a death grip. "Please!"

"Dani, holy shit. I don't! I don't hate you." He kisses her deeply as he hugs her hard, cutting off her pleas. When he pulls away, he looks up at me. "What else do you have?" The venom I expected in his voice is non-existent. He'll never understand how grateful I am for that.

I hesitate. "Pictures. He had a lot of them. Dani growing up. Taken from a distance. Like he was watching her." I wince as Dani explodes into a fresh wave of screaming sobs.

"She doesn't need to see those. Anything else?" he asks, looking up at me.

I shake my head. "I think I've ruined enough lives for one day."

"You didn't, Robby." Nick stands with Dani in his arms. He leans into me. I wrap my arms around him and hug him.

When he pulls away, carrying a trembling Dani from the room, I look at everyone else. I expect looks of hatred. Anger towards me at the very least. What I'm met with is exhaustion. Waves and waves of it. I walk slowly back to my chair and slump into Luke's waiting arms.

After a few moments, Ryan looks at me. "Thank you."

I look at him bewildered. "For what? Destroying your entire family?"

He smiles, though it's pained. "No. For finding out the truth. For dedicating yourself to finding it. For not hiding anything. You know how close this family is. As part of it, an important part of it, just as important and loved as everyone else, you know how strong we are. And you know that this is only one more thing to make our bond thicker."

"I don't care whose sperm Nick was conceived with. That boy is my son," Ethan says with conviction.

"And he's our brother," Jason says just as forcefully as his father.

"He's all of our brother," Chase says.

"That isn't changing," Taylor agrees.

"This family is everything to me. It's strong," Ryan says to me. "And it's staying that way."

I watch him for a moment. "There is one more thing. I..." I look at Jessa. "...think I figured out the real obsession with Jessa. And why he was so obsessed with her and making an heir."

Jessa looks up at me. "Why?" she asks quietly.

I give her a sad smile. "Circumstance. Coincidence." I look at Ryan then my screen. I pull up a side by side of Jessa and Nick's mother. I say nothing.

"The thought crossed my mind when I looked at the newspaper clipping," Lyric whispers. "But… it's undeniable."

"You look a lot like Nick's mother," Taylor says quietly.

I nod. "So much so that I think Lucinio wanted her as a way to replace both Nick and Nick's mother. It's just a hunch, but I think the hit on Nick's parents was more about Lucinio wanting Nick. I don't know if his mother was the intended target; if she was even supposed to be killed, but I think in the end, Lucinio wanted his son. I think he probably spent time looking for him, but the rivalry with the Crane Mafia really amped up when he found out Nick had been adopted by the Crane family."

"And then when he realized he couldn't get Nick back, he tried a bunch of ridiculous shit until it finally ended with us coming face to face," Ethan finishes.

Jason hugs Jessa tighter and runs his fingers through her hair. "When he found out about Jessa, he saw the resemblance."

"And wanted her for himself to replace the woman he lost and probably never got over," Ryan finishes. I nod. "It doesn't matter. None of it matters. All that matters is we know the bigger picture. We know the whole story. We know the missing pieces. Now, we go forward. We address it. We take Lucinio out once and for all. And we continue building the already strong bond we have as a family."

I collapse in relief as everyone takes in all of the information and processes it. We're all silent as we deal with everything in our own way.

Lyric chuckles. "I guess through Nick, Alex and Josh really are brothers. I mean, if they're his half brothers…"

Ryan grins. "I didn't think of that."

"Matthew Lucinio fucks up again," Lyric says with a soft smile. I feel the mood in the room lift slightly as Lyric leans on Taylor's shoulder. He hugs both her and Nicole.

I'm very suddenly hit with more exhaustion than my brain can deal with. My body refuses to allow me to stay awake another minute. I don't blame it. I don't know how much sleep I got, but I know it wasn't enough.

I have no hope of stopping it. Laying my head on Luke's shoulder, I let myself succumb to the rest I need. Even if it's just an hour while everyone processes, I'm okay with that. I close my eyes and yawn. Seconds later, I fall into an odd sleep.

It's not restless. It's not really peaceful.

It just… is.

Chapter Twenty Six

⚔ Dani ⚔

I whimper as Nick lays down with me in our bed. I cling to him, terrified that if I let him go, he'll run. Nick kneels on it and lays down with me. He never lets his grip on me go as we both cuddle into each other.

"I really didn't know… I didn't know any of that…," I whimper into his neck as I bury my face in it.

"I know."

"I thought some of the mannerisms were similar… His eyes… I should've known. I'm so sorry."

"Dani. Don't. It's not your fault." He kisses my shoulder, my neck, my cheek, and my lips. "Don't."

I look up at him. "I'm so scared that you're going to blame me for him killing your parents. He's my dad." The tears make their way down my cheeks. My nails dig into his shoulders. "I'm sorry."

He reaches up and wipes away my tears with the pad of his thumb. "It's not your fault. You weren't involved. Is it my fault that my biological father has tried to kill everyone in this family? Somehow?"

I shake my head. "God no."

"Then why would I blame you for the actions of your father? It's not your fault. I don't love you any less."

It's like my heart grows wings and flies out of my chest. All I can do is cry and hug him tighter. He runs his fingers gently through my hair as I shake and tremble against him. I run my hands up and down his back, knowing he needs some kind of comfort, as well.

After a long while, Nick takes a deep breath. "It's not every day you learn your father is one of the most hated fucking men in the world."

I snuggle into his neck. "I know... It's not every day you find out that your father killed your fiancé's parents..."

His fingers tangle in my hair. "Today has been one fucked up event after another." He kisses my forehead before slowly pulling back just enough to look at me. "Are you okay?"

I shrug and sigh. I look down at his chest and rest my head just underneath his jaw. He rests his chin on my head and hugs me tighter. I lock my arms around him, taking a few minutes to compose my thoughts.

"I guess... I don't really know how to feel," I say quietly. "I don't remember a lot about my parents. I remember that I loved them. I remember bits and pieces that I've mentioned." I sniffle. "But learning who he was. What he did..." I feel the tears again burn my eyes. "The timeline." I look up at him. "The night he fought with my mom and killed her. I don't know what she had on him. I never understood what he was screaming about or why she kept saying that she's leaving with me. But... it coincides with..." I blink back the tears as I look down.

"It coincides with my parents' murder." He hugs me tighter and kisses the top of my head. "I think he fled the night he killed them. And whatever your mother kept saying she had on him must have been evidence that he had done other things. What it is, we may never know."

"I was just so young. I almost wish he had found me just so I knew more about him and could help you more." I deflate in his arms. "And I feel so bad knowing that he was responsible for taking your family from you."

"Dani. Baby, look at me." He tugs on my hair until I look up at him. He wipes my eyes and kisses me softly. "It wouldn't have changed anything. He still would have killed my parents. He still would have killed Carter Rudd. And maybe you still would have witnessed it. Maybe you wouldn't have. Maybe you would have been a hardened mafia princess. Or

239

maybe you would've been like Arianna and had a serious sense of right and wrong. But I do know one thing." He runs his thumb along my lip.

"What?"

"He never would have let you go. Even if you had run like Arianna did. He would've hunted you down. Mafias don't just let people walk away."

I furrow my brows. "But… your mom."

"I don't think it was anything more than an affair. The fact that he did let her go and allow her the annulment tells me that there was more going on than Robby was able to uncover. And again. That may be something we never know the entire story of. Jessa always says to me that everything happens for a reason. Ryan and Taylor are always telling me that coincidence doesn't exist. And they're all right. Everything. There's a far larger design at play. Everything we went through, it all brought us here… to each other."

I smile weakly and kiss his jaw. "That's a very strong way to look at things."

"The point is, you can't let events like that define you. You know the truth. You know we all still love you." He kisses me deeply. "You know I still love you. I don't blame you for your father's actions. And you can't either. That's on him. Not you. You don't choose your parents."

"I just don't know how to feel about having a father who's a dangerous criminal. And I really don't know how to react to the fact that I know he killed someone. I saw it. And that he killed your parents."

"It's hard. But it's something that you have to let go. You have to look at it like the guy is a bad guy. He did some bad things. But it has nothing to do with you. If you allow yourself to think about all of his crimes and the people he hurt, his actions will destroy you. Just like knowing everything I've done will."

"It's different, though… You're one of the good guys."

"Don't mean I haven't done bad things."

I shake my head. "It still feels very different." I chew the inside of my cheek. "So…, you're saying I need to focus on the here and now. Not on him and a life that doesn't involve me."

"That's my girl." He kisses my forehead as I cuddle back into him.

"What about you? Are you okay…?"

"The shock has worn off. When I first heard it, I don't really know what I felt. So many things were going through my head that I broke down. Now that I know, I guess it just doesn't matter to me. I was adopted by a very loving family who treated me like one of their own kids. I'm angry at my mother a little, but knowing what I know about Lucinio, I don't really know that I can be angry."

"I feel like you can be," I say quietly. "I'm angry. I'm angry that he killed your parents. I'm angry he got involved with that man. I'm angry that my world has been taken over by mafias, and that I can't have a normal life."

"Dani. We can have all of that. There were several years where things were quiet for this family. Ryan was basically just running businesses. Establishing himself. Making law enforcement contacts. We all lived a pretty quiet life." He hugs me tightly. "We need to eliminate him. Things will never be normal with that fucker around."

"I'm sorry he has to be your dad."

"He's not. Not to me. Ethan. He's my dad. The only two things I care about that have come out of this situation is that we now understand why he's hell bent on destroying this family and getting to Jessa. The other thing is I've gained two incredible family members out of this. Josh and Alex. Ryan has long considered Alex a brother. He's close to Josh now and considers him family, too. Just as he does Chase and Taylor. But…" he shrugs. "They really are. Through me. And that's something that's incredible to me."

"I wonder how they'll feel, though. Knowing this. I don't really know a lot about them, but I know they've been through so much."

"They have. They truly have. And honestly, I guess I don't know how they'll react. When it all comes down to it, they went through a lot of what they went through because they weren't me. It looks like Matthew decided that he wanted his first born to take over his mafia. When that didn't work out for him, he took it out on the two sons he did have."

"I wonder what made him decide he wanted you."

"I don't know that I'd ever really be able to get an answer to that. Short of having Matthew right here. There's a lot of questions I'd like to ask him. Things I think only he would be able to answer. I'm not going to let them burn at me, though. I have other things to focus on. Like finding

Krins and Lucinio and destroying them for all they've put you and me and this family through."

I can't help but feel a small sense of comfort at the low vibration that comes from his chest as he talks. What really brings me that feeling I need, though, is his arms wrapped tightly around me. The sexy twitch in his bicep. The overwhelming feeling of protection that washes over me.

Nick is my safety. He's my heart. My home. Where I belong. I lean up and kiss him deeply and hard. Where the overwhelming urge came from to need to feel his mouth on mine is something I don't quite understand. But if there's one thing I've learned from this family since I've been a part of it is to not ignore instincts. Right now my instincts are saying that we both need this.

So, I grip his shirt and kiss him with everything I am. I pour so much feeling and every fiber of my love into it. I don't want him to have even an ounce of doubt about my love for him. I don't fully understand why I'd think he would. He just told me he wouldn't. That doesn't seem to matter to my heart, though. I need him to not only know it, but also feel it.

Nick's hands trail to my ass. He grips it as he deepens the kiss and rolls over on his back tugging me on top of him. I straddle and press close. My fingers spear his hair. I'm unable to get close enough to him.

Nick slowly tugs my shirt up and off me before wrapping his arms around me and sucking lightly on my tongue. I moan softly into the kiss as I close my eyes. He unclasps my bra and throws it somewhere after he pulls it off. Being away from him for only seconds is torturous, but the clothes we have on are keeping me from the skin to skin contact I'm craving.

Nick sits up as I kiss him and takes off his shirt. My mouth is on his as soon as he tosses it. He grips my hips and flips me onto my back. He covers my mouth again and kisses me deep. I arch into his hands as they skim down my body. He squeezes my tits and tugs my nipples.

"Fuck! Nick!" I scratch my nails into his back and grip his shoulders.

He groans against my neck and nips my collarbone as he kisses lower. I feel him tug my button on my jeans. He unzips them and rips them down my hips while his tongue lavishes my nipple. He nips and kisses along my chest to my other one and does the same thing.

242

My fingers find the button on his jeans, but he grips my wrists and holds them above my head. He sucks hard on my nipple, then kisses his way down to my quivering and overly excited center. I arch into him trying to get his tongue where I need it.

He teasingly licks my clit. "Mmm…"

I buck up into him. "Nick!"

He gives me an infuriating chuckle. I can feel him smiling against my pussy as he slowly licks. "What?" He speaks against my clit, sending vibrations through my entire body.

I try pulling my wrists free to tangle in his hair, but I have no chance against his strong grip. I arch into him again, begging for his tongue. "You know what! Nick, please…"

I feel him smirk as he sucks my clit into his mouth. Hard. "Please what?"

I tug against his grip again, but he only holds my wrists firmer. I tremble and moan. I try to spread my legs further but can't because my jeans aren't even to my knees. I'm trapped. Completely at his mercy.

Exactly where I want to be.

"Your tongue. Please…" I close my eyes and squirm under him.

"So sexy when you beg for me." He dives into my pussy hard and fast, thrusting his tongue as he swirls it and shakes his head.

I nearly fly off the bed as I scream. "Ah!"

Not being able to spread my legs wider has only managed to make everything feel far more pleasurable. My pussy clenches tight around his tongue as I pulse for him and thrust into him. His tongue sinks a little deeper and feels like every sinful desire I've ever had.

My thighs tremble. My stomach quivers. My entire body shivers in pleasure as I writhe and thrust my hips into him. He nips my pussy and sucks as he lightly scrapes his teeth around me. My eyes roll back in my head as waves and waves of ecstasy crash over me. I can't even find my voice.

"Come for me, baby." His deep voice sends new sensations through me.

"Nick! Yes!" I arch into him as he thrusts and licks my pussy. I come hard, jerking my hips into him. I pulse and clench as I writhe and moan.

"Christ, you taste good."

243

I shiver as he slowly licks me with low hums and moans. He kisses my pussy as he lets go of my wrists. He kneels next to me and tugs off my jeans as I pant from the intense orgasm. I watch as he pulls his off. His perfectly large and thick cock springs to attention, and I suddenly have a whole new craving.

As soon as Nick lays down, I pounce. I take him in my mouth and suck softly before sliding him further and further in my mouth. When he's touching the back of my throat, I pull back just as slowly while I scrape my teeth lightly along his vein.

"Mmm…," I hum as I reach his tip. I lick and suck along his length.

He tangles his fingers in my hair and arches into me when I take him back into my mouth. "Fuck, Dani."

I let him take control of me and bob my head up and down on his dick at the pace he wants. I reach down and tug on his balls lightly as I roll them in my hand. I suck and hum and moan around his dick. I feel him thicken and throb as his breathing quickens and grip on my hair tightens.

I look up at him with a shy smile and watch his abs clench. He pushes me down until he's touching the back of my throat. I swallow around him. He throws his head back and comes hard, spilling all of his warmth into my mouth. I greedily swallow it all with a low moan.

I lick him and kiss up his body to his neck. He grips my hips and guides me down over his length as he thrusts into me. "Oh, God…"

He trails his hands up to my tits and tugs my nipples, making me arch and groan. He smiles. "Ready to take a ride?"

My eyes widen. "Ride?"

His smile only grows as he slowly slides his hand down to my ass. "Yes. Ride." His eyes blaze their way down my body and back up, setting me on fire. "You might want to hang on for this."

I tilt my head slightly, but do as I'm told. I grip his arms, but before I fully understand what's about to happen, Nick starts slamming into me at the same time he lifts me up. His dick slides all the way out before he slams me down and pounds himself deep, hard, and fast into my pussy.

I throw my head back when he hits a depth he hadn't yet reached. "Ah! Oh! Holy God!" I grip him tightly.

He thrusts, burying himself so deeply inside of me that I'm positive he's created his own path to his new home deep within. I feel like he's hitting my stomach with every hard thrust of his devilishly delicious cock.

"Holy… fuck…, baby." He slides me along his dick, hitting every spot of pleasure in my body.

He continues thrusting into me as I bounce on him. My pussy pulses hard and clenches tight. I place my hands on his abs and tremble around him as I spread my legs wider. I moan as he sinks even deeper.

He slaps my ass before gripping it hard again and bouncing me on him until I'm screaming and writhing.

But his punishing pace doesn't let up.

"Nick! I'm gonna… Ah!"

"Come, baby. Come for me."

I scream his name as he watches me. "Nick!" I come hard for him clenching his cock in a vice-like grip. "Ah!"

"Oh, God…" His eyes roll back in his head as he continues thrusting rigorously as I come, not letting up for a second.

"I'm… It's… Oh!" My eyes roll back in my head as I try to stop myself from succumbing to the immense gratification he's bringing me to.

"Oh… shit." He moves me back and forth over him again and comes so hard I feel like it flows completely through me.

I collapse on top of him as my pussy pulses and quivers while I come a second time. Our hips jerk against each others. His arms wrap tightly around me as we pant and spasm. My fingers dig into his shoulders as I moan and whimper in a state of complete rapture.

Refusing to let each other go or lose the connection, we stay wrapped in each other as we both fall into an exhausted sleep.

✕✕✕

I shyly sit in Nick's lap in the living room. He settles me between his legs and smiles as he kisses my neck. I snuggle into him as he wraps his arms around me. I'm still getting used to the fact that Nick and I are so affectionate in front of everyone else. Even though all of the couples in this room are just as affectionate as we are.

245

To me, being a creature of privacy and never really having a relationship I was proud to flaunt anyway, all of this is still foreign to me. But the one thing I know is the time I've had with Nick and this family has been the best time of my life. Nothing can compare to experiencing the real love that a family offers. Or the true love that a soulmate can give.

Soulmate. I've never really understood that word. It seemed like something made up by Hallmark. Who honestly finds a love so bone deep that you'd really do anything for them? It seems so farfetched.

Yet here I am in the lap of the man who stole my heart. My soul. Who breathed a life into me that I really didn't realize I needed. Here I am sitting with a family I've always wanted, but didn't believe would ever be mine.

Everyone looks up at Ryan as he stands. The exhaustion he feels is evident in every part of his being. The way he stands with a slight slouch. Ryan never slouches. Everything about him is commanding.

Looking around the room, it's the same with everyone. Everyone is tired. Like no one has slept in weeks. Truthfully, they probably haven't. If they are stressed and on edge as Nick and I have been, then they've been tossing and turning throughout the night, eventually falling into a restless sleep like we did. Even the guards in the room look ragged.

Ryan takes a breath as he begins. "We're going in with everything we have this time. The last two times we've gone against him, he's outsmarted us. The first time, though it was many years ago, we lost a lot of men." Something dark passes over Ryan's eyes before he rubs his eyes and refocuses. "The last time he got away with a plastic surgery scheme. That's not happening this time. I have a surveillance team out there with all of the technology we have at our disposal watching him."

"I just sent a second team," Luke says. "Robby was uneasy and wanted every angle to be watched. I told him every angle is being watched, but he felt like there could be vantage points missed."

Ryan nods. "Can't be too careful." He looks at me. "I'm taking everyone with me. Nick and Jason. Taylor. Chase and Lyric are staying with you."

I nod. "I understand." It's a reiteration of what he told me already.

"I'm leaving an arsenal of weapons. More than just handguns. I didn't get to teach you more than the basics of weapons handling, but if you have that down, you can shoot anything. Stay away from the shotguns.

The kickback is harder. It'll knock you on your ass. Chase will give you an AR-15. Lyric knows how to use it just as well as he does."

I look nervously at Chase and Lyric. They both smile and put me at ease. "I won't let you down," I say as I look back up at Ryan.

"I know." He looks to the rest of the room. "We know Jessa has been a direct target in the past." We all watch as she curls into Jason. "And it's partially because of that reason that I've called in crews from all over the States to come in and help with this. There will be over a hundred guards guarding this house. Excessive?" He shrugs. "Maybe to some. To me? My family is priority. And I'm not taking chances with this fucker."

Taylor gently untangles Nicole from his side as he stands. "For the first time in… well, ever, I'm about to enter a territory I've never really been involved in. I'm going to lead a team into a raid. And instead of arresting the bad guys, I'll be taking shots."

One of the guards gasps. "Taylor, we have enough guys. Our job is to protect you. That includes your job," the guard says.

"I know. But there's also a time in everyone's life where they have to step up. Might not be to this extreme, but in my case? He went after my wife. Twice. Me. Everyone I love. We need everything and everyone we have. So, my team. We're all carrying grenades. Our main goal is to pave the road. Nothing stands in the way of getting to Lucinio."

Robby stands and pulls a whiteboard into the room. He clips a map to it. "This is the blueprint for the house he's renting. It's under Mitch Buchanan. I don't know what his obsession with the name is. He's probably just fucking with us."

Nick groans. "Fuck. I don't know why I didn't put two and two together before. Maybe it's because I didn't know everything until last night. Baywatch. I never missed an episode."

Ryan tilts his head. "Are you telling me you think he's been watching you that long?"

Nick shrugs. "He had to have been. Baywatch didn't air until I was taken in by dad."

I watch Ethan's entire friendly demeanor change. I'm once again reminded where Ryan gets almost all of his attributes from. Ethan stands. "This ends." He looks at Ryan. "Now. I dealt with the truce for long enough out of respect for you and this family. But you should have listened to me."

Ryan puts a hand on his shoulder. "I know, dad. The truce with him only existed because of my friendship with Alex. When he came after Jessa, it ended there. Had I known half the shit I know now, I would have listened to you."

"There's no point in dwelling," Ethan says as he rubs his forehead. "We need to end this once and for all. Our family won't be safe with that deranged psychotic on the loose."

"So…, other than me, Lyric, and Chase and the surveillance crew…" I look at Ryan. "...what exactly is the plan?"

"I'm glad you asked," Ryan says. "We'll have our two surveillance teams watching their every move. I have a lot of guards coming in from around the country. They'll be arriving throughout the day. We hit tonight with everything we have. We overpower. So far, all surveillance seen is eight guards. So either he's cocky as fuck, which we know he is, or he doesn't know that we know he's here. Surveillance spotted him. They've been watching him. They've been listening."

I watch as Robby points to the blueprints. "We have entry points here." He points to the back part of the house. "Here." He points to the front door. "And we have one here. That's the garage."

"What about that patio?" a guard asks.

"No access," Ryan says. That entire wall is glass. We can be seen coming in. Don't want to tip him off. Unless he shoots through it, though, he can't get out from there. We'll have four teams. Usually we have five people to a team. This time? We'll have ten. The house is large. We have a lot of ground to cover inside. Surveillance can watch outside and tell us what's coming."

"Basement?" another guard asks.

"No." Robby says. "Blueprints don't show a basement or an attic. There's a crawl space. Surveillance doesn't see anyone up there. They also can't see a basement."

I watch as Ryan takes everyone through every single step of the upcoming battle. Nick lightly rubs my thigh as he listens. I can feel the electricity crackling through the room from the guys, and a cold dread from all the girls.

I find myself stuck somewhere in the middle. The need to protect the family that's accepted me so wholeheartedly seems to be the one that's overpowering everything else. I snuggle into Nick. He wraps me tightly in his arms. I make eye contact with Arianna, who's curled up as she chews her lip nervously.

I feel the complete fear that her and all the other girls are feeling. The fear that our loved ones will be irrevocably changed by what will happen tonight.

That they may not make it out alive.

Chapter Twenty Seven

⚔ Nick ⚔

I strap on my bulletproof vest and sigh.

Jason looks down at me. "You know it's going to work out in our favor. We have almost a hundred guys with us."

"That's not the problem." I strap a gun to my thigh and make sure the one at my hip is loaded.

"Then what is?"

"I feel that all too familiar feeling. The one that nearly destroyed me the last time. The one where I'm consumed with such hatred and revenge that I feel nothing."

"It's different this time, Nick. You're different."

"I almost lost everything then. My whole fucking family. And all I could think about was the kill."

"Not this time. It's different. This time you have a woman waiting for you to come home. We've all come a long way. We're better."

I strap my shoulder holster on. "I don't know."

Ryan walks up to us. "Ready?"

I nod, choking down the familiar thick black hole before it takes over my soul. "As I'll ever be."

There's a few moments of silence that falls between the three of us. Ryan hands me an AR-15. Taylor, Luke, and Robby join us.

I chuckle darkly. "We all look like the fucking S.E.A.L.S. going in for some covert mission."

Taylor gives me a humored smile. "We pretty much are."

Robby glares. "This ends tonight."

Luke nods. "Fuck right it does."

I look up at Ryan. "He got out last time."

Ryan's dark eyes meet mine. "Not taking chances again. He's in there. Surveillance has been on him all fucking day."

"Since yesterday," Robby puts in.

Shane finishes strapping on his shoulder holster. "He hasn't moved. He's in there. He's in the upstairs office."

I nod. "Keep the X-Ray cameras on him."

Shane checks his gun. "We got the X-Ray, night vision, audio. He so much as farts, we'll know about it."

"Good. I don't want a fucking repeat of the last two times we've dealt with this asshole," I growl.

Ryan puts a hand on my shoulder. "Nick, look at me." He waits until I finally sigh and look up at him. "We're older. We aren't kids anymore. We know what we're up against. We have enough guys to completely overpower his ass."

I nod and let out a breath. I close my eyes a moment and think about the beautiful woman I'm going to be calling my wife soon. I think about Jessa. Her fear of Matthew. How knowing he's alive sent her into such an intense panic attack it nearly killed her. I think about everything he's put my family through. I think of my brothers; parents. The only family I've ever known.

After I calm myself down and remember the reasons I'm doing this, I let myself get into mission mode. I force my mind clear and focus on what lies ahead in the immediate future. Take out Lucinio. Protect my family; my girl. I nod and open my eyes.

Taylor pats my shoulder. "Good to go?"

I nod. "Good to go."

"Good. Luke, take Team Two. Get in position. Taylor. Team Three. Team One... on me." Ryan's voice gets as dark as I feel right now. He catches my eye as he rubs the worn out, brown leather band our grandfather gave him. He does it subconsciously, but watching him do it brings me comfort. It means he's in mission mode just like the rest of us. I follow him and Jason. Luke and Robby take Shane. The rest of our team falls into step with us. We quickly get into position.

I crouch next to Ryan and take in our surroundings. I swallow hard. My stomach clenches. I look at Ryan. "It's quiet."

Ryan nods. "I know."

"Surveillance says he's still in there. Six guards." Shane's voice comes over the earpiece as I look around the property.

I shake my head. "No. Something isn't right. It's too quiet."

"We go in and clear the house. Our team out here can see if anyone leaves or shows up," Luke says into my earpiece.

Ryan reaches over and squeezes my shoulder. "We need to do this. We run it just like we run anything else. Careful. Methodically. We stick to our assignments."

I feel myself panicking slightly as I look around. "There's no guards out here. They're all in there. Why?"

Jason follows my gaze. "Nick. We have backup out here. Sixty guards. It isn't like before. Trust the team."

Taylor pats my back. "We have to. It's our only option."

I can't shake the feeling no matter how hard I try, but I force myself to. I have to be calm. I won't get out of this alive if I'm not. And I have to. I won't leave my family or my soon-to-be wife behind unprotected.

"Teams, now's the time. He's on the move," Cal, a surveillance guard, says.

Ryan nods. "On my count... Three... two... one... Enter!"

Everything immediately falls from my mind until nothing else exists except my team, my family, and the people trying to hurt them.

Nothing else matters to me.

All I see is the guards I need to kill. It's like tunnel vision. Ryan's orders faintly hit my ears. I'm vaguely aware of our teams moving through the house. Only one thing matters. Lucinio. No more hurting my family. He's done.

"First room. Top of the stairs. Two guards," Cal says.

"Outside the room or in?" I ask, zeroing in on the stairs.

"In. They're flanking him," Cal says.

252

"Pointless. I'm coming for you, you fucker," I growl.

I follow Ryan up the stairs. Taylor's team joins us after clearing the bedrooms upstairs. He takes the lead. Taylor kicks open the door. I hear shots ring out and watch two bodies hit the floor. Matthew Lucinio stands in front of us, his back to us. Me, Taylor, Ryan, and Jason all level our guns at him.

I give him a furious glare. "Turn around."

"Now, you son of a bitch," Ryan snarls.

"Whatever the hell torment you have planned this time for my wife ends fucking now," Jason growls.

Matthew chuckles dangerously as he turns around. "You guys really have no idea who you're fucking with, do you?"

We all stare in shock. The man in front of us isn't Lucinio. But I know that voice. I'd know it anywhere. It's hard to forget the hard, emotionless timber of the man who killed my parents. The man who tore both mine and Dani's lives apart.

Taylor shakes his head. "Krins?" he asks in disbelief. Adam Krins gives us a victorious grin as he keeps his hands in plain view.

"What the fuck is happening?" Ryan bellows. "Where's Lucinio?"

"Oh, come on. You don't think he'd make shit this easy, do you?" Krins gives us a sickening smile.

I nearly choke. I knew. I fucking knew. "Son of bitch," I say.

Krins smirks. "Nickolas. How *is* my daughter?"

"Not like you'll ever get the chance to go near her, but rest assured. She's great," I growl. "One thing we don't understand. Why? Why'd you do it?"

He stands there cockily. Calmly. He smiles sickeningly. "Why did I kill her mother? Simple. Because she discovered who I was. What I'd done. She had evidence. She had bags packed. She planned to run. Take my little girl away. We fought. I shot her. I wanted to take Dani with me, but she was afraid. She was hiding. I didn't have the time to find her. I had to get out before getting caught."

Ryan shakes his head. "Why not just grab her? You were obviously stalking her. We've seen the images you had on your laptop of her growing up."

Krins glares at Ryan. "Being a father, I thought you'd understand. I couldn't let my little girl be involved in this life. Dani is the one thing

I've never compromised on. When I found out she was the one who witnessed the murder of Carter Rudd, I did all I could to get to her. Protect her. Just when we found her again after she disappeared, she was in your clutches." He turns his glare to me. "I should've killed you when I had the chance. Just like your parents."

I'm vibrating with anger, but I choke it down. "You tried. You couldn't find me." I look down the barrel of my gun at him. "I've been waiting twenty-eight long years for this."

"You seem awfully calm for a man who's about to die," Ryan says.

"I know my role. I don't like any of you, but at least I know my girl will be safe. You better be prepared, though. Lucinio is coming at you with all he has."

"What do you know about it?" I ask dangerously.

He laughs manically. "I've been involved with the Lucinio Mafia for years. But I'm sure you already know that if you got your hands on my laptop. I made a very bad deal many years ago, and they bailed me out. I've been indebted ever since. My time has come to an end. I've accepted that." He becomes serious and looks at Ryan. "But I'm also not stupid. Keep Lucinio away from my daughter. For what it's worth, I hope you beat the fucker. I couldn't get out from underneath his clutches. As a father, though, speaking to another father, protect my girl."

I glance at Ryan and see the immediate switch. He knows as well as I do that this shit isn't Krin's fault. While I want to take that shot and am wrestling at not doing it, I also know that Krins could do us a lot of good alive. If Lucinio wants us to kill him, maybe it's better we do the exact opposite. It's not like we haven't gotten enemy mafia bosses on our side in the past.

At that moment, Krins' body jerks. We all jump back as blood splatters from his head. He falls to the ground.

"What the fuck?" Ryan asks bewildered.

"We got company! Lots of guys are coming up from the basement!" Cal yells over the radio.

"Basement?" Taylor asks, looking at me as we all try to figure out what the hell just happened. "There's no basement!"

"It's a fucking setup! All teams together on floor one!" Ryan commands. He looks at me. "We fucking needed him."

254

"Fuck!" I point my gun at the shattered window, but I don't have time to search outside for whoever just shot the only lead we have to Matthew. We all turn and run down the stairs, ready to take down Matthew Fucking Lucinio for the final time.

"Well, Dani won't have to worry about him anymore," Taylor says, staying at my back.

"Fucking right," I growl as I run. "I'm just pissed because we needed him."

We meet our teams down the stairs as a bookshelf slides open. My eyes widen in horror as the next seconds unfold. Shots are fired all around me from both sides.

I fall to the ground to cover myself and start screaming at our team. "Stop! Stop fucking shooting!"

People all around me are diving or falling to the ground.

"Cease fire! Cease fire!" Ryan yells using hand motions as well as his voice.

"Stop! Everyone fucking stop!" Alex demands.

"Hold up! Stop shooting!" Josh commands, waving frantically.

For a few moments, all I hear is the rapid beating of my own heart. After I catch my breath, I look up. "How many did we lose?"

Ryan shakes his head. "None. We stopped it before anyone got hurt."

I look to the ceiling and send up a small prayer. "Thank God. Thank fucking God." I jump to my feet as everyone else brushes themselves off and looks around.

"What the hell are you guys doing here?" Alex asks, as confused as I feel.

"Us? What about you?" Ryan asks, just as confused.

"You told us to go after Krins," Josh says to Ryan. "That's what we were doing. We tracked him here. So, I'll parrot Alex. What the hell are you doing here?"

Ryan glares at them both. "Going after your father. Where is he?"

Alex looks like he's about to start laughing. "Our father? He's dead. Stress getting to you? Have you lost your damn mind?"

I shake my head. "He's not. He's not, Alex. We didn't have time to tell you."

"Robby got information that led to some fucked up shit," Taylor says.

Josh looks at me like I've grown a second head. "What? I shot him! Point blank in the fucking head! You were there!"

Ryan shakes his head and glares at Josh. "You shot a guy who he paid off and put through plastic surgery to look like him. Robby found the records. Now, where the hell is he?"

Josh's mouth drops. "How the fuck are we supposed to know? We thought he was dead until five fucking seconds ago!"

"You guys show up in Chicago when I get intel on your father. Fucking convenient."

I put a hand on Ryan's arm. "Ryan. They didn't know."

He pulls away. "Yeah? How are you so sure?"

Alex returns his icy stare. "Fuck you! How many years have you known me? Come on! Just say it! You think I fucking betrayed you!"

"Enough!" Jason's voice carries above all of us and immediately silences everyone. "You both will stop it right the fuck now. You both are brothers. Family. We all know Alex and Josh wouldn't betray us. They both hate their father just as much, if not more, than we do. You're fucking tired, stressed, and we have a bigger problem."

I nod. "We don't know where he is. Or how the hell he got away."

Ryan and Alex both take deep breaths before looking at each other.

"I'm sorry, bro," Alex says.

Ryan shakes his head. "You don't need to be. I'm the one who can't think straight these past couple days."

"It's been a really messed up few days, Ryan. I get it, but I wish you would've talked to me. When did you find out about our father?" Alex asks.

Ryan takes a deep breath. "With certainty? Yesterday. But the suspicion has been there for a couple months. I didn't want to go to you until I knew for sure."

"Fuck," Josh breathes out. "How the hell could this have happened and us not know about it?"

"An excellent question for you to ask." We all whip around, looking for the man behind the voice. The man who has been the bane of my family's existence for years.

"Matthew…," I growl dangerously.

256

"Over here on the screen." Slowly, we look at the large wall to wall TV. Sure enough, Matthew Lucinio's ugly fucking mug is plastered on the damn screen.

And he's waving.

"Couldn't face us like a man, huh? Had to go hide?" I glare viciously.

"Ah... Nickolas. All grown up. Tell me. Do you still pine for mommy and daddy? Or did Ethan Crane manage to turn you into the perfect killing machine for me?"

My blood turns to ice. I feel the fire that had been in my heart fill my eyes. "You son of a bitch!" I lunge for the screen, but Jason and Ryan catch me and pull me back.

Matthew laughs. "Calm down, sharpshooter."

"What the fuck do you want?" Alex barks.

He shrugs. "Obviously my plan failed. Fuck. All of them have somehow been thwarted. I thought I'd be able to take out at least some of you with that explosion I set up with Zekeih's wife." He shakes his head.

"What the hell did you want with Zekeih?" Taylor growls.

Matthew looks at him like he's stupid. "You aren't the brightest one of them, are you? Zekeih takes you down. You're an integral part of the Crane Mafia operation. Kill one of his main stars. Watch his act crumble. Zekeih was weak. Just a pawn in the grand scheme. I figured you'd kill him after he pointed the finger at Adam Krins for me. But he couldn't even get that part of the plan right."

Taylor growls low as his eyes blaze. "So, you'll kill innocent people in this big picture just so you can do what exactly? Rule the world?"

Matthew laughs. "Wouldn't that be nice? Maybe that will be my next goal. But the first step is to get rid of all of you." He glares at the three of us and Josh and Alex. "I wanted to bring you all together and have you kill each other. Figured Nick would be the last one standing. He's always been the strongest of the group. The survivor. I guess I underestimated how smart you are. Won't happen again." He says it so casually it makes me want to throw up.

I laugh. "Me, the survivor? Sure I survived the streets of New York. But did you forget you fucking poisoned Josh and brainwashed him? Tried turning him into a soulless killing machine? I protect my family. I'm a protector. You want a survivor? Josh is the survivor, you arrogant motherfucking pricksickle. I'm honored to have a brother like him."

Josh looks at me a little surprised before he looks back at the screen. He crosses his arms over his chest and shoots daggers at Matthew. "You didn't answer the question. What the fuck do you want?"

"The demise of both the Crane Mafia and whatever the hell you turned the Lucinio Mafia into would do nicely. But… I'd also like my rightful heir to take his rightful place at my side." His cold eyes meet mine, sending chills down my spine. Then he turns to Jason. "Maybe then I'll take my sexy plaything and show her how a real man fucks a woman."

"You aren't getting anywhere near her," Jason says through gritted teeth.

He gives Jason a sickening smile. "Last I saw you, you were fucking my sexy little plaything. When was that? Last night? In Ryan's home? My, how time flies."

It's Jason's turn to lunge for the screen. He howls as Ryan and I hold him back. "Stay the fuck away from her!"

Ryan steps forward as I pin my brother against the wall. "We all know Jessa isn't the play here. She's just the prize. What's the real play? Is it Nick? You know he's not going to play into your hands."

Out of the corner of my eye I see Josh and Alex share a confused look. "What?" Josh mouths to his brother. I can feel my heart break slightly at what they're about to find out, but I have to focus right now. There's time for family reunions later.

He chuckles. "So brave, aren't you? Everyone including my three fucking sons look to you for leadership. Well, guess what? I'm bigger than you are now. Took me years, but I'm big enough to take you completely out."

Ryan shakes his head. "Not fucking possible."

"More than possible. Tell me, how are all the wives doing? Nick? How's Dani?"

"Touch her, and she'll fuck you up. I won't need to." I shoot him the same icy stare Jason is as I let him go and turn back to the screen.

He laughs. "Always the cocky, overly-confident one. The hothead. So much like me. I know she's guarding your family with Chase Shaw and little Lyric Sharpe."

"Stay the fuck away from her," Josh growls. From the corner of my eye, I see Alex grip his shoulder to keep him from lunging forward.

"Stay the fuck away from all of them," I growl just as dangerously.

Seeing straight through the anger coursing through my body isn't easy. But I've learned well. I shove it all down and glare hard at the screen. I stand next to Ryan. Jason stands on the other side of me.

"For now, son. For now."

Josh looks at Ryan. "What the fuck is going on?" he asks low.

Ryan shakes his head. "Later. Focus."

Matthew laughs. "Oh, you mean you didn't know?" Matthew howls with laughter. Manically.

"Know what?" Alex asks through gritted teeth. His fists are clenched at his sides as he stares down his father.

Matthew gives both Alex and Josh a demonic glare. "Nick here… He's the rightful heir to the Lucinio Mafia. My son. True son. The one I had with the only woman I've ever loved." Matthew smiles at me. "Thank you, by the way, for giving me the opening I needed to finally take down your mother's murderer, son. I never could stand that fucker. Not after what he did. He was only supposed to kill the man who stole you both from me. If I hadn't needed him, I would have done it myself long ago."

"Son?" Josh looks at me in utter confusion.

Before I can respond, Ryan steps in with a low whisper. "Later. There's so much shit we have to discuss."

Matthew cups his hand over his ear. "What was that? I couldn't quite hear you. Are you planning my demise?"

I can see Alex's anger burning in his eyes. I can feel the shift in Josh. Both of them are seething and entering the same dangerous territory that I long ago passed. They don't need the entire story right now. They both understand the priority. Taking down Matthew Lucinio.

Once.

And.

For.

All.

"I don't really understand all that's going on, but I don't care," Josh growls at the screen. "I shot you once, you son of a bitch. You can bet your ass I'll do it again."

"You failed the first time. Obviously, I'm still here. Can't even tell your own daddy from a fucking clone. Worthless. And here you are leading a mafia. More like a little band of misfits and fuck-ups just like you." He glares just as hard as Alex. "Both of you. I don't know why I wasted my time on either of you, when I had him." He points to me.

"You can fuck a spike if you think I'll have anything to do with you," I say darkly.

"No thanks. I have a sexy little thing at home waiting for me. But I'll gladly take Jessa and Lyric as appetizers. On second thought, maybe just Jessa. Lyric is damaged goods after losing my heir, Jaxon."

"You evil son of a fucking bitch!" Jason yells as he lunges for the screen again. I grab him.

"Cool it!" Ryan commands. Jason growls but calms down staring viciously at Matthew.

"You're not getting anywhere fucking near Lyric. You got me?" Josh growls venomously.

"Fitting name for what would have been a strong boy. Have you knocked her up again yet?" Matthew continues as if the outburst he caused never happened. "No? Pity. She's probably too fucked up. I can still take her as a spare, though."

"Motherfucker!" Josh yells. Alex pulls him back again and whispers something I can't hear. It calms him but his glare is still vicious. Matthew just laughs.

Ryan folds his arms over his chest. "You seem to know a lot about us. You're obviously near if you shot Krins. You must also know that I pulled more guys in from all over the damn place to guard my house. You aren't getting anywhere near anyone. Not Jessa. Not Dani. Not Lyric. None of them."

He shrugs cockily. "Not yet. But I will. I have what I want. Right now. You see, while all you guys were busy trying to get to me, I escaped through a hidden passageway." Matthew gives us an evil and very calculated glare. "And in the spirit of respect and all that shit, I'll be honest. I didn't take that shot…"

I'm immediately on edge as I start glancing around. I suddenly have a sick feeling, but I don't know what it is or why. Jason and Ryan are near me. Alex and Josh are here. Taylor is standing behind me. Luke is next to him. Shane stands next to Luke. Robby is…

260

"Robby..." I quickly look around the room, then meet Ryan's eyes. "Where's Robby?"

"Robby? You mean him?" Matthew asks, his voice laced with fake innocence.

We all look at the screen and see Robby laying on the ground. His hands are cuffed behind his back. Matthew kneels next to him and grabs his head, yanking it back. His mouth is gagged. He looks unconscious.

"No! Fuck! Robby! Get up, baby! Come on!" Luke screams as he takes off running. I grab Luke's arm as he tries running out the door, but it takes me, Taylor, Ryan, Shane, and Jason to hold him.

"That's what he wants! Luke, stop! He wants you to charge after him!" I yell.

Matthew laughs manically once more. "I do. I really do want that. But you won't get to him before I put a bullet in his head. This is the one that figured me out, right? Little chloroform in the middle of that chaos. Pay off one of your preciously loyal guards. And this. This is what we have. The little prick that found me." We watch in horror as Matthew takes out a gun and stands.

"No!" Luke screams. "Let him go! Robby! Get up! Get up, baby!" Robby lays motionless, and Luke lunges for the door again.

Alex and Josh join in and grab him, holding him back, though none of us want to. Unfortunately, we all know a trap when we see it. We don't know where he is despite all of the security we have set up; all the surveillance we have, we all know if we walk out that door, we could be walking into an ambush.

Matthew shoots. My heart stops beating.

I try to catch him, but Luke drops to his knees, shaking and crying. "No! No! No! No!" He looks up at the screen. All of us are kneeling next to him. Luke's expression becomes dangerously menacing. "I *am* going to *find* you. And I *will kill* you. You think Ryan is dangerous? You just fucked with Satan himself."

His voice sends actual chills down my spine. It's dropped an octave and sounds fucking demonic,. Maybe it's not Ryan that everyone should fear. Or me. Maybe unleashing Luke on Lucinio is the way to go.

I chuckle despite myself. The truth is, we're all right there with him. He took one of our own. Do that and we all become the most demonic sons of bitches in the world.

Matthew kneels down next to Robby. "I look forward to it."

"I'm coming for you, you fucker." I stare at Luke a little in awe.

"Mmm... Luke?" Robby says weakly as he groans. My eyes snap back to the screen.

Luke's eyes widen. "Robby? Baby, are you okay?"

"I... I think so." Robby looks up. We all can see the glimmer of fear in his eyes as we all try to process the fact that he's still alive. "What happened?"

Luke shakes his head choking back the tears. "Don't worry about it. It doesn't matter. I'm coming, baby. Okay? I'll find you."

Matthew grins. "You have until tomorrow morning. Sunrise. I'll have what I need from him by then."

The screen goes blank. Luke stares at it. All of us are quiet for a long moment. I can hear people catching their breath. I reach up with a shaky hand and start rubbing my own chest as my heart starts beating again. Ryan closes his eyes and runs his hands through his hair vibrating with the anger that all of us feel.

Finally, I give Luke's arm a squeeze. "We'll find him."

"If he's telling the truth about being bigger than Ryan..." Luke looks up at us.

"Then we need to combine our forces." Josh meets his eyes as Luke looks at him.

Alex stands, pulling Luke up with him. "I assume Robby is your boyfriend?"

Luke nods. "He's everything. My everything."

Josh stands and attempts to smile, but none of us feel like smiling. "We'll get him back. You have Ryan and all of his forces. And you have me and Alex and all of ours."

"No one gets left behind. Especially when that person is family or the love of your life," Alex says, voice heavy with emotion.

"We'll find him, Luke," I say as I put a hand on his shoulder. Luke shakes us off as he nods.

"All clear out here. You all are safe to exit," a guard says over our earpieces. Luke doesn't wait any longer. He wipes his eyes and storms out the door.

I look at Ryan. "He's going to tear this city apart."

"Wouldn't you?" Ryan asks, watching Luke.

"Didn't say I wouldn't. But we need to move. Save him from himself."

Ryan nods as we all follow Luke out of the house. I call Dani as we're on the way home, thanking God that she's okay and safe. I'm lucky. Hell. We all are lucky our women are okay.

I glance at Luke sitting in the passenger seat next to Ryan. He hasn't said a word. The muscle in his jaw twitches. The further we drive, the tighter his jaw becomes. He's clenching his fists so fiercely, I can see the blood he's drawing from his nails digging into his palms.

"We'll find him," I say, though I know it's a wasted effort.

He says nothing. I know instinctively that our biggest fight won't be with Matthew Lucinio. It's going to be making sure Luke doesn't destroy the entire universe in his quest to find Robby.

Chapter Twenty Eight

⚔ Luke ⚔

When I walk into the house after the raid, I feel like I'm on fire. An inferno of rage steadily pulses through my body. I can feel the blaze shooting from my eyes. I know how scary I look. I know how dangerous I appear to be. And all of that is confirmed when everyone in the house backs away from me.

Including my own mother.

Nick comes in behind me. I watch Dani leap into his arms and hug him tightly. I try not to be pissed off as he hugs the love of his life close. They all do. They all should.

Mine is gone. Missing. Taken by a disgusting and vile fool who has no idea who he's messed with. No idea in the slightest.

I try to let the love in this room calm me, but it's not the easiest thing in the world to do.

Next to me, Josh hugs Lyric as close to him as he possibly can. She's wrapped around him like an octopus. "Fuck, Lyric. What are you doing here? I'm so fucking glad you're here," he whispers into her neck.

"I'll tell you later. Right now, I'm just... I..." She shudders against him.

He runs his fingers through her hair. "Shh... I don't care why right now. I'm just glad you're here. I found out a lot of shit tonight. I'll get guards on your brother. It's not safe for you to go back to Gainesville right now."

Lyric just nods into his neck but doesn't let him go.

I take a steadying breath and walk to the den at the back of the house and pace back and forth with my hands locked behind my head.

No one is safe.

I pace for several minutes growling and grumbling. "Where the fuck did you take him, you son of a bitch?" I mumble. "Where *would* you take him?"

"We'll figure it out."

I spin on the voice behind me. "Why the fuck would he do this? Why cause so much heartache and pain to one family?"

Josh shrugs. "I don't know. My suspicion? A little to do with being the biggest and most powerful mafia boss in the world, and a lot to do with the fact that the Cranes stole his son."

I sigh and shake my head. "There's so much you don't know about that. So much you need to." I sit in the chair nearest to me.

Josh sits across from me. "In time. Now isn't that time. We need to figure out where Robby is. But... what I do know is that somewhere along the way he found out about Nick and that he was adopted into the Crane family. I'm sure that's all stuff we'll figure out. But the priority here is Robby."

"I just don't understand. Why him? Robby hasn't done anything to him."

"Luke, he doesn't follow rules. There's never been any rhyme or reason to his actions. Now, I know Robby found a lot of shit. But the concern isn't with what he found right now. It's with finding him. Alex and I are here. We know that fucker better than anyone. We can go through all of our resources. Records. Properties. We'll figure it out."

I look at him. "Josh, I don't think you understand just how pissed off I am. I want to tear apart the world."

"I do know. I've been there. But I learned something. All of that anger and energy that's coursing through you right now, it needs to be put into something useful. Like finding Robby." Josh stands. "We can't do that without you."

I nod and stand. "You're right."

"We'll find him. We need to piece shit together, but we'll find him."

I follow him into the living room where Ryan is explaining what happened to everyone. Josh sits down and pulls Lyric into his lap, wrapping tightly and protectively around her. I stand next to Alex at the back of the room with my arms folded over my chest. Not a single person in the room looks like they're able to stand on their own two feet. Everyone is beyond exhausted.

But I know this family. No one is going to sleep until we bring Robby home. That thought is the only thing that's keeping me sane right now.

When Ryan finishes explaining to everyone what happened, he turns to Alex and Josh. "I know you both have questions."

Josh shakes his head. "We can wait. That's not the priority."

"We know Nick is our brother by blood. We don't need more than that right now. All of that can come later," Alex says.

Nick looks up at them both. "You aren't pissed that your entire life has been spent with an abusive motherfucker because he felt you weren't good enough or some shit?"

Josh laughs. "He would've been abusive to us either way. Because of you or not. We've moved past that, Nick."

"You know we love you and this family like our own. Only difference is now we know we share blood," Alex says. "I don't blame you for his actions. Neither does Josh. We'll deal with that and how everything was found out later. Right now, we need to find Robby."

Josh looks at Ryan. "We'll call in our team from L.A. Gavin, Damon, and Lance might take a bit. I'll have to pull them from another mission. I'll pull in more guards, though."

"Robby is number one right now," Alex says as he pats me on the back.

"Thank you," I say quietly.

"Last thing," Ryan says. "We've had a guard betray us."

Everyone falls silent, but my anger boils. I glare. "I'll figure out who," I growl.

"I already know," Ryan says. "Cal. We had two guards working with him come to me and say that they didn't know what to make of it or how he knew, but right after he told us we had company, he took off."

I shake my head. "What?"

"We don't know how he knew, Mr. Massena."

I look up as a young guard we just recruited from the FBI leans against the doorframe. "How he knew what?" I ask.

He crosses his arms over his chest as Ryan turns towards him. He shrugs. "We don't know how he knew there was anyone coming. We had cameras and equipment all over the damn place. We never saw the basement. It didn't show on any of the tech we had with us. We didn't see anyone coming up on the house. When he yelled that we had company, we were all confused. He took off running. Two of the guards chased after him."

"Did they catch him?" Ryan seethes.

He shakes his head. "No. At least not then. He disappeared. But I asked a couple of the guards who were in the house with you. They saw him. One second he was there. The next second he wasn't. No one knew where he went. He disappeared in the gunfire."

"That has to be when Robby disappeared. Right after we brushed off, Lucinio popped on the screen." I look at Ryan. "Robby was right next to me. I never checked to see if he still was when Lucinio came up. I knew he was okay after the shots. That's all I cared about."

Ryan nods and looks back at the guard. "Anything else? Anyone else disappear? What do you mean, at least not then?"

"It was just him that took off and disappeared. But I know you'll want to talk to everyone. Everyone else is accounted for. The two who chased after Cal did find him. He'd been shot about a block away from the house. And one more thing. Just before Krins was killed, Cal said he had to take a leak. Couldn't hold it. He took off before we had a chance to stop him. Came back just after Krins was killed. I questioned him, but that's when he started screaming into the radio that we have company and took off running. I can't prove he took the shot, but..." He shrugs.

"But everything fits." Ryan closes his eyes and pinches the bridge of his nose. "He said he paid off a guard. It would make sense, but I want everyone questioned."

"I'll take Taylor. We'll question the guards," Alex says. "Josh can stay here with you and call in our team. He can also help narrow down where Robby might be."

Josh nods. "I have ideas. Lyric just asked about the docks, and I'm thinking that's where he probably is, but we need a plan. I need Lance. If Robby has his phone, we can track it. It's just going to take me time to get him here, and it's time we don't fucking have."

"Do it," Ryan says. Taylor kisses Nicole and follows Alex out of the room. Ryan looks down at Arianna. He leans down and kisses her softly. "We'll find him."

She nods and looks at me. "I'm so sorry."

I walk to the chair and kneel in front of her. I take her hands in mine. "We'll find him, Air. I promise."

I kiss her cheek as I stand. Josh is on the phone with Lance. Ryan is pulling out a map of Chicago. Jessa is curled into a ball so small huddled into Jason's side that she's barely visible as he engulfs her. Nicole is burrowed in Breetana and Chase. Dani is wrapped like an octopus around Nick. Lyric is cuddled tightly into Josh.

I look back at Arianna as she watches her husband quietly. I tug her up before sitting and pulling her in my lap. She snuggles into me and immediately bursts into the tears she's been fighting to hold back. I hold her close as much for her as I do for myself.

I need her to center me because if I don't, I'm going to explode into a massive hypernova with a serious chance of destroying the entire universe in my wake.

For the sake of life in this galaxy and beyond, not finding Robby isn't an option.

And he better be alive.

If he's not?

I don't want to go there, but all I can think is...

...God have mercy on Matthew Lucinio...

Because I won't.

The End

Next In The Crane Family Series

The dark and sexy Crane Family Series concludes with *Love In The Dark*.

Being a gay man in a law enforcement community has never been easy for me. It's a secret I've kept ever since I admitted to myself what I've known my entire life. Guarding that secret when I became the right-hand man to the most powerful mafia boss in the world, and also my sister's husband, was even more important.

I couldn't allow those in my command to think differently of me because of my sexual orientation.

Then I met Robby. Sexy. Handsome. Smart. So perfect in every way.

When Robby becomes the target of the Crane Family's ultimate enemy, I'm faced with losing the only man I'll ever love. Damn if anyone thinks that's happening.

As an ATF agent, I've had to cross lines to take down the bad guys. As Crane Mafia's second in command, I'll do what needs to be done to protect my family.

The world thinks Ryan Crane or Josh Lucinio are dangerous when backed into a corner. As a man in love... I'm about to become the darkest force this world has ever seen to keep what's mine safe.

~ This book is a steamy MM/Mafia romance dealing with dark and violent themes, including kidnapping and vulgar language, that may not be suitable for some readers. ~

Order *Love In The Dark* Today!

The Crane Family Series

Available Now

The Reluctant Mafia King
Sweet Lies
Billion Dollar Love Story
Be Mine
Protecting Her
Dangerously Forbidden Love
His Heart
Love In The Dark

Box Sets Available

The Crane Family Series

Other Books By Melony Ann
The Beautiful Dream Series

Available Now

Loving You
My Love, My Heart
Softening Lyric
Undercover Temptations
Captain Charming
Breaking Boundaries
Crashing Into You
Tactical Inferno
Ravishing Our Queen
Cherished By The Texan
Unveiling Our Passions

Box Sets Available

The Beautiful Dream Series: Box Set: Part 1
The Beautiful Dream Series: Box Set: Part 2

The Deimos Trilogy

Available Now

Connor's Legacy
Aryan's Alpha
Kade's Redemption

Box Sets Available

The Deimos Trilogy

The Forbidden Temptation Series

Available Now

The Detective's Forbidden Temptation
The Running Back's Forbidden Temptation

The Lucinio Family Series

Available Now

Rising From The Ashes
The Player's Rebel
Encrypting My Heart

Multi Author Series
Piper Falls: Firehouse 49

Available Now

Ignite My Fire by Melony Ann
Regain My Fire by Kindra White
Playing With My Fire by D.L. Howe
Fight My Fire by Darley Collins
Against My Fire by Anneke Boshoff
Relight My Fire by Louise Murchie
Harness My Fire by Ayana Lisbet
Quench My Fire by Havana Wilder

Let's Be Friends

Follow me on

Bookbub

Facebook

Goodreads

Instagram

Tik Tok

Visit my website
www.melonyannauthor.com

Subscribe to my newsletter and get a FREE never-seen-before NOVELLA
just for subscribers!
https://www.melonyannauthor.com/exclusive-content

Join my Facebook Reader Group!
Jason's and Melony's Sizzling Book Nook

The official Crane Family Series Playlist on YouTube
https://youtube.com/playlist?list=PLGEiD5wbQmDc78K7gNeODh-
janqmIFiie

Dedication

You're our hearts and souls.

Acknowledgements

Brad - Friendships and relationships just seem to go up in flames. And somehow, through all of the chaos, there's you. I love you more and more as each second passes.

Laura - When the darkness creeps in, you're the sunshine that breaks through the clouds. You're the warmth that keeps us all from freezing. But most of all, you're the arms that keep all of us together. You're the light to the dark and one of the most amazing people I've ever met. I love you more than I ever believed possible.

Jay - Sometimes I question where exactly you came from. It's almost like you appeared at the perfect time on a mythical white unicorn. What started off as this amazing friendship has blossomed into something incredible and beautiful. I know some call what we all have crazy, but I don't care. It's so right. It's perfect. It's an amazing love story that I wouldn't change a moment of. I love you beyond reason.

Ayana - Thank you for always having the right words to lift me up when my mood gets low.

Anneke - Thank you for having my back and continuing to believe in me when I start to doubt myself.

Jason - I'll be forever grateful you dropped into my DMs because what we have now is one of the best things that's ever happened to me.

To the Bookstagram Community.

To my family.

To all of those who believe in me and support me.

To all of those who don't.

Cover by: Carter Cover Designs

Edited by: Alyssa Skaggs

About Melony Ann

Melony Ann began writing short stories and poetry as a child. She continued honing her craft over the years until she took the plunge and began publishing her work, despite having severe anxiety.

Melony writes contemporary romance stories that are full of suspense and a lot of steam.

When she isn't writing, she is loving her family and working to make her life something she deserves.

Melony believes that if her writing can inspire just one person, then all of her hard work is worth it.

Her hope is that her writing allows each and every one of her readers to escape for a little while. To dive into a different world one book at a time.

www.ingramcontent.com/pod-product-compliance
Lightning Source LLC
Chambersburg PA
CBHW051536260626
47170CB00003B/961